MW01279821

# MYSTERIES
# ON THE
# MATANZAS

*Unexplained River Murders*

A Novel by

ALEXANDER MAXIMOVICH, M.D.

Mysteries on the Matanzas
Copyright © 2021 by Alexander Maximovich, M.D.

All rights reserved. No part of this publication may be reproduced, distributed, or transmitted in any form or by any means, including photocopying, recording, or other electronic or mechanical methods, without the prior written permission of the author, except in the case of brief quotations embodied in critical reviews and certain other non-commercial uses permitted by copyright law.

This literary work is fiction. Names, characters, places, events and dialogues are used to provide apparent authenticity. These are factious products of the author's imagination and not from or about real people, living or dead. The story should not be construed as accurate or real events. Any similarities to actual people, locations or actual events are purely coincidental.

No part of this story may be copied by photography, electronically or pasted on to other new of old types of media without prior written permission of the author and publisher.

Tellwell Talent
www.tellwell.ca

ISBN
978-0-2288-4851-6 (Hardcover)
978-0-2288-4850-9 (Paperback)
978-0-2288-4852-3 (eBook)

This book is dedicated to lovers of crime mysteries, science fiction, monsters, trivia and sex.

*In memory of David Alden Brinton, M.D.*
You were my dear lifelong friend and professional
partner for forty-three years.
I miss your daily reflections on patient medical challenges, your
Mission in Brazil, religion, life-force and the hereafter.
Paraphrasing one of Dr. Brinton's saying —
*Life without faith, nothing seems possible,*
*Life with faith, everything is possible.*

*Individuals having any advantage, however slight, over others, would have the best chances of surviving and of procreating their kind.*

Charles Darwin

# Foreword

I received one of the most prestigious journalistic recognitions in America. I have a gold medal encased in a brown wooden plaque on my office wall for "Public Service." This was administered by Columbia University.

Most stories focus on the events of one individual. This story is different and involves several people, events and more. It's not about me as the reporter. I believe good luck is prepared opportunity. I took the initiative to cascade me to success.

As a boy from East Palatka, I wanted to write about history and present day news. I spent one year at St. Johns River Collage, Palatka, then at Valencia Collage of Journalism, Orlando. The college wasn't named after Valencia, Spain, but for the Valencia oranges that are grown over much of central Florida.

As an independent investigating reporter, I started my journey to this story of my life. An encounter with the lower St. Johns Sheriff on the Matanzas River Inlet overpass gave me my literary run for the eventual Joseph Pulitzer Prize.

This story (book) is about capital crimes, medical genius, love and infatuation, law enforcement persistence, the world's first Oceanarium of ocean life and most importantly the mythical megaannums-years-old monster, which named itself "Yao." Let the events unfold in Northeast Florida.

—Richard Ward Angel

# Introduction

## Present Day

**The forty-horse-power outboard** engine sputtered and then started.

"Thousands of river crossings with thousands of interested tourists are taken to see this historic National Park Landmark."

This day was like all others, with the visitors hurrying from the tree-lined parking lot to make the next river tour boat to cross. As the people boarded, they got a clear view of the legendary Fort Matanzas. The fort on Rattlesnake Island is square in shape with fifty-foot-high walls and abuts a thirty-foot tower.

"Welcome to the Fort Matanzas National Monument Park. I'm your senior tour guide, Theodore Roosevelt Smythe. Where have y'all wan-na-be historians traveled from?" asked Ranger Smythe.

"Connecticut, Michigan, New York, Alabama, Maine, New Jersey, Illinois, Ohio, Indiana Georgia," the responses were shouted out.

"And where in Michigan are you from?" Ranger Smythe asked as he pointed to one person.

"I've moved around a lot in Michigan—Traverse City, Ann Arbor, Lansing, Troy and now just across the street. I'm staying in a condo in Crescent Beach," answered the blonde-haired young woman at the rail of the ferry tour boat.

"Well, thank you. But we don't have enough time for you to have your own tour about how you got here. Yet that was a good segue for me to come back to this Monument Park," jumped in Ranger Smythe. "The Spanish named this river and built this fort in 1742 out of coquina. Which is what, anyone?" The Ranger's hands extended outward to the tourists.

"No answer? It's the shellstone y'all have walked on to board this boa and it will be the ground y'all will walk on to enter Fort Matanzas."

Mumbling came from the crowded boat deck.

"How is it made to be useful for construction?" asked the blonde Michigander.

"Finally, a good question on the final tour of the day," huffed the now irritated and irritating Ranger Smythe. "Crushed limestone from burned oyster shells and mortar mader the walls. Close set pine tree pilings were driven deep into the salty marsh ground to create a stable foundation."

"And was this fort to protect St. Augustine and Fort Castillo de San Marcos from foreign invasion from the southern Matanzas River Inlet?" asked the young woman.

"I'm guessing it came from—" He pointed his index finger. "Have you been on this tour before, Miss …?" the ranger sneered.

"Alisa. No, I haven't, Mr. Ranger Smythe, sir."

"You are correct, Alisa. The Matanzas River is the only ocean inlet to give direct access to St. Augustine from the south. Several centuries of history has led to the establishment of Fort Matanzas as a National Monument."

The white-bearded ranger then looked at the tourists' faces. "Let's get back on track. When debarking, we'll be entering the premises of historic tales of murders surrounded by religious hysteria, hatred and domination. Finally, no one is allowed to remove any stone fragments from the site for souvenirs under fear of federal prosecution—to the full extent of the law!" he yelled out.

Alisa heard his voice fade away as she questioned herself, *how did I get here?*

\*\*\*

**Crescent Beach, Florida** was a quiet beach resort area consisting of condos, a few storefronts, restaurants and private homes—the typical Florida seaside community. That's why Sheriff Gary T. Sellack transferred to Northeastern Florida, specifically to patrol southern St. Johns County, southern part of St. Augustine, Anastasia Island, Crescent Beach, the town of Marinescape, 6.5 miles south to the Flagler Estates and Palm Valley, where St. Johns and Flagler Counties meet.

Sheriff Gary and team also patrolled the Matanzas River running through the southern part of the county, which also was part of the Intracoastal Waterway. Gary has been happily working and living for more than a decade. That was to end. In less than a week's time, the Matanzas River would be home to murders, rapes, physically and psychologically damaged survivors of attacks and vandalized pharmacies, including a medical clinic.

"Sheriff Gary T. Sellack, why did you move down to this southern part of St. Johns County?" asked a local newspaper reporter when Gary first took the law enforcement position.

"Just call me Sheriff Gary. I was ready for a change from the high intensity of the Orlando and Jacksonville Law Enforcement Agencies. I needed the less hectic environment of this county, for which I've always held a special place in my heart, since I grew up in the area."

He didn't reveal his real reasons, like to decrease his internal stress, hopefully lower his blood pressure without meds, decrease his heart palpations, sleep without nightmares, stop his excessive alcohol consumption and not think about his two divorces.

"Sheriff Gary, the media has labeled the recent unknown perpetrator or perpetrators of these multiple crimes collectively as the 'Matanzas Monster.' Any comments?"

"Not at this time."

"Have any comments concerning the Florida State Police and FBI getting involved?"

"I'll let them make their own comments."

Sheriff Gary's local police force was normally only involved with solving petty crimes. Sheriff Gary was painfully aware of his local law enforcement team's deficiencies and lack of capital crime experience. On the other hand, he was very familiar with such atrocities, having come from two prior large metropolitan areas. Sheriff Gary's police force included a CSI team and director, limited laboratory facilities and a medical examiner (M.E.). This professional was the exception. The M.E. had previously performed many autopsies in different state counties.

All of the above-mentioned events would soon reoccur. Suddenly, Sheriff Gary and the CSI team were to be under intense scrutiny from residents, media and outside law enforcement agencies to solve and stop the "Matanzas Monster." With little success in making progress in their cases, they'd be forced to consult a highly respected and recognized professor of marine biology, ichthyology, genetics and animal reproductive endocrinology. Unknown to Sheriff Gary at this time, a human reproductive nurse and a Marinescape assistant from out of state would be included in the investigation's web of persons of interest.

"Is this consultant actually involved in the recent crime spree?" asked Sheriff Gary of his CSI director and team.

"Their answers to my questioning are quite elusive. I think someone is guilty of at least impeding this team's criminal investigation, which would reveal the source of the current crime spree."

Crescent Beach and Marinescape would nevermore be a quiet resort haven.

***

**As the National Monument Park** tour boat began the return trip to the mainland from Fort Matanzas, Ranger Smythe continued his monologue.

"Historically, this river has fostered human life and death for at least 1,000 years. In 1492, the European invasion of the continent began. Slaughtered Native inhabitants and European bodies have floated on this river to the Matanzas River Inlet. Thus the name Matanzas is so appropriate.

"The Floridian Indian population was about 300,000 people. Around the Matanzas River, the Timucua Indians were probably 40,000 strong. These Natives were called heathens, savages or 'child-like.' Appearing godless, they needed the teachings of Christianity, or so said their European conquerors." The ranger paused.

"Does anyone know how the Western continents got their name?" he asked. "No answers, no guesses?"

"Someone put it on a map?" Alisa sheepishly conjectured.

"A segue for me again by the Michigander," Ranger Smythe smiled. "In 1507, a cartographer or mapmaker, named Martin Waldseemuller decided to create a New World map. For the first time in history, he would show the entire known and suspected unknown world, including the newly described lands across the ocean from Europe. Waldseemuller had read of Amerigo Vespucci, who had sailed with Columbus. Vespucci was commissioned by King Ferdinand and Queen Isabella of Spain, separately from Columbus, to explore beyond Columbus's findings. (Footnote Vespucci)

Vespucci actually recognized that what Columbus had discovered was a new continent. On his death bed, Christopher Columbus still believed the islands he'd found were off the coast of India or China, so Columbus called the indigenous inhabitants 'Indians.'

The ranger hesitated again, "Any questions, no?"

"The German Martin Waldseemuller used Amerigo Vespucci's accounts in *Cosmographia Introductio* and named these land masses of North and South continents after this explorer.

Following the practice of naming sea going vessels female, so did Waldseemuller name the new lands? Latinization and feminization of the name 'Amerigo' makes it "Americus," which became America and then South and North America," he finished explaining as the tour boat docked. (Footnote Indian History*)*

\*\*\*

**"Not mentioned** by Waldseemuller was Vespucci's reporting of wild and bizarre new plants and animals, especially a fast and elusive animal. It was comfortable swimming or running upright. When seen on land pursuing its prey, it seemed almost man-like. Vespucci described it as 'very tall, possibly twice my height, with a large, irregular and bulbous head, thick scaly skin and bright reddish eyes.' He called it 'Rio Lagartija,' Spanish for 'Female River Lizard.'" Ranger Smythe finished his tour monologue, docked the vessel and opened the boat's gate.

(Author Note) Films such as the *Alligator People*, *The Blob*, and *Attack of the 50 Foot Woman* supplied audiences with adventures of fascination, monstrosities of man and nature and tales of outer space's new life forms. This book continues this motif. The story includes hate, love, multiple crimes, murders, mysteries, and frustrated police investigators. There's even a little wetness of mythic of Merfolk or Merpeople.

\*\*\*

***Mysteries on the Matanzas*** story characters will eventually accept the unacceptable, the unbelievable and some will just accept it with blind faith. There are explanations and trust that resulted in man's grotesque interventions with unrealized consequences. (Footnote Homo sapiens viewpoint)

# Chapter 1

---

## *Water*

**Water envelopes my face.** Why? I'm underwater. I look up and see light reflecting on the water's surface. Spotlights, flashing red and blue colors were barely visible. I must be ten or twelve feet down. My arms and legs are so light and weightless. This must be what it's like to be in outer space. Yes, these are my air bubbles coming out my mouth. Up, up past my face as I try to yell. But all I speak is in "gurgle." A swish of something goes by my head. A tail of hair goes one way and then the other. I do believe they are of human form. Wait. It goes by again. There's one going by my feet. Where are its...? My tucked-in shirt is slightly flapping. A momentary sparkle catches my eye from on my shirt. I stare and my vision clears to show a star. A five-pointed star ... no, it's a badge with a name and number. I can't make it out. Something continues to swim all around me as I settle downward to be standing on the bottom of a river bed or lake. Finely formed greenish scales, long multi-colored hair ... oh yes, and plump, bobbing breasts with red nipples all zip by me. My mouth opens as a cherry-like nipple moves closer to my face. Hark, no luck capturing that one; maybe the next one. The gentle current makes me want to walk on a — river bed. I'll walk with the current and never lose sight of the breasted, now clearly visible half woman, half scaled fish tail. Oh, what brilliant colors of scales they have. They match its hair color. They're mermaids. They have shimmering red, orange, yellow, blue and my favorite—green

1

scales. All bring their smiling faces within inches of my lips. Their waist-long hair hits my cheeks with each pass. What else can I do but smile back? No talking, just a whooshing water sound in my ears, like waves hitting a river shoreline. I think I love that blue mermaid, no, the green one … no the blue. I… I could follow anywhere. Her blue eyes mesmerize me, blue hair, her blue body scales and large …

"Buzz … buzz … buzz." Suddenly, I watch the river's water level go down like water down a bathtub drain. I'm collapsing to a reclining position on the river bottom. The mermaids are swirling around my head faster and faster until the river bed becomes almost dry. "The mermaids are…disappearing with that noise."

What is that? A male mermaid, a merman, with claws—long, sharp claws?

***

"Buzz … buzz, ring, buzz, ring … ring."He opened his eyes and saw the white popcorn bedroom ceiling with the sight and rhythmic swooshing sound of the ceiling fan. The first morning's multi-colored sunbeam came through the warped window pane like a prism and caught the corner of his eye. He felt a drool dripping down his left cheek. Turning on his side, he saw his cell phone, beeper and the red flashing light of the landline phone base. All on the bedside stand, he grabbed the cell and landline phone together, answering both at the same time."Yes, Sheriff Gary here." He said in a deep, stern voice after clearing his throat. The beeper sounded off again and vibrated at the same time. He grabbed the beeper before it vibrated off the side table.

"It's me on both phones … and you also beeped me?" The Sheriff hung up the landline and clicked off his beeper.

"We got a '911' to dispatch. A suspected floater in the Intracostal Waterway," answered Deputy Sheriff Keith nervously.

"Well, good morning to you too at …"—he looked at his watch—"at 6:07 a.m. Hey, wait, I see a telegram delivery boy running to my front door … and a Fed Ex truck, a US Postal delivery truck and wait … even a pony express rider racing down my street to my house and dismounting his horse at a full gallop. Now running to my door!" snapped the sheriff.

2

"Sorry, boss, for all those messages. I'm quite shocked that a possible homicide has occurred in our district. My first response, instinct, thought, reaction was that you'd want to know right away … seeing as you're familiar with such crimes, since you previously worked in Jacksonville," rapidly and erratically spoke the deputy.

"First, calm down, relax. This call relayed a possible floating body, accident, homicide or something. We don't call it until we get there, right?" Sheriff Gary asked.

"You're right, Boss Gary."

"Stop calling me your boss. I'm a county employee, just like you."

"O.K., bo … Sheriff," mumbled Deputy Sheriff Keith.

"Now, text me the location and …"

"I'll get your usual, on my way, Sheriff," added the deputy.

Gary rolled again on his back, thinking…*Was that a prophetic dream? Oh, my mesmerizing mermaids must be mingling in my mind mercifully and mystically.* With a loud groan, he flexed his body into a "V," rotated and jack-rabbited out of the bed.

*'I should get me a good divorced woman and find a day job with no weekends. Would I be bored?'* Gary pondered this as he stood looking out his bedroom window. *Could I keep my oath to myself of not drinking or smoking?*

This was out of the ordinary for this lower St. Johns County, as compared to Jacksonville or Orlando, where daily body count adds up and anticipated. In Florida, Jacksonville was the fourth largest city by population with 1,000,000 people. Orlando was number three, with greater than 1,500,000 people. One would expect these larger cities to have higher violent crime rates, not Crescent Beach with a population of less than one thousand year-round residents. Sheriff Gary had no rapes or murders during his twelve years on the force in that small, quiet community. That's why he took the job.

"Keith, an alleged murder victim may have actually succumbed to one of many causes," stated Sheriff Gary. "Deputy Sheriff, list them for me as I drive to the possible crime scene."

"Accidental drowning should be included, heart attack, stroke, falling with significant head injury, excessive blood loss and ah … ah."

"People having unresponsive cancer treatment, a person with poor respiratory health getting pneumonia, dementia, Alzheimer's, diabetic complications," continued Sheriff Gary. "And suicide," they both stated together.

"Many deaths are never explained beyond filing paper work with the District Attorney. No actual police footwork is done. No in-depth investigating," added Gary. "No police action following a preliminary and superficial autopsy final report stating no signs of suspicious acts or violence leading to the person's demise. Typical coroner's conclusions have no multiple organ failure consistent with old age. If prior medical records reveal to the medical examiner that the deceased had symptoms within the last seventy-two hours that explain the death with no foul play, then an autopsy may not be performed. The above factor would lead to no expected county prosecutor involvement in the case. In many urban areas, there are too many cases with too little resources and manpower to expect all cases of death to be investigated.

"In a small community like ours, Crescent Beach," Sheriff Gary said, "we don't need or have the resources, the experienced personnel or any reason to suspect a violent crime to occur here in our peaceful coterie."

"Ah, excuse me, Sheriff. What is a co-ter-ra?" questioned Deputy Sheriff Keith.

"A coterie is like our small group of people … our defined society of Crescent Beach," explained Gary. "In the pursuit of a homicide case, the investigation depends on a state, county or city detective and the coroner or medical examiner. The coroner, COR., is an elected or appointed individual. This individual may be a veterinarian, dentist or ordinary person with no medical experience whatsoever. No experience in performing autopsies, understanding of pathology or medical accreditation. Let's compare COR to a medical examiner, M.E., who is a state licensed and medical board certified doctor and usually is a pathologist."

Sheriff Gary slowed down and put on his right blinker.

# Chapter 2

## Sight

Seventeen Years Earlier

**I'm going to get you,** you slimy bugger." She got down on her hands and knees. Her hands swept under her bed from side to side, toward and away from herself as she tried to grasp it.

"You're a fast and feisty critter, aren't you?"

The blonde-haired girl had dreamt of this moment—night dreams, daydreams and actually acting out this event with her dolls. That would prepare her for success, for the real thing. She envisioned making the event true one day soon. She had a gift.

"Got Yah, little guy," Alisa said through a smile. The wiggling between her fingers and palms excited Alisa. Her imagination went wild. "I've seen this moment many times before, but a little different each time." Alisa sat cross-legged (or Indian style). "I've read about you, again and again," she spoke to her captive in her cupped hands. "In fact, slightly changing my mind's sight has made our meeting more perfect."

No reply came from the captive. Wait …."Croak."

"Oh, you understand, don't yah?"

She quickly brought her hands to her pursed lips …

"Alisa!" Pause. "Alisa!"

*Not Now, Mom,* Alisa thought. She opened her hands and kissed an empty palm. Her eyes opened wide. *But it was so real.*

"Thanks, Mom. You made me lose my prince charming!" Alisa yelled to her mom.

"Sorry, Alisa, you'll have another chance," her mom called back.

Alisa sighed as she looked down at her bedroom's beige-colored carpeted floor. She re-cupped and opened her hands several times. "Don't worry, my little amphibian, reptile or whatever you are. Soon we will have our glorious union. My sight guarantees that. We're only a kiss away …"

***

Present Day

"Alisa, still looking for your amphibian-reptile to be a prince to kiss?" her mother asked.

"No, Mom. I also gave up on a four-leaf clover, Santa Claus, the Easter Bunny, a pot of gold at the end of a rainbow and a lucky rabbit's foot. It wasn't too lucky for the rabbit! I'm going to be realistic and drive south to look for my job." (Footnote: Rabbit's Foot)

# Chapter 3

## *Speed*

**"I don't believe it,"** she said as she looked in her rear-view mirror, then to her car's speedometer and back to the mirror—now filled with red and blue. "My trip odometer shows I've traveled only 135 miles." She slowed the white Volkswagen Beetle with a black convertible top. She stopped on the shoulder next to an I-75 South highway sign. A silver Dodge Charger Ohio State Police car followed behind her with a rooftop row of blue "bubble gum" flashing lights and flashing red lights on the grill.

She opened her driver window. With license, registration, and proof of insurance all in hand, she watched her favorite color flash in all her car mirrors. *I feel like I'm in after school detention—all those smiling faces as they freely whisked by.*

After what seemed like an hour, the driver's door finally opened on the ominous predator vehicle. A person stood upright and put on a wide brim hat with a plastic protective rain cover.

*It's partly cloudy and blue-gray sky out … no rain. What's the purpose of the hat wrap? Oh, now the officer is putting on dark sunglasses. Whoa, what a giant of a man*, she thought as John Wayne, Dwayne Johnson and the Hulk all in one strutted to just behind her open car window. His waist was at her car's roof line. Having seen his utility belt, she automatically, for no particular reason, started doing an inventory. Keys, cuffs, short black night stick—called an asp, which can telescope out, a semi-automatic

7

firearm secured in a snapped down holster and two magazines holding a lot of bullets. He had approached her car with his right hand resting on this holster. He finally leaned forward to see her face, hands and to look in the rear compartment for anything dangerous or illegal.

*Should I slump in my car seat and look helpless or look up and do my Cameron Diaz, Heather Graham ... no, Katie Scarlett O'Hara imitation?* Questioning herself.

"How's the Autobahn today?" he asked in a stern voice. "Need your driver's license, registration and proof of insurance, ma'am."

Shaking them in her outstretched hand, the captured and helpless young girl passed the papers into his massive hand as he looked at each one.

"Ma'am, do you know why I pulled you over today?"

"You wanted to see what the new Bug's interior package looked like?" she smiled.

He leaned down and looked over his sunglasses at her. The officer definitely wasn't smiling.

*I'm still wondering why the sunglasses on a sunless day?* she thought.

"I'm sorry. I'm normally quite respectful of authority. It's just, I'm quite nervous right now." She hesitated and sheepishly smiled up at the officer.

He didn't move or speak.

*Is he assessing me? What does a northern Michigan girl know?*

He stood up and walked slowly with her papers back to the flashing blue lights on the clearly marked patrol car.

*How did I not see this predator vehicle?*

After waiting a night and a day, in her mind's timeline, he returned to her car.

"Your license shows your name as A-l-i-s-a. Is that A-Lisa or Ah-Lisa?"

"Which do you like?" He looked discerningly. "Lisa, Officer, sir? Yes, Officer," she whispered. She nodded her head and leaned her buxom chest toward the open car window. *I knew I should have worn my low-cut blouse.*

He looked at her license and then back at her face.

"In your license photo you have glasses and brown hair," he stated.

"Yes, I'm a natural blonde," she said as she fluffed her hair. "But I like to occasionally change it up, just for the fun of it." Alisa smiled. "Oh, I have contacts now."

"Well … you do remind me of that actress … what's her name?" the patrolman questioned.

"Maureen O'Hara. No, maybe I'm Amy Adams like?"

"How 'bout Julianne Moore … Molly Ringwald or Nicole Kidman?" he said.

"Rene Russo … Jane Seymour?" she fired off.

"No," he said.

"Isla Fisher, Emma Stone, Alicia Witt? Really now—am I like Kate Winslet? Rachel McAdams? Maybe Kirsten Dunst?" she continued.

"I'm going way back now. Ann Margaret, Tina Louise or Rita Hayworth?" he said.

"What about—"

"Stop Miss!" the patrolman took a deep breath. "Do you know how fast you were going?"

"Actually, I goosed-it just a little to get back in the right lane so other cars could—"

"You were going ninety-four miles per hour and the posted—"

"Oh my, I thought this wee Beetle Bug topped out at like … seventy-five?"

"Ma'am, ma'am, since this is your first speeding ticket in the Great State of Ohio"—he looked down at her girlish half smile—"I am writing you up for eleven miles over the posted speed limit. I'm not writing you up for your actual radar-determined speed of ninety-four miles per hour, or twenty-four miles over the posted speed limit." The patrolman still did not smile. "This infraction requires a mandatory appearance at the Auglaize County seat. That's at the downtown Wapakoneta Court House. If you as the speeder are determined to be hostile, I'll be obliged to arrest and place you in its county jail. There you will wait in jail, until the judge is in session at the Wapakoneta County Court," the enormous patrolman explained. "Do you have any questions?"

"Oh no, sir, I'm very cooperative, sir. I deeply appreciate this merciful consideration you have passed my way," she said, squirming in her seat.

The officer sternly stared at her, questioning if she was sincere or a smart ass.

"If you wish to fight this ticket in court, I'm informing you as a courtesy that the actual radar-determined speed is posted on this ticket."

The State Trooper stopped and tilted his sunglasses down again.

*He looked into my eyes … my soul!* A shiver shoot down her spine.

"On the back of the ticket is a phone number to call to pay your fine within ten days if you have no dispute."

"Thank you so much, Officer Burns."

He turned and walked away, likely not hearing any of those last words. *Luckily he didn't know about all my other speeding tickets,* she thought as a smile broke over her face.

Unbeknown to her, Officer Burns had first used his on-board ANPR, Automated Number Plate Recognition technology, to run her license plate number and obtain its history. Then he inserted her driver's license into his Datalux, Mobile Computer Solutions for information concerning her driving record, personal history and any criminal record such as arrests, convictions, jail time and outstanding warrants for her arrest.

The Highway State Trooper did identify Alisa Favour with a list of all the prior issued tickets in all traveled states—not only speeding tickets, but also unpaid parking tickets in several college and university communities, resulting in arrest warrants issued in several Michigan cities. There would be a costly waiting "prize" in jail if or when Alisa was pulled over for another moving violation in Michigan.

"This day is lucky for me." Alisa grinned and pulled slowly out in front of the still lit-up parked Highway Patrol car. She continued southbound on I-75 at the legal speed limit. She felt lucky in more ways than she knew, at least for now.

# Chapter 4

---

## Trust

**"I know what you've been doing ...** what you've been trying to accomplish." The man walked closer. "Look at my face."

He paused as the watery eyes turned toward him.

"Haven't we been good together?" His hands moved back and forth between him and the entity he was speaking with. "Hasn't your life been good? Do you want this relationship to end? Do you? Well, you're jeopardizing everything we have." He put his hands on his hips. "Don't look away from me—I know you understand. Think of all the things I've done for you. I can make this thing you want happen. It will happen. It's just a matter of time."

The man heard some mumbling, guttural and hissing sounds from the watery-eyed face.

"Right now, only I know what you've done. If you don't listen to me and continue being careless, everyone will know," he said seriously. "Then it will go ridiculously bad and out of my control, to the point where I won't be able to help or protect you."

The wet, dripping, expressionless face stared past him at something.

"You know you can trust me. Who else can you trust? Don't be this way. Don't turn your back on me! Come back here. We need each other. You can't do it on your own in this country." His speech became a whisper ... and then he was alone.

"Professor, who are you speaking with?" a woman's voice asked from behind the building.

"Where are you, Professor?"

He turned by the north corner of the windowless building and saw her walking toward him.

"Ah, there you are," she said.

"I was just thinking out loud, that's all." The professor smiled. He lightly placed a few fingers on Jennifer's shoulder and directed her toward A1A with him by her side. Suddenly, they both heard a loud splash from the river behind them. She partially turned to look back.

"What was that?" she suspiciously asked.

The professor turned her back as they approach the road.

"Probably just a breaking wake from a passing boat on the river," he explained. "Let's pay attention to the traffic."

"Will you come into the park's waiting room? You do know you have a schedule to follow? You've asked me to keep you straight on for the day," relayed the front desk admission assistant, Jennifer.

He looked back over the paved road, shrubs, and trees, beyond the research building to the calm river with no surface movement except for a river's current. There were no waves, no circling ripples, not even a solo leaf floating by from a warm off-land breeze.

"You are correct, Ms. Jennifer with the cute ponytail. What would I do without you?"

"Thank you, Professor. Do you think I look prettier with my brown hair in a ponytail"— as she turned to strike a pose with her head skyward— "or when I have pigtails, like yesterday?"

"Ms. Jennifer Lynne Longing, with your smiling face, outgoing personality and positive attitude, your hairstyle, whatever way you wear it, only complements your entire package as a desirable woman." The professor opened the door to the Marinescape Park's educational and entertainment facility. "I'm sure you'll have many young suitors to choose from."The grinning and not shy Jennifer handed the professor a typed paper schedule.

"What I need from you, Jennifer Lynne is to mail out an employment search for a marine assistant to lighten my daily routine here at Marinescape." The Professor flipped through the papers. "I need help doing all the maintenance duties so that I have more time for research projects. Send out e-mails or fliers to all the colleges and universities offering marine biology degrees."

"That sounds like a lot of research and extra work," Jennifer pouted.

The professor gently placed a finger under her chin, bringing her eyes up to his at six-foot-three-inch height.

"You do this for me … I'll help you next time with whatever you need."

Jennifer's smile came back and she nodded.

# Chapter 5

*Inlet*

---

**Dispatcher Mary Jane** had confirmed that the source calling in on the 911 was a reliable local resident.

"I sent the dispatcher call to M.E. Doctor Ian MacGrath to inform him of the floater," Deputy Sheriff Keith announced.

"A suspected floater has been reported," corrected the Sheriff as he drove the community-owned, all-wheel drive SUV Ford Expedition toward the National Fort Matanzas National Monument Park in Crescent Beach.

Gary had really wanted the Ford F-150, which shared some of the same body frame and mechanical components as the Expedition, but a county voting council member had a brother-in-law who owned a Ford dealership near St. Augustine. He had a surplus of the afore-mentioned vehicle, so that's what Sheriff Gary drove, stamped with "620 St. Johns Sheriff" on it, one of their four-vehicle fleet.

The same council member also argued that if anyone on council needed such a large vehicle, and it wasn't in use, they could "borrow" it, even if it wasn't for law enforcement business. Gary had to admit that the Expedition was a comfortable vehicle for his large frame compared to his previous ten-year-old Ford Bronco.

"The report is correct, Sheriff." Deputy Keith looked down on to the deceased.

"Good job. I'm almost there." His vehicle's lights and siren were on to alert traffic of his approach and subsequent passing of them.

Crescent Beach was a quiet and friendly community that when the sheriff passed pedestrians and bicyclists would wave.

The Sheriff arrived at the west Matanzas Inlet parking lot and saw the St. Johns County Ambulance's rhythmic flashing red lights. He wondered if this was another homeless veteran who had lost all hope of a normal life after an American overseas military tour. Maybe a drunken boater who fell overboard … or a deadly heart attack or stroke occurred in an un-expecting beach walker.

As Sheriff Gary got out of his vehicle and stepped along the wooden boardwalk to the sandy south and west river shoreline of the inlet, he saw two paramedics turn away from the shore and walk toward him. The paramedics were already at the accident or crime scene, in case the victim needed medical attention, as per police dispatcher protocol. He went under the already placed "Do Not Cross" yellow police crime scene tape.

"Morning, Sheriff, no work for us here," reported one of the paramedics as they passed.

Gary nodded to them. He looked up and to his left to the white concrete structure. Several spectators had collected on the Claude Varn Bridge, which crossed this Matanzas Inlet. They could be watching the comedic sparring … diving gregarious pelicans. No, they were rubbernecking from the bridge to gawk and get a bird's-eye view of the dreadful dead body or the crime scene of someone's loved one. And, of course, all these vultures were on their cell phones texting, talking and taking videos or pictures. To be the first to post an awful event on social media brought some kind of status. Sheriff Gary did notice an out of place hat among a sea of baseball and university-styled caps on the bridge. An average-height man stood out because of his beige-colored straw fedora hat with a red feather coming out of the black hat ribbon. Or was it a Panama straw hat? Gary couldn't tell because of the easterly rising sun behind the bridge.

"What do you have?" inquired Sheriff Gary.

"Unidentified woman, found like this, naked, face-down in the water." Gary and Keith both looked down at the body. Keith handed one large cup of coffee to Sheriff Gary. Neither man looked up as they took a sip of their coffees. Deputy Keith held his breath.

"Large, regular, one cream, no sweetener —just as I like it, Thank you, Deputy."

"She needed to lose weight," Deputy Sheriff said as he shook his head.

"Is that the way a professional would phrase his observation?" questioned Sheriff Gary.

"No, Sheriff. I should list her physical characteristics," the deputy responded quickly. "We have a female whose five-foot-two-inch and one-hundred-seventy-five-pound. She has short, irregular cut, multicolored hair in salt water. She has black hair under both her armpits, red buttocks cheeks and shoulder bruises, Sheriff, sir."

"Right on with that summary of the victim, Deputy Sheriff Kermit Keith."

"Sheriff, please don't use my first name in public, just the initial," whispered Keith. They looked straight-faced at each other.

"No clothing or identification found near the body or the shoreline. I'm guessing she's in her mid-twenties," sourly responded Deputy Sheriff Keith. "The crime scene has been secured."

From behind them, two voices called out.

"Untouched body?" asked Medical Examiner MacGrath.

"Hi, guys," added CSI Assistant Tara as she walked past them.

"Only touched by the paramedics for vital signs," volleyed the Deputy Sheriff Keith.

Looking at the slightly bobbing body in the shallow water revealed the red buttocks checks and shoulder bruises.

"She surely didn't take care of her body," remarked M.E. MacGrath. "I can't image this lady in her early thirties was swimming for needed weight loss exercise?"

Sheriff turned to Deputy Keith, who expecting Keith to apology. The incident went unacknowledged.

"No crown hair missing, no cuts, no disfigured limbs, no blood or foreign objects in the body, body orifices or around the body," Tara clearly stated as she recorded her observations.

"Let's move the body to the shore and onto a cart," commanded the M.E, "once CSI Assistant Tara stops photographically documenting our victim's scene. Can someone help Tara enclose the body and move it to the CSI van?"

"I.D.?" asked Gary again.

"Yes," yelled out a patrolman jogging to the sheriff's side. "I ran to get the car plates on the car found in the parking lot. I saw the flashing dash security light in this White Camaro, so I called the car's tracking system. I also found this purse."

"Nice thinking, patrolman."

Deputy Keith took the purse and found her driver's license, "Thirty-three-year-old, single woman, blonde, blue-eyed, from Ohio."

After looking at it, Deputy Keith handed it off to the sheriff, who glanced at it and then gave it to M.E. MacGrath, who then handed it off to CSI Assistant Tara, who bagged it and labeled it with the date, location found, time, and personal signature.

"Any ideas when, how, why?" questioned Sheriff Gary.

"Probably a drowning; however, you know I can't say anything officially until I have this unfortunate young woman on my examination table. She'll 'talk' to me under my inquisitive eyes and knife." This was the doc's usual response.

Meanwhile, Tara was smiling at Deputy Keith. He nodded back at her.

Gary looked around the area. "I want an even larger surrounding area searched, including the trampled parking lot and shoreline under the bridge, plus another two hundred yards for any significant trace clues," the sheriff called out.

"Patrolman, would you please continue to secure the area until our CSI team is done?" asked Doctor MacGrath as he looked to Sheriff Gary, who nodded in agreement.

"Sheriff, could these indentations in the sand be footprints?" the same patrolman asked.

The Sheriff and Doc walked over to the shoreline near the bridge.

"Tara," shouted MacGrath as she was still smiling at Deputy Keith, "photograph, measure and make a cast of the best-preserved footprint you can find, include the surrounding area to show the possible perpetrator's direction." Tara ran over with her orange CSI bag to perform the proper collection process and preservation of the potential evidence.

Gary, next to Doc MacGrath, looked up and saw the same fedora hat looking down.

"If they're footprints, I'd call them size twenty or larger, like from clown's shoes," Tara answered. "I'm going to use my leased 3-D printer and compare it to the usual casting system." Tara turned from facing Sheriff Gary and found Deputy Sheriff Keith by her side. She jerked back in surprise. "Whoa! Why so close?"

"Sorry I came up on you like that."

"You were quite stealthy, Kermit," Tara said with a smile.

"Please whisper that around the team, Ms. Co—i—tus, I mean Coitan."

"Quiet— that's not funny."

"I guess we both have our secrets," grinned Deputy Keith. "Make sure to maintain your chain of command when reporting your findings, Miss CSI."

"Is that why you're being so jerky?"

"I enjoy watching you work; every minute move seems so personal. I feel I really know you, all of you. I hope to hear from you later, Miss Assistant Crime Scene Investigator Tara," added Deputy Keith. "Maybe I should start a *Miss CSI* magazine."

"Oh, that was a night of mistakes on my part," Tara whispered. "It ended that night … no more, nada. But don't worry. I now know what to get you for the Christmas exchange—a rubber inflatable doll." Tara used her hands to demonstrate inflating chest balloons.

"Ha, you're exactly who I'd want to be in my magazine. Your face is welcoming; you have stylish hair, attractive and smart clothing and a right-proportioned body. The reader would love to read about your inventive idea of using the 3-D printer for capturing temporary evidence." Keith's lips were only "cells" away. Their breathing pattern became in sync. She licked her lips.

"That would include me being clothed?" Tara remarked as Keith held his breath.

"Fully clothed, your tight laboratory garb, at all times, at least for the publication," he said.

"Of course, as you are now." Tara tapped her index finger on his nose and turned away.

"I'll expect an update on this situation of ours," he said as he started to follow her.

"I'll relay any new findings through my superior, CSI Director Leon," she said. While walking away, Tara turned and faked a smiled at Keith.

"I was referring to you personally," he replied as he caught up to her. "I was thinking the two of us should meet for coffee, tea, snack, dinner or something we both like."

"Sheriff?" The patrolman pointed to the shoreline under the bridge.

"Tara, go look at what the patrolman may have found," directed the sheriff.

Tara took her orange CSI evidence bag over to the patrolman. A blue scarf was wrapped in a frond of seaweed.

"A probable good find, Patrolman," Tara said. She pulled out an extendable pointer from her bag. "Sheriff, we found a long, wispy blue scarf." She held it up.

"A blue scarf that looks shredded, wispy, but still together." Gary looked a little shocked.

"What the hell. Blue, shredded scarf, like blue hair?" responded Gary with a face of loss.

"I'm sorry, what did you say?" asked Doc MacGrath.

"Nothing important," Gary lied.

"I thought of another possibility for the large sand impression, like a fin," he said as the patrolman knelt down next to Tara. She looked at him. "These sand prints could be from a scuba divers flipper, swim fins or a sea monster." The patrolman grinned.

Tara looked at him, studying his face, "Really ... patrolman ... a sea monster? What's your nam?"

"I'm Patrolman John Brenner, Miss CSI Tara Coitan, like the mineral."

"No, that is spelled without the letter 'I' Just Tara is fine.

"It also could be explained by drying sand expanding and flattening with time."

"That's an excellent suggestion as an explanation for these large footprints." Tara moved closer to John. They leaned toward each other, as if gravity was pulling them together, until their shoulders touched.

"Oh, I'm sorry about that, Tara," John said as they both stood up and hit heads.

"Oh, I'm sorry about that," laughed Tara.

Not far away, behind them, Deputy Keith frowned at seeing them together.

"Doc, time of death?" Gary looked at Doc Ian.

"Well, with a body on land, normal human body temperature minus the victim's body temp, divided by 1.5, would give time of death, plus or minus one or two hours. That depends on air temp and ground temp. Now if the body was in the sun or water, the water temperature—"

"O.K., I get it. You can't be that accurate. Just an educated guess based on the liver temp you just got with that temperature needle," the irritated Gary asked again.

"Well, the body was in cold brine water, like being pickled. I can't say at this time because the body core temperature of the victim has been affected by varied ocean water temperatures of the tides and the mixture with the Matanzas brine and warmer fresh water temperature," rambled on M.E. MacGrath.

The sheriff started to walk away when he heard a response over his shoulder. "It was probably four to six hours ago."

"May I interrupt? Her wristwatch stopped at 6:06 a.m.," the patrolman observed.

"Very astute, Patrolman ... your name?" the sheriff asked.

"Patrolman John Brenner, badge number—"

"That's good. Do you want to make some overtime?"

John nodded with a growing smile.

"Don't smile. You'll probably be bored. I want you to walk along the shoreline, up to the National Park tour boat dock, across the boardwalk and A1A to the ocean shoreline and back under the bridge, ending at the death scene," instructed Sheriff Gary. Call the office when you're done and tell Mary Jane the extra time you spent here."

"If I find trace evidence, should I contact CSI Assistant Tara to process it?" John asked.

"Ask Doc MacGrath what—"

"Contact CSI Assistant Tara," Doc replied.

"Yes, sir," the patrolman responded. He saw Tara walking to the CSI vehicle carrying her orange bag. He jogged over to her as she opened the Ford's door.

"Tara? Can I have your contact phone number in case I find more evidence?" he asked. "That's alright. I'll just call Mary Jane." Tara turned around.

"No, that's not necessary, Patrolman Brenner." She looked at his eager face. "Please feel free to call me at my private cell phone number."

"I'm John." He extended a hand. "In case you forgot."

"I'm Tara, John. I didn't forget your name." Their eyes exchanged unspoken emotions.

# Chapter 6

## *Another*

**On another shoreline,** another woman continued her speed-walking while listening to Lady Gage's "Bad Romance." Her ear buds still allowed her to hear the relaxing waves lapping, the passing A1A traffic beyond the sand dune on her right and extraneous noise on her left. This eastern Atlantic Ocean beach was still part of the Matanzas National Monument Park. The beach and dunes were protected from future development, for all to use.

She walked by and read the welcoming sign: "All who come this way may enjoy its Nature." She approached the Inlet Bridge. A sand dune rose about ten feet, covered with sea grass.

"This is a great site for the Atlantic loggerhead turtles to migrate to lay their eggs in sandy sea grass. Are any of you little guys out this morning?" she called out.

This shoreline wasn't far from where the CSI team had just left.

With the diurnal ocean tides, the high tide water on her left had shrunk the beach to less than six feet wide. As she went under the Matanzas Inlet Bridge, she heard a faint splashing sound.

"Ah," she said as she looked around, "must have been waves on the bridge's supporting pylons." Suddenly, she felt some wet, scratchy hands grab her from behind and under her arms and she was pulled into the water and disappeared.

\*\*\*

**The Matanzas Inlet** crime scene had been cleared of the patrol cars, the ambulance, the CSI van with the body and the last of the crime scene tape, which had been removed by Patrolman John. Even the bridge spectators had dispersed.

Sheriff Gary was the last to leave. As he approached his vehicle, he heard a voice from behind.

"Sheriff, may I have a word?" Gary turned to see the red-feathered fedora first and then the speaker's serious face on a medium-size man.

"Yes?"

"I'm R.W. Angel from the *Palatka National & Local Newspaper* and supplement." He extended a hand with no reciprocal response. "I was wondering if you could answer a few—"

"No comment at this time," Sheriff Gary snapped. "You should know we need time to collect the evidence, analyze the evidence and develop our theories to explain the evidence."

"I'm an independent reporter for the major newspaper in Putnum County, which I mentioned, is also published as the *Palatka Daily Florida News*. I'm a small fish among large established carnivorous fishes at the newspaper. There's no future in reporting 'a newly found family recipe for spicy cornbread or chocolate fudge pie.'" I'm hoping to break a story first so a larger newspaper will notice me, like the *St. Augustine Times* or even the *Orlando Sentinel.*"

"What's in it for me or the sheriff's department," Gary suspiciously inquired of Mr. Angel.

"I'll only write what you tell me, verbatim," Mr. Angel stated as he crossed his heart.

Sheriff Gary grinned at that hand gesture.

"You make one—"

"I'll make no mistakes, no assumptions and no yellow journalistic lies for media coverage." The twenty-five-year-old reporter tapped his heart. "Of course, if you want me to write something questionable?"

"Don't make me sound like an idiot or uneducated," the sheriff said. "You may quote me: 'There is no official comment at this time, on the recently found body on the Matanzas River Inlet. I can't remember a single unexplained death in the lower St. Johns County villages and towns since I joined this Law Enforcement Agency, which was twelve years ago. More information will follow.' Off the record, don't use the word 'force.' It's too intimidating to the public. Make sure to use 'agency' when writing about law enforcement." Young Mr. Angel went to shake hands with the sheriff, who again only gave a head nod.

"I'll send you a copy of my article," he said as he opened the door of his white and red convertible. Sheriff Gary stopped.

"What are you driving, a baby elephant or a twelve-foot extinct dinosaur?" He walked over to the vehicle Mr. Angel proudly stood next to.

"This beautiful girl is from the last century, a 1959 Metropolitan." Angel ran his hand along its warm, vibrant red, smooth fender covering the front protruding headlight. Gary looked in the open-topped, two-passenger-bench-seat car.

"Do you get tickets for driving too slow?" Gary chuckled.

"Sheriff, you'd be surprised," the smiling reporter said as he sat in the car. "It's a three-speed manual and I've gotten up to sixty-five miles an hour …, legally, of course."

"No radio. You have manual canvas top, roll-down windows, trunk the size of an airplane overhead bag—"

"Sheriff, I have windshield wipers, a heater, covered outside spare tire, forty mpg, classic looking red *M* logos on each wheel cover and car front fender—"

"Enjoy the ride and as you mother would say, 'Drive safe.'"

Angel started up the 1.2 liter, three-cylinder Austin motor and rolled down the road, gaining speed with the wind. No James Bond car seen here.

*** 

Sheriff Gary shut his eyes, trying to remember the last time there was an unexpected body found in Crescent Beach … actually, the last time any body was found in lower St. Johns County.

"Sheriff Gary!" crackled the Expedition's intercom. "We have another floater. It's at the fishing landing cutout just west of the 206 Verle Allyn Pope or Crescent Beach Bridge near our headquarters," broadcasted the dispatcher, Mary Jane.

"Call the paramedics, Deputy Keith, CSI team and the M.E. again."

24

"Already done, sir," confirmed Mary Jane.

"What would I do without you, Miss Mary Jane?" the sheriff said sincerely.

"Why thank you, sir. I didn't realize you thought of me like that. Please call me Jane."

***

**Just a short distance** from the first crime scene, Sheriff Gary drove north on the two-lane Road, A1A Oceanshore Boulevard turned left and crossed the bridge. After some hesitation and breath holding, he exhaled.

*I'm not in Jacksonville. I'm not in Jacksonville*, he told himself. He got out of the vehicle and took in the view of the Matanzas River-Intracoastal Waterway site just south of the S.R. 206 Pope Bridge. He saw the same participants from the Matanzas Inlet accident-crime scene re-collected at Estuary Park. Their dialogues and expressions were a little more disgusted as each repeated their routine. One significant difference was found—heel-dragging marks in the sand, suggesting someone had tried to save her on land or she ran into the water and was dragged back to the shore. Why save her? Why go into the water? She had hair and a blue sundress soaked. Deputy Keith had immediately found her purse and identification by some fishing gear.

"She's thirty-four-years-old and from Ohio."

Patrolman Brenner, standing next to Keith, added, "The only parked vehicle in the area is that unlocked white Chevy Camaro to the west. The same color and make of car as at the first crime scene." The sheriff gave the patrolman an "Oh really?" look and turned away.

"Ah ... I found a dashboard car pass for the Summerhouse. Dispatch Mary Jane called the resort and found out she was housed there for three months," added Brenner.

"This is our inventory bagged at this crime scene so far," said CSI assistant Tara, who handed the list to Sheriff Gary.

"A tipped over folding chair, her purse with money and credit card remaining, bait bucket, sandals, sunhat, sunglasses and an unopened *Vernors* pop can. Also a fishing rod with no hook on the line," read Sheriff Gary.

25

The paramedics again had nothing to offer the victim and packed up and left with their lights off. Deputy Keith was speaking with the black-haired Officer Brett and smiling. The doc knelt by the lifeless body. Tara was placing crime scene identification numbers by the evidence and clicking a thousand photographs in color and black and white. The sheriff watched as Tara knelt next to a short cluster of shoreline reeds. She pulled out what appeared to be torn white underwear—*An assault gone deadly?*

"You know what these reeds are named?" asked Keith.

"I do. The British call them Bulrushes; Americans call them cattails or punks," she answered.

"Another name would be corn dog grass or water sausages," Keith added with a wide grin. "I prefer one of those names myself."

"Why am I not surprised you would know that trivia?" she replied.

"Tara, come on over here, please," requested the doc.

"Is that a fish scale? Right there at her right temporal hair line?" observed MacGrath.

"I'll photograph, bag and label it, Doc Ian," summarized Tara. "In the lab we'll reveal what it is. Isn't that rather large for a fish scale?"

"I heard some of your conversation on intracostal vegetation with Deputy Keith," said the Doc. "The story of the Intracoastal Waterway is quite fascinating. It extends from Boston to Key West on the Atlantic side, continuing on to the Gulf of Mexico side to Brownsville, Texas. Three thousand toll free nautical miles of waterway with a minimal depth of—"

"Doc, you know I expect significant findings by tomorrow, on both cases, right?" interrupted Sheriff Gary. He was used to interrupting Doc's rambling trivia. Dr. Ian MacGrath just looked up and smiled at him. Doc was used to ignoring Gary's frequent interrogations for information.

"Can't you see me in a chair along the river, fishing or relaxing in a boat and holding a rod? Because that's what I'll be doing when we solve these cases, by tomorrow, before the weekend!" framed Gary authoritatively.

"And which weekend are we referring to?" fired back Doc MacGrath.

"Do your best, as you always do," both Sheriff and Doc said together.

"Sheriff Gary," called Tara, "I've determined that the suspected heel-dragging was toward the river, ending at or in the water." Tara looked at Gary. "She was dragged into the water, where I found the torn underwear."

Gary turned and walked back to his SUV. Once in it, he reclined the driver's seat and closed his eyes. *Two separate drownings on the same river, close to each other, on the same day!*

"Oh yah ... both victims have Chevy Camaros. What are the chances of that?" Sheriff Gary blurred out. "A blue scarf ... a blue sundress ... a blue mermaid? Am I becoming psychic or psychotic? Oh, it's going to be hard not to smoke a pack or drink a bottle of Jack today."

# Chapter 7

## *Third*

---

**Within minutes of reclining** in his car seat, he found himself underwater again, walking slowly on the river bottom. I've been here before. I'll wait expecting … they are … whisking hair by my face. There's her head and body.

I look up and see sunlight reflecting and refracting on the water's surface. Several smiling mermaids swim by, back and forth. Do their breasts seem bigger? They brush against my bare body parts … my head, arms, lower legs … wait!

"I'm totally naked," I gurgle as I look down! "Whoa, my snake is awake and at attention." I struggle to cover my privates with my hands, but my arms keep floating up. I start to hear music. "Is that just in my head?" Air bubbles pass up beyond my face. "I'm in the water, but I can see blue sky and hear a song."

*Birds fly free*
A female form appears and starts walking on the river bed toward me.

*Fish swim free*
*This river runs free; they all know how I feel.*

The female silhouette has no tailfin. It's ... she is walking next to me. I can't make out her face, as it's covered in flowing hair and shadows. The rest of her naked body is clearly visible and...

"What? You love me? Who are you?" I again try to cover my erect member to no avail.

I'm becoming overwhelmed by bubbles. I spin slowly around.

"Where are you?" I gurgle. At a distance, I see my favorite blue mermaid swimming my way and frowning directly at me. She swiftly turns away.

Suddenly, all I can see is ... no, it can't be ... three naked women holding hands. Still under water, I approach them. They turn into three naked dead women floating up as if they were reaching for the surface, the sun, some air. Their bodies are turning into skeletons.

Out of the corner of my left eye, I see a half-man, half fish with claws swim toward me. I shake my head. No, no, no ...

It turns back to the mermaids, who are looking down at us. Their heads are mere skulls devoid of ... their hair detaches and floats away. A flapping sound becomes louder and louder.

"Is that a dragonfly ... under water? Is that a helicopter above the water's surface? It looks like a Coastguard helicopter coming down to me."

"Hello, Sheriff?" Gary opened his eyes, as he was still partly reclined in his vehicle. "It is a Coastguard helicopter," he smirked.

"Sheriff, Sheriff Gary, can you hear me?"

"What now?" He grabbed the dashboard mic. "Another body?"

"Well, yes, sir."

"What the hell? Now where is this one?"

"It's on the ocean side, back at the Matanzas Inlet opening. The body was rolling back and forth in the ocean's low tide. The first responders brought the body up on shore. No vital signs found," reported Mary Jane apologetically.

"You're telling me that after we left the first crime scene, during daylight, this third alleged drowning occurred?"

"Sorry, sir, I'm just relaying information from the Coast Guard helicopter's observation, as they just passed by the Inlet."

The sheriff exhaled and hesitated. "Damn it all! I'm sorry for attacking you, Jane. Forgive me?" asked Sheriff Gary. "Jane thanks for doing your job. I owe you a coffee or something."

"Oh Deputy Keith, I thought you were already out at the crime scene," said a surprised Mary Jane as the deputy walked into her semi-private office while the sheriff listened. "I came back to get some notes I made on the first two crime scenes that I left here for transcription." The deputy leaned over her back, smiling and placing his face near hers. "You're looking quite beguiling today." He moved over and placed a hand on the back of her chair, motioning to wrap her shoulders without actually touching her.

Mary Jane grinned and acted shy. "I've had no time to transfer script to type."

"What's on the air?" he asked as his face came close to her right ear.

"I picked up the Coast Guard helicopter chatter. Here, I'll put it on speaker," said a still-smiling Mary Jane. She played the recording:

*"Did you see that? Let's go back for another look."* The twin engine Sikorsky MH-60T Jayhawk turned south 180 degrees like a dragonfly hunting a mosquito. The copter was typically used for search and rescue, law enforcement, military readiness and marine environmental protection. The copter's base was in Palm Beach County for fuel, maintenance and new copter production. The crew of four was excited.

"This baby can fly up to 207 mph straight line, so let's giddy up."

"Pretty funny, don't you think, Deputy?" Mary Jane turned her face left to look at him eye to eye from her chair. He was staring at her face, which was surrounded by curly reddish-brown hair.

"Whatever MJ, may I call you MJ?" asked the still smiling deputy. Mary Jane's breathing quickened and she answered with a couple of blinks, without pulling her face away.

"You're alluring face glows like the morning sun." His whispered breath tickled her left ear. "Your cheeks are reddish, like the sun reflecting on opening tulip pedals. This sight is reserved for only a special person to wake up to and see each morning." He exhaled into her ear.

The radio recording sounded again.

*"There it is, Captain, right in the shallow surf,"* the audio recording continued. One could hear the helicopter's whooshing blades slow down to a hover.

*"We'll go down lower. Can you all see?"*

*"Yes, sir, thank you, sir."* Two of the four crew members stood in the open cargo door.

"*Those are fine-rolling, back-and-forth breasts,*" a crew member commented.

"*This surf is safe and secure,*" announced the captain. "*This will be a moment we'll have only between us.*"

"*Captain, I think we need to reassess the situation. I think this body is lifeless, sir.*"

"That's the end of the audio." Mary Jane continued the whispering mode.

"This will be a moment we'll have only between us," mimicked the deputy.

Suddenly, an incoming call came on.

"Keith, are you at the new accident-crime scene?" the sheriff loudly asked.

"Yes Sheriff. Did you hear all that recorded conversa — I heard on my way." He stood upright and headed out. He stopped at the car door in a daze and turned back with a smile and a nod. He saw her bewitched, bothered and bewildered face, at least in his mind. She gave a small wave.

# Chapter 8

## Driving

**Alisa started to relax** after driving over the Ohio River's Brent Spencer double Decker Bridge at Cincinnati into northern Kentucky, continuing her journey toward her dream of a professional life in a water world.

The highway patrol seemed to be more lenient about driving over the posted speed limit. She passed Covington, Fort Wright and Fort Mitchell as the highway became free range ... to speed. Then the Florence Mall tower appeared.

"Oh, I really don't have the time—don't need anything— don't have the money. Too late, "I've missed the exit. Good-bye temptation." Kentucky's southbound I-75 began to straighten out as the I-75 and I-71 split approached.

"Let's pick up the pace a little," she softly spoke to her car. She was already going nine over the posted speed limit. "All I need is to tag a rabbit and keep close." Soon she saw a black Mustang followed tightly by a black Audi and a white 150 Ford pickup. "Here we go," Alisa said through smiling lips. "I'm going right between the Audi and 150. Don't worry, boys; I won't drag this express convoy down."

Alisa probably had driven over 300,000 miles in multiple cars in her lifetime—different cars at different schools and part time jobs. She felt she was meant to be driving a car; that's why driving had become second nature to her.

"I think I must have genes that recognize a vehicle as the place of my conception, my home, so to speak."

This is explained by "imprinting," which she had learned about in class. It was a biology professor, Professor Blabla or whatever his name was, who explained a study involving Mallard ducklings. It showed they learned important sounds while in the embryonic stage of life, still un-laid, un-hatched in an egg. They heard sounds from their mother; these conversations started at seventeen days after the duckling's conception. Alisa remembered the open-ended question to the students:

"Do animals, including humans, act the way they do from inherited genetic instruction, like a blueprint contained in every living cell of the organism? Or could their behavior have been learned from a mother's uterine talk? Many call this instinct. Or was it within hours of birth that lifelong behavior began? This is called imprinting or learned behavior from observing Mother and others of similar species."

"Maybe I have a combination of imprinting and observed driving behavior from both of my parents, relatives or friends," Alisa exclaimed out loud. "Whatever, I have this need for speed."

\*\*\*

**When Alisa wanted** something, she became a boulder. No budging on the issue. No changing of her plan of direction.

When it came to learning to drive, she told people she'd taught herself to drive. This was as soon as she could reach the floor pedals and see over the steering wheel.

"I was nine years old," she'd say while look at a disbelieving face.

Alisa would drive her mom's car on an accessory gravel parking lot behind her workplace while her mom was working. It was easy enough to do. Her parents always left the car keys under the driver's floor mat for either parent to use. They never locked the car.

"No need to," her father would say. This idiom was good for Alisa.

So once in the car, keys in hand, Alisa practiced on her non-school days and summer vacation. She was very observant of her parents' driving and listened to them arguing about if there was a law against what her dad had just done. Once Alisa became confident with her new skill, she was tempted to drive the three-and-a-quarter miles home to show off to her friends. Her adolescence "showing off" desire said yes, but her developing maturity told her no. She never did.

When driver's education class came around in high school, she could have been the instructor. Her mom acted amazed at how comfortable Alisa was behind the wheel with her driver's permit. Alisa passed with an 'A' and received her license at the first go-a-round with the written and the officer accompanied road tests. After the ride-a-long, the officer commented to her mom, "You have a fine driver here, ma'am. The best I've been with so far this year." One month later, Alisa got into a parking lot accident at the North Kent mall, which resulted in a painful insurance increase for the car her dad had bought her.

Alisa never told her mother how she became so proficient at driving. The first car her parents bought her and survived the above accident was a pre-owner 289, 210 horsepower convertible red Mustang.

It was only after Alisa had paid off the auto debt to her parents that she came clean. While her mom was making dinner, Alisa sat down at the kitchen table and casually mentioned that she had driven the family car without their permission.

"I know," her mom said without turning away from the sink where she was cleaning vegetables. "I saw you driving in the back lot with a look of concentration on your face, dear."

Alisa immediately hugged and held on to her. "Now, your dad's response would have been a different story, so our secret." Not being the alpha driver led to less mental focus and judgment.

***

**Alisa had time** to reflect on her education while driving. In high school, she was the center of attention, the one all the girls looked up to and asked for an opinion. There was immediate reward from daily drama, excitement and having the ultimate power of her high school social group. Being a cheerleader and on the prom queen's court for three years was the position all the girls wanted the added benefit of being invited to the "cool" parties and desired by the "cool" boys. Many young men and boys wanted to date this bodacious, voluptuous, long-haired, blonde beauty.

Her educational path after high school to a career still remained arduous. She realized in her senior year that her socialization skills were not reflected in grade point averages, so very few colleges were open to her.

Alisa regretted starting college while living with her badgering parents, whose criticism and quizzing during nightly dinners was tiresome. The counterpoint was a convenient, short commute to the community college with no living expenses and free meals.

She transferred to Grand Valley State University as her average went up through the boring social science, social behavior, psychology and French classes. Still, Alisa had no enthusiasm or definite career path. She just fell toward a general degree in Literature, Science & Arts.

During her time at GVSU, Alisa went on a group canoe wilderness trip and discovered she was interested in wildlife. She enjoyed learning about environmental concerns, animal and plant life cycles, especially their reproduction. The handsome and captivating group guide helped intensify this interest. Alisa still had shoulder-length hair. She stood at five-foot-four, had a shapely body and a generous chest. Boyd, the guide, presented with wavy, sandy beach-like colored hair and tanned skin. He was a confident, trim, six-foot male who dressed as if he were a *GQ* outdoor model. Unfortunately, their first date went badly. He misread Alisa's early interest in his wildlife knowledge as an open gateway for him to try to freely ravage her.

"Not to be, Boyd, the embodiment of Mr. Giacomo Girolamo Casanova," she said as she skillfully diverted his advances and octopus hands, to his frustration and anger. Alisa had developed such defensive moves back in her Riverview High School days.

Her next stop took her northward to Northwestern Michigan College (NWC), achieving an associate's degree in Science and the Arts. Was it fate, coincidence, serendipity or destiny stepping in? The biology and environmental science classes launched her boat with no turning back. She visited the Great Lakes Maritime Academy, right there on the West Bay of Traverse City. At the academy, she read on a bulletin board, the flyer advertising for an assistant at Marinescape, Florida.

She went from the light blue, white and black colored "Louie the Laker" (GVSC) social sciences, to the green and white "Hawk Owls" of

NWC biology in Traverse City, to the green and white of the "Spartans" of Michigan State University (MSU) in East Lansing.

*** 

**Alisa smiled** as the Kentucky countryside whipped by.

*My Zoology B.S. from State will secure a position in a zoo or in the fields of aquarium science, marine animal behavior management… like Marinescape!*

"No! Not me. Not again!" Alisa cried out and hit the steering wheel. She watched in her rearview mirror as two marked Kentucky State Police Chargers raced off an overpass entrance ramp.

"But I'm in the 'rocking chair.' I'm supposed to be safe!" The first trooper passed the Audi and Mustang and waved them over. Alisa's nanosecond decision and reaction time to slow to seventy-five miles per hour forced the F-150 to quickly go around her Beetle.

"He mustn't have seen the cops," Alisa whispered. She held her breath. The second trooper passed Alisa and NASCAR-ed the F-150's bumper!

"Ah-ah-ah-ah," she said as her brain reminded her to breathe.

"Praise St. Christopher, the patron Saint of Travelers. Thanks Hermes, the god, for quick traveling and thinking." She put the car on cruise. About half a mile ahead, she saw the three rabbits pulled over by the two state troopers. She saw their disgruntled faces as she cruised by at the posted seventy miles per hour. The traffic was light going southbound from then on.

"I could bump the speed up a few miles per hour, up to seventy-five. No, I'm close to the Tennessee line. I'll wait. What a beautiful day for driving … Whoa!' Filling her rearview mirror was the front end of a Kentucky State Trooper car, the Charger predator, bumper-tight like a hitched trailer, maybe three feet back. Alisa kicked the cruise back down to seventy.

"Oh, how far is the state line? Stop looking back there. He's definitely there. Oh man, I really need to pee. The dark green and white mile marker showed fifteen miles to the state line."Alisa fidgeted and adjusted the seat belt, checking the speed, fuel, oil, and temperature.

"How's my speed? Be cool. He hasn't pulled me over and no lights. So he's not going to pull me over. He's just trying to make me nervous. Trying? I'm sweating my pee out. Turn on the air conditioner too max.

There's the state line." She glanced to the rearview mirror. Yes! He was in the median and turning around to go north!

Wham! Like in the comic strips, the cop is gone.

Wham! The state line is crossed.

Wham! There's Tennessee Welcome Center and getting to the blessed bathrooms.

Just like the sweet City of Oz.

# Chapter 9

---

## *Four*

**"Well what now?"** Sheriff Gary asked on his car microphone.

"Good morning, sir. An apparent break-in and robbery at the A1A Pharmacy north of your location," relayed Mary Jane.

"Is there another body?"

"Sorry, Sheriff, we only have an unconscious person, a man. I texted you the address."

"Mary Jane, good morning, I now owe you two dinners for my rudeness," the friendly Sheriff Gary answered.

"Sheriff Gary, you really don't owe me anything, sir."

Sheriff Gary mentally took an inventory of what had happened in the last two days as he turned his vehicle around and drove north to the new location. First, a floater was found at the west side of Matanzas River Inlet Bridge. Second, a dead woman was found at the fishing park at the 206 bridge crossing the Matanzas. Third, a woman's body was discovered on the ocean side of the Matanzas River Inlet Bridge within six hours of the team leaving the first crime scene. Each crime had the same modus operendi and similar collected evidence.

Now a robbery and an unconscious man found at a pharmacy off highway A1A, which incidentally abuts the Matanzas River.

***

**Gary flashed back** to when he played on the river, especially at the Matanzas Inlet, the mixing bowl of ocean and river. Many times he would take his twelve-foot wooden rowboat with its small outboard motor from his uncle's dock on the river. He had been explicitly told never to float near the inlet's tidal pool.

"Stay away from the inlet, young man. Never go under the bridge. You'll be drawn out into the ocean," Gary's mother would say in a threatening voice, finger pointing at him like a bobbing chicken head.

Gary would stand there nodding his head. "Yes, Ma," he'd agree as he fidgeted with thoughts of getting in his boat named the *Blue Mermaid*.

"The Atlantic Ocean is deadly! Do you understand?" Gary would continue to nod his head. "No, you do not understand! This is the Atlantic Ocean, thousands of miles—"

"I do know, Mom; 41.1 million square miles." Gary and his mother had this scolding conversation many times.

"You know it's thousands of feet deep."

"I know, Mom. An average of 12,881 feet deep, like 2.4 miles deep."

"That's exactly my point. You could drown out there and we'd never find your body to mourn your death." His Mom would start to cry.

This would only fire up her zeal to reinforce her point of view. Gary would stand there looking frustrated and acting like a beaten dog.

"Oh no you don't, young man. Once that undertow catches you, you'll—"

"Be gone forever," they'd both say together.

"Are you mocking me? That's right. You'll be lost to me and your father forever. You're a young man, but you'll always … still be my baby." She'd start to cry harder and pull Gary to her chest for the ritual hug.

Once the homily finally ended, Gary would run to his moored *Blue Mermaid*, jump in the bopping vessel and release the lines from its posts, except for a single noose. He'd start his twenty-five-horsepower Mercury, two-stroke engine. After three gas line bulb pumps, he'd choke up the engine and give one quick starter rope pull. The engine would cough once or twice, sputter or pop. There would be a puff of smoke and the smell of oil and gas would fill his nose. Then the choke off and the engine would cleanly rev up. He'd grab the tiller tightly while flipping off the remaining post noose and be off, straight away to the Matanzas Inlet to "investigate" the daily river changes and washed-up treasures.

"How far are you, Sheriff?" the intercom squawked.

"I'm five minutes or less."

These were fond memories for Sheriff Gary. There was a special girl who'd often ventured out with him on the *Blue Mermaid* to the Inlet. Tanya lived close to Gary's uncle on Barrataria Drive, just before the road's circle end, on a tract of land running perpendicular to the Matanzas River. This made her pick up and drop off quite easy. She had the same wanderlust as Gary. This red-haired sparkplug was always challenging young Gary to do more. They played pirates, dolphin finders, Rattlesnake Island treasure hunters and Mr. and Mrs. Robinson Crusoe.

"What did you bring to eat today," asked Gary.

"Our usual, a sandwich surprise and bottled soda," smiled Tanya

Several times they were caught in brief rain downpours. During one of those passing deluges of rain, Gary experienced his first spontaneous, consensual kisses.

"That was great. Can I have another?" Gary asked with a poor puppy expression. Tanya came back with a suction cup kiss and upper body hug, which almost tipped the boat over.

"Let's pull up on the island with our towels," suggested Tanya kittenishly.

Gary experienced his first girl exploration and touching of each other's private parts that day.

"I love you, really I do." Then they did a dual wrapping of limbs. This was followed by Gary's first premature ejaculation with a girl.

"No reason to be ashamed; it's primal and natural," she said, making light of the event.

Tanya would be the girl Gary compared all future women to.

As they lay on their towels, Gary stared at the white clouds above.

"What should we do now?" he asked.

"I know I want to travel, care for animals. How about you?" Tanya squeezed his hand.

"I want to be with you."

"No, I mean in the future."

"A boat captain and run the Intracostal Waterway or a fireman to rescue people."

Those were great river trips for the two young "detectives." Gary and Tanya knew this river better than most local people.

One day Tanya and her family were gone. Gary motored past her house in the *Blue Mermaid* and saw a "House for Sale" sign with "Sold" over it. He wondered if he would ever see Tanya again. Was she O.K.?

***

**The Sheriff saw** three roadside walkers, all waved at him and his train of thought changed to questioning how many times he'd driven State Road A1A alongside the Matanzas River. Thousands of times…?" Gary had patrolled and answered calls from south St. Augustine, Crescent Beach, Dolphin Family Fun and the town of Marinescape, continuing southward through to Flagler County.

He stopped at a traffic light and watched people crossing A1A. Every day pedestrians and bicyclists risked their lives on this road to thoughtless drivers. Drivers had listed many excuses. "I'm already late; get out of my way. I live and work here. Do you?" The tourist driver was tolerated because their money was needed, but did they have to drive in front of 'me?' They'd look left and right for their destination, but not straight ahead, where they were going. Then there was the retired driver. "No need to be in a rush. Ten miles under the posted limit is a safe speed."

Finally, all locals recognize the snowbird driver, who migrated south for the winter. They'd drive thinking of the 101 things that were more important than the road, like the cell phone. "I'm excellent with my Smartphone. I have conversation, text, instagram and tweet while steering with my knees, pinky finger or elbow, which allows answering the phone within a second of its first ring, beep or vibration."

***

**The Sheriff arrived** at this fourth Matanzas River crime scene.

# Chapter 10

## Trivia

**Georgia** was a peach to drive through. In fact, Alisa had just finished eating their state fruit as she crossed into Florida. Even though people complained about driving around Atlanta, Alisa drove right through the downtown by the Atlanta Airport (ATL) in less than thirty minutes.

"Well, my short time through Atlanta depended on the time of day, if there was road construction, and driving in the HOV lane." Alisa spoke out loud as if there was a passenger present.

"Welcome to Florida," she read and then broke out into song. "Oh what a beautiful morning, oh what a beautiful day ..."

Alisa pulled off into the Florida Welcome Center. "Just in time for another potty break. A brisk walk to the facilities is in order."

Alisa had noted that each Welcome Center and state highway rest area contained interesting state trivia, like the state bird and other state factoids. She had always liked picking up trivia anywhere she went. For example, the Florida state animal is the Florida Panther, the state beverage is orange juice, their fruit is, of course, the orange, the state heritage horse is the Florida cracker horse, the state marine mammal is the manatee, the state pie is key lime, the state reptile is the American Alligator and the state saltwater fish is the Atlantic Sailfish; in fact, Stuart, Florida was the nation's capital for the sailfish. Alisa's favorite saltwater mammal was the

Dolphin, her favorite saltwater reptile was the loggerhead turtle and her favorite state song was between "I Am Florida" and "Suwannee."

Alisa had decided to overnight in Jacksonville Beach, just east of Jacksonville. Once leaving I-75 and turning on I-10, she again started to think about unique state symbols. Michigan had a state children's book, *The Legend of Sleeping Bear*, a state fossil, the mastodon and state reptile, the painted turtle. "I'm very interested in reptiles and marine life," she said, still speaking to her imaginary passenger."

Ohio has a state beverage, tomato juice. The state fruit is the tomato; the state fossil, the trilobite; the state frog; the American Bullfrog; the state prehistoric monument, the Newark Earthworks; the state reptile, the black racer; and the state rock song, "Hang on Sloopy," which was proposed to the Ohio State Congress by the late, great Ohio State University football coach, Wayne Woodrow "Woody" Hayes. My favorite unique trivia for Ohio is the state native fruit, the pawpaw. The typical person's response is 'What's a pawpaw?' About a five-inch long, light green fruit on a tree, usually in forests. I've even tasted it. The fruit has a tropical citreous flavor of mango and banana, yum, yum.

Kentucky has a state agricultural insect, the honeybee; a state bluegrass song, the "Blue Moon of Kentucky"; a state dance, clogging; a state drink, milk; a state fossil, brachiopod; a state gem, freshwater pearl; a state horse, thoroughbred; a state mineral, coal; at state musical instrument, the Appalachian Dulcimer; a state soft drink, Ale-8-One; a state song, "My Old Kentucky Home"; a state sports car, Corvette; a state theater pipe organ, Wurlitzer; and a state game animal, gray squirrel.

\*\*\*

**Alisa thought again** about her work interview at Dolphin Family Fun and Marinescape.

"Let's read that flyer," she said while fueling her Beetle. "This work opportunity describes me."

She'd found this marine mammal and aquatic life research facility on the internet. Also listed were several underwater viewing tanks for research, the site for Hollywood studio films and commercials, tourist entertainment and education.

"I'll have driven about 1,300 miles if I go straight through. I'll take any position at Marinescape for at least a summer internship. If I work hard and over-the-top enthusiasm on my part, it could lead to a full-time marine position. Whoa, do they have every Florida State Trooper on this stretch of I-10?"

Soon she'd be on I-295. Incredibly, she'd only gotten one speeding ticket the trip. That is, only one speeding ticket per state per year while traveling the I-75 corridor. Fortunately, she never accumulated more than eleven points during a three-year period, so still no judge interaction and intervention.

Alisa shuddered down her spine thinking about her highest speeding ticket.

"A ticket for forty-five miles over the speed limit in Ohio did result in a backseat police squad car ride to the Marion County jailhouse."

Alisa had hoped for an officer in a good mood who would let her pay the fine right there on the roadside. No such luck. The backseat ride meant either waiting to stand before the judge to dispute the ticket or paying the fine in the old "caught and release" scenario. After getting her freedom back, she'd had to find a taxi to take her back to her car on the side of US 23, just east of Marion. She'd sat at a curb outside the police station. *No problem waiting for the taxi to arrive. It's better than jail time.*

"I'm sorry I had to ticket you, bring you to the county seat and fingerprint you," the officer had said, looking down beyond her breasts to her fingertips. "They seem clean."

"Yeah, they are. Thanks," Alisa had answered without looking at the officer.

"At least you didn't have to wait for the judge. He's not in court for another four days." Alisa had nodded.

"The cabs can take a long time to come here to the county buildings." He'd hesitated. "You know, I could take you back to your car. I just need a quick sandwich. I could get you one at the same time, if you like. The deli is right around the corner. Then we'll ride back to your car within minutes. Well?"

"Will that be another backseat ride?" Alisa had quickly asked the officer, who again was looking down at her bountiful breasts.

44

The trooper said, "Well, we could—" Just then a taxi had pulled curbside and stopped.

"Thanks, but no thanks." She'd opened the cab back door. "I've already spent enough time in my life in the back seat of men's cars." The car door had closed behind her.

***

**Alisa exited** for Jacksonville Beach. "It's going to be a beautiful night to sleep in Florida."

Once on highway 212/ 90, she headed to Beach Boulevard, across the Safe Harbor Intracoastal Waterway Bridge, left on to 1st Street N, and then to the Four Points by Sheraton/ Marriott.

"I'll get an ocean view and balcony or bust! Oh, I forget about Georgia's unique state symbols. Georgia state crop, the peanut; the state dog, any adoptable dog; the state folk dance, square dance; the state fossil, a shark tooth; the state language, English; the state marine mammal, Right Whale; the state possum, Pogo Possum—the cartoon character; the state prepared food, grits; the state reptile, Gopher Tortoise; the state school, Plains High School; the state song, "Georgia on My Mind"; and one that can't be forgotten, what every meal needs, the state of Georgia vegetable, Vidalia Sweet Onions."

***

**Alisa sat** in her parked car next to the Sheraton watching the ocean waves. Opening her car door and stepping out, she felt the warm ocean breezes surround her and fill her nose and lungs.

"Wow, how exhilarating is this?" This would be her first night enjoying the sight and sounds of the ebbing Atlantic Ocean.

"O.K., looking around … there's the Moonlight Movie Theater. I just passed a Walgreens drugstore, the Sheraton and Joe's Crab Shack, all within walking distance." Alisa smiled.

"I'll check in, have a light dinner and then sleepy time with an open balcony door," she laughed.

45

Alisa had no trouble checking in and getting a seaside room with a walkout balcony. Smelling fried food, she walked up the wooden walkway into the entranced of the crowded and noise Joe's Crab Shack.

"We're almost ready for round two of Joe's Crazy Crab Shack Trivia Fun Shots," a D.J. announced. "Pick a partner and create a funky name. I'll be by to pick up your names. This is your chance to win some crazy Jell-O shots or whatever shots of whatever you're drinking!" the D.J. squealed out the speakers. "Sorry, folks, for the last ear drum buster."

As soon as Alisa sat down by herself, two girls sat on either side of her.

"Hi, she's Brandy."

"She's Candy!" They pointed to each other.

They both giggled as they pointed at each other again, then high-fived each other and giggled again,

"You're Candy ... you're Brandy, I got it," said Alisa. "Hi, Brandy, Candy, I'm Alisa." She greeted them again and tried to look at them as their eyes swirled around the large open bar and restaurant.

Candy offered a hand. Their jovial attitude must have been lubed up by joy juice, Alisa surmised.

"Will you join our team? Please? Please? O.K.? O.K.?" They each repeated the other.

"What's our funky, crazy, sexy name going to be?" laughed Candy.

"How does 'The Three Twin Packs' sound?" giggled Brandy. "No, wait for it, The Three Twin Peaks?"

Alisa looked at them in confusion.

"You know ... we each got two." Brandy pointed to her breasts.

"Yeah," Candy mirrored Brandy's action.

"Wait. How about naming us the stooges?" Candy boisterously shouted out.

"You mean like the Three Stooges? The last century's slapstick comics?" asked Alisa.

"No, the amazing rock band, you silly girl," they both said asynchronously.

"I suggest the 'Tri-Colors,'" Alisa threw out.

"I don't get it," the two blurted out.

Alisa pointed to Brandy's black hair. She then pointed to Candy's light brown hair. Then, using both hands, she pointed to her own blonde hair.

They looked at each other and nixed it.

"Boring," was Brandy's response.

"Yes, I agree, boring," mimicked Candy.

"I got it," proclaimed Brandy.

"She's got it," Candy said, nodding her head like a bubblehead.

"I think 'The Pussycat's Meows,'" said Brandy as she stood with her arms up in a victory pose.

Candy started to purr, purr, and purrrrr.

Alisa looked down, giving in.

\*\*\*

"**O.K.,** all, this is round two of trivia. It's going to be a little more difficult. It's time to separate the cheese from the cracker. What did I just say?" The D.J. laughed. "Ten questions, ten answers you'll write down. When we're done, you'll trade your treasured answers with another team to check. Are there any questions, ladies and gentlemen? No? Let's go.

"No. 1... How many grooves on a single record? [Two, one on each side]

"No. 2 … In 1975, Gary Dalh created a national craze. It was in a little box and cost $5 dollars? [Pet Rock]

"No. 3 … What year was the last official live Beatles concert? [1966, Candlestick Park]

"Are you guys massaging your brains?" asked the D.J.

"No. 4 … Name of the little dog on the Cracker Jack box? It's the game with numbers that old people play. [Bingo]

"No. 5 … What's the common name for circum-orbital hematoma? It's commonly seen after a fight. [Black eye]

"No. 6 … George Washington Carver from Georgia is the inventor using this protein with many other uses. What is the best known of them? I know this is a nutty question. [Peanut butter]

"No. 7 … How long in time is a 'jiffy?' It's a really short part of a second. [1/100 of a second]

"No. 8 … If you saw your 'doppelganger,' what did you see? It's like looking in a mirror. [Someone who looks like yourself]

"No. 9 … Who invented the wooden coat hanger, the hide-a-way bed and the dumbwaiter? He wrote a declaration that was read on the July 4, 1776 celebration. [Thomas Jefferson]

"Finally, no. 10 … Who or what are Inky, Blinky and Pinky? For triple bonus points, what is the fourth member's name and their colors?" [the ghosts in *Pac-Man@*, Blinky is red, Inky is blue, Pinky is pink and the fourth ghost is Clyde, who is orange.]

"Boy, you're smart for a girl," said Brandy.

"Yeah, you like wrote the answers, like right away," Candy remarked befuddled.

"Girls, did you want to change any of my answers?" Alisa politely asked the other two.

"Brandy is happy with your answers," said Candy.

"Ditto for Candy," added Brandy.

"Pass your answer sheet to the nearest team."

The DJ gave out the correct answers. The correcting teams then handed back the answer sheets to the DJ.

"We'll have a musical interlude while the correct answers are tabulated. Enjoy the theme song of the TV show *Jeopardy*, titled 'Think.'

"Hold on to your hats ladies and your private parts, gentlemen. In third place with eleven correct answers is the 'Four Guys Hanging.' In second place with fifteen correct answers are the 'Guys and Dolls.' The second and third teams will each receive ten dollar gift coupons. Drum roll please. With a whopping twenty out of twenty-two possible points, including bonus points, this winning team gets to choose forty dollars cash or equal value in food or drink gift coupons, it's 'The 'Pussycat's Meows!' Kitty, kitty, kitty … come on and accept your purr-fect gift vouchers."

After all the hoopla, clapping, whistling, wolf calls and off-color jokes had stopped, four guys came over to the girls' table.

"Hey, young ladies, we're here, the Thunderstruck: Rip, Kip, Chip and Burp. We were fourth to you bodacious Pussycats. Get it? Fourth? Four great guys who Thunderstruck the ladies."

"My pseudonym name is Burt, not Burp," one of them said.

"We're also first in 'other' special games. We heard your 'meows' and came running. We'd like to satisfy y'all winners' needs, like drinks, appetizers or whatever gets your cat fur riled, if you know what we mean."

The trio had Cheshire cat grins. Burt had a closed-lip smile.

"Why, aren't you the gentlemen," bubbled over the top Brandy and echoed Candy.

"Thanks, guys, but we won all the drinks we need," remorsefully Alisa sighed.

"We were referring to something more, like the human needs of a man and a woman," Rip explained as he swung his arms around in the direction of the newly gathered group.

"I've got an early work day tomorrow." Alisa got up and started to walk out.

"I'll escort you out of this male testosterone radioactive field," one of the guys said with his same friendly smile she'd seen before.

"I'll step out with you for some fresh air," she agreed. They came to Joe's decorated deck.

"I'm Alistair."

"Alisa." She stopped and shook his hand. They actually looked eye to eye.

"I thought you were Burp."

"The team wanted Burp. Kip, Rip and Chip wanted me to be Bip ... eh, no," Alistair smirked. "Burt was our compromise."

"I've never met an Alistair before."

They continued to walk toward the Sheraton on the beach.

"My father named me after his favorite British athlete, Alistair McCorquodale, who was an Olympic medal-winner cricketer. He said McCorquodale was the greatest batsman and bowler in the game, at my dad's time."

"I was named after my mom's favorite flower, the alyssum, which is a sweet, fragrant flower that attracts very colorful butterflies. The alyssum carries the myth of being a healing plant. My mom thought I'd be a healer or supporter of life."

"I agree," Alistair broadly smiled. May I hold your hand again?" Alisa offered her right hand. He caressed it softly with his left hand and brought it slowly to his face.

"What are you doing? What do you...?"

"I agree with your mother that you do smell sweet and have become a fragile blossoming flower." He kept eye contact with her. "I believe I'm being rejuvenated just by touching you. Your positive aura is very strong."

The two trailed past the hotel on to the beach. They both had taken off their shoes and swung them in their opposite hands.

"We're making a splendid melody together ... the low tide surf and our splashing feet," he said.

Alisa bumped his shoulder and smiled. She stopped and pulled down his hand to stop him walking.

"Is something wrong?" he asked.

Without answering, she grasped his other hand to turn him face to face. She stared and slightly cocked her head.

"I was just trying to determine if you were sincere or full of shit." Squinting, she tried to pierce deep into his consciousness. Neither blinked for a while, finally, Alisa blinked first. She had thought all she needed was an open window, a big comfortable bed with fluffy pillows, and the sound of the ocean's rolling surf to fall asleep, but ...

"Where are you staying?" asked Alisa.

Alistair looked to the Sheraton.

The gentle breaking waves quietly sang out "Oh, mystery of life, I have found you."

# Chapter 11

---

## *Pharmacy*

**North of the 206 bridge**, Sheriff Gary and Deputy Sheriff Keith had gathered outside the South St. Augustine River Pharmacy.

"Is the janitor still unconscious?" asked Gary.

"Yes," answered one of the paramedics as they moved the Native American man onto a gurney and to the ambulance's open rear doors. The paramedic had started an IV and placed a facial oxygen mask on the victim.

"Is the blood on his T-shirt sleeves from you starting the IV?" asked Assistant CSI Tara.

"No way, we're not that messy, no matter how fast we're working." The paramedic looked at Tara with give-me-a-break face.

"His vital signs are stable and I think he works—"

"He works as a midnight janitor at this pharmacy, according to the store manager. This is one of the few drugstores not open for the 24/7 shift." Deputy Keith interrupted the paramedic as he approached the group.

"You could be on the cover of *Miss CSI* magazine," Keith whispered into Tara's left ear.

Tara just shook her head. "I could change the name to *Entrepreneurial Women* magazine, spotlight on Miss CSI." Tara turned away from Keith with a big smile on her face, which he couldn't see.

The group noticed that the man was beginning to move his arms.

"Steady now. How do you feel?" asked one of the paramedics as he bent over him.

"What's your name, sir?"

"Yuma. Yuma Manta," the Native American answered. "How do you think I feel? Why does my left arm hurt?"

"Oh, that's where I started your IV for fluids. It's a way to give you medication quickly if you need it ... you know, life supporting meds,"

"I know what an IV is for, numb nuts. No, I mean why do both my upper arms hurt?" Yuma moaned back.

Tara slowly lifted Yuma's left arm.

"No detectable reason. All looks in order. Wait a second." Tara looked into the sleeve of his T-shirt. Deep in Yuma's armpit was a bruise. Tara looked under his right arm. The same deep bruise was there.

"Doctor MacGrath, come look at this," called out Tara.

Keith watched the cute, brunette CSI Investigator intensely.

"Found something of interest, have you?" Keith asked with a broad smile.

"Deputy Keith, could you help me pull off Mr. Manta's T-shirt?" Tara snapped photos of both arms, up to the armpits.

"We'll just cut it off," the deputy suggested.

"No, you won't," Yuma commanded loudly as his arms came back to his body and he crossed them. "I don't have many T-shirts." He had become quite agitated.

"Oh, no, I didn't mean the T-shirt. I meant your arm." Keith grinned at Tara.

"That's not funny, Deputy."

"I'll say it's damn sadistic, not funny," roared Yuma.

"O.K., no problem," Tara quietly and slowly said. "We'll slip the shirt off you, onto your IV-set arm, and over the IV bag.

Doctor MacGrath stepped over and examined both armpits. As she waited for the doc's assessment, Tara's eyes went back and forth, as Keith had moved in next to her ... very close to her again. Their shoulders touched, like they were conjoined twins. During their years of professional meetings at crime scenes, there had seemed to be more than just their work. They shared a friendly banter, yet they'd never dated. Their lingering look, gentle touching, and smiling promised a romantic future. Each time they met, a little more personal interest showed. Their voices became softer and more intimate.

"Tara, notice anything else?" Doc sternly asked, noticing she was more interested in Keith.

Tara re-examined the bruises. On closer inspection, she saw scratches in four parallel lines. It was the same under each arm.

"And?" the doc pushed her for more.

"Yes, all are parallel, each two to four inches long. The longest scratch has a dot of clotted blood and—"

"And a green foreign body in the longest scratch," added the Doc.

"Sorry, Doctor MacGrath, I overlooked the potentially important clue." Tara was now not smiling.

"Even minute bits of evidence can make the difference in solving a case," added doc.

"Is it Mr. Manta's blood or the perpetrator's?" asked Doc.

"I'll take photos with measurements before and after removal. Then I'll prep, package, label and register the new evidence." Tara opened her orange, small suitcase-sized utility bag. She waded among the multiple pockets and folding shelves of the bag and found several wrapped swabs, sticky evidence tape, narrow tipped tweezers and glass slides with their test tube holders. She laid them out on the extended platform.

"Now, Mr. Manta, I'm going to touch your two bruises. There's a little clotted blood that I need to retrieve for evidence. I'm removing the plastic cover from the swab."

"I'm not a child. I understand what and why you're doing what you're doing. I'll accept this pain for future justice," Yuma responded.

"There will probably be a lot of pressure, not really pain." Tara spoke softly and had a swab and tweezers in hand.

"Ah, call it what you want!" groaned the muscular Yuma, who was now wide awake and trying to get off the gurney.

"Please lay down again, sir, for just a moment longer. I'll be as careful as I can under your other arm," Tara tried to reassure him. "I'm picking out a tiny piece of something and—"

"Ouch. Ouch! That's nature's way of signaling to me that I'm still here," Yuma yipped.

"We're done. Thank you, Mr. Manta, for your patience and cooperation." Tara slightly smiled at his disagreeable face. Her test tubes and evidence bags were appropriately labeled with the usual specimen number, date, time, photo number and location site. She signed that it had been collected by her. Tara secured the evidence in the CSI vehicle and joined the rest of the crime scene investigation forensic team, who were dressing up so as not to contaminate the indoor crime scene.

The pharmacist followed the CSI team into the store. He immediately went behind the broken glass above the countertops and locked cabinets.

"All seems to be in order, undisturbed and undamaged, except for the glass, thank God," the pharmacist relayed out loud to anyone who might be listening. He continued to examine each narcotic and expensive medication self. "It's just as I left it at closing time."

"Let's check the broken glass fragments for blood and fingerprints," Tara said loudly as she carefully collected all the glass shards.

"Since I see security cameras, where would the recorders be, sir?" asked Sheriff Gary.

"They're not connected. Just for show. We never have crime," answered the pharmacist.

"You should see this, Sheriff Gary," called out a husky voice of uniformed Officer Brenner from one of the regular non-prescription pharmacy aisles.

The CSI team leader, Director Leon Mendelssohn, had just entered the building and went over to the officer. All the contents of aisle Four's shelves had been completely wiped off and were now on the floor. Leon looked at the reference cards above the disturbed shelves. "This card is labeled 'Vitamins, Minerals and Natural Supplements.' Why pick this aisle?" he asked the people present. "What's on the floor?"

"Small bottles and boxes of vitamins, more vitamins, vitamin supplements and herbal supplements," Tara repeated out loud quickly.

The patrolman knelt next to Tara and nodded his head in agreement as she lifted her arm up, hitting Patrolman Brenner's head looking down.

"Sorry." Tara smiled at John. "I was instinctively raising my hand to speak … you know, like in class?"

"It's pretty funny. Actually, I think it's quite cute," complimented the patrolman.

"How will we know what, if anything, has been taken?" Tara inquired of Director Leon.

"That will be the pharmacist's job to let us know."

"You're having quite a day, Miss CSI Tara."

"What?" A shocked Tara quickly turned toward the direction of the voice. "Oh, it's you right next to me, John." They looked at each other while still kneeing. They continued to study each other's face as they stood up.

"Excuse me for my reaction, I thought you were someone else," Tara slowly answered, still keeping eye contact.

"I recognized you by your beautiful sparkling blue-green eyes and your always smiling face." John spoke while they kept their eyes locked.

"Well, I … why thank you … John," she shyly answered.

Further evidence was obtained, including all the janitor's clothes, his fingerprints and blood, to eliminate him as a suspect. Multiple samples were taken from his clothing while he wore them and after he removed them and replaced them with a supplied jump suit Mr. Manta had in the drugstore cleaning closet. Samples were taken from around the outside of the store and surrounding area. Special attention was concentrated on where Mr. Manta was found unconscious in the store.

Tara pointed to his neck. "May I also have your necklace and bracelet, Mr. Manta?"

"No. These are my heritage, my legacy, my identity," Yuma sternly said, shaking his head.

"May I at least lay them on my CSI bag's shelf, photograph and swab them?" He agreed to her request.

Tara became obsessive-compulsive. She wasn't going to stop her meticulous evidence search until she found something remarkable. She felt a need to re-instill CSI Director Leon's and Doctor MacGrath's faith in her investigative abilities. Her diligence did pay off. Tara looked at both of Yuma's armpits a third time.

"Are you starting all over again?" asked Yuma, resisting her trying to lift his arms.

"I'm playing a hunch," Tara said without looking at his face.

"Well, I'll play," he said as his arms went limp. "What will I win in return?"

"We'll find out who your assailant was, Mr. Manta."

"I was more interested in winning a date with you or at least a kiss." He waited for her response. She stopped and just stared at him. He was a rather handsome man at six feet, with black wavy hair in a well-kept ponytail and he was a well-spoken Native American with no accent. He winked at her and smiled. Tara gave a small laugh.

"Do you need any help here?" asked Deputy Sheriff Keith.

"Oh, no Deputy, we're moving to some shade. I'm just following up on a hunch." She proceeded by pulling out light spectrum glasses, which revealed images undetectable to the human eye in ordinary white-sunlight. The ultraviolet light lit up the shadowed armpit. "Yes, as I hoped." Tara saw a rare find, a partial finger print on the dark, bruised armpit skin. Tara sprayed the area with highly sticky cement and then placed tape over the area to capture the image before it disappeared. The image was then relayed onto a glass slide and photographed by her high-end digital camera at different angles and with different light wavelength filters. The slide was then placed in a nontransparent plastic paper envelope. The gathered data would be reviewed in the lab.

"Got it, "Tara proudly smiled at Yuma. She also noted a slimy texture to his chest wall and lower arms. She repeated the previous steps and captured the slime by swabbing and gently scraping it into a test tube.

Tara continued her findings, including another speck of suspected blood discovered by a florescent reagent used to detect blood. This too was transferred from Yuma's upper arm to a test tube by a swab. "It's positive for human—wait, no, it's negative for human blood. What kind?" she asked in a whisper.

"Director Leon?" she called. He turned and walked over to Tara. Dr. MacGrath also walked over upon hearing the word "evidence."

"One, there appeared to be a partial fingerprint in the largest armpit bruise that I captured. This bruise is consistent with a finger grab. Two, I collected transparent, slimy fluid that covered his shirt and oozed through it onto his chest skin and his armpits," Tara added.

"I agree," stated Leon. "These are things that could have been easily missed. Nice job, Tara.

"What's your third item?" waited Dr. MacGrath.

"Look at this blood test reaction. Is it human blood or not?" Tara paused.

"I don't know," puzzled Leon and Ian, "Quite intriguing. Make sure to package it in an airtight container so it doesn't lose its freshness."

Mr. Manta's examination was now concluded. He got up and walked close to Tara. "We'll talk again, at your favorite seaside restaurant. You pick the place. We'll meet at the South Beach Grill, World Famous Oasis Restaurant, the Salt Water Cowboys or Red Frog McToad's Grub Pub. I believe I deserve something for giving in to your probing." He walked away.

Tara smiled with no reply to his remarks. "Hey, wait. We need a urine sample from you," she called after him.

"Perfect, you can help me with that." Yuma laughed and grabbed the collection container.

"The only way for you to maintain the chain of evidence is to come in the bathroom with me." He laughed again. Tara watched him go into the drugstore.

Later, Yuma would refuse to go to the local hospital for further examination and possible X-rays of the bruised areas. "I'll go if Miss CSI comes and holds my hand," he'd offer. When Yuma came out of the pharmacy restroom with his yellow evidence for Tara, he asked her a question. "Did you happen to look at the river shoreline behind the pharmacy?"

"Ah, no, I didn't. why?" She left Yuma and walked the Matanzas shoreline. "I think I see the clown or scuba divers fin footprints in this soft earth. Oh, this is even better." Tara found scales, which had probably rubbed off, on the rocks placed on the shoreline to prevent shore erosion. She looked around, but Yuma was already gone.

No other blood drops were found on the floor, ceiling, or surrounding disturbed shelves of pharmaceutical inventory. However, near the shattered pharmacy glass window was a pool of standing, slightly tainted-green water and what appeared to be a partial foot or shoe print on the floor tile.

"John does this water image look like the beach print you found yesterday?" asked Gary.

"Manta, are you feeling better?" a baritone-voiced Leon asked. "Just a few questions, Mr. Manta, before you leave, if you don't mind." With no hesitation, Leon proceeded to ask. "Do you remember anything about the attacker?"

Yuma shook his head.

"How about before your attack occurred? See anything out of the ordinary, a movement, a sound or a strange smell? When you were attacked, feel anything strange?"

"Ah, yes, yes I do remember something," he anxiously answered. "The smell of water, a smell of fish and my back felt wet, damp … ah, ah, that's it."

"Any other wet areas?" Leon called out to Sheriff Gary through the drugstore's open front door. "Any water stains or collections in there?"

"Maybe, maybe some faint outline of wet spots, Leon," replied Tara. "I'll photo shoot these areas with different light filtered lenses."

"By the direction you're moving, Tara, these spots suggest steps with a two-and-a-half to three-foot stride." Deputy Keith joined in next to Tara step for step. "You've worked hard today. Coffee, tea, Danish or"—he raised his eyebrows and nodded—"you know?"

"I've got a lot more to do back at the lab," Tara smiled.

They glanced at each other. Then their eyes went back and forth, resting on each other like a pendulum coming to rest being unable to resist gravity, eyes searching the other's face.

"I must admit, I get lost in the sea of your emerald and deep blue peepers," Keith added. "Can't stop for a quick nibble on the way to the lab?"

"You almost sounded like a poet until 'peepers?' And 'deep blue' and a 'nibble' … is that for food or something else?" Tara quizzed him.

"Deep blue seems more … more romantic. I'm open to nibble suggestions."

Sheriff Gary stood against his Expedition and called over Director Leon as he wrote down a few notes. "Leon, have any ideas on this crime scene?"

"My team needs, as always, to analyze all the evidence back at the lab."

"I do believe all these crimes are related because of the water factor. It's been quite a forty-eight hours of crime in our quiet waterside communities. I see I won't be going fishing in the near future, will I?" frowned Sheriff Gary.

Doc MacGrath joined the twosome. "Did someone mention fishing?"

"These four cases will keep all three of us and our team busy as bees in a beehive," summed up doc. "Now talking about bees ... Did you know the world and we locally, are losing our honey bee population? Their numbers have markedly decreased for no apparent reason. That means our flowers and vegetative food plants will stop —"

"Right," interrupted Gary. "No rod and reel for me," he lamented.

Yuma saw Tara standing by Deputy Sheriff Keith. He leaned against a palm tree but stood at attention when his eyes met Tara's. He gave her a salute and motioned his arms from himself to her. His view of her was broken by Sheriff Gary, who was walking toward him and mumbling.

Gary lifted his head and saw Yuma, who immediately started walking to his parked car.

Gary followed, "Mr. Manta, I'm just checking you didn't remember anything else, even if small."

Yuma stopped and turned. "I am part of a proud Nation. We're a proud people. Don't think for a second that I'm ignorant of the way government officials have treated my people in the past centuries. I'm quite versed in my rights as an American citizen. Yes, we are American citizens! I'm also college educated. I went to Flagler College and got a double degree in cultural anthropology and—"

"Wait! I'm so sorry if I've somehow offended you. I'm just trying to find the perpetrator of this crime, the one who attacked you. No disrespect to you and your Nation," apologized Gary.

Yuma hesitated. "No, I'm sorry. I'm a little sensitive and feeling vulnerable right now. What did you ask?"

"Remember anything? Here, just sit in your car and relax. Close your eyes if you like. Try to visualize the assault," encouraged Sheriff Gary.

Yuma shrugged his shoulders as he shook his head, "No ... nothing. I see no person. I hear no one approaching. But ... I hear heavy breathing, heavy like a panting dog. It makes no sense to me. I saw no dog. As I said before to the other guy, I smelled something ... not a dog. Some smell that was more than water, more than just fish."

The sheriff listened, wrote notes and stared at the victim—the witness and waited.

"A quite familiar smell, I have a very good nose. It was like when I take my kids to the zoo."

"Thanks, Mr. Manta. This may turn out to be very helpful." They shook hands.

As Sheriff Gary started to walk away, Yuma called out. "Sheriff, this is way out there." He looked around as though he were going to reveal a secret. "There's a Spanish legend, based on a Floridian Native American's oral folklore. It's a tale of a water beast attacking men who violated the surrounding nature. We call it 'la garra' or 'el despertar lagarto.'"

"And that translated would be?"

"The Claw or the Walking Lizard,"

# Chapter 12

## *Clinic*

**A white Cadillac** pulled into the paved parking lot surrounded by high palm trees and low manicured bushes abutting the Matanzas River. The mostly hidden bright and swollen face of the sun highlighted the tree tops. Nurse Patti looked out her car windshield. The clinic was unusually dark. For whatever reason, the landscape lighting wasn't working.

"The last person to leave the clinic is supposed to turn on the outside light timer."

She looked around in a circle to see through all the car windows. No other cars in the lot.

Breath holding began. "No people in the lot. As usual, I'm here first." Talking out loud made Patti more comfortable and secure. "Who wouldn't be nervous after two days of news coverage of three women found dead along the Matanzas ... and this clinic, only fifty feet from the riverbank? Why should I be nervous?" Breath holding was how Patti responded to stress. "Now Patti, let's take a deep breath in. There is no Matanzas murderer, at least not here." She exhaled slowly as she opened her door.

"A normal woman would be nervous with only one murdered woman ... alone ... at the bank of the Matanzas River ...in a dark parking lot." Still looking around, she stepped out of her car and slowly walked toward the front door. She had left her car door open for a quick retreat. Her revolving 360-degree viewing of her surroundings confirmed her aloneness. "Now, just because the woman always goes in a dark room or building as the audience yells 'don't go in there. He's waiting for you!" Patti started to pant. "This is why I shouldn't watch those teenage horror movies."

Still talking out loud, Nurse Patti had been part of the Matanzas River Couples Fertility Clinic for over eight years. She'd always wanted to be a caregiver. First, she became the neighborhood nurse, then the playground nurse and then an animal healer of her son's dog. Once she experienced her own live birth in a friend's screened-in porch and welcomed a new life, she knew her calling was to be involved in bringing new souls into the world. Each soul brought to life was surrounded by one or more angels. Better yet, she could help new lives to start by getting involved in the reproduction of animals or humans. Maybe she could do both. Suddenly, Patti stopped, wide-eyed, with her mouth gapping and breath held.

"Ah … ah … ah," came out softly. The front door was ajar. "What do I do? Go in? Stay out? Call the doctor on call? Call 911? Maybe the door was left open by accident last night."

As Patti stood in front of the dark clinic entrance, she looked off to the side in the shrubbery and saw that the light control box had been torn out. "Explains that..."

She looked in through the glass pane windows on either side of the partially open door. "Normally the clinic is open at dawn, seven days a week. Today it's different. There are no inside or outside lights on, the front door is open, and there are no cars in the lot. Women getting murdered right here on this river … Hello, I'm here!" Patti bravely and foolishly slid into the office front door without touching it.

"Again, normally the inner office door is also closed. Not today. To be an act of bravery, you have to be first scared, to quote the History Chanel," *is this foolish, stupid or crazy, as the media will later report my death?*

As Patti thought, she became dry mouthed and instantly formed armpit sweat.

"What the heck. Probably one of the doctors came in early to dictate patient notes or review today's patient charts for procedures. But where's his car?"

Patti walked further into the office, turning on as many lights as she could find. She walked down the main office hallway and then turned into the back corridor. There she found the scary explanation for everything.

Medication boxes were strewn across the floor. The medicine closet door had been torn off, actually snapped off its hinges, splinted along its lengthwise boards!

"Who would do this?" Her hand lingered over a medication box.

"Should I call the police? Hell, yes!" Patti ran out of the clinic dialing 911 on her cell.

"Don't you dare look back, just keep running!"

A gymnastic leap put her in the Cadillac and she reflexively locked the doors. She typed out the address to the 911 operator and told her she was O.K. Patti rhythmically looked in all directions, double checking the Matanzas River bushes and trees.

"Are they on their way? I feel the presence of evil," she said in a whimpering voice.

"Yes, ma'am, the officer is only a couple of minutes away."

"Only one officer is coming?" Patti gurgled out as she blew her nose and wiped her eyes.

Within less than seven minutes, the first police car with rolling gumballs of blue lights arrived. Patti closed her eyes. *I'm alive.*

"I'm Patrolman Brenner," he said as he tapped on her window. "Please open your car window, ma' am."

"The clinic was broken into. I'm the first one here. I'm the head nurse, Patti Albright," she panted through a sliver of an opened window.

"Anyone hurt?" She moved her head and whispered unintelligible words.

"I know you're nervous, ma'am. Which is it, yes or no?" the Patrolman patiently asked.

"No. I'm the only one here," she smiled slightly. "I'm not hurt."

"Anything touched, broken, or stolen in the clinic?"

"Medications were thrown onto the floor." She now spoke in a normal voice and opened the car window all the way.

More vehicles pulled into the parking lot with lights flashing.

"Ma'am, please wait here in your car. We'll have more questions for you later."

The same CSI team assembled as had at the prior four crime scenes.

"Hey, Doc, we got to stop meeting like this," smiled Sheriff Gary with Deputy Keith standing behind him.

"Hi, I'm a lab assistant, Rick. I'm pulling the crime scene duty today. Tara is running several items in the lab … gas and liquid chromatography. The state lab laser spectrometry results are due to arrive soon, maybe today. Also, we're getting an expert opinion on some bizarre preliminary evidence we've collected,"

"Nice to meet you, Rick," Sheriff Gary greeted him with a nod.

"Oh, is Doc still close-lipped on his results, Rick?"

He only shrugged his shoulders. "Have to ask the doctor."

After the clinic was declared safe by Patrolmen Brenner, Keith had Nurse Patti follow him through the office from front to back.

"I count these meds at the end of every day," Patti said in her professional voice.

Deputy Keith turned and stared at her.

"Oh, yeah, sorry, I'm a little frazzled. The only medications missing are the gonadotropins, the injection kind."

"What kind of meds are those? And could you spell that?" He wrote on a pad.

"Fertility meds to assist a couple achieve a pregnancy when they're having difficulty conceiving naturally." Patti smiled with her hands on her hips.

"No other uses for those meds?" queried the deputy.

"Well, there are some people who use them for hormone replacement or falsely believe it will lead to weight loss," Patti now spoke more comfortably.

"No other items are missing as stated by the other personnel and physicians who have now arrived to work," completed Patrolman Brenner.

"Good morning, Officer … Brett," Keith said, reading her badge. "Aren't you taking your detective exam soon?"

"Why thank you, sir, for remembering."

"Yes, you've kept your boots clean and shiny." He spoke through his grin. "I'm now being serious. If there are any questions you might have concerning the exam, we could answer them over coffee or a little bite of dinner. Any personal questions that might come up, I'm here for you."

She forced a smile.

"Or just someone to talk to, who understands you're pre-exam stress, someone to complain to."

"I feel a little uncomfortable, sir, seeing as you're my senior officer and all." Officer Brett stood erect with her hands behind her back, staring at Deputy Sheriff Keith.

"I respect those feelings. If anything comes up, my cell number is with the dispatcher."

Deputy Keith turned to Nurse Patti. "In case you get anxious after this morning's experience, you can call me anytime. We can discuss feelings or other things over coffee, a bite of dinner or whatever would relax you."

Keith saw Patti look over to Officer Brett.

"Maybe we should talk about it at a later time."

"Here is my business card with my personal number on the back."

# Chapter 13

## Special

**Her eyes popped open** and she saw rays of morning sun spray across the room's white ceiling and walls. Warm air and the sound of splashing beach waves excited Alisa's senses and inspired her to spring into action, out of bed and run enthusiastically to the mini balcony rail.

"What a glorious day this has already become." She looked up and down the straight beach. There were a couple of walkers splashing each other with their feet and laughing.

"I'm fifty to sixty feet high. I should be able to see nine or more miles out into the Atlantic Ocean on this exhilaratingly clear day." Her white monogrammed bathrobe opened as she hopped up and down, holding on to the balcony rail.

"I think we're more like eighty feet high and can see eleven or twelve miles out," said the gentleman's voice from the bathroom.

"Alistair, you're already dressed? I was going to order room service," Alisa protested.

"We both have our journeys to continue this morning," said Alistair as he walked out onto the balcony and stood next to her. They hugged as if never to separate.

Alisa planted a deep kiss on him that locked their lips like a hungry lamprey eel. Alistair gave her one last squeeze, bringing her to a complete exhaled breath. With increasing speed backward, Alistair picked Alisa off the floor and the two fell onto the bed, enveloped by soft pillows. He pulled a bed sheet over them.

"Oh, Alistair, you're so … we fit together so, so well," she laughed.

They re-explored each other's bodies.

"I don't know why you got dressed, Alistair." She undressed him and brought their naked bodies together again to become one. After twenty minutes or so (Who counted?), the sheet was flung off the bed and they stared at the white ceiling with mile-wide smiles of satisfaction.

"I really got to shoot to the down—" Alistair started to say.

"I think you just did," she said through a grin.

Alistair rolled on top of her, kissing her neck and face. "As I was saying, I need to shoot down to the lobby. I've left my business card with my private cell number. May I have yours?"

"You foreigners are so formal. Of course you may." Alisa sprang up in her natural beauty, unabashed. Her pale buttocks wiggled and her breasts followed gravity as she bent over to write her number.

Alistair jumped up at attention with his pants shackling his ankles. Like a duck, he waddled up to her and placed his card in her teeth. He caressed her private parts and bumped her with his semi-limp member. They swept each other's bodies with venturous goodbye hands and kisses.

"You're so incorrigible," laughed Alisa, slapping his naked buttocks with a loud echo.

He pulled his pants up, re-groomed himself and gave her a final goodbye kiss and grope.

After the door closed, Alisa ran, jumped and did a mid-air half spin over the bed onto her back with a spread eagle landing. "He doesn't know how special our encounter was for me," she said as she pretended to make a Michigan-winter snow angel in the white, airy comforter. Alisa rolled back and forth with crossed arms pressing together her breasts. Then her legs went straight up, followed by bringing her knees to her chest in a fetal position.

"I have some morning time for beach shell exploration. My appointment isn't until this afternoon. It will take no more than three hours to get there, depending on if I have any distractions."

Alisa continued to roll from side to side on her back as she talked out loud.

"That leaves time for breakfast and whatever. Maybe I'll stop at a cheesy tourist trap. Maybe I'll find a venue with a predacious exhibit. I feel vulnerable. Too bad I don't know of a nude beach nearby." Alisa started to laugh out loud again. "Naughty, naughty."

After a refreshing beach walk, she packed her things and had a light breakfast snack. Then she was "back on the road again" with her off-key country twang singing voice. She stood by her Beetle, which she called Libby, with respect to her deceased cat.

Traveling on State Road A1A to 202 westbound, Alisa stopped for gas. A very friendly young man pulled in for gas next to her pump.

"This expressway you're about to enter is called the J. Turner Butler Boulevard, or JTB. That's my nickname," he said as he pointed to his car's decal.

"I can see that, but it is kinda understated. I see a JTB decal on the trunk lid, under the door handle, on the back wheel well fender and behind *The Judge* logo."

"Don't forget on the hood scoops. You know, however you see me … front, back, side, you'll know it's me." He grinned widely, leaning on an extended arm to the fuel pump housing.

The space between them became silent.

"It was named after a lawyer and Florida legislator who helped to establish the Jacksonville Expressway Authority," the young man expounded.

"Really…" She listened with a smile and watched the fuel pump gauges go up.

"We could retire over there at the Coffee Shoppe and commiserate about the time we've lost not knowing each other until now," he suggested as he pointed left.

"Hey, I'd like to, really, but I'm on a tight schedule," explained Alisa.

He walked toward her and stood by her car pump. "Man, I really have to go. Sorry." Alisa finished pumping and jumped into her Beetle and was gone.

She looked back as she entered the JTB expressway. The young man's beat-up orange GTO also turned to drive west, several cars behind her.

In a short time after crossing the Intracoastal Waterway on the Arthur N. Sollee Bridge, Alisa was on the southbound I-295 and then the south

I-95. She felt a little panicked and repetitively looked in her rearview mirror for the creepy GTO. *(Appendix GTO)*

"A car named after him or vice versa, JTB." *What a silly name*, she thought as her bladder filled from the perceived stressful situation. "I think it stands for 'Jerk,' 'Tiresome,' 'Bully.' Well, it is a male testosterone thing, so 'Jaw,' 'Triceps,' 'Brainless,' or 'Jeopardy,' 'Tricky,' or 'Brawn.'"

Alisa played this mind game to avoid thinking about the orange-muscle-car-monster gas station guy. "I'll beat the pretender Casanova. Guys want it to mean 'Jiggles,' 'Toys,' 'Beat offs,' ha, ha, ha. Why not 'Just, Turn, Back! Just There, Bladder.' This exit for bladder relief," she smirked.

"Man, this parking area is crowded to the max. Is every Floridian tourist at this rest area? Of course, the last available space is in the last row. I'm right next to this forest and dog run. I might as well squat here and save the quarter mile run to the Welcome Center restrooms."

Alisa looked around and saw no orange monster. She locked her Beetle and assessed her fastest route to the restroom.

Just as she started her walk through what looked like a used car parking lot, a large brown and silver RV with a black-colored Beetle in tow pulled up next to her.

"Nice car you have there," a handsome, black-haired man in his mid-forties said as he leaned out his driver's window. "Is that the new Bug?"

"Yes, it is," answered Alisa as she squirmed. "Sorry, I need the restroom that's way over there, seemly in a different state."

"Hey, I have all the comforts of home in here," the still smiling man suggested. "I'll just put this monster in park until you're done."

Alisa hesitated. *A monster*, she thought assessing the vehicle's many large windows. She took one more look at the Welcome Center and inadvertently saw an orange car slowly going up and down the lanes. "That old beat up GTO?" she mouthed.

"Pardon me, what did you say?" the RV driver asked.

"Nothing … nothing important, Well—Alisa looked back and forth between her two choices—"sure, but please turn the engine off." She turned back toward her car and walked around to the front of the RV.

Another car, a hunter green convertible Jaguar XK8, pulled up diagonally in front of the RV's front window.

"Alisa, is that you?" a familiar young man's voice rang out. She turned toward the man getting out of his car. "It's Alistair."

She cheerfully ran and hugged him. "What are doing here?" she asked before giving him a big wet kiss on his lips.

"Same as you, I'm looking for a parking space so I can hit the 'Johnny Boy.' I'll drive to the front. You hit the restroom and then wait in my car while I go."

As they left, Alistair looked to his wide windshield rearview mirror and saw two faces behind the RV's front windshield.

"Are we playing *Centipede* like the 1981video game?" His car looped around each aisle getting closer to their goal.

From the opposite direction came a rusted out orange GTO, which slowly passed them.

"Wow, what an angry face," observed Alistair. "Does he have enough logos on his car?"

"Oh, he must be very frustrated." She crossed her arms as well as her legs and grinned.

Alistair's plan worked fast enough so neither had an embarrassing moment before reaching to the restroom.

As Alistair drove them back to her car, he asked, "What was with that RV? Were you actually going into that possible capture pit?"

She shook her head thoughtfully. "Close. I was on the verge of massively wetting myself in the parking lot!"

"Weren't you afraid of those two smiling Grinch faces?"

"Two faces?"

"Hey, forget about it."

"Where are you going from here?" she asked, putting a hand on his right thigh.

He looked down to his leg. "I don't remember." They both laughed. "I'm going to a meeting down in Fort Lauderdale."

"You're pretty 'Austin Powers' like in this fancy British Jaguar. You should have a British or Scottish flag painted on its hood,"

"Nice thought. I'll give it a … not!" They both laughed again.

"I never got to ask what you do." Alisa squeezed his thigh.

"We could just stop at a sleaze motel along the expressway and talk about my boring job under the sheets," he suggested.

She slapped his thigh with a resounding, "You know what I like."

"When I drive the Jaguar, it feels alive." (Appendix Jaguar)

"And I feel that there's something alive right here," she said as she rubbed his lap. "It's alive, alive."

Alistair's face looked at hers with a questioning look.

"It's from Mel Brooks' film *Young Frankenstein*."

"Oh, yeah..." They laughed again.

"What do you do, Alisa?" he asked and then kissed her.

"I'm hoping that will be determined in the near future at Dolphin Family Fun, Marinescape." She kissed him back.

"I myself am only a surgical instrument rep for Olympus and Striker," Alistair frowned.

# Chapter 14

## *Aquatic*

**Less than a half a mile** up the river and across SR A1A from Patti's fertility clinic, another closed overnight pharmacy was broken into. Only oral vitamins and fertility meds were stolen. Again, multiple shelved contents were thrown on the floor. The locked counter windows and a door were broken into. No perpetrators were found when police responded to the building's alarm system. This was another pharmacy with fake video camera monitors. Incidentally, both robbed pharmacies were owned by the same person.

After the police left the fertility center, Patti confirmed with her employer that she, her son and two other female clinic employees could still go on their planned daytrip to the Dolphin Family Fun and Marinescape.

"You'll find Marinescape quite exciting," she told the others.

Patti reflected on the land between the waters leading to Marinescape and the first time her parents vacationed at Crescent Beach. Hard-packed sandy ocean beach with miles and miles open to adventurous vehicle drivers, bicyclists and walkers. This drivable beach almost made tracks to St. Augustine. There were protected sand dunes covered with sea grass for the egg nesting of turtles. "Life grows by the inch and dies by the foot," said the sand dune sign posted along the dunes. It meant our foot. Dunes covered by sea grass along wooden boardwalks leading to the beach from resorts and private homes helped accomplish the posted goal.

Nesting started in May for the loggerhead and gopher sea turtles. As a young girl, this nesting experience stimulated Patti's interest in the science of reproduction in animals and later in humans. On the other hand, a bored Patti would fish with her father using shrimp and crab bait.

Patti loved kayaking along the Matanzas River. Being proficient and strong enough, she'd kayak south four miles to an unnamed building. She'd rest on a provided bench by the tall, windowless building and wonder what it was. Across A1A stood the ocean side Marinescape campus, one of her favorite places to visit. This had motivated her to kayak from Crescent Beach to the shoreline of this unknown building and then walk over to Marinescape. After the fact, Patti told her angry and scolding parents what she'd done. Patti rationalized that if it had been city streets to the Marinescape, she would have bicycled there. The ruling came down. No more kayaking for Patti.

After Patti received her driver's license, vacations at Crescent Beach became more fun as she drove the length of the river and stopped at a small river park right off of A1A, the Frank B. County Park, with two picnic tables, shade from two palm trees, a Johnny-O-Portland and a groomed beach for swimming.

"I like to swim here in the river compared to the creature-infested ocean," she told her resort friends. Later she would be proven wrong,

Patti had a particular local boy she chose for water play, kissing, hugging and more. The two decided to name the park Pleasure Park. Later, the park name would be proven wrong. Patti had learned not to tell her parents, just in case another rule was made. The irony of the Pleasure Park was that she would later work just up A1A at the Matanzas River Fertility Center!

One day the two were lying on the ground and looking up at the palm tree's fronds.

"Glenn, what kind of palm tree is that above us?" Patti asked.

"You have the Sabal palm, the Roystonea *regis*, Everglades palm and my favorite is the Bismarkia nobilis."

"But what kind is that tree?" She pointed straight up.

"I don't know." He rolled on top of her bikini-covered body. "But I do know what kinda tree trunk you're feeling right now."

\*\*\*

**The Dolphin** Family Fun, Marinescape and Marine Animal Aquatic World had aquariums larger than Olympic-size swimming pools, except these aquariums were also twenty feet deep. A man stood peering down into one of these pools where bottlenose dolphins swam back and forth. "I know you can see me and the treat I have for you," said the six-foot plus-tall man toward the water's surface. He stretched his right arm out. Taking turns, the dolphins jumped out of the water and retrieved a dangled fish from his fingertips.

Feeling a tap on his left elbow, he turned and looked down to see a young woman in her mid-twenties, dressed in an airy blouse and brown-colored Bermuda shorts.

"Hi, I'm Alisa Favour. I have an afternoon appointment. I'm a graduate student hoping to supplement my education in marine and ocean mammal studies, focusing on their lives and environments." Alisa stood there with a very attractive, smiling face full of anticipation.

"Sorry, I filled that position two days ago," the handsome man responded.

"Oh, no," Alisa said in a whisper. "Would you need another marine intern? I've come over 1,300 miles to be here."

The man stared and slowly turned his head, still staring at her. "O.K.," as he nodded his head. "My expected intern will not be her for another five days. If you prove yourself **extremely** worthy of the position, we'll see." he said with an expressionless face.

"I've read your published works and about your lifetime commitment to understanding these animals and helping the mammal and aquatic life survive in their daily environments, which have been altered by industrialization," Alisa smiled while speaking and gained eye-to-eye contact.

"Well, young lady, maybe I should hire you as my speech writer or public relations representative," responded the man as he turned away, still feeding the dolphins.

"I feel I could contribute to helping you achieve your goals and those of Marinescape. I've designed my multiple college programs to enable me to assist someone like you and I'm meant to help and improve a place like Marinescape."

The afternoon sun highlighted the man's red-brown hair. He simply stood there.

Alisa started to feel uncomfortable and desperate. "I know you have a qualified individual coming for the same opportunity; however, I'm not like others. I have more drive, enthusiasm and willingness to work for you, with you, for Marinescape, Dolphin Family Fun and any research project you're involved with. I'll accomplish even greater things with you."

He still remained silent, but he did give a little head nod.

*There's hope*, she thought. "Not only would I bring all this"—she waved her two hands toward herself—"but also my deep interest in ocean life reproduction, especially amphibians, reptiles, mammals and the environmental effects on their ability for healthy reproduction and offspring."

The man suddenly extended his hand. "Since you're here, I'm Professor Rory Maxwell," he said as he watched her face.

"I've waited so long. Ah, call me Alisa." She excitedly shook his hand vigorously.

"I think we can say we've been introduced."

"Oh, I'm sorry." Alisa stopped and released his hand.

"Quite a firm handshake you have. Well, I admit I know some things about my field of interest; however, I can't promise it's what you are looking and hoping for," answered Professor Maxwell. "I am the appointed advisor for the three facilities here as the marine biologist, PhD., M.D., and D.V.M. at Marinescape, Dolphin Family Fun and the research facility of Marine Animal Aquatic World or MAAW."

He was tall and slender with blue eyes and dark red-brown hair combed straight back, which piled up into ridges like hills and valleys of countryside. "You can call me Professor or Doctor Rory Fergus Hamish Lachlan Maxwell, the IV."

Alisa looked at him with a look of fear on her face.

"Just getting you wet behind the ears with a little MAAW humor. Call me Professor, Doctor or Max, 'Hey you' is also fine," Max grinned. "There is a caveat. You must prove yourself during this short probation work period. Let's walk a little to introduce you to the residents and the facilities. You saw me feed three of our bottlenose dolphins; Moe, Shemp and Curly."

"The Three Stooges," Alisa laughed. "Bottlenose dolphins are the most common type on the shores of Florida. I bet you named them for their playfulness."

"You already understand the ways of Marinescape humor," Professor Maxwell laughed.

They walked shoulder to shoulder along to the next aquarium.

"That's a lot of seawater to filter, re-circulate and replace nutrients in," Alisa remarked as she turned toward Max.

"Yes. Alisa Favour, These are truly daily technical challenges, oxygenated ocean salt water with nutrients containing no man-made toxins."

They both smiled as they continued to walk.

"We regulate and maintain specific percentage of each element and nutrient, just like the mixing bowl of salt water and brackish at the Matanzas Inlet is great for newly created life forms to occur and reproduce," explained the professor.

"Have you named the sharks I see in this tank?" Alisa asked.

"What species are these four sharks, Alisa?" he asked'

She leaned over the tank wall to try to visualize them. Max watched her.

"Let's go to the lower level," he suggested as he walked to a stairwell. Alisa hurried along.

"Dolly, Molly, Holly and Jolly are their names," he told her as the two looked through glass portholes in the tank wall.

"They are," as Alisa listed "hammerhead shark, sawshark, bramble shark and—

"Let's move on to the next window," quickly interrupted the professor. The four sharks followed them, swimming in circles.

"Oh, how slow am I?" Alisa moaned. "That's the same sand shark."

"What makes these facilities very, very special?"

"All these questions on my first day at work, no, the first hour at work!" Alisa stopped. "I'm working here as your apprentice or intern, right?"

"So far that is correct, Miss Favour," he answered as he lightly tapped a finger on her shoulder. "Back to why this facility is so special, Alisa."

"This Oceanarium was the world's first and largest marine mammal facility, Hollywood film site and family theme park. More than just an outside pool, tank or aquarium," Alisa relayed authoritatively.

"Very good, extra facts: all these fish and mammals we mentioned were conceived and born here at MAAW," proudly stated Max.

"An incredible feat in itself," added Alisa.

"And this includes the world's first three bottlenose dolphins conceived and birthed in captivity," Max stated.

"I get it, using these world-famous namesakes, 'Dolly' and 'Molly,'" agreed Alisa with confidence.

"So you are versed also in non-aquatic animals," noted Max,

"I'm very interested in reproduction of different species. But why 'Holly' and 'Jolly?'" queried Alisa.

"Jolly for the animal's exceptional inquisitive spirit and quite playful nature. Holly's name was for her earlier-than-expected birth, the day before Christmas. This place has high standards to be mirrored by future institutions. As I have said already, you should be my spokesperson," smiled Professor Maxwell. "Oh, by the way, you have proven yourself worthy for the assistant managerial position here. Congratulations!" The two smiled and shook hands again.

Then teary-eyed, Alisa grabbed Max and hugged him. "Thank you so much for fulfilling my lifelong dream, Professor Rory Fergus … Ham … Lak … Lal … Lackland Maxwell the IV."

They both laughed as she continued to hug him.

"Now don't thank me yet," Max said as he held her at arm's length. "You will also be responsible for the Dolphin Family Fun—and Marinescape weekly lecture series."

"Yes, just bring it on!" Alisa moved her arms toward herself and Maxwell nodded his approval.

"Then you'll guide and monitor the interactive Marinescape, Dolphin Family Fun experience where visitors get to swim, touch, feed and play with the bottlenose Dolphins."

"I'm open to all I can do and experience myself." Alisa rubbed her hands together. "Professor and Doctor Maxwell, I'm putty in your hands."

"When you have proven your commitment and won my trust, we will venture across the street. There, behind closed doors, you'll see the unknown, the unaccepted, unique, unbelievable and scientific firsts of nature," the well-versed experimental marine biologist, veterinarian, geneticist, ichthyologist and herpetologist whispered.

She gave him a shadow of a smile.

# Chapter 15

## *Evidence*

**It had been five days with six crimes** having occurred in south St. Johns County over only a six-mile stretch. Sheriff Gary had stopped thinking about going fishing in the near future. All departmental staff involved with solving theses crimes were to meet at a community center just off A1A. All the shades were drawn on the windows and the doors would be locked to the general public once all attendees were in the building. A temp dispatcher was covering Mary Jane's position in the police station with direct communication to Deputy Sheriff Keith.

The crimes to be reviewed were not on a TV show where everything fell into place by the end of fifty-two minutes, with strategically timed commercials. There were no large rooms, no multi-story building with a secure lockdown facility. No state-of-the-art center with TV monitors on the wall and all crime solving laboratory technologies on site. No multi-computer connections to large, pull-up results from anywhere in the facility from a main monitor.

This one room had several rows of chairs, a couple of tables and two wall-mounted chalkboards. The investigative staff brought their own food and beverages. Sheriff Gary greeted each as they entered, starting with Deputy Sheriff Keith, who brought Gary's coffee. Medical Examiner Ian MacGrath, CSI Director Leon, CSI Assistant Tara, Assistant Laboratory

Director Rick, Officer Brett, Dispatcher Mary Jane and Patrolman John Brenner entered.

Gary stood at the front of the room and used the chalkboard, since the center had previously been a multi-grade schoolhouse. He listed the crime scenes in order of occurrence. When he finished writing, he hit a chair with a wooden pointer he'd found in the chalkboard's grooved metal holder or rail.

"Good morning. Thank you all for showing up so early to participate in this soon to become productive meeting," Sheriff Gary looked to the room's ceiling. "The State Police and FBI both have decided to run their own investigations. They expect to receive all our collected evidence. But this is not a two-way street. These two high power Law Enforcement Agencies will share their collected clues and conclusions only on a 'need to know' basis. Where we're concerned"—Gary's right arm waved around the room—"we're low level, inexperienced, small town, ticket giving and petty crime constables of the community who don't need to know. I believe information must flow both ways or not at all. The rest of you faithful crime solvers must decide for yourselves."

"For myself, I believe —well, you'll know where I stand.

"Presently, as found on the media by Mary Jane, the State Police have two drug-dealing, repeat sex offenders in custody. The FBI stated they had a solid lead to a repeat sex offender recently released from the United States high security penitentiary in Coleman, Florida only thirty-five miles south of Ocala. Neither of these agencies can be correct," Deputy Keith stated as he showed his teeth, baring a grin of anger and disgust.

"Thank you, Keith. I hope we can prove you correct," the sheriff said. "That's why I called all of you together. We all have evidence that, once put in line, I believe will show these crimes to be linked."

"And then Gary will finally get to go fishing," Ian MacGrath threw out to the group.

The gathering laughed, even Gary.

"Here's our list of crimes, not to be released to the media. We will contribute what we know is new concerning each crime. Thus we'll all be on the same page.

"**Number one** crime scene was on the Matanzas River side of Inlet Bridge. She was floating face down." Gary tapped the blackboard with the pointer.

"She was a twenty-four-year-old, five-foot-six-inch, 140-pound, brown-haired Caucasian female. A friend of the victim told us she swam early and every day since gaining weight. Why she swam naked remains unknown. Her folded clothes on the shore seemed untouched. Near the body, footstep impressions were digitally recorded," spoke Keith.

"That would be size twenty to twenty-two. No other surrounding area evidence found," added Tara.

"Her cause of death was drowning," stated M.E. MacGrath. "Fine scratches were found on both outer hips. No evidence of pubic or crown hair removal. Her vulva had bruising of both labia majora mounds at the vaginal opening. There was evidence of internal lower vaginal trauma. No upper vaginal trauma by the cervix. There were three trapped fluid pools in her vagina including unnatural fluid to the vagina, not identified as yet, prostate secretions with prostaglandins, common in male ejaculatory fluid and seminal vesicle secretions, normally mixed with sperm. No sperm was found."

"If a man had a vasectomy, we would find no sperm. Could that be the explanation?" asked Tara.

"Tara, that's and excellent observation. What do you think, Rick?"

"Sperm uses fructose, citric acid and acid phosphatase in its metabolism and these factors decrease with each ejaculation."

"That's important for the ladies to know when—" interjected Keith.

"Deputy, let's stay on track," interrupted Sheriff Gary.

"Once a man has had a vasectomy, no sperm is present, so that would mean no metabolic use of fructose, citric acid and acid phosphatase, so they all remain and become elevated over time." Rick paused and looked to the deputy. "Would that be true Deputy Keith?"

Keith put his hands up and shrugged his shoulders.

"Don't hold us in suspense, Rick," Tara said with a raised and excited voice.

"The seminal fluid fructose, citric acid and acid phosphatase were all of normal levels, thus not from a vasectomized man," answered Rick. "Questions? No?" He sat down.

"Thanks, Rick; continue, Doc," directed Gary.

"We still have the additional unidentified clear, green-tinted vaginal fluid. This fluid has been sent by Rick LaGrande to the state crime lab. They, in turn, have sent it to the USDA's lab, the United States Department of Agriculture. They've sent it to the US Fish and Wildlife Service. We're waiting for their final analysis report and conclusions," Doc added.

"The upper vaginal fluid has a normal pH of 8, which is alkaline. The lower vaginal secretions have a normal vaginal pH of 5, acidity. A pH could be 6 with her menses or 8.5 from natural cervical secretions at her ovulation," stated Doc.

"However, salt water has a pH of 7.6 to 8.4 and was detected in the entire vaginal canal and has affected possible additional vaginal evidence. There were a few cells in the fluid. Again, with no sperm found, normally having a pH of 8; with no blood, which normally would have a pH 7.2. No vaginal cells, normally has a pH 5 to 8. So I'm running a series of additional lab analysis on our own," stated Rick. "The young lady was midcycle and had just ovulated, as determined by blood hormone levels. Under infrared light, green fluid was found with small fish scales. Also, I saw bacteria." Rick sipped some water. He held up the water bottle. "pH is 7."

Everyone had a good tension-releasing laugh. "I cultured the green fluid and found"—Rick looked around the room for dramatic effect and saw everyone looking at him, who had a smile to his face—"salmonella. I then cultured the other two victims' vaginal fluids and found the same salmonella."

"I went back to our three victims' bodies," Tara stepped in. "I had Rick culture their swabbed scratches. All salmonella positive."

Sheriff looked around but no other person came forward.

"This case is moving forward with the salmonella identification, green fluid under infrared lighting, vaginal trauma and unknown fluid to be identified at outsourcing," listed Sheriff Gary.

"She was most likely held underwater and drowned during an attempted rape," added Doc. "Her completed autopsy confirms this, as salt water was in all five lobes of her lungs. This would happen in a swimmer in panic mode trying to catch her breath in repetitive waves or while being pulled deeper in the water from below."

"Any new theories—evidence supported theories?" Gary asked. "I know none of you are familiar with cases like these. My assessment is an assault gone badly. A crime of opportunity where the perpetrator saw the victim swimming nude and his animal instincts took over with no considerations for the consequences.

"Just received, the US Fish and Wildlife lab suggest we consult an ichthyologist or marine biologist," interjected Rick. "There's one just south of here on SR A1A."

"**Number two** crime scene: The deceased woman was found at a popular fishing site on the west side of the Matanzas 206 Bridge."

"Victim is a thirty-four-year-old, five-foot-two-inch blonde female on vacation. No significant evidence found at her nearby Summerhouse condo," spoke Keith. "The victim is another assault. She had torn underwear found in the nearby water grass. Either she was dragged into the water, dragged out of the water or both, as suggested by heel tracks in the sand. Since there were no signs of a struggle while being dragged, like interrupted and sporadic heel marks, she was probably already unconscious or dead. Fishing gear near the body support that her intent was to go fishing. No fingerprints found at the previous Matanzas Inlet scene or this Bridge 206 scene," reported Tara.

"Doc will tell us about the victim's examination."

"This victim's findings were similar to the first one we just reviewed. She drowned. There were the same alkaline and citric acid fluids in the entire vaginal canal. Again, no sperm found. The green fluid, which could only be seen with infrared visual assistance in the first victim, was visible with the naked eye at the vaginal opening. This evidence connects the two crimes. Visual and anatomical autopsies have revealed no other significant evidence except that she was midcycle and had fine scratches on her inner thighs."

"X-ray body imaging and ultrasound revealed no bone fractures, no dislocations and no ruptured body organs. Finally, at the autopsy, cultures of her internal female genital tract revealed her organs, cervical canal, endometrial cavity, fallopian tubes, ovaries and peritoneal fluid were negative for sperm but did show all sites positive for salmonella. Different from victim number one is that cultures from victim number two were positive for salmonella in her crown hair, hands and under her fingernails," added Rick. "Scales in this victim's crown and pubic hair found by Tara would suggest some kind of aquatic animal origin. Not a typical size or shape fish scale for this part of Florida, so I sent it to my old college friend at the Maryland Aquaculture and Fish Farm.

"Nice work, Rick," added CSI Director Leon.

"Unfortunately, no additional evidence was found after walking the areas around each crime scene again," commented Patrolman John.

"Oh, I should include that no significant new evidence or non-victim fingerprints were found in either of the two victims' cars," added Tara.

"My guess has changed to a hunch," stated Gary.

"What's the difference?" asked Patrolman John Brenner.

"A guess is just that. A guess is grabbed from out there somewhere in space." Gary waved his arms skyward. "A hunch is surrounded by facts yet to be proven."

"Really, I don't see any difference," whispered Keith to Dispatcher MJ.

"These two crimes were on the Matanzas River; both victims assaulted, drowned and the same vaginal foreign fluids reveal their connection," responded Gary.

"There was a difference between the first two victims and this **Number three** victim," interrupted Ian. "The woman in this crime scene had very little water in her lungs, suggesting she was dead before going into the water. If she was unconscious when pulled underwater, her vocal cords and epiglottis wound have relaxed and her lungs would fill with water. I'm certain she didn't drown. I believe she died before getting wet."

"So, Doc, how did she die?" asked Leon.

"There was massive cardiac muscle ischemia and muscle fiber death from three of four major right and left coronary arteries and the left circumflex was 100 percent blocked. Very unusual for a thirty-two-year-old woman to have such heart disease and blood vessel closure. Another explanation could be 'Capture Myopathy' as found in some wild animals that have been captured, restrained and die shortly after."

"So massive heart attack from shock and blood vessel spasm?" asked Keith as he smiled.

"Thanks for further adding to our confusing crime riddle, Doc," Gary smirked.

"We have victim **number three**, a Crescent Beach resident woman of 125 pounds with black hair and the same findings of assault," continued Gary. "A perpetrator so fast he's not seen committing the crimes … a serial sexual predator of Olympian swimming or running caliber and speed and strength."

"Does it have to be just one person? Does it have to be human?" Tara posed the question.

No response from the group.

Leon broke the silence. "On the same line of thought as Tara's question, there have been many water creatures attacking or capturing young women." Leon cleared his throat. "In classical music, the Czech, Antonin Dvorak, composed the symphony *The Water Goblin*. This was based on events that became a fairy tale poem called the "Vodnik." The creature was an evil underwater goblin that came to the water surface to capture a young female. It then took her to the lake's bottom to procreate." Leon looked around the conference room, ending on Tara's smiling face. "Just keep an open mind."

"Maybe mutant predatory fish, amphibian, snake, reptile wanting to procreate?" said Tara.

"Maybe a mermaid —" Gary whispered.

"Say what, Sheriff," startled Deputy Keith asked.

"Nothing...."

"Just for information," volunteered MacGrath, "in 1912, three dead victims were brought from the sunken *Titanic* to Halifax, Canada. The mortician was the first in North America to use toe tags to identify the deceased.

"On to the next case, **Number four**." Gary pointed to the list on the chalkboard. "The pharmacy robbery with a surviving assaulted victim and actual potential witness."

"I believe I will be the lead on this particular case," started Tara.

***

"**Hello**, this is the temp dispatcher, Deputy Sheriff Kermit Keith. Please tell Sheriff Gary Sellack you have another reported body," blared out the call over Keith's belt radio speaker, which was heard by the entire conference room of investigators, now all smiling at Keith.

# Chapter 16

## *Marinescape*

---

**On AIA in the community of Marinescape** stands the Marinescape-Aquatic Theme Park. It opened in1938, making it the oldest Natural Marine-Aquatic Theme Park in the US, maybe the world. Contained within was an Oceanarium to provide a marine-mammal habitat as close as possible to the animals' true-to-life natural living environment.

This habitat allowed for close scientific observation, photographic documentaries, safe marine-human closeness, visitor entertainment and education. The Marine Animal Aquatic World building, MAAW, came later as a research facility. Marinescape's large animal swimming tanks allowed visitors to walk outside around the top of the water and view the ocean life environment while maintaining safety for the spectator and the marine life. Better yet, Marinescape created the world's first double-decked visitor viewing opportunity through glass portholes below the water's surface, placing spectator "ocean floor" and face-to-face with the ocean creatures. Unfortunately, several devastating hurricanes forced Marinescape, Marine Animal Aquatic World to change from its original goals to less ambitious ones, because rebuilding was too costly.

\*\*\*

"This sunrise sky is so emotionally inspiring over the solemn ocean," Alisa whispered. Small rolling waves were like muscle fasciculations under the skin when one's muscles fibers twitch. The sun slowly raised above the eastern horizon clouds.

"How magnificent ... yellow to white to brilliant blue." She continued to watch the sky change from the parking lot's breaker wall by the ocean. A breeze passed over her face like a breath of invigorating energy and inspiration. She felt like anything could be forgiven. This new day promised that any problem could be solved as the young lady turned to pass through the Marinescape entrance.

"Good morning, Max," greeted Alisa cheerfully.

"It's a new day, a new start. Many things to resolve and create," the professor proclaimed. "We need to re-evaluate the seawater filtration and recirculation systems."

MAAW scientists had to develop new and revolutionary water and nutrition systems for the World's largest man-made, self-contained, on-land ocean marine swimming areas for future marine life.

"We put these marine animals in this environment, so we need to make sure their 'home' is safe, clean of man-made pollutants and has daily flowing biologically nutritious salt water," recited Max. This will ensure their longevity. It does encourage healthy reproductive offspring."

"All marine life is driven to continue its species by passing on their genetics," added Alisa

"You're right on." Max touched her nose and turned to stare out at the sunrise with her. "Nice weather on this side of the state. Hopefully, no repeat of a tropical storm or hurricane hitting the Marinescape faculties as in 2016. That was the last severe hurricane to hit us since 2004. It decimated the Oceanarium. When originally rebuilt, no viewing porthole existed. So MAAW designed changes to be more visitor-friendly, with interactive participation, including dolphin communication and touching." Max continued walking and lectured.

"I'm excited to start my rounds," fidgeted Alisa.

As the two walked toward the main redesigned Oceanarium, Alisa saw a sign: "Absolutely No Admittance."

"Professor Maxwell, what's with this closed-off area?"

"It is a security pen, an area for violent marine animals. Some animals get so out of control, they start hurting those around them and themselves.

They need to be confined until we can resolve their anger issues, to be safe and sociable again."

"An anger management place like 'Go stand in the corner' or stay after school or go to your room," Alisa grinned.

"Let's go in," he said as he unlocked the gate.

"Wow, that is a massive fence over the aquarium. No one or thing is getting out of there."

"This very expensive, twelve-gauge stainless steel mesh was installed with electrification if additional security was needed."

"Oh, I've been shocked by static electricity, so that would keep me from touching that wire."

"The electric shock you got is measured in the same way as this electrified wire energy. Voltage and amps sent through the wire and then you. Amps are the measurement of resistance offered by the wire gauge, you and whatever body part touches the wire. What really hurts or even kills are high amps. Your static electric shock was high voltage but very, very low amperage.

"This was installed by the same company that placed electrified fencing around the US Department of Prisons in Coleman, Florida. This aquarium wire top can have its voltage and amperage adjusted with a capacitor controlled in millisecond pulses of shocks for the aquatic animal to remember and still survive the shock. Of course, amperage needs to be kept low."

"Have you ever used this pen?"

"Used twice, with the animals being successfully rehabilitated for their return to the Marinescape 'Oceanarium.' Shall we go back to your daily assignments, Assistant Alisa Favour?"

# Chapter 17

## Patti

**Nurse Patti,** being the last to leave the clinic, turned on the outside light's timer and locked up the fertility clinic's front door. As she was about to leave, the clinic's front-desk phone rang.

"This Saturday morning's work won't end," she said as she turned around and stared through the window at the phone. It stopped ringing. She turned back around toward her car. Then it started to ring again. Patti felt negligent if she didn't answer the call.

"The call must be important." She unlocked the front door and answered the phone.

"This is Deputy Sheriff Keith. I was calling for Nurse Patti."

"This is Patti. You just caught me. I was on my way out. I'm going south to Marinescape Park with some fellow workers and my son."

"Well, have fun. I called for your assessment of the missing clinic items."

"Yes, I have that list," answered Patti. "I was going to email it to you tomorrow."

"Thank you, but could you just tell me right now and include everything?"

"O.K., all meds were of injection form. The ones we use to increase chances for ovulation. All our stock meds of Bravelle, Menopur, Gonal-F and HCG are missing. And, of course, the many injection needles that are needed to use these medications."

"So this thief must know what he or she is doing. It's a patient, nurse or doctor?"

"Sorry, I can't answer that," spoke Patti.

"Can you answer this for me?"

"If I can, Officer Keith, I'm on my way to meet friends ... at Marinescape."

"What kind of person would use these meds?"

"It would most likely be a woman to increase her chance to release an egg or eggs. Rarely, her male partner could use the meds for himself to potentially increase his sperm quality. If only HCG had been stolen, you might be looking for a fanatic overweight person who believes that the HCG will mimic the increased metabolic caloric demands of pregnancy. Unfortunately, this isn't true and the person won't experience weight loss from just HCG shots."

A long pause occurred on the phone.

"Hello? Are you still there?"

"You're way over my head with that egg-sperm thing, Nurse Patti. Let me know if anything else shows up missing," Deputy Keith responded.

"I'm so sorry for rambling on so much."

"Oh, no, Nurse Patti. I love listening to your voice, if you don't mind me saying so."

"Why thank you, Deputy Sheriff Keith. That has made my day."

They both laughed.

"Hope to speak with you soon, Deputy Sheriff Keith."

"Maybe we can meet later?" asked Keith softly. "And just Keith is fine, Patti."

***

**Patti,** her son and friends drove southbound on A1A in her white Cadillac into the parking lot of the Dolphin Family Fun and Marinescape Park.

"Here we are, people, at the world-famous Marinescape Park," Patti announced.

"What's that across the street?" Patti's son, Blaze asked.

"That's where Marinescape's research and aquatic medical facilities operate."

"Can we go there? I'm sure they'd love to see you three young and pretty nurses," Blaze grinned.

"Your son has learned the ways of the world with his use of flattery," said one of the nurses as they all got out of the car.

"Oh, Blaze, you're growing up too fast." Patti shook her head. "I doubt we can go there."

"I'm a healthy, adventurous young man of almost eleven."

"I wonder why Marinescape Park is in such a small community of Marinescape?" one nurses asked.

"Tax benefits? It allows for more political control of all the Marinescape facilities?"

"Marinescape formed the Marinescape community, Dolphin Family Fun and Marine Animal Aquatic World and incorporated this area for just those reasons," Patti added. On a less serious note, let's start our new Marine adventure. Take notes—just kidding." The four walked toward the official Marinescape Park entrance and stopped in front of a large stone wheel. It was approximately three-and-a-half feet in diameter. As the small group stood by the stone, a man observed their presence from a second-story conference room window above the entrance. The group stared at the etched stone's face. The wheel showed a timeline of life on earth.

"Life began 1.2 billion years ago as chemicals reacted and became a non-membranous single cell. Then a membranous single cell formed; some had the ability to move. From this came invertebrates, fish, amphibians, reptiles, land and flying dinosaurs and finally the development of mammals," read Patti.

The circular written pattern required some neck bending to follow. The circle of life led to Homo sapiens, with man's historic development covering only a fraction of the circle. The script ended with "Present to Future" life forms. Patti had read out loud the entire stone tablet script to the group.

"Looking backward and forward 1.2 billion years, today's science can only predict possible new life forms on earth or beyond, unknown when they will or if they have already appeared," finished Patti.

"And those new life forms are the exciting future," added a deep male voice from behind the foursome.

They turned in unison and smiled.

"And why is such an attractive and inquisitive group of people here today?" he asked.

"And you are?" suspiciously asked Patti.

"My apologies. I am Professor Rory Maxwell, marine biologist here at Marinescape.

"It's nice to meet you, Professor Maxwell. We're REI nurses— Reproductive, Endocrinology and Infertility nurses from the Matanzas River Fertility Center just up the road. This is my son, Blaze. We're on a day outing for fun," Patti stated. Maxwell shook hands with them all. "And education," added Blaze. "To find out more about marine animal reproduction," he pronounced with a grinning face. "We're involved with IVF," his excited voice added.

"Well, the three of us are IVF nurses." The nurses smiled together.

"Do you know what IVF is, Professor?" interjected Blaze.

"Well, maybe I need you to help me out and explain it to me, Blaze." The professor knelt down in front of the boy to be face-to-face.

"I can. In vitro Fertilization is one of several ways of bringing sperm and egg together, in a glass container (actually, a non-allergic, nonreactive type of plastic), for the purpose of achieving fertilization," Blaze spoke authoritatively.

"Blaze, do you know what fertilization means?" The professor now sat cross-legged and patted the ground next to him. Blaze flopped down, mimicking the professor.

"It's the making of new life with God's help," smiled Blaze.

"He's had an interest in how things come about and work since an early age," Patti stated as she put her hand on Blaze's shoulder.

"My favorite movie is *Frankenstein*, the original black and white, 1934 version by James Whale. My Mom and I read Mary Shelly's 1818 novel *The Modern Prometheus* together. You know that Frankenstein wasn't the monster, right? It was the creator-scientist Victor Frankenstein… oh, and I loved Mel Brooks' in his movie *Young Frankenstein*."

"My son and I have discussed the moral issues brought up by the novel and the films. We felt the scientist was morally misled and misunderstood, while we felt compassion for the monster," Patti embellished.

As Max, Patti and Blaze continued to converse, the other two nurses politely excused themselves from the group and entered the park.

"Well, we've taken enough of your time, so—"

"May I offer you and your son a personal tour?" smiled Maxwell.

"Oh yeah," immediately answered Blaze, "and like the research building over there?" He pointed across A1A.

"I'm Patti and you already know Blaze. Please forgive him for being so forward."

"I encourage forward and open-minded thinking. I'm Max. You never know, maybe someday I'll be mentally challenging the two of you."

The three walked into the park.

"Why did you pick us out of the incoming visitors to speak with?" She looked up to him.

"I noticed your group stopped to read the Circle of Life tablet. Ninety-nine percent of the visitors never even notice the stone, no less read it. They just walk in the entrance."

"Yes, we're all interested in—"

"Everything," interrupted Blaze.

"Blaze, I was talking." Patti stared at him.

"I can see we might become friends … special friends, with common interests." The professor stopped for a triangular hand piling. "Friends interrupt friends."

Blaze looked back and forth to his mom and the professor. "Yeah, I like this guy."

# Chapter 18

## Alive

**Between the Matanzas Inlet and** the River Pharmacy robberies and Yuma's assault, another assault took place along the river.

"Miss, are you O.K.? Are you hurt in any way?" a paramedic asked her. He tried to have her lie down on his gurney, but she refused. She preferred to sit down on the open backend of the ambulance while they took her vital signs.

"Of course I'm hurt," she angrily complained.

Her blood pressure was slightly elevated at 140/90 with a pulse rate of 100 bpm. "Please show me where," the paramedic patiently asked.

She had both hands grasping her head and moved her head back and forth. "Right here, can't you see? The shock, the fear, the embarrassment is just too much to bear." She started to cry. "You're a man. You just can't imagine what almost being raped does to a woman. A lifelong mark it leaves. You remember it all like it just happened, over and over in your mind."

The paramedic sat and listened. He laid a hand on hers, but she just moved it away.

Her miniature schnauzer sat at her feet and watched her. When the paramedic moved along the side of the ambulance, the dog barked.

"Izzo, be quiet now."

"Her vitals are stable and no visible signs of trauma," reported the first responder.

"I can hear you. I'm right here in this damaged state. And who are you?" she complained.

"Deputy Sheriff Keith, Miss. Can you tell me what happened?"

"It's Mrs. Beatrice. Everyone calls me Beatrice, but you, young man, may call me Bee."

"So, Mrs. Bee, could you tell me what happened or what you remember?"

"Oh, I remember it all. Well ... I'm collecting my thoughts. I want to get it right the first time." She closed her eyes. "Izzo, that's my dog and I was walking along the river shoreline, as we always do in the early morn. I watched a car go by on the A1A. Speeding, I'm sure. I almost got its license plate number. Of course, there were no police around—"

"Mrs. Bee, could you—" the deputy asked again.

"You're so impatient! Izzo turned and started barking. I went to turn and someone grabbed me ... no, he carried me ... no, lifted me by squeezing my shoulders, like a baby's doll ... no, a manikin. Lifted and turned me toward the river."

"Deputy, have you discovered the suspected body?" asked Dispatcher Mary Jane.

"Yes, I have and the paramedic has found her vital signs stable. I'm speaking with her right now," he responded into his shoulder intercom. "Correct the reported incident to an assault, sorry, Miss Bee, for the interruption."

"Yes, I'm alive," she said as she leaned toward his shoulder microphone. "Can you hear me? And I'm a Mrs., not a Miss ... and I'm alive, thank you very much."

"Mrs. Bee, were you able to struggle free?"

"Oh no, Officer, I didn't want to. I haven't been held like that, by a man, for decades."

Tara stepped out of the police vehicle and stood next to Deputy Keith and slightly smiled at Mrs. Bee's remark. Izzo didn't not bark or growl but wagged its tail. It jumped up on Tara's pant leg and licked her patting hand.

"Wait, I don't think I went into the water, but I'm wet." She stopped and started waving her arms in opposite directions, in smaller and smaller circles before coming to rest in front of her chest. Deputy Keith, the paramedic, a patrolman and Tara watched.

"Any other de—" Keith was stopped by her right index finger in the air.

"We proceeded into the water backward until I was waist-deep. He was always behind me and held me gently. He kind of bent me forward." Mrs. Bee began to smile. "He pressed me against him, doggy style. I'm sure Izzo was watching and panting. Bad doggy, bad," she scolded her dog. She hesitated to catch her breath. "He swung me from side to side like a rag doll." Bee looked at the deputy and the others around her. "I expected the worst! Yet he stopped. He turned us back toward the shore and then walked us in slowly and set me carefully down. It was a beautiful sunrise in my face." Her face changed to a frown. Looking at her dog, she smiled. "Izzo, you were such a good guard dog." She scratched behind both his ears. "Barking and jumping on him." She stopped and picked him up.

Doc MacGrath, who had been watching them from the police vehicle, stepped out. He approached the woman. "Does your dog bite?"

"No, my dog does not bite."

The doc extended his hand to pet the dog and quickly withdrew. "Is this your dog?"

Mrs. Bee looked puzzled "What?"

Tara, standing behind her, gave a little laugh that changed into a cough. "Excuse me," she said, cupping her hand over her mouth and looking downward. Tara was quite a movie buff and had recognized these three lines from a Peter Sellers movie.

"May we look more closely at Izzo, his mouth and nails?" Doc patted the dog's head. "Tara, please examine the dog for evidence of the perpetrator." As Doc held the dog, Tara swabbed its face, eyes, ears and nose. The calm dog let her examine its mouth, teeth and tongue and comb through its thick, hanging down mouth hair. Finally, Tara gently scraped each of the dog's long nails. Izzo just panted and occasionally licked Tara and Doc's hands.

"Thank you, Mrs. Beatrice," Tara smiled.

At first glance, they both saw what looked like fish scales on Mrs. Bee's shoulders.

"Tara"—the Doc pointed to Mrs. Bee's shoulder—"please includes this evidence and any other particles you find on her blouse. We should take Mrs. Beatrice's clothing with us."

"You surely shan't undress me!" Mrs. Bee said in a disgusted voice.

"We'll have Rick do his magic with the evidence in the lab," added Ian MacGrath.

"Izzo likes you," Mrs. Bee declared as the licked Tara's gloved hands.

"We'll have you step up into the ambulance for the paramedics to complete your physical exam, unless you prefer to go to the hospital," asked Tara.

"We really would like you to give us your clothes, and we'll give you some fashionable green scrubs to wear for now. We'll return your clothes at a later date," instructed Director Leon.

"Is it important to identify and capture the kind young assailant?" Mrs. Bee thought for a moment. "I could just as easily undress right here for you. You've all seen a beautiful mature woman before. Will I meet that kind man again?"

"Oh no, madam, inside the ambulance is our protocol, if you don't mind." Tara led her to the vehicle. "I don't know if you'll meet your assailant in the future."

Mrs. Bee stepped out a few minutes later, redressed in surgical green garb. "I feel like I'm on a medical TV show dressed like this."

Leon had been observing Officers Brett and John scrutinize the crime scene for evidence of the assault. "Anything interesting…?" Leon called out.

"Look at these depressions in the soft sand. They're consisted with Mrs. Bee's description of the perpetrator's movements," observed Officer Brett.

"Also, the shoreline vegetation has been broken and torn away at the perpetrator's water entrance and exit," added John.

"I'm on it," said Tara as she walked to the described areas.

"Make sure to culture the area for Rick's lab work-up," called out Doc.

Deputy Keith walked over to a kneeling Tara, who now had the evidence bags in hand. "There you are posing for another potential front page of *Miss CSI*, bent over at a crime scene, "Keith whispered.

"Do you only speak to me in whispers because you're embarrassed by what you say to me?" Tara spoke out loud.

The deputy looked around to see if anyone reacted to her statement. "I feel we can be more intimate," he again whispered.

Tara started to walk away.

"I caught the Peter Seller's *Pink Panther* movie reference you giggled about."

"Do you think it was intentional by the Doc?" Tara asked.

"Oh yeah, movies, something else we have in common," he smiled.

Izzo suddenly ran to Keith's left pant leg and started to pull him toward Mrs. Bee. She chuckled. "Look how much Izzo likes you. He's a good judge of people." Mrs. Bee nodded her head. "Izzo wants me to get to know you better."

Sheriff Gary waved Keith over, "Group text all the investigative members to meet on this Friday, 7:00 a.m., for the continuation of our crime scene evidence summaries of each case's progress. This time we'll meet at the city hall. Please bring all evidence written on slips of paper to tack up to a cork board. Please refer all media inquires to Sheriff Gary or Director Leon."

***

**Tara** decided to check on how prior assault victim Yuma Manta was doing. It was a small community, so the investigators wore many hats. Now she was a social worker. She was told in broken English that Yuma was at Jackson Memorial Hospital.

"What happened?"

"He got fever, throw up," an elderly Native American woman said.

Tara drove to the hospital and was now standing at the foot of Yuma's bed. He opened his eyes and smiled a "Welcome, Tara, nice to see you" smile.

"I knew you couldn't stay away," Yuma said between intermittent coughing spells.

"What's going—"

"Nausea, vomiting, went to hospital, salmonella septicemia, IV antibiotics. I'm getting better and don't count this as our date." Yuma laughed at his succinct list of events. "I'm not up to being my best for you, if you know what I mean?"

Tara just crossed her arms and nodded. "So you're getting better?"

"Wow, you're a beauty no matter what mood you're in!" he exclaimed.

"Sorry, Mr. Manta, I need to answer this text message. It's from Doc MacGrath: 'Need you or Rick to culture all of Mrs. Bee's evidence, especially for salmonella.'" Tara read the text out loud.

"Sounds like the same damn Iyola who attacked me and is still spreading its salmonella crud."

Tara stared at Yuma.

"Yes, I was listening. Thank you for that. Iyola in my language means snake."

"I learned your language; I'll tutor you in a few words in my language."

***

**Doc** MacGrath decided to revisit the three corpses in the county morgue before the second evidence meeting.

"I need to listen again to each of you ladies, in case there are any hidden secrets to tell me." He picked up his previously dictated and typed notes. Doc first read his findings and conclusions while looking at the three lifeless bodies lying adjacent to each other on cold, stainless steel carts.

"Oh Miss, you were plagued by chronic glucose poisoning." Doc looked over the obese first victim. "And you, young lady, went fishing to only to become bait. And you, the fittest and healthiest, chose the wrong beach for your morning run." Doc looked up and saw that Rick had come to his side. He started to read his original descriptions out loud.

Ian would begin a visual exam before the dissecting part of the autopsy. "Much can be learned by meticulous, magnified exams of the victim's clothing, body surfaces and all natural body orifices."

The two re-evaluated each typed line. Signs of trauma and original photos were also re-examined. Being suspicious and open to all possibilities were the examiner's most valued tools. Suspicion will lead to additional lab and microscopic tests to be performed beyond the routine tests. When the coroner suspected a natural cause of death, it was quickly completed and paperwork filed. Doc McGrath, being a pessimist, never assumed natural causes.

As Doctor MacGrath re-examined the three corpses' bodily orifices, he began his usual trivia oral dissertation as he grabbed a speculum. "More than two millennia ago, the Egyptians described an instrument design to examine each bodily orifice, such as the eye socket, nasal, oral and ear canals, vaginal and anal openings. I will use modern day modifications of the Egyptian embalmer's tools."

He completed the findings on all the victims with some insightful remarks by Rick. Doc MacGrath then called Sheriff Gary. The two decided to wait to review new findings and conclusions to be included at the official team meeting the next day.

"Rick, do you have culture results for the latest assault victims?"

"Of course, Doc, it was done within two hours of Tara telling me of the new evidence."

# Chapter 19

---

## *Befuddled*

**Doc walked** into Sheriff Gary's small office. He started with the cliché, "Gary, I have good news and bad news. I couldn't wait until tomorrow morning."

"Hit me." Gary put his fisted hands up like he was going to spar with Ian.

"The good news is the three victims were attacked by the same perpetrator(s) and died in similar fashion. Two drowned with lung water salinity the same as the salinity of the water they were found in. The third had salt water found in her orifices the same as the water she was found in. I feel she died of a heart attack and then was pulled into the water. They all have bruises of their inner and outer thighs, vulva, upper arms, arm pits, and lower backs. They all have different degrees of what I said, but still generically the same."

"Then rape with the purposeful downing?" injected Gary.

"Not necessarily. Each had only mild vaginal and vulvar bruising, but no high vaginal internal cuts or tears. No trauma to any other orifices. No foreign objects. No blood. No fingerprints." Doc stopped. "Don't look so disgusted."

"Did you try everything, every little known technique to bring us to a final conclusion?" Gary asked, staring at Doc.

Ian stood with his hands on his hips in front of Gary's desk. "Yes, even shook each corpse's hand." Doc stared back. "Everything…? Did you know there are over a hundred different methods available to make prints and blood visible, depending on the surface being examined? Rick and Tara have used iodine fuming for porous surface and ninhydrin on nonporous surface. Then for things not visible to the naked eye, they used superglue vaporization chamber, ultraviolet light, black light with fluorescent powder or solution and even a newly discovered method of turmeric powder."

Gary gave MacGrath a shoulder shrug. "O.K. May I continue?" asked Doc. "No pubic hair, no sperm. The good news is that I did discover two very interesting findings. All three victims had the same injuries, with armpit bruising and parallel scratches. The same scratch pattern was on the attacked employee, Mr. Manta, at the CVS Pharmacy. Secondly, the three women had a peculiar collection of lower vaginal fluids. No sperm was present. The perpetrator didn't have a vasectomy, as shown by lab tests. Other explanations include that he has a very low sperm count, is a retrograde ejaculator, meaning the sperm goes backward into the bladder or he has a very short penis, a penile-urethral tract anomaly called hypospadias, so sperm spills out at the base on the penis into the salt water."

"How about if he's a premature ejaculator?" added Gary.

"Or just has azoospermia, meaning no sperm at all?" added Ian.

"The vaginal fluid contained a few white blood cells and red blood cells, but not typical cells for a human. The fluid glowed bright green under UV light. I sent our two samples to the state police lab. They, in turn, sent the samples to the College of Veterinarian Medicine, University of Florida. Finally, we found all evidence samples positive for salmonella."

"Your conclusions, Doc?" asked Gary.

"I'm starting to think Tara and Director Leon may be on the right tract with their non-human perpetrator. I'll bring coffee and bagels for our meeting."

"What? Law enforcement officers only eat donuts," joked Sheriff Gary.

\*\*\*

**Doc** MacGrath, Director Leon Mendelssohn, CSI Assistant Tara Colton and Lab Assistant Director Rick LaGrande sat around Doc's desktop computer. The computer's table was cluttered with colorful charts and images.

"People, I'm befuddled. It's blood; it contains red blood cells, some sickle cells, and lymphocytes. Yet the serum is green. The RBC didn't react with the usual ABO antibody reagents for blood typing," sighed Doc.

"I know. I even referenced dog, wolf, cat, large feline, snake, salamander, frog, eel, dolphin, manatee and shark, with no luck matching their blood type," continued Tara.

"You forgot trolls, goblins, hobbits, abdominal snowman, sasquatch." Rick looked to Tara, who had her hands on her hips.

They all laughed, including Tara.

"Another amazing fact is that the blood contains a hemoglobin count of 24 and higher grams per deciliter, as compared to humans, with normal female 12 to 15, and normal male at 13 to 17 grams per deciliter," added Rick.

"No matches with the partial fingerprint or palm prints?" asked Gary of Tara and Rick.

"No, because there are no whorl patterns found in our multiple impressions and images made at the crime scenes, so there's nothing to compare for previous perpetrators on IAFIS, Integrated Automated Fingerprint Identification System," retorted Rick.

"No IAFIS for bizarre creatures, Rick?"

"Funny one, Tara," said Rick as he pointed at her.

"And my partial print in Yuma's scratch blood was a bust," the disappointed Tara reported.

"The veterinarian school's final report offered that our collected cells, green fluid and scales were consistent with a rare animal source, like maybe a crossbreed animal between a crocodilia, crocodile or alligator, salamander, lizard, armadillo or snake. It's possible that it's a marine mammal or creature with lymphoma or leukemia," summed up Rick.

They looked at each other, speechless after CSI Director Leon had read their conclusion. "The conclusions led the involved university staff to suggest that our team consult a marine biologist, ichthyologist—fish scientist—and/or a herpetologist, which is a reptile scientist and present all the facts currently available to the consultant(s).

***

Friday morning, the group met in a city hall room with closed window shutters, locked doors and a patrolman outside the front door to guarantee privacy. The goal was to summarize all the evidence and facts, get all team members on the same page and ultimately solve the listed crimes. Sheriff Gary pinned pieces of paper with crime scene location, name and summarized information from Doc's meeting a day earlier.

"Again, I stress that we,"—Gary looked around the room and pointed to all the members— "will not leak any info to the media. Only I or CSI Director Leon will speak with the media."

The first three homicides were quickly reviewed again. The team agreed the three crimes were related.

The fourth crime scene was Mr. Manta, six-foot, light brown skin, Native American. He was at the first of four known pharmacy robberies. The list of stolen items included all stock of CoQ10, B6, B complex, calcium, zinc, magnesium, folic acid supplements and prenatal vitamins. No narcotics or sleep medications, no Tylenol Sinus or ephedrine was stolen, which are commonly used for illicit drug manufacture. "I also received a note from the second pharmacy break-in that clomiphene citrate or Clomid, an oral fertility medication, was stolen."

The **number five** crime was a fertility center and included only fertility meds, injectable with needles, and oral Clomid.

The **number six** and **seven** crimes were other pharmacies with similar vitamins and drug thefts.

The **number eight** crime scene and the fourth woman to be apparently assaulted with no significant injuries, was Mrs. Beatrice and her dog, Izzo. The dog had cells, scales and green blood on him, as seen under regular light microscope. There was no need for infrared lighting.

All events took place on or very close to the Matanzas River. Geographic forensics showed the plotting of the crime scenes going almost straight along a north-south line. This gave a 95 percent confidence interval that the listed sites factor was true—that factor being the Matanzas River.

All break-in scenes showed extensive unnecessary destruction at the scene and demonstrated massive strength of the perpetrator(s).

"Four women had signs of vaginal manipulation or some kind of attempted entry. Three are deceased young women whose blood work confirms that they all were potentially fertile, with ovarian follicles or recent ruptured follicle found at autopsy. We looked at the older female survivor of an attack and discovered that her follicle stimulating hormone, FSH, was very high at 51, predicting fertility potential extremely low and a less than 1 percent chance of pregnancy in one year. She stated that she'd had no menses for more than five year and was postmenopausal. Yet she looked quite young. The conclusion is that the perpetrator was looking for a fertile female," summarized Doc.

"Rick cultured the found scales; the three deceased women's swabbed bruises, scratches and vaginas; cells and blood droplets found with Mrs. Beatrice's clothes and the mouth, hair and nails of her dog, Izzo. Finally, bacteria found in Yuma Manta's hair and armpit scratches were all re-identified as salmonella typhimurium and consistent with Mr. Manta's salmonellosis from a sick human or animal source of salmonella."

"Yuma Manta's salmonella septicemia is near resolution and his projected hospital release is tomorrow," announced Tara.

"With all this evidence, the team's perpetrator profile includes someone who liked the dawn or sunset, was taller than six-and-a-half feet and liked water, specifically the Matanzas River," continued Sheriff Gary. "Probably near his or its home."

"Abnormal blood work, maybe a lymphoma patient," stated Rick. "I ran other endocrine blood work and found a high testosterone level of 3,900 ng / dl (nanogram per deciliter). A normal human male's total testosterone level is from 240 ng to 950 ng/ dl." Rick perused the group.

"Then this perpetrator is male with an abnormal skin scale shedding condition, lymphoma and a significant salmonella infection," offered Director Leon.

"Humans have a rare inherited condition called ichthyosis," started Dr. MacGrath. "In the aquatic world, shedding scales is common for fish, lamprey and hagfish species. There's an extinct prehistoric dinosaur called an ichthyosaurus, Greek name for fish-lizard. This dinosaur may have become an unidentified walking terrestrial or land animal that eventually returned to water for marine life as an amphibian or reptile. This precursor reptile became the present-day dolphin and whale. The word 'dinosaur' came from Greek, meaning 'terrible lizard.' Now amphibians like salamanders start life with gills and then as an adult breathe through their skin," lectured MacGrath. "A large surviving prehistoric reptile includes the Chinese salamander, which is six feet in length and—"

"Thank you, Doctor MacGrath," interrupted Sheriff Gary.

"Partial fingerprints with none of the typical six ridge patterns used to identify human fingerprints have already been discussed," stated CSI Director Leon.

"So we have a genetically abnormal individual, very tall, carries cancer cells which it is immune to, carrying salmonella and a scaly fish lizard who wants to mate with an ovulating human woman or attempts to have underwater sex," stated Gary as he scanned the room of investigators for additional comments. "Oh, who also has green blood with very high hemoglolin and testosterone counts, yet no detectable sperm, anything else?"

"We do have a murderer committing multiple break-in robberies, multiple assaults and destruction of property," added Deputy Keith.

"And a rapist," commented CSI Assistant Tara.

"Have we revisited other crimes in the area that have a similar profile?" asked Gary.

"There are none, the entire State of Florida, the East Coast, the Gulf of Mexico... none. We'd have to go as far as Jacksonville, Orlando or Miami to equal levels of our crime spree," said the frowning Rick. "The State Police have checked their records. The FBI has searched for any weird unsolved FBI cases. The prior statements of possible perpetrator(s) have been retracted by both of these law enforcement agencies.

"So finding the malicious culprit is left up to us." Gary walked to the front door and unlocked them. He opened the door to see the vigilant officers. "Officers Brett and Brenner, you are relieved of this duty and can pursue your regular duties."

"Officer Cecilia Brett, you look quite sharp and professional this morning," smiled Officer Brenner.

"Officer Brett, have you taken your detective exam yet?" called out Deputy Sheriff Keith.

# Chapter 20

## Selection

**Before I give** your mom and you the special backstage tour, Blaze, I want you to tell me what you want to be when you grow up," Professor Maxwell asked.

Blaze looked at his mother. "It' your show, Blaze," Patti reassured him.

"Speak freely, young man." Max nodded to an outside picnic table. They approached the table and sat down. Then Blaze spoke up. "I think a lot. I'm pretty serious. There are good and bad people in the world. Some kids want to be G-Men. Others want to be M-Stars. The good kids go for the right, the wannabe government men. Or they wanna be mobster's stars. They're naturally mean to all people."

Both adults looked at each, wondering where this train of thought came from. "And you are?" asked Max.

"Well, look at me." Blaze stood up and struck a pose with arms apart and fisted hands in front, like a boxer. "I'm one of the good guys."

The threesome walked through the main entrance and past the gift shop and open air aquariums exhibits, talking as they walked. Professor Maxwell explained each of their purposes until they finally reached the outside wall by the wavy ocean. From an elevated white wall, they looked down and outward in unison. "See those sand dunes covered with sea grass, Blaze?" They looked. "Alisa! Hello!" He was surprised to see her on the shoreline. "Alisa is a new Marinescape assistant intern. She is making sure these grassy six-to-ten foot dunes will be a great location for loggerhead turtles' annual migration to lay their eggs in the dunes bases."

"Not much room for them to do their laying," said Blaze as he turned his head sideways and looked up and down the shoreline.

"With the diurnal ocean tides, the high tide water left the beach on Alisa's left less than six feet wide. Thousands of eggs will crack and squiggling bodies will dig out of the sand dune and race to the ocean water," enthusiastically described the professor.

"Who's that girl again?" Blaze asked with more interest as Alisa walked closer to the wall. He leaned slightly over the wall to study her and her windblown blonde hair. "Hey, Alisa down there, are you having fun?" He waved furiously. "I'm Blaze."

"She's my intern assistant who wants to work up to a marine biologist, taking care of aquatic animals and helping them bring new life into their watery world," explained Professor Max while staring at Patti.

"Hey, Alisa, I think I want to be like you. I have helped bring new life ... breeding gerbils. They had many babies in my Habitrail. I'm like my mom, making babies come to life in the lab."

Alisa looked up to Blaze as they both pointed at each other, smiling.

"Well, I'm the head nurse in charge of running a fertility and IVF clinic—patient instructions, scheduling egg retrievals and embryo transfers," Patti explained with a flushed face.

Maxwell just grinned.

"They loved running through those clear yellow tubes," laughed Blaze. Blaze stopped talking and looked down to his scuffling feet.

"What's wrong, dear?" Patti put her hands on her son's shoulders.

He put both hands in his pockets and wiggled from her grasp.

Max kneeled down and gently pulled Blaze's hands out of his pockets and took hold of them. "You can tell your mom and me. We're all friends here," reassured Maxwell.

Blaze looked up to Max with tearing eyes. "I helped make a lot of babies ... but ... many were born weird. All wrong in their arms and legs and dying," he sniffled. "We had to get rid of the gerbils, the entire Habitrail setup."

Then Patti mouthed "ugly, monsters" to Max as she shook her head.

"It is not your fault. It is part of nature the result of what is called overpopulation. It can happen with any animal, even us humans. In nature, those things happen when there are too many babies to feed or there is not enough space for their growth," explained Max. Animals may decrease overpopulation by eating their young or abandoning them to outside predators. Nature selects animals best suited to survive in the present environment. This group will continue to breed. The poorly formed ones will usually not breed. Your Habitrail's environment led to "selecting out" the weakest gerbils." Max lightly touched the boy's shoulder.

"The moms and I didn't know it was too crowded. The moms just make weird babies who couldn't make more babies or even just survive in the new place?" said Blaze, wiping his eye.

"Yes, you're right," Patti said as she hugged him.

By now Alisa had come up from the beach and was standing next to Professor Max.

"Alisa, I'd like you to meet Patti and her son, Blaze." All shook hands. "Why don't you take Blaze with you, Alisa, so he can see what you do each day? If any little work items pop up, let Blaze help you out. He is a very inquisitive young boy." Max winked at Alisa.

"That would actually be me. I'm a friendly, likeable and interesting young man," Blaze corrected the professor. He leaned forward and said in a low voice, "And I find you quite interesting. Ah … your work, I mean."

The professor and Nurse Patti walked off together talking. Alisa's eyes watched them. Or was she only watching Max?

# Chapter 21

## *Appearance*

**Hurry, Mom,** we can still make the last boat," yelled back Blaze.

The certified National Park Ranger Theo R. Smythe pulled the tour boat from the dock and began his tourist spiel. His loud voice rang out over the river's breadth and engine noise. "The Matanzas River at St. Augustine is referred to as the Matanzas Harbor of America's oldest ongoing historic city and port. It's the 'backdoor' to St. Augustine. This made the river a strategic necessity for controlling the early Spanish colonists' safety at St. Augustine. Spanish engineers and laborers built this most southerly aspect of the 'backdoor' defensive structure as Fort Matanzas, which you see growing before you as we approach. From the fort, one can see the Matanzas Inlet, covered today by a highway bridge. Thus, the Spanish soldiers could 'close the door' to foreign invaders."

"What do you think, Blaze? Do you like history? Giving people information like this tour guide?" Patti asked.

"I don't think so. The less people know about history, the dumber their questions. The less they know, the less they care about it and they start talking about nonsense—"

"O.K., Mr. Negativity. You understand that Professor Maxwell and Alisa both gave you information on their tours? Were you dumber, less uninterested with their 'rambling' talks?"

"No." Blaze looked at his feet, a common practice of his when embarrassed. Patti placed a finger under his chin and lifted it.

"So you do like history?"

"This eighteenth-century monument was the controlling point of foreign boat traffic on the river from the Matanzas Inlet north about fourteen miles to St. Augustine," T.R. Smythe explained.

"Today, we appreciate that the Matanzas River supports an extensive tidal marsh habitat. The preserved areas include salt marshes, mangrove tidal wetlands, oyster bars, estuarine lagoons, upland habitats and marine animal environments."

"Always look at someone's eyes when you speak with them. Remember, Blaze, information stays with you. Someone could take all your physical possessions, but they cannot take what you know, your knowledge," Patti whispered.

"You can stop the lecture, Mom," Blaze said loudly.

Ranger Smythe stopped his lecture. People turned to look at Blaze. Patti put her hand up.

"Sorry, sorry, just a misunderstanding, Mr. Ranger; please continue." Both Patti and Blaze shrank down to the size of barnacles, hoping to not be seen but to be ignored.

The ranger cleared his throat. "Unfortunately, the Matanzas River faces several pollution issues, which helped invasive biological species to grow, one of many polluting contaminates coming from St. Augustine's urbanization," spoke a young woman who now took over the tour lecture as Ranger Smythe took over the boat's steerage. "Hello, I'm Frieda Nelson, assistant to Senior Ranger Smythe. Did I hear a question before the interruption?" she asked in a heavy Eastern European accent. "No? Then let us continue. The Matanzas River was named by the Spanish forces for being an infamous 'massacre' site. Pedro Menendez de Avilés of Spain led a group of several hundred shipwrecked French Huguenots to slaughter somewhere near this present site of the Matanzas Inlet in 1565. Menéndez had been ordered by the Spanish royalty and Church that in the New World, all Protestants and others who refused to convert to Catholicism should be executed."

The boat came to dockage on the west shore of the river.

"Myth has it that over the centuries, many people have died 'accidentally.'" as Ranger Nelson put her fingers up and twitched them like quotation marks. "They died near this same spot, as if Menendez de

Aviles' ghost was still active. Well, we've landed. Let's debark and take a closer look at this 450-year-old fort." Nelson led the group to the boat's exit and narrow boardwalk. "Watch your step as you leave the boat onto the dock. If anyone needs assistance getting off the boat, just ask one of us rangers. I'll be here waiting on the head of the boardwalk for your return."

The tourists talked among themselves as they looked to the fort. The last few individuals were still on the dock.

"Hey, look in the water," one man yelled. Then more people joined in. "There!"

A long dark shadow moved along the dock, under it and back to the other side. More people returned to the dock. The rangers asked everyone to return to the shore.

"What is it? It's swimming by kicking it's ... webbed feet ... fins?"

It again disappeared under the dock and the moored boat. The dock slowly started to list away from the boat, sway, buckle and drop into the water. The moored side of the tour boat submerged, with half the pontoon boat remaining above water, like an aluminum iceberg. Screaming people ran back to shore and the fort. The National Park Rangers assisted all visitors off the collapsing dock and boat.

"Everyone go back toward the shore and safety. Is everyone O.K.?" the Ranger Smythe asked loudly as he looked around. "Count the people," he instructed Nelson.

The Ranger Smythe then noticed that Ranger Nelson was dripping wet. "What happened to you?"

"I don't know. As the boat started to severely list, I leaped toward the shore and found myself in the water." Smythe handed her a towel. "I was so close, but the soft shoreline kept giving way with each handful of sand and shells I grasped." Her panting became normal breathing. "I did feel something wiping, then touching my feet. That sensation powered me to scrabble up and get on solid land."

They both looked down at her Bermuda shorts and saw the multiple small skin scratches and torn clothing.

"Mom, what just happened?"

"I don't know, son."

Several cell phone cameras were recording the event.

"What happened to the back of her shorts and legs?" asked Blaze.

# Chapter 22

---

## *Frenzy*

**With their feet** up on the sheriff's desk, Sheriff Gary and Deputy Keith drank their coffees. The sheriff's nameplate was face-down on his desk. They both looked at the single telephone between them. Their eyes slowly moved up and met. They both placed their right hand on their snapped-down hip weapon holster. Neither would blink, both in a frozen but ready pose.

"Ring, ring ... ring!"

They both jumped forward, but Gary got to the phone first.

"Hello. Sheriff's Department, Sheriff Gary speaking. Ugh. Oh. Ugh. It's a real lead? Tara has a real lead, Deputy Keith. She's asking if you're able to go out on a date Friday night."

"I'll take that phone, smart ass, sir." Keith grabbed the phone, started whispering, and turned away from the sheriff.

Gary got up, walked past "The prior statements of possible perpetrator(s) have been retracted by both of these law enforcement agencies. So finding the malicious culprit is left up to us." Tara in the next room, and patted her on the shoulder.

"No, I was not calling to make a date with you."

Doc and Rick sat with Tara reading medical journals or at least the abstracts.

"Hey, Doc, two weeks and we haven't had a crime. Not even a bicycle theft," complained Gary. "Murder, robbery, assault and break-ins are all over in less than five days and now nothing. Nothing new, not even one new clue or lead. We're back to normal with the State Police and the FBI having pushed us aside." Gary turned to see Mary Jane run in from her office. "Sheriff, everybody … you have to see this on the TV.

*"**Breaking News** coming to us from the Matanzas National Monument Park at Crescent Beach. Our reporter Miranda Vera de Cruz la Hoya Cardinola is live onsite.*

*"Thank you. We're here at the Matanzas Fort National Park, where frenzied tourists are describing a very strange sighting and life-threatening experience,"* spoke the reporter into the TV camera.

*"Ma'am, what did you see?"*

*"It was horrible. I thought I was going to die! An alligator at least twenty feet long tried to climb out of the river on to the dock. It was looking right at me. You know they can run—"*

*"Thank you, ma'am, and what about you young boy?"*

*"Oh man, it was so cool! This thing swam along the dock, round and round and then pulled the dock underwater. It pulled half the boat down with it. I ran along the shore with this swimmer who I saw at the dock, to follow where—"*

*"Blaze, that's enough."* A woman pulled him away from the reporter.

*"Sir, how about you … can you describes what you saw?"*

*"It was a dark slender shadow, maybe eight … no, more than ten feet, swimming along and under the dock as we all departed the tour boat. Then it disappeared under the dock. The dock began to sink. I have video on my cell phone."*

*"They claim to be lucky to have survived. We have several of the surviving tourists' videos. Go ahead and show some of the horrifying footage."*

The police investigative staff watched the videos.

"I can't believe the reporter said, 'lucky to be alive—survived,'" Deputy Keith angrily repeated. "They're just building fear and panic in the public."

"We all have to get to the park to question all possible witnesses on that tour," commanded the sheriff. "And get all the cell phones."

113

\*\*\*

"**M**ax, wait up," called out the running Alisa. "How am I doing so far? You can't expect me to be fine-tuned yet; it's been only two weeks. Just tell me how to be better and …"

Facing Alisa, Max placed both hands on her shoulders.

"I want to be the best intern you've ever had. This is the perfect job for me. I don't want to mess up this opportunity!" Alisa surprised Max with a bear hug.

He immediately raised his arms. "I followed the work routine you gave me. I followed your example to be able to explain why I do everything I do, not just because I was told to. I probably improved some of the small steps—"

"Alisa, take a breath. This is not a race. You have done better than I expected. Relax and enjoy the marine animal interactions. It is not always about finishing the job faster each day. It is also about quality and enjoying the journey."

"O.K., I'll continue on my 'journey' for excellence in my job of interacting and spreading food and good health care of the animals," Alisa smiled. "Oh, who was that woman and boy?"

"Excuse me, Professor Maxwell, you must watch the breaking news on our TV in the Marinescape's reception area," relayed staff member Jennifer.

\*\*\*

**Eleven minutes later,** the sheriff and the CSI team were at the National Monument Park entrance off A1A. Several State Police vehicles blocked their entry, while two officers stood in front of the yellow "Do Not Cross, Crime Scene" tape.

Sheriff Gary pulled up in his clean large white Ford XLT Expedition; a green logo marked St. Johns Sheriff. An officer approached Gary's open window

"Good morning, Officer. I'm Sheriff Gary Sellack of the St. Johns County Law Enforcement Unit, with my CSI team for the purpose of investigating this suspected crime scene."

"Sorry, Sheriff, we have strict instructions to keep out all media, gawkers and unauthorized law enforcement officers, which specifically includes you and your team by name," the State Trooper sternly stated. "So you and your entourage of vehicles must exit the premises immediately."

"I'd like to speak with the officer in charge," Gary said as he started to open his SUV's door.

The trooper quickly stepped forward and forcibly closed Gary's door. A second trooper stood behind him. "Please, Sheriff, don't cause an incident." They stared at each other. "I do understand your frustration." The officer paused. "For authorization to enter this site, call the State Police main office in Jacksonville and ask for the Commander in Chief on duty. Now you and your team must exit promptly to avoid serious consequencences."

Gary thought for a moment of his options. None, he remembered his last encounter with the Jacksonville Commander in Chief; only bad words had been said and it resulted in bad feelings between them. He backed up his vehicle to A1A. He put on his red and blue lights without the siren as he performed a U-turn to go back north. With his windows still open, he motioned with his arm for Keith to follow "Back to the station." Gary passed each car parked on the shoulder and waved them to also follow.

Back at their small station, the team regrouped and Gary explained the situation. Then the room was silent.

"Sheriff, remember the Fish and Wildlife's recommendation?" Tara asked. "Consult an ichthyologist and marine biologist?"

"There probably is such a person at Marinescape and Marine Aquatic Animal World," several team members spoke in unison.

"Let's see who will be going with me to see the consultant and be bored by scientific mumbo jumbo language." Gary looked around the room.

***

**About twenty men** collected in a large domed glass room wearing multicolored draped clothing on their shoulders. The several younger men stood behind the much older, seated men. They faced each other in an elliptical-shaped arrangement. Near the center of the group sat men with large decorated head gear and painted faces. The older members preferred to sit on a blanketed floor cross-legged. The oldest men wore side streaming headdresses of feathers, leather skins, strips of animal fur and colorful beads.

"We call upon the elders to speak up so we may learn from them," spoke Yuma Manta loudly. "We believe it is time to pull off our 'resting' blankets." Yuma dropped his. "You all know me." He walked around acknowledging the faces that looked up to him. "Help us identify this new threat and protect our young femmes (women). The Spirit of the Great Yaha (the Great One) has given the Timucuan tribal hommes (men) the honor to remove this threat to life. We need to stand strong and together." He stopped and looked to the center of the room. "We wait for the elders to speak." Yuma moved to the back of the room.

\*\*\*

**Patti** watched Blaze as he turned the book's pages at the kitchen table. He would pick a letter out of the alphabet and take a journey. From the beginning of the edition, he would look at the many pictures. *Compton's Encyclopedia and Facts Index* was well known for its pictures with explanatory comments. If he was interested, Blaze would read more. If not, he would move on to the next picture. He did this pictured adventure three or four nights a week. Patti laughed to herself. Sometimes he read straight through to bedtime and missed his favorite TV programs.

"You know, Blaze, when I was about your age, I too read *Compton's*. I wanted *Britannica Encyclopedia*, but my mom said it was too expensive."

Patti looked out to their back yard through the kitchen window while preparing dinner. "Blaze, why do you like reading encyclopedias?"

"When I open the next book, I feel I'm a traveler through time and getting there 'faster than a speeding bullet.' You know, Mom, like Superman for finding knowledge. I think it's like when we go to Marinescape together. I know Professor Maxwell and Alisa always have things going on and she lets me help her."

"She lets you do what things exactly?" Patti suspiciously queried.

"She lets me do little ... safe things with her."

"Your face sparkles when you say her name. You kind of like her, don't you?"

"Well, who wouldn't?" He looked back down to the next encyclopedia page. "When we're with Max, you look at him a lot. Do you like him, Mom?"

Patti just smiled and tapped his encyclopedia's open page.

"Alisa looks at me a lot too. Do you think she likes me too?"

Patti looked out the kitchen window again.

"When are we going back down to Marinescape?"

"Soon," Patti softly said. "Soon, he ... the professor asked me some questions when you were with Alisa. I ... we have some things to talk about."

"Yes, Alisa and I have some things to talk about," he mimicked his mother.

***

**Rick** rushed into the lab. "Doc MacGrath, Doc"—Rick saw him sitting at his desk, slumped over a medical journal. "Did I wake you? Sorry."

Gary heard the commotion and walked in. Keith, Brett, and Mary Jane followed. Mary Jane watched Deputy Keith's every movement.

Rick summarized the latest news. "The State Police and the FBI both have closed the three Matanzas river deaths as 'accidental drownings.' The three pharmacies and the fertility center break-in crimes are listed as unrelated to the drownings. The State Police and FBI consider these cases to be drug addicted thieves looking for money and drugs. They classified them as independent incidents. They've left these issues for the local law enforcement agencies to follow up on and solve."

Gary spoke after Rick. "And finally, the communication from both, separately, is that the last attempted assault on the woman walking her dog was a harmless, failed assault, prank or complete fabrication from a woman looking to be on the local TV networks and social media. Whatever, this also is a local police matter."

The small collection of personnel looked at each other.

"A lot of people are going to be upset," said Doc while getting up.

"Who's upset?" asked Gary as another latecomer, Leon, stood next to Gary. "In other words, the investigations are back to us." Gary put his hands on his hips.

"What about the National Park incident and sketchy sighting of something swimming?" asked Patrolman Brenner.

"Good question. I think that will eventually be thrown in our lap to wrap up as well," responded Gary.

"Interesting follow-up ... the young female Ranger Nelson was scratched by that swimmer and reported to the Flagler Hospital Urgent Care Center in St. Augustine two days later. She had several infected scratch tracks on her legs. Guess what was—" Tara was interrupted.

"She had positive salmonella by slides and cultures," answered Rick.

"Thus showing we're on the right scratch track," added Keith, followed by a few moans.

"As it should be; fortunately, we've wasted no time. Our work continues," Leon stated.

"Oh, the US Department of Agriculture sent their final report. The foreign object we sent in is from an aquatic animal with traces of fresh and salt water. Their conclusion—very large, ordinary fish scale!"

"No way!" shouted Tara as she walked around the room in frustration. "How does an ordinary fish climb out of the water, into the pharmacy, get under Yuma's T-shirt, scratch both armpits and then get back into the river?"

"Knocking shelves, taking only vitamins, without being seen?" added Director Leon. "Wait. The flopping fish has to first break into the pharmacy building."

"Rick and I know it wasn't an ordinary fish scale by its silver-dollar size," Doc MacGrath said. "That's why we sent it to them."

"Also, the scale wasn't like a single shingle on a roof. It was similar to a melted sheet of material where the outline of prior, separate scales had grown together," added Tara.

"It would be a great to patent that scale for a waterproof diving suit. You can't tear it," excitedly explained Rick.

"How did we get this sample?" interjected Keith.

"It just rubbed off, like our own skin does with friction, except our single skin cell is a quite small, micro slice. These scales one can see with the naked eye," said Rick.

"I guess the non-human green blood droplet, no human blood type, high hemoglobin and very high white blood cell count weren't worthy of the authorities' comment?" added Doc.

"And, of course, the unclassifiable fingerprints, palm prints and large clown-sized footprints weren't explained," Tara cheerfully added to the list of unexplainable facts.

Officers Brett, Brenner and Dispatcher Mary Jane had listened since the beginning of the listing of unexplained facts. They all looked around like deer flashed by a car's headlights.

Mary Jane's phone rang. "Sheriff Gary, a woman is on the line. She's walking along the Matanzas River and saw something in the water. She thinks it's following her."

"There we go, team. We continue our own investigations. We need to get to this walker. We also need to get to the Matanzas National Park crime scene and any witnesses you can find. We'll see who'll have egg on their face. We'll see who will be left behind the yellow police crime scene tape now," stated Sheriff Gary.

As the group dispersed, Keith caught up with Tara. "How did you find out about Ranger Nelson's salmonella?"

"I have an old friend from the Flagler Hospital lab. He figured I'd like to know," Tara answered. "We both were at Flagler College together in laboratory science."

"How good of friends were the two of you?" pried Keith.

Tara just walked away.

\*\*\*

**The several elders** looked to each other. One decided to speak. "The Timucuan Tribe, of which you young biros (men) disrespectfully called yourselves hommes, represents our proud past, present and honorable future."

Yuma moved to the front. "I apologize to the elders for my—"

"Young people have been disrespectful because of their kneeling to the white Francais (English) and Espanol (Spanish) men," interrupted the elder. "We once filled half this southern Native Nation. But the white chiefs have disrespected us many times. Again we have been disrespected by them not recognizing our tribe but only the combined Miami and Seminole Tribes."

"We have learned not to trust the white invaders of our land to do the right thing," spoke another Elder.

"It is left to us to stop the killing of our land and soul-bearing animals."

"Yuma, you are correct that our nias (women) are in danger." He paused. "Our past has been passed on by our glorious spoken words to tell us of a Protector, of the Great Yaha's gift to Mother Earth and the Timucuan people."

A third Elder now spoke. "This Protector may change its shape and form. It comes from the Efa (sun) and Acu (moon) becoming one." The room of Native Timucuans was silent. Not a breath could be heard. "It will protect as in the image of a Cuyu (fish), Iyola (snake) or as one large Cuyolabiro (fish-snake-man)."

"As a good, honorable man, Yuma, the Protector will not harm you," the first elder added.

"But I was attacked by this Protector," Yuma questioned.

"That is because you were in a disrespectful place to the Mother Earth and its souls," the Elder answered with staring eyes. "You happened to work there for the disrespectful white man."

# Chapter 23

## *Premonition*

**Sheriff Gary reminisced** about going fishing while he reclined in his office chair with his hands behind his head. "Oh well, it will happen soon." He picked up the local newspaper and read for a short time before falling asleep. He found himself again under water. This seems familiar. A few small fish swimming by in between the river bottom plants waving with the slight current. I see a snake slithering on the surface in my peripheral vision. I soon realize I'm stretched out and floating near the river bottom. It's quite relaxing. Some hair swishes by my face. I twist left and my favorite blue mermaid is hand-motioning me to follow. The mermaid swims to the surface and pops her (its?) head out. I do the same. I look around and hear a 'dulce Melos,' a sweet melody.

Suddenly, a high-pitched sound, like my police vehicle's siren, starts up to the point of hurting my ears. I move to see the blue mermaid on the west shore. The Mermaid points to the opposite eastern shore of the river, where several buildings can be seen. Between the buildings, I see jumping dolphins. The siren sound diminishes to a hum.

I must be in the Matanzas River. I look back to the mermaid, but it's gone. I look back toward the buildings. The dolphins have been replaced by a tall irregular shadow. It dives into the river and swims toward me.

\*\*\*

**"What the hell?"** Gary said out loud.

"Sheriff, did you say something?" Mary Jane asked. "Are you O.K.?"

"Yes, Mary Jane, I am. Thanks for caring," he said as he came out of his stupor.

"I do care," she replied. "More than you know," she whispered to herself.

Deputy Keith texted Tara: "Are you too busy for break?"

Tara responded: "Yes."

He then texted Officer Brett: "Do you need help on your detective exam?"

Brett texted him back: "No thanks, sir."

Keith decided to walk over to the dispatcher's desk. He saw Mary Jane sitting next to Gary.

"Well, my default is …" He looked around.

"Real Jeopardy, so it is." Keith sat down in front of the TV in the office's back room.

"Our final Real Jeopardy category is animal myths. This is an unusual question for this program, so think out of the box for this one," the host stated. "We will be back after this commercial break."

"Darn, the program is almost over," frowned Keith.

"I see all the contestants have their wages in."

"The final Real Jeopardy: the oldest living reptile at 350 million years old with a 231-million-year-old relative, named originally by Floridian Spaniard." The host looked to the contestants. Let's see your answers.

"What is an alligator? What is a caiman? What is a serpiente? The correct answer is 'What is Lagartija or Lagarto?' The translation is the lizard man."

"Hello, Deputy Sheriff, sleep on your own time." The sheriff kicked Keith's chair and then the two men walked through the police station's front door. "Do you know what, Keith?"

"I do, Gary, sir."

"We have to go to Marinescape," they said together.

"We should meet with that biologist, fish specialist guy or whatever he is. Those over-educated nerds have always irritated me."

"I think that too, boss … ah, sheriff," said Deputy Keith as he brought up a clenched fist.

\*\*\*

Mary Jane was now alone at her desk, so she turned on the desk radio.

*"Hey, Jimmie John, what have you heard about this Matanzas River freakin' monster? Sounds like a fish that got away story. I think it's a Hollywood stunt perpetrated by that downriver Marinescape Park."*

*"Well, I think it's a way to get a cheap date,"* answered Robbie Rodney, second member of the Ear Shot Shocker Morning Bunch Show.

*"Now really, deer slaying fools, this is a real fear for women on the Matanzas River and should be taken seriously."* Fannie Fay, the third member of the morning show team, bantered. *"You can flush that idea down the toilet, Robbie Roy. O.K., listeners, call in to give your voice some airtime,"* called out Jimmy John Jackson. Keith walked into MJ's partial office. "What are you listening to, MJ?"

"A radio food station for a recipe, I'm trying to find my favorite dinner menu."

"What about you, Deputy?"

"I actually was listening for any media updates on our Matanzas River dilemma. I know you wouldn't want to disappoint me, MJ. Anything you prepare for me will be good." Keith placed his widely separated hands on her desk to bring his face closer to hers.

"Any important news for us?" asked Doc MacGrath as he and Rick walked in.

Keith stood up and greeted the two. "Let me turn the volume back up."

**Breaking News:** *"Northeast Florida should be getting ready for another possible hurricane hit, or at least a heavy tropical storm, in the next twenty-four hours. All usual hurricane precautions should be taken. Special risk areas include two-or-higher-story buildings on the ocean shoreline and low lying land near sea level. How will Dolphin Family Fun and Marinescape prepare and protect all the marine animals, especially the unusual and rare species?"* the weather newscaster posed the question.

# Chapter 24

## *Hypothetical*

**The Cadillac had become** a familiar sight in the Marinescape Parking lot. He saw the pair exit their car from his elevated office window. Max paged Alisa to the front door to let them in without paying an entrance fee. Eventually they would be issued their own special entrance pass as Professor Rory Fergus Hamish Lachlan Maxwell's guest investigator and researchers.

Blaze had developed a real work ethic. As a result of this, Alisa asked Max if the facilities' administration would consider paying the kid for his work. Max had reviewed Blaze's contributions with the financial advisor and decided to pass their decision by his mom, who then asked Blaze.

"I feel privileged just to be behind the scenes with the professor and Alisa." He'd rather be free to be educated than have a structured job for money. This made Patti very proud to tell Max and Alisa. In fact, Blaze would rather spend the day with Alisa than play with his friends.

Max did tell Patti that Blaze's volunteer work still could turn into a paid part-time position for his maintenance work with a minimum wage. If Blaze were paid, Patti realized she would be responsible for filing for his tax I.D. and filing taxes, getting a social security number, etc.

As usual, Alisa and Blaze went on their own separate way and Patti and Max went to his office so they could discuss some of Max's ideas.

"Alisa, may I ask you some personal questions?" Blaze smiled as they went to the underground Oceanarium walkway.

"Whoa, I know you're going through puberty, but …" Alisa put up her hands.

"No, not about that, but since you brought it up … no, we'll leave that for another time when I've shown my worthiness."

Alisa stopped walking and grabbed his arm. "Way, way later. Maybe never," She grimaced while shaking her head.

"Thanks for your confidence in my character," he smiled. They both started to laugh. "I was going to ask about Professor Max. Can I? And you have to promise not to tell him I asked about him, O.K.?"

She hesitantly nodded her head slightly. "If I know the answers."

"Have you ever seen Max without a turtleneck or a buttoned-up neck? When you saw him swimming in the aquarium, were all his wetsuits collared up?"

She nodded her head in agreement. "Peculiar, isn't it? And his hair never changes from the flowing backward ridges and furrows."

"Like the back of an otter," added Blaze.

"But it is hair, not fur, skin or scales," Alisa added.

*** 

**Up in the office**, Patti answered some commonly asked fertility questions about getting pregnant with donor sperm and donor egg. Max made some statements about the similarities between human and animal fertility, conception, and newborn survival.

"I like working in the field of human fertility because I can make a difference in a couple's lives by helping them achieve pregnancy with their own gametes, sperm and egg or maybe just one of them and donor," proudly presented Patti.

"You get the same satisfaction when it is with only donor sperm or donor egg?" asked Max.

"Definitely, because the couple, especially the spouse with the donated gamete replacement for themselves, is showing how much they love each other and want a family," remarked Patti. "The genetics are still half the couple's. The chromosomes mix to result in a new entity, soul and human, which the woman will bring to life. The couple will raise the child with

125

their way of thinking and social mores, customs and values. That's just as important, if not more as genetics, don't you think?"

He nodded while listening. "Established animal species and new species have their continuation through reproduction," said Max as he looked around the room and behind himself.

"Is there a problem?" Patti asked as she also looked around the room.

"No. I felt something. I heard a calling out, but it's nothing. The aquatic world's biggest problem is man, his pollution, his continuous waste of aquatic life and resources. This waste is also generic. No specific person. No one wants to take the blame or the lead to correct the problems, to help in the way an individual might make a small difference." Max was becoming angry.

"Why don't we take a walk around the facilities, Max? Get some fresh air," Patti said as she got up.

"We can in a minute." Max looked at her and hand motioned to sit back down.

***

**Alisa** and Blaze finished checking the water tank's salinity, mineral additives, herbal supplement levels and the inhabitant's food status.

"Is Max married?"

"No," Alisa casually stated. "Well, as far as I know."

"Does that make you happy, Alisa?" as Blake leaned toward her.

She smiled and fidgeted. "It doesn't make me unhappy."

"He acts as if he and my mom get along all right." He watched for her reaction, but there was none. "Have you seen Professor Max have fun or play sports?"

"No," answered Alisa. "But I think he considers taking care of the aquatic animals as fun. I know I do. He'll swim with the residents. I've only swam with dolphins and porpoises."

"I'd swim in there, especially as part of your animal care team, Alisa." Blaze pretended to do the breaststroke.

***

126

**"Do you have** many donor egg recipients?" Max asked as he looked at a turbulent ocean.

"Several couples a month, with 60 percent to 80 percent successful live and normal birth rates. It depends on the male having a normal semen analysis and wash of his sperm, and the woman recipient's general health, uterine health, history of miscarriages and other fertility issues," explained Patti matter-of-factly.

Max got up and started pacing the edges of the rectangular room's periphery. "I assume you would do donor sperm and/or donor egg together. What about single women or single men?" Max stopped and turned to look at Patti as he asked.

"Yes to all those situations except for donor egg and a single male. In our fertility group, the team would have to review the feelings and acceptance of each team member concerning that topic, since all the team would participant in the IVF case. Most importantly, the embryologist would have to be on board. All donor eggs are frozen and require the embryologist to do what's called intracytoplasmic sperm injection or ICSI, to bring on fertilization. That means the embryologist mechanically injects a single sperm, chosen by him for normal shape and movement. This is seen under a special light microscope with video camera assistance. The sperm has to be inserted in a precise way and location in the egg to increase the chance of fertilization success."

"And if the team doesn't agree?"

"There are other IVF facilities willing to perform their requested procedures. The cost for everything including the growing of the fertilized eggs, now called embryos, which would—" "Does not matter about the cost; it was only a hypothetical question," Max interrupted again. "Patti, let us take that walk you suggested."

# Chapter 25

## News

**"This news media mess** all started with that single woman's phone call to the police station. Keith, why don't you and another team member follow up on the call?"

"O.K. Sheriff, I'll see who I can find." Deputy Keith only looked for one specific person. That would be Tara, sitting with the Doc and reading journals. "Tara, interested in a road trip?"

"Is this work or pleasure for you?" Tara asked.

"Definitely, whatever you want. He hesitated. "It's an interview with another woman and her dog."

Tara looked to Ian, who nodded.

Once they called on the dog lady, she agreed to take her dog for another walk and show Deputy Keith and Assistant Investigator Tara her suspicious spot.

"The best time to see it is just at dawn. Your eyes are all narrowed down from the rising sun. We may not see anything because the sun is already pretty high in the sky." She frowned as the dog pulled her along the river shore.

Tara whispered to Keith, "Does the sun rise in the east? We're looking west and the sun is too high to make any difference."

"You know, it's already too bright," she answered in frustration because the deputy didn't understand. "This is the magical spot." She swung her arm back and forth, pointing to the river. An occasional car passed the three and her dog barked at each one. They walked southbound on A1A. The river's surface undulated with rollers and shadows from passing boats mixed with the small wind surface waves. "Only when I looked away from the river did I hear a splash or the dog started to bark at the river."

After walking about a half mile, Deputy Keith felt they had seen enough. "Ma'am, I believe we've seen what we came to see."

"But we haven't seen it yet. You should come back tomorrow morning. I'll call you when I'm going to go out!" she exclaimed.

"Ma'am, you're right, the best we can do now is wait for your call and then come back."

"Can I have your cell phone number?"

"Sorry, ma'am, you'll have to call the dispatch number here on our card." The deputy handed her a labeled police business card. She looked quite disappointed.

"Do you need a ride home?" Tara asked her.

"No, thanks, my dog and I enjoy walking together."

After Keith and Tara got back in the police SUV, they both shook their heads. "Sorry for dragging you out here for nothing, Tara."

"She believes there's something out there and she seemed to develop a bond with whatever it is," observed Tara.

"Only because it hasn't killed her!" laughed Keith. "I believe we have five minutes to stop for a donut, bagel, coffee or tea."

"O.K., but remember it's only for that, Keith," she said, looking straight ahead.

The twosome reported by radio back to Sheriff Gary.

"We need to collect our thoughts and compare notes, Tara."

"Just keep driving, Deputy. We can do that as you drive with both hands on the wheel."

"Is that 10 and 2?"

"It's a non-incident call, Sheriff. I took care of it," the deputy said.

The next day, the sheriff brought in several local newspapers—Jacksonville, Palatka and Orlando. "Deputy Keith, I want you to see the 'non incident' report you handed in yesterday. I have a copy of the *Palatka National & Local News*, who asked me for a quote yesterday. I read him your filed report verbatim, Deputy Sheriff Keith."

## Tourists Meet River Monster and Almost Die.
## Dog Saves Master's Life from Sex Crazed Monster.
## Local Police Say Matanzas River Safe …
## Local Residents Ask State Police, FBI for Help.

"These headline stories don't sound like a 'non incident' to me, Senior Deputy Sheriff Keith. And how did you take care of this?" huffed Gary.

"The dog lady must—"

"I especially liked the quote the 'non incident' lady gave the media: A County Sheriff, I think, and a woman, like his girlfriend, talked with me for a minute. They ignored my wonderful guard dog, Bo Baby. This dog is what saved my life! They did nothing to reassure me that I was safe. When they walked away, I'm pretty sure they said I was crazy.'"

"Gary, we didn't see anything out there," apologized Keith.

"She said she'd call the next time she was going to walk her dog. We walked the river shoreline with her and saw no obvious shoreline evidence or occurrence, Sheriff," added Tara. "She must have gone to the media because we didn't satisfy her need for attention."

"Do you think? I could see how she would mistake you two as being a couple on a date." Gary put his head between his hands. "Any minute the State Police Chief Commander or State Attorney General will be calling. Wait, maybe I'll be speaking with the governor for the first time. Good morning, Governor, " mimicked Gary. "Oh, thank you, Sheriff Gary T. Sellack for complimenting our department and *ruining my day, Sheriff!*" Gary slammed his opened hands on his desk.

"Hopefully I didn't ruin your chances for re-election, sir?"

After a long silence, Keith and Tara turned around. They saw the entire team milling around in the next room. After Tara left the room, the rest slowly dispersed.

Doc MacGrath walked over to Gary. "All of us are committed to prove our team's worth. This low point in our investigations will be corrected by eventually bringing us to the truth."

"I left the big urban police workforce for exactly this reason—the constant ridicule by other officers and higher ranking officials criticizing me. The media was always on my back. Why didn't I know? I must be hiding something. You become their fool. When you're right, they want to know why it took so long to tell them. It's all starting again." He sat down at his desk.

"Rick, let's go review our autopsies and lab evidence once more." Ian waved to Rick.

"Tara, let's go back to the first crime scene at the Matanzas Inlet," Leon called to her.

"We'll go to the second crime scene at the 206 bridge," said Officer Brett with Brenner followed her.

Later that day, Deputy Keith entered the station's main room with Yuma following. "Sheriff, Mr. Manta was hoping to speak with you."

Yuma sat in a chair in front of the sheriff's desk.

"Yes, Mr. Manta, please speak freely."

"My Timucuan Nation Council met after the media frenzy about the Matanzas River creature. Our Nation has lived along this mother of life, Matanzas River basin, for many centuries. The present elders of four generations passed on their oral legends to the young ones, of which I am one."

The deputy had time to re-collect the team around the seated Yuma. He proudly relayed his message from the elders. "The river's new life is not always from happy spirits. This new life may also be pure evil. Some are angry with the purpose of bringing retribution for man's disregard of nature's innate value. These beings, as seen by several elders, may be a snake or lizard with legs or even a combined fish-snake-lizard-man walking upright." Yuma looked at the doubting faces.

"One must remember bizarre tales of flying fish. Then they were found off the South Africa coast," added Doc MacGrath. "Remember the Scottish and Chinese tales of flying dragons and ocean man-eating monsters found out to be squid and octopi?"

"There is always some thread to truth," added Yuma. "I come to relay that my Nation knows there is something out there that is more than a fish, lizard or snake. It has been in the river longer than any of us has been alive." Yuma hesitated with his head bowed down. He looked up toward Tara. "Hombre Lagarto is one of its names. The room was silent as everyone decided what they were willing to believe.

# Chapter 26

## *Dolphin*

**Max saw Alisa and Blaze** seated and eating snow cones. Blaze pointed out to the ocean.

"How do I know if that's a dolphin, porpoise or just a big fish, Alisa?" Blaze smiled as he crowded in to her.

"Don't look at me like that and give me space. Think of me like your older sister."     Max remained undiscovered behind them.

"Well, dolphins have longer noses, bigger mouths, more curved dorsal or mid-back fins and longer, leaner bodies. Porpoises are more portly," answered Alisa. "Dolphins and porpoises jump with arched bodies. Fish jump in the air with flatter and wiggling oval-shaped bodies."

"Dolphins are more gregarious than porpoises, so they live in groups. Porpoises are more likely to be solo," spoke up Max. "Good morning, you two. Those pods of jumpers you're looking at are most likely dolphins. There are thirty-two dolphin species plus five closely related river dolphin species, but only six porpoise species. We should go over to the Oceanarium so we can take a closer look at how they differ. Dolphins and porpoises are warm-blooded marine mammals, like us. Fish, amphibian and reptile species, on the other hand, are 99 percent cold-blooded. Yet they both live in the ocean. As all mammals, they have lungs. Fish and reptiles have gills"— Maxwell placed his right hand on his turtleneck collar—"right here to extract oxygen from passing through water."

"So gills and lungs let them breathe air," Blaze concluded.

"Dolphins have lungs and are marine mammals. They are warm-blooded, have hair, give birth to live young and lactate or breastfeed them from mammary glands," added Max.

"Another difference is that marine mammal's sperm fertilize females internally. Fish fertilize externally by releasing eggs and sperm into the water, called spawning," spoke up Alisa.

"Can different animals fertilize each other even though they're different?" asked Blaze.

"Different groups called species, normally don't not—" Alisa stopped. "But different species have been interbred, right?""What about,"

"Now Blaze, intra-breed reproduction occurs within the same species population. Interbreeding is between species producing offspring called hybrids," answered Alisa

"Professor Maxwell, I welcome any corrections you may make as I list a few hybrids."

Max crossed his arms, grinned and nodded. "Go for it, Assistant Biologist Alisa."

"I will start with the most commonly known hybrids," said Alisa. Male horse and female donkey will give a Mule. Tiger and lion get a tigron. Wolf and dog get a wolfdog; this may have been the origin for the werewolf."

"I've seen those movies," said Blaze excitedly.

Domestic cow and the American bison get a beefalo. Sheep and goat get a geep. Male camel and female llama gets a Cama.

Grizzly bear and polar bear get a Grolar bear. Zebra and any horse get a Zebroid.

Serval, a large eared wild African cat and a domestic Siamese cat get a savannah."

Yak and domestic cow get a Dzo," added Max.

"What about the dolphins breeding?" Blaze asked.

"You cross breed a bottlenose dolphin and false killer whale and get a Wholphin," smiled Alisa.

"A very perplexing question concerning interbreeding species is about humans," said Professor Maxwell. "Are there two species of Homo sapiens-sapiens (human) and Homo sapiens Neanderthalis? Could they have interbred? Or do you classify them as subspecies? So if they interbreed as two species, would you get Homo sapiens neanderthalis sapiens? If these were subspecies then intrabred in the same species, would you just get Homo sapiens?"

"That is way over my head." Alisa placed her hands to her head and slightly shook it.

"Wait, would that be a mixed or blended human?" Blaze interjected.

"Max pondered the issue. "Right one, Blaze"—Max tapped his shoulder—"for a later date." Maxwell started walking. "Incidentally, the orca or killer whale is actually the largest member of the dolphin family. All of them can echolocate which means they can detect objects around them using sound waves to echo back to them."

The threesome came to the open-top Oceanarium.

"Trust me," Alisa said, "that would be like a cop's radar gun." She frowned.

Max waved to Alisa to call a dolphin over to her while they looked down into the enormous ocean saltwater tank. Alisa pulled out a whistle and blew. In seconds, three playful bottlenose dolphins were circling and started to jump. She rewarded each with a small fish.

"Can I feed one?" Blaze hoped.

"Yes, you may. Dolphins and porpoises are carnivorous, so they eat fish, shrimp, squid and even jellyfish," Alisa rattled off, "Hopefully not young boy's fingers."

Blaze gave her a worried look.

"These mammals are extremely intelligent. They have large, complex brains and a structure in their foreheads we call 'the melon,' which generates sonar or sound waves to bounce off objects to navigate their underwater world," relayed Max.

"As Professor Max has shown me, it comes down to their faces. Remember the TV show *Flipper* and his famous grin? Well, Blaze, you may have seen some TV reruns. Do you remember the dolphin with its elongated beak, or snout?"

"Yeah, I've seen it on the rerun channel, or a kids' channel."

"It has a larger mouth," continued Alisa, "with cone-shaped teeth, curved dorsal fin and long, lean body, up to ten feet. The porpoise has a small mouth and a short, flatter snout with spade-shaped teeth, a triangular fin, like a shark, and a plumper, shorter body, less than seven feet.

"Hey, you mentioned *Flipper*. Many other TV shows and commercials were filmed right here at Marinescape and Marine Animal Aquatic World," interjected Max.

"Come on, Molly, Dolly and Polly, talk to me," called out Alisa. "Dolphins are the talkative ones, with their whistling and clicking sounds through their blowholes. This is how they communicate with each other underwater."

"Porpoises do not make audible sounds that humans can hear, probably due to structural differences in their blowholes," added Max. "We know all these facts from the National Oceanic and Atmospheric Administration (NOAA) research."

"Cool! When I'm on the beach with my mom and I see a curved dorsal fin or a jumping pod of mammals, I'll be able to tell her what they are." He then started making a clicking sound with his tongue on his hard upper mouth palate, intermingled with whistles as he circled around Alisa and Max. All three laughed.

# Chapter 27

## Closer

---

**"Thank you, Mr. Manta,** for you and your elders' insight. We'll let you go so we can digest this information," directed Sheriff Gary.

Yuma got up and nodded his head to the sheriff and the others. He stopped next to Tara. "I know you believe me. You saw the evidence first-hand," He leaned over and whispered, "Mother Earth is calling us together," as he extended a hand. Tara hesitated and then shook it.

Gary waited for Yuma to leave and close the door. Deputy Keith walked over to Tara and began his own whispering.

Sheriff Gary asked, "Anything the two of you have to share? No? Now that we've all had a moment to reflect, I believe all the cases are related. We should also include the two dog walkers and the National Park incident, which was originally closed to us. That gives us a total of eleven, maybe twelve, cases. I want everyone to return tomorrow morning with their contribution that will crack this group of cases wide open. I know the State Police and FBI are mistaken."

The next morning, Tara and Keith came in together with coffee, tea, bagels and pastries. Several team members watched them pass and then whispered to each other.

"All right now, I'll start the list of why these cases are related. All crimes occurred in an eleven mile stretch of the Matanzas River from Marinescape north to the fertility clinic. Three dead women, an assaulted woman and man, a break-in and theft of the fertility clinic and three pharmacies and three suspected river sightings and possible assaults with the additional National Park tour guide sighting." as Gary looked around the room.

"All six women involved were five-foot-two to five-foot-four in height, all had blonde hair and were on the river during the early morning," summed up Deputy Keith.

"The perpetrator is very comfortable in the water and swims very fast," said Director Leon.

"This perpetrator either has the world's record of underwater breath-holding, aqua lungs or gills," added Ian.

"It must be a carrier and immune to the bacteria salmonella bongori, found in cold-blooded animals, especially reptiles," continued Tara.

"But cold-blooded animals don't have a hemoglobin of 25 to 52," added Assistant Rick.

"That would explain our perpetrator's exceptional oxygen carrying capacity and unbelievable underwater breath-holding," smiled Doc Ian. "There are countries with high malaria infection rates, like Central and South America. Blood with high biliverdin comes from the breakdown of hemoglobin. This green blood from biliverdin gives an animal protection from many types of malaria. Maybe, the same is for our perpetrator?"

"Those few species that fit this description are some salamanders and reptiles. This is the same green blood found at the crime scenes," stated Leon. "When a hemoglobin cell sickles, as in the human condition called sickle cell anemia, it's believed to give the advantage by decreasing the risk of malarial infection of the deformed sickle RBC."

"We're getting closer." Gary rubbed his hands together. "I know where we should go. Crackle! Hiss! Sheriff Gary?"

"Yes, this is Sheriff Gary."

"We have a call from the National Park Service at the Matanzas Fort concerning vandalism," relayed Mary Jane.

"Why call me? Wouldn't the park ranger take care of the incident?"

"The ranger thought you might be interested, since it involves the Matanzas River."

"O.K., tell the ranger we're on our way. Brett, you'll be with Deputy Sheriff Keith. Patrolman John, you'll be with me," tallied Gary.

"Tara, you'll be with me," added Leon.

The three vehicles arrived to at least twenty people standing on the site. An attendant pointed through the open air hallway of the information building to the docked pontoon tour boat. A single capped man sat on the boat.

"Brett, John, you two detain the lobby people and question them on what they saw," ordered the sheriff. The rest of the CSI team boarded the tour boat with Gary and Leon.

"Good morning, Ranger Smythe," greeted the sheriff. "This is my crime scene investigative members, Director Leon and his assistant, Tara. They all acknowledged each other.

"I'm Ranger Smythe."

"What's your concern?"

"Good morning and welcome to the National Monument Park. I'm so glad to see all of you." He started the motor and freed the mooring ropes. The covered tour boat pulled away from the eastside dockage. "We followed our routine crossing of the Matanzas River on the first morning tour to Fort Matanzas."

Gary looked back and saw Brett and Keith questioning and containing the tour witnesses, now surrounded by media reporters and photographers in the National Park's small lobby.

"Did you also happen to invite the media today?" Gary asked.

"No, but they've been hanging around since the Matanzas Monster scare hit the newspapers' front pages about the prior incident with the west shore dock damage."

"So what's the problem?" Gary inquired again.

"As you all can see, as we approach the arrival dock … wait, it's no longer present," Ranger Smythe sarcastically stated. "This happened here before. But you may not remember, Ranger Smythe that only the State Police and FBI were here," said Gary.

"I figured the Sheriff's Department wasn't interested or just defaulted to their expertise," Smythe said.

"You obviously didn't know the St. Johns Sheriff' Department was restrained from entering this site. But why worry? They both concluded it was just a 'shoddy dock that broke away in the Matanzas River brisk current.'"

The ranger seemed to ignore the sheriff's chatter. "The river goes down to approximately fifty feet very quickly at this spot. It was difficult to repair the prior damage. This morning the boat approached the dock. Uncommonly turbulent water appeared around the dock like a swarm of fish. We were just short of tying the tour boat to the dock when the dock started wiggling back and forth, snapped with a loud crack and disappeared into the deep black flowing water!" Ranger Smythe stared into Sheriff Gary's face.

"I'll look at the shoreline," Leon stated.

"Are those clown footprints Tara identified and had labeled at the first crime scene? Or maybe they're from a skin diver's webbed flippers."

"They go from the fort, along the river and back to where the dock was," Leon noted. "We'll call the State Police diving squad to investigate."

"They already came and found nothing," Smythe complained.

"Then we'll hire private divers to re-examine this prior dock site," Gary decided.

Ranger Smythe beached the pontoon boat and the team debarked.

Meanwhile, in the National Park's lobby, the two police officers had finished questioning the tourists. They confiscated five cell phones that had recorded the disappearing dock from the boat. The two officers watched one tourist's phone video.

"Look here, you can definitely see something swimming by, then around the dock and then disappearing with the sinking dock!' the tourist proudly displayed.

"We'll return each phone after we copy the recordings. Please give your name, address and phone number. Tell us if your preference is to have it mailed to you or if you'll come to the station to retrieve your phone," explained Deputy Keith. "Thanks for your cooperation and patience."

As each tourist left the building, the reporters surrounded them and shot questions. After all the tourists had left, the tour boat returned with the team.

"Did someone walk Rattlesnake Island for any shoreline evidence?"

"I could go," volunteered Patrolman Brenner.

"Yes, John," answered Gary. "Go from Fort Matanzas down to the southern end of the island, which ends opposite of the Matanzas River Inlet."

As the three police vehicles left the tree-lined parking lot, the Divers Interstate Inc. van arrived. Sheriff Gary stopped and got out to speak with the two divers. He explained the crime scene and his concerns. "I'd be very careful. This perpetrator must be very strong to rip the dock away," Gary surmised.

"We will. We have very high lux (luminance) underwater lamps, spear guns and deferring electrical rods," they stated confidently. "We'll report to you later today."

The three law enforcement vehicles drove up the A1A and then back to the station and small lab. The team noted multiple SUVs parked along both sides of the road. When nearing the station, several TV-labeled vans also filled the parking lot.

"The crazed media wants the Matanzas Monster story to explode in our district. The bounty hunters have staked their zones. Director Leon or I will be the only official spokesmen for the department, O.K.?" Gary entered the station's front door and Rick handed Gary the most recent, special edition St. Augustine newspaper.

### Gill Man Sighted
1950s movie **Creature Existence** proven with sighting
Monster still alive, claims barely alive tour boat observer!

"Let's bring the team back together, Rick." Gary walked into their small area with desks and eraser-able easels. Each team member saw the taped up newspaper headline as they entered the room. Gary rewrote on the easel the known facts.

"Sheriff, breaking news is showing the National Park dock sinking," interrupted Mary Jane.

The group went to the back room TV and saw a dark shadow passing the dock before the dock sank.

"Well, a tourist has decided to give their cell phone video to the media rather than the police," commented Sheriff Gary.

"They probable received money for it," said Deputy Keith.

"Back to our perpetrator who left its blood samples at two crime scenes. It revealed a very high red blood cell count of 100 grams per deciliter. It's three times greater than a normal human's value. The white blood cell count of 32,000 per microliters is also three times a normal human's. This probably explains why he or it can hold its breath for an extremely long time underwater … and tolerate carrying salmonella bacteria."

"There were other cells in the blood. Oval and tear-shaped cells, commonly found cells in fish, amphibians, reptiles and bottlenose dolphins, according to the US Fish and Wildlife Services and the Florida Oceanography Coastal Center," added Rick. "The scale patch is also consistent with fish, eel, snake, amphibian, reptile or a genetic mutant of one of these animals."

"I would expect that all these animals have gills," expressed Tara.

Doc MacGrath agreed. "The gill is also a unit of liquid measurement equal to—"

Gary interrupted the doctor. "So basically you're saying the perpetrator is not human?" Gary could barely squeeze out the words from his mouth. "These conclusions are all very confidential, understood?"

"You were saying a gill equals?" Rick whispered to Ian.

"My calculations from—"

"Gentlemen," Gary looked at the two whispers. "Do we all need to hear your conversation?"

They shook their heads no.

"Are we all now listening?" the sheriff asked. They both sat straight up.

"Tara?" Gary waited.

"My calculations from the footprint evidence for size, depth and stride of step in the sand, so far …" Tara hesitated. "My estimate of the individual is that it has a weight of four hundred pounds, seven to eight feet in height, with webbed feet and clawed toes."

"I've reviewed all of Rick and Tara's conclusions, and I support them," said Leon. "Look at the photos." He passed them around—"of the *Creature from the Black Lagoon Legacy* movie series of the mid-1950s. The studio photographs from the original movie set show an actor putting on a green foam head and green rubber body suit-costume, clawed hands and clown-sized web clawed feet, which are actually modified flippers. This all could be worn by our perpetrator."

"We've all seen such a creature's rubber full-head mask being sold at every Halloween costume store," announced John. Everyone in the room turned to him. "Did I speak out of turn? Should I have raised my hand?" John sheepishly raised his right hand.

"We're all impressed by your obvious revelation."

"I've taken my nephew Bradley to Marinescape and Dolphin Family Fun and there's a marine biologist on staff," John continued. "This biologist and his assistant gave us a tour. It's down the road, south of us on the Matanzas River and in the community of Marinescape."

"The trilogy of Marinescape, Dolphin Family Fun and Marine Animal Aquatic World has a Professor Rory Fergus Hamish Lachlan Maxwell the IV, who has a PhD., M.D. and D.V.M.," relayed Doctor Ian MacGrath. "He's also published and knowledgeable in marine animal biology, oceanography, ichthyology or fish science, herpetology or reptile science, animal reproduction and their endocrinology."

"Wow, Ian, you've found someone with more degrees than you, Medical Examiner Ian MacGrath, Bachelor of Science in Pathology and M.D.," ribbed Gary.

"You forgot to mention my degree in reciting nonessential and worthless trivia."

"Doc, your trivia is timely and interesting." Tara hugged Ian and looked to Sheriff Gary, who looked to dispatcher Mary Jane, who looked to Deputy Sheriff Keith, who looked to Officer Brett, who looked to Patrolman John Brenner, who looked to Tara, who looked back to Keith, who looked to Mary Jane, who looked to Rick, who looked to Tara. Leon, who was married, just sat there and waited with crossed arms.

"Those of you who are interested may come with me to visit this balloon-size headed and esteemed Professor of Bla, Bla, and Bla," stated Gary.

"Oh, don't forget that the suspect has green-colored blood. In low volume, it's seen under ultraviolet light; when the blood is concentrated, it can be seen with the naked eye," said Rick. "In amphibians, the green color is from the green biliverdin, a break- down product of red hemoglobin," added Rick. "You know, like when you get a deep bruise in your skin or muscle, the color changes from black, blue-red, to green and finally yellowish before being completely absorbed. Anyway, the biliverdin would make the skin or scales of the suspect green in color."

"Oh yeah, now I get it," several team members remarked.

"The divers from the National Park are at the front, Gary."

"Gentlemen, did we get lucky?"

"Yes, Sheriff, we did. Here are pieces of the wooden dock. We separately bagged them." He held up bags of slimy green and brown goo.

Tara and Rick took the specimens.

Deputy Keith moved in close to Tara. "You and I should be watching this trilogy of *The Creature from the Black Lagoon* movies together," whispered Keith. "I got them at the public library. Of course, its viewing would be strictly for research purposes only."

# Chapter 28

## Breathe

**Alisa and Blaze watched Max** swim in the country's largest Oceanarium. Alisa looked at her watch and then back through one of the lower-level portholes with Blaze. These underwater windows allowed them to see marine animals in their deep-water activities as if in the ocean. It would be great for scientific research and tourist entertainment. The two watched Max.

Max swam among sharks, stingrays, loggerhead turtles, eels and other less aggressive fish.

"How does the professor swim underwater without being afraid?" Blaze asked Alisa. "Look how he runs his hands along a stingray's and shark's backs. Look now, he's holding on to the shark's body and is being pulled as the shark swims."

"I don't know, but he's quite elegant as he swims." Alisa looked at her watch again.

"Max actually touches them all. I think he's playing with them and they don't seem to mind and aren't threatened by his presence," Blaze laughed.

Max wore a dark, rough-surfaced, green upper half wetsuit from the chin down to the waistline, a tight, dull-turquoise three-millimeter swimsuit bottom to just above the ankles and truncated flippers that looked like webbed flat shoes.

"Alisa, I noticed you glancing at your watch. How long has Max held his breath?"

"Hey, look! Max just grabbed that hose lying behind those rocks," noted Alisa. "Ha, that's an air hose. Now I don't know how long Max can hold his breath."

"Well, how long would you guess … about?" Blaze pushed Alisa.

"About nine minutes! Wouldn't that be impossible? I can only hold mine for about forty to fifty seconds. How about you, Blaze?"

"Ah, a minute if I just doggy paddle. Blaze looked up the Guinness World Records on his cell phone. "The nonmoving underwater breath-holding contest winner was for twenty two minutes and twenty two seconds. After hyperventilating with pure oxygen thirty minutes for the dive, one person lasted nineteen minutes and thirty seconds. So nine minutes is remarkable."

"Well, I think anything longer than three minutes is a big deal to me!" said Alisa.

"Tap, tap!" They both slightly jumped back as Max placed his hands and face on the bubbled window glass. All looked at each other. Max made a boisterous underwater laugh and turned away from the porthole quickly swimming back and forth several times in a comedic fashion. He finally pointed to himself, to them, and to the water surface.

When Max met them topside, he was clothed in his usual turtleneck shirt, long pants and wide, khaki-colored Crocs.

"We thought you'd set a world record for underwater breath-holding," blurted out Blaze.

"What did you record me at?"

"Nine minutes before you refreshed with the bubbling rubber hose," Alisa shyly answered.

Max smiled at the two. "I can hold it longer. Most people can hold their breath twice as long underwater as when they're on land. Untrained people who aren't afraid of being underwater typically have their pulse rate drop 10 to 20 percent. Professional divers, especially in cold water, will drop their pulse or heart rate 50 percent. Their heart rate slows so less oxygen is used and the person can spend more time underwater."

"Were you ever a professionally trained diver?"

"No, it just came naturally to me. Where's your mother, Blaze?"

"I think she was reading a book on an ocean view bench."

"Go ask her if she wants to go on a tour given by a qualified guide."

Blaze ran off as Alisa moved in close to Max.

"How's my quality of work so far, Professor Maxwell?"

"Aren't we being formal, Miss Alisa Favour?"

"I just wondered if I needed to improve any aspect of my work. Have I made good use of all my attributes?"

"Your quality of work has been exemplary, Miss Alisa. Your special attributes have been noted since our first meeting."

"Do you ever feel that you'd like to review work subjects, scientific topics or something with me? Like one colleague to— or just friends?" she asked bashfully.

"From our first meeting—"

"We're all here; let's get going," shouted Blaze excitedly.

"I want to take the three of you on a historical enlightenment tour from the center's conception to the present day status in the community, if time permits and you're not tired."

"Oh, we're all full of energy," Blaze answered.

"Then I'll take you all across A1A to the research facilities on the Matanzas River, the Marine Animal Aquatic World facilities I designed."

# Chapter 29

## Specialist

**The heads from each department** boarded the county-supplied sheriff's SUV. Gary drove and Leon rode shotgun with Ian MacGrath in the back. All watched out their windows as multiple parked vehicles lined the Matanzas River side of A1A state road. They also observed many pleasure and fishing boats of all sizes, from rowboats rigged with outboard motors to enormous yachts on the river. The smaller boats were managed by fishermen casting nets, with chumming or chopped fish in a bloody mixture. Powhatan Indians of the Native American Virginia Algonquian Nation were present, known for their expert technique in catching sharks. The larger boats were manned by scuba divers armed with spear guns and electric water rods.

"Look at all these yahoos," commented Sheriff Gary. "I'm sure some of these 'Glory Bounty Hunters' have illegal explosives to throw in the water and the aquatic poison Biolyzes, the chemical pesticide to kill insects that also acts as a neurotoxin for paralyzing fish."

"By the end of the week, I expect we'll have some idiot accidentally creating their own crime scene," added Leon. "Hopefully not a crime involves a death."

"I hope my services won't be needed," a serious Doc added.

Gary turned on the local Free No Bull public radio station and a voice rang out:

*"The craze and fear concerning the Matanzas River monster continues to grip Northeast Florida and the nation's interest. Local families and tourists are still fearful to be on the Matanzas River. Stories have now surfaced of unconfirmed monster sightings on the Matanzas River into St. Augustine. Sightings of the water monster include the northeastern coast down to Daytona Beach. Curious tourists and expert shark hunter boats fill the intracostal waterways passing Crescent Beach, Marinescape, and the Palm Coast to Flagler Beach,"* crackled the AM radio.

The SUV crossed the Matanzas River Inlet Claude Varn Bridge on A1A. In the middle of the inlet, the three passengers saw a sixty-five-foot Coast Guard cutter. On deck were bulletproof-vest-wearing law enforcement authority officers armed with handguns and M4 assault rifles. There were sharpshooters on the ship's upper deck. There was also a large fire hose cannon at the bow.

"Here we are, gentlemen … Marinescape," spoke out Gary. He parked in the posted sign area.

## No Parking
## No Standing
## Fire Lane
## No Firearms or Alcohol on Premises

Before the three could disembark the sheriff's phone rang with its ringtone, "Smoke on the Water."

"I changed my ringtone," Gary said to the surprised passengers as he put his phone on speaker.

"Hey, Rick here. The park's partial pieces of wood the divers retrieved have been examined. I found large green flats of scales stuck in the wood. These scales were the same size and shape as the prior single scale. Also, Tara looked at the green goo. It was microscopically chock-full of the salmonella organism."

"The goo has similar minerals and enzymes found at the three deceased women's crime scenes," Tara added. "But I found moving flagella-like bodies, like primitive sperm. It's like the gel evacuated by fish for external water fertilization,"

"Tell me how you came to that conclusion," CSI Director Leon asked.

"I called my old school mate who works in the Fish and Wildlife lab and face timed the goo. He felt confident making the diagnosis."

As the three walked toward the park's visitor archway, a man wearing a shirt with "Manager of Marinescape Tours and Gift Shop" on it came out to meet them.

"Good morning. May I help you? Is there a problem?" he nervously asked.

"Good morning," responded Gary and Leon. Doc nodded. "We were looking for a Professor Maxwell."

# Chapter 30

## *Beginning*

**Follow me closely."** Max looked back and saw Blaze right on his heels. Max turned and placed his hand on Blaze's shoulder. "I was just joking, Blaze." He looked at Patti and then Alisa. All were smiling.

"Marinescape opened in the late 1930s. Its founders envisioned a place where marine life mimicked the natural ocean world. The center opened under many names. Its purpose was to film scenes for motion pictures and newsreels. Originally all underwater filming was done with stationary cameras, so what was to be filmed was forced to swim in front of the camera. At this facility, several people developed a hand-held portable underwater filming camera. The camera could follow the swimmer, fish or marine mammal, providing a more exciting audience viewpoint.

"On opening day, over thirty thousand guests crowded the entrance. Immediately, the developers realized the facility was the most unique in the world. This location would be for filming movies, newsreels and then later television shows and commercials. It probably was the world's first Oceanarium."

"Would I have seen any of these movies or TV shows?" interrupted Blaze.

"They made popular movies with the Olympic gold medal winners. In 1955, a film about a 'Creature' was made right here. It's a popular science fiction film trilogy. One of the three men who actually played the 'Creature' was Ricco Browning, who created and co-produced the dolphin

TV series in the 1960s, which was filmed at this facility. Then in 1981, a TV series was made about the first dog in history to scuba dive, which was again filmed right here," relayed Max.

"He has seen these on the rerun channels," interjected Patti.

"Oh yeah, I think I said that already, Mom."

"O.K., I already said there have been many name changes, ending with today's name of Marinescape. The public's interest turned in 1943 to Jacques Cousteau's co-invented Aqua-Lung. This breathing device is used by scuba divers at Marinescape. They study complex aquatic marine animal behavior and communication. They pioneered methods for animal care, water environmental standards, better aquatic mammal communications and response to human-given commands."

"I can communicate with dolphins." Blaze clicked his mouth and whistled.

Max being tall bent ninety degrees at the waist and placed his hands, with palms together, in front of his face. Then he began to oscillate his upper body up and down and move in a serpentine fashion. "I'm a bottlenose dolphin hearing your calls."

"The first successful dolphin live, healthy birth in human captivity occurred right here in the late 1940s," Max continued. "The dolphin was named Spray.

"Between 1950 and 1960, Marinescape was Florida's number one most popular public attraction, having more than 500,000 visitors per year. The park was best known for exhibiting multiple aquatic life activities and showcased 'educated' dolphins and porpoises performing in elaborate guest viewing stadiums. The mammals would execute never-before-seen behaviors, like major aerial maneuvers in response to verbal, sound and hand-arm commands. This ocean education, research, training and amusement park became present-day Marinescape, Marine Animal Aquatic World and Dolphin Family Fun.

"Marinescape and Marine Animal Aquatic World have been hit by at least by tropical storms or worse in over thirty weather events since its opening. The average sustained wind has been 102 miles per hour. The most recent devastating hurricanes to hit Marinescape and MAAW were Charley in 2004 and Matthew in 2016. The Marinescape Park, research facilities and community were massively damaged. Many of the favorite exhibits couldn't be rebuilt because of cost and land shifts. The loss of the Oceanside beach, public swimming area, car driving beach, the world's first and largest Oceanarium, the multiple underground viewing portholes of natural ocean life, accessory aquatic mammal training tanks and the original forward-thinking aquatic genetic and reproductive research facility were all severely damaged.

"With the construction of up-to-date facilities, the staff focused on education and intimate marine animal with visitor interactions. The Dolphin Conservation Center has become a facility for viewing by scientists and tourists alike. We call it 'edutainment,' combing education and entertainment," cited Professor Maxwell.

"I like that term, 'edutainment,' quite witty in itself," complimented Patti. "How long have you been here, Professor?"

"I was drawn here twelve years ago. I designed the high security containment aquarium, which Alisa has seen and the high security research building across A1A." His voice became quieter.

The three leaned inward to hear him finish his sentences.

"Professor Maxwell, you're quite a storyteller in your own right," noted Alisa as she moved in next to him.

"Are you going to take us to that research lab now?" Blaze asked as he squeezed the professor's hand to squeeze in between him and Alisa.

"Yes, if you are still interested, we can go across the street. The Marine Animal Aquatic World story continues with the 2011 Marinescape Dolphin Conservation Center being purchased by a Georgia corporation, now renamed Dolphin Family Fun. The MAAW name actually now only applies to the research facilities. We still have much more than just bottlenose dolphins, with my interests in animal reproduction.

"Professor Maxwell, three gentlemen want to speak with you," the tour manager said "They have parked illegally."

The men walked over to the professor once the manager inadvertently identified Maxwell by speaking with him.

"Rory Maxwell?" Sheriff Gary sternly asked.

"Yes." Max extended a hand, which was ignored.

"Is there a place we can sit and speak in private? We have a few timely questions for you."

"I surely will respond the best I can to your timely, thought out and important questions."

# Chapter 31

## *Meeting*

**"Sorry, ladies and Blaze.** We'll continue our discussion later," Max apologized.

Max and the three men found a small conference room on the first floor of the tour center. Max held the door open for the three. As he closed the door, he saw the sad faces of Blaze and Patti and a low hand-wave by Alisa.

"We're from the local St. Johns County Law Enforcement Unit. This is CSI Director Leon Mendelssohn, Medical Examiner Doctor Ian MacGrath and I, the lower end of St. Johns County Sheriff Gary. T. Sellack."

"I'm Rory Maxwell, Biological Director for the aquatic animal life here at Marinescape and facilities. I will not bore you with my list of degrees, specialties, subspecialties, areas of special interest, field development or my well-known areas of expertise and list of publications. That must be why you are here."

The three just stared and said nothing.

"So, gentlemen, how may I help you? Please ask your questions."

"I'm sure you've seen the newspapers or heard on the TV reports about the so-called Matanzas Monster," answered Gary. "Some media have called the strange phenomenon 'Fish' or 'Gill Man.' Do you have an expert opinion about these media concoctions? What is the likelihood of such a thing existing?"

"I've seen some very peculiar and prehistoric looking aquatic animal life forms in my career," began Professor Maxwell. "Peculiarities are commonly revealed, as they are in your law enforcement profession, in science. People can deduce things under duress. People wish for such extraordinary outcomes or media events. Maybe they say things to become the center of attention. Scientifically, to every one's surprise, there have been supposed extinct sea and land creatures discovered alive—"

"Specifically, can there be such a thing as a Gill Man?" the sheriff interrupted.

"The problem with a Gill Man is basic. Aquatic animals need air, just as we land animals do to survive. Air contains oxygen and other gases. We have lungs, which take the oxygen out of the air for us to use. Marine mammals, like dolphins, porpoises and whales do the same because they have lungs. On the other hand, fish need to be in water to run water through their gills to remove oxygen from the water, instead of just breathing through lungs. Thus, for a gill creature to do these media-described activities on land seems clearly unbelievable." The Professor put his open hands in front of him.

"But wasn't there a time in evolution when a fin and gill swimming fish became a fin and leg developing amphibian for land ambulation?" Doctor MacGrath asked. "This animal could move and breathe on land as well as in water. So wouldn't this new animal's life change from gill lungs, Professor Maxwell?"

"Doctor, your thinking is correct or maybe the new life form will use both gill and lung," complimented Maxwell. "This is one of the theories in the steps of evolution where natural selection was at work. In fact, the suspected time period started between 410 million to 360 million years ago. It was called the Devonian geologic period or age." The professor was very relaxed and verbose. "We would then need to accept this new animal form of gills and lungs and then only lungs to survive the great dinosaur die off. You can ascribe whatever caused the dinosaurs' trail of death and still allow this mythical gilled, standing, walking, swimming 'Gill; Man' to survive the horrific cataclysm to present day."

"If we watch a developing human embryo, wouldn't we see a brief stage when the embryo would possess gills in the neck area?" CSI Director Leon added.

Professor Maxwell only addressed this specific question. "Ancestral characteristics are often presented in an organism's embryonic development. It is true the human embryo does go through a stage where it possesses slits and arches in the embryonic neck, which at first glance resembles gill slits and gill arches as is found in fish. However, these structures are primitive and never develop into functional gills. This similarity to gills does support the idea that humans share a common ancestry with fish. That is all that can be concluded."

"So are you saying there's no possible way there could be any truth to the media stories of the Gill Man?" questioned Sheriff Gary.

Professor Maxwell turned away from the three inquisitors and looked out a window to see a turbulent ocean. "Well, I could make an argu—" The sheriff's belt radio blared into the small room. "A woman claims to have been attacked by a seven-foot man in a wetsuit," Mary Jane called out. "It's the north end of Palm City, on the Matanzas-Intracoastal Waterway. A moored cruiser named *Ride Me Easy*. It's just south of the town of Marinescape. Officers Brett and Brenner are arriving at the scene as we speak."

"Why call me? That's at the border of St. Johns and Flagler Counties."

"They figured you and your team are the most knowledgeable about the Gill Man in the state of Florida," surmised Mary Jane.

All four men looked at each other with the mention of that name.

"I was going to say, I could argue that there are many ways to mimic your desired Gill Man's appearance without involving the complexities of natural selection and millennia of time," Max continued, pointing with his right open hand to the sheriff.

"Tell the officers we're on our way," clicked off Gary. "Maxwell, thank you so much for your time and our education on topics in which you are so very well versed. You have given us the opportunity to rethink the media's hullabaloo about what you would consider not real," Gary stated his verbal bologna sandwich. "This was very instructive for us and we'll use your insight in solving our cases. We'll return for more information, education and mythology."

As the three got into their SUV and closed the doors, Sheriff Gary spoke. "We have to check out this arrogant son of a bitchy prick. Anyone with multiple names and degrees just means they're more talented at creating watertight, shit-filled excuses for the nonexistence of anything. My decades of police experiences tell me he's hiding something; my intuition says don't trust him and what comes out his upper hole."

"I think you have successfully picked up the professor's form of rhetoric and elocution. I'll get Tara and Rick on his case," Leon said.

"We'll unwrap where Max came from, where he has traveled to, his prior relationships, his actual educational history and the exams he cheated on … and why his mother doesn't like or trust him." Gary nodded. "And add salt to all his body's openings.

"I'm going to call Mr. R. W. Angel at the Palatka newspaper and tell him that the professor claims there's no possibility or truth to the existence of a Matanzas Monster," spat out Gary. "We might as well use this cocky Maxwell to our advantage and calm down the media."

# Chapter 32

## *Genes*

**"How does one dolphin** become two?" Blaze quizzed Alisa.

"It's called reproduction. That's what your mother does at her workplace."

"I help people get babies," Patti said. "I help couples who are having trouble conceiving or keeping their pregnancy."

"My gerbils had no trouble getting babies," Blaze smiled.

"Remember, right here at Marinescape was the world's first healthy, live dolphin birth in captivity. That's nature's way of creating new life, like Max told us," summarized Alisa.

"I had so many births, very fast." Blaze continued looking to his feet.

"We all talked about this before," Patti said.

"They made babies so fast, but the babies started being born goofy looking." Alisa and Patti both knelt down to see Blaze's tears stream.

"They were born all messed up: no arms, legs and big bags bulging from their bellies. They just dragged themselves with their two front legs, as their backs were in knots. I must have done something very wrong with the Habitrail? Maybe their food was bad or—"

"Stop Blaze, we've told you that you did nothing wrong. The gerbils were limited to reproducing with only their confined group. It's called 'inbreeding.' There was little mixing of their genes. The genes were too alike to each other," Patti tried to reassure him.

"Genes?" Blaze wiped the tears off his face.

"All living things have genes, starting with a single living cell, such as viruses and bacteria, which can give you a sore throat. Ants, bees, fish, dogs, favorite lizards and dinosaurs, birds and right up to humans, like you, me and Alisa, all have genes," explained Patti.

"Do Professor Max and the dolphins have them?"

"Yes, we all do. Genes are very, very small packages of information. So small we can't see them with our naked eyes," continued Patti. "These packages give instructions to cells to make little parts, which will add up to bigger parts being put together to make all the life forms on earth."

"Like building blocks, Tinkertoys, Legos, Erector Sets, right?"

"Exactly, son," Patti patted Blaze's shoulder. "Each organism has a mixture of different genes. These genes are organized in groups called chromosomes. That's what makes us all different, like your baby gerbils. As an example, we'll use a building block as separate genes. When the original building blocks are too similar or are the wrong building blocks or we're just missing blocks, then the chromosomes start making mistakes with the building blocks for the larger animal parts, like arms and legs, which can come out wrong or goofy. So you see, it wasn't your fault. This is called a mutation. It may result from what's called inbreeding, the mating of animals too close or the same genetically," summed up Alisa.

"I get it. I needed to add new gerbils to the group," Blaze surmised. "So I have two different colored Lego sets, one set making a red brick dinosaur another set making a yellow brick dinosaur. Now, if I mix the Lego colors together, I make two new multicolored dinosaurs and they'll genetically be different."

"Another consideration is how we act with each other," brought up Patti.

"That's one of the things done by an anthropologist," chimed in Alisa. "Social or environmental anthropologists study human characteristics and how people interact with each other. This type of work can also be applied to other animal groups, like your gerbils."

"Yeah, like my lizard with other lizards and with me."

"You are a smart and inquisitive young man," complimented Maxwell as the three entered a high-ceiling room. "Now that your mother explained genes to you, the next idea is evolution, introduced by Charles Darwin. Ever hear of him?"

"Maybe ..."

"Charles Darwin showed the whole world that—"

"Do I have to learn more today? I think my brain is full and leaking out of my ears."

"Hey, why do not we all take a break?" volunteered Max. "I will buy all of you your choice of a beverage, popcorn, candy corn, hotdog or ice cream. How does that sound?"

After everyone devoured their snacks, the four sat and looked out at the calm ocean.

"No surfacing mammals," observed Alisa.

"No fins or playful jumping pods," said Blaze, trying to outdo Alisa.

"That's a game Blaze and I play—trying to outdo the other's observation," explained Alisa to Patti.

"Max, I'm ready to go into the secret research lab." Blaze pulled on Max's sleeve.

"Before any of us venture into the high security lab, we first all need to have the same background basis." Max smiled down at Blaze.

"Oh boy, here it comes," Blaze frowned.

"Do you remember the name—"

"Charles Darwin," Blaze finished his sentence.

"Charles Darwin showed that animals that adapted and survived environmental changes had the best chance to reproduce and continue their same kind," explained Max.

"I know," Blazed mumbled.

Patti wanted to speak, but Max put his hand up to her.

"The weather can affect an animal's survival, like the cold, hot, rain, or no rain. Also, whether they eat or are eaten by other animals is called natural selection. The unique chromosome irregularity possessed by the surviving animal can then be passed on to the next reproducing generation," added Alisa.

"This was quite a deep conversation," Patti exhaled.

"Can we continue our tour over at the research facility, Max?" Blaze frantically bobbled his head to the others' amusement.

# Chapter 33

## *Cruiser*

**"Now that Director Leon,** Medical Examiner MacGrath and Sheriff Gary are here, would you please repeat what happened to you, Mrs. Kimberly?" instructed Deputy Keith.

"O.K., I'm lying here in my recently purchased dark blue top, yellow with splashes of light blue on the bottom." She spun around once. "So I get in my reclining massage Zero Gravity lounge chair to sunbathe." She proceeded to lie down on the aforementioned chair with her legs straight in the air. She then slowly brought them down to place her feet on the deck on either side of the chair base, in a spread-eagle fashion. "Right here at the back of my husband's cruiser." She paused in this position and looked skyward, placing a finger at the corner of her slightly gapping mouth. Suddenly, Mrs. Kimberly stood up and did a pique turn on her toes, ending with a curtsy. "I used to be a ballerina. Do you like what you see?" She smiled at the four men.

"Very nice, Miss, but could we go back to the assault?" suggested Sheriff Gary.

"What was nice?" she frowned. "My appearance"—both hands went down her body—"my two-piece bathing suit, my thoughtful pose, my spin and special presentation for y'all?" She came within inches of Sheriff Gary's chest. Her fingers twitched around his shoulders, moving inward to his badge on his chest, but not touching him.

"Ma'am, please, back to describing the assault," Gary pleaded as he stepped back.

"If we must, I got up to get a beverage, since I was hot, hotter and hottest." Mrs. Kimberly went a few feet, turned and came back with an imaginary beverage container. She lay back down on the chair. Then she got up and walked over to Sheriff Gary. "I used to be an actress." She curtsied again. "As I turned my back to the boat's stern, someone or thing grabbed my breasts, bent me forward and started to hump, hump me, humping me like I was his bitch dog. He or it was a very, very big dog!" She then bent over in front of the group of men and started to twist her bent over body up and down and to the sides. "I became his folded, squirming rag doll." One of her breasts became free of her bathing suit top. "Oh no, gentlemen, such an embarrassing accident, isn't it?" She stayed bent over and slowly replaced the breast into her bathing suit top with one opened hand, after looking to each man first.

They didn't reply, only watched.

"I used to be a magazine model." She struck a pose with a finger in the air like in the movie *Saturday Night Fever*. Then she started to take a bow and looked to the men. "I better take precautions." She cupped her hands over her breasts as she completed her bow.

Deputy Keith would later swear that "she squeezed her breasts during the bow" as he recounted the incident to other male team members not present on the cruiser.

"Did he pull your bathing suit off?" Doc MacGrath asked.

"Oh yeah, ripped my damn new bikini bathing suit bottom right down to my ankles in one movement! I think he'd done it before." She again bent over straight-legged and started to pull the bottom suit off.

"Mrs. Kimberly, you don't need to show us," said Gary as he cleared his throat.

"However, we will need that bathing suit bottom for evidence," smiled Deputy Keith.

She grabbed a towel, wrapped it around her waist and dropped the suit on the deck.

"Do you want to get it or should I kick it to you?" She waited. "Shy, are you?" She kicked it to the deputy.

"Can you describe this person?" asked Gary.

"I don't know. Maybe it was a man in a full wetsuit with flippers? He was panting heavily, like he was having difficulty breathing. And the green wetsuit or his skin; scratched my shoulders."

"I'll need to swab a sample and culture those scratches," the doc said.

"Since you're a doctor, I can take all my clothes off ... in private, of course. Do you need a more personal exam for evidence?" she coyly remarked.

"You're absolutely correct. You will need a complete exam. You'll need to come down to the police station lab so that my female assistant, Tara, can be present for the exam. Mrs. Kimberly, do you feel injured and that you require a visit to the emergency room? Especially if he penetrated you?" Doctor Ian MacGrath finished.

She shook her head. "I can wait to visit ... ah, Tara."

"How tall are you, ma'am, about five-six?" the sheriff continued.

"I'm closer to five-foot-five. I can fix it to be six or seven inches if you need that."

"So the person behind you was—"

"Oh man, he was seven or seven-and-a-half feet." She raised her hand up as high as she could reach. She grasped her towel at her waistline and hopped several times to raise her hand even higher on her tippy toes. She looked to her bikini top to see if it was still secure. "Scary high, like I was about to be squished." The victim shivered.

"If you know his height, you must have seen his face," said Deputy Keith.

"His height is a guess. His gloved hands were scratchy and kept me bent over, so I kind of only caught a side glimpse of an ugly face or mask. Yuck!" She spat on the boat's deck. "I did get a good look at his left leg and member."

"And?" enunciated Sheriff Gary.

"A quite muscular leg covered with big green fish scales. In fact, his body, of what I saw, was colored green!" She spoke louder and with more anger as she was reminded of the rape.

"So you did see his whole body?" M.E. MacGrath asked in a slightly excited voice.

"I don't know, but what I did see was scaly and green."

"Then what happened?" interrupted the sheriff.

"I tried to fight him off and keep my legs really tight together, but he kept humping, squeezing me and panting … ha, ha, ha, ha." She lifted both arms and moved them back and forth in a humping motion again. Faster and faster! "Then … then I felt a warm liquid drip down my legs as he gave a horrible groan, a painful and pathetic groan that faded off." Now her arms pointed to the horizon. Her face followed. Her whole body froze and became statuesque.

"That was quite a dramatically expressive climax," smirked Keith.

"Why thank you." She only slightly bowed. "I'm an accomplished stage actress, you know," she smiled.

"Yes, you already told us. Any movies we may have seen you in?"

Sheriff Gary stepped in between the now-glowing actress and Cheshire-Cat-smiling deputy. After Gary cleared his throat loudly, he continued the inquiry of the emotionally distraught victim. "Do you need to take a break?"

"No," she said as she flipped her hair back and lifted her face to the sky. "I'm O.K. I'm getting over it."

"Is that liquid still on your legs, Mrs. Kimberly?" Doc asked.

"Hell no, would you have left it on your leg? It stunk, his whole body stunk, like a dead skunk, no a day old-fish on a sunny beach. Disgusting, stinky, nasty, putrid, rancid, foul, fetid, rotten, yet somehow alluring and—"

"What did you do with this liquid on your legs?" interrupted MacGrath.

"Oh, I wiped it off with a towel."

"Where's that towel now?"

She pointed to a wadded up white towel on the deck by a side railing.

"We'll need to take that towel as evidence." Leon photographed, bagged, labeled, dated and signed the bag.

"Keep it. No amount of washing will be able to remove my memories of the abuse." She again gave the men a profile-posed head looking skyward.

"Grace Kelly … your pose is a striking image of the actress," Keith excitedly realized.

"Why thank you, Officer. You must be a man of class and culture." Mrs. Kimberly smiled at him.

"Please"— Gary shook his head—"please continue with what happened next."

"Nothing, I heard a splash and I knelt down crying." Tears started to roll down her cheeks.

"Where was your husband during this assault, Mrs. Kimberly?" asked Deputy Keith.

"He's in Jacksonville. He thought this would be a quiet place for me to relax. He's still there on business. I called him and he's driving back in haste to my side." All her answers and body language now seemed quite dramatic, like for a movie screen test, exaggerated, over the top.

"And what does your husband do?" asked Gary.

"Ah, export and import, I guess. I don't really know or care to know."

"How long have you been moored here on the Matanzas River-Intracostal Waterway, off Friends of Washington Oaks Garden State Park?"

"Three days, maybe four."

"How did you name your cruiser?" inquired Keith.

"The Ride Me Easy … was my husband name after me," Mrs. Kimberly said proudly.

"May I ask a personal question?" inquired Doc. She nodded. "Are you on your menses?"

She shook her head. "I'm certainly not. I wouldn't be out here, dressed like this." Her hands swept down her body. "I'm a day or two before mid-cycle. My husband and I are trying to get pregnant. Why?" she quizzed.

"Possibly important information," responded Doc.

"May we see your shoulders and back?" Leon politely asked. "We'll also need your bikini top and bottom, since he touched both pieces of clothing."

She walked into the cruiser's first cabin and came back out wearing a bathrobe. She held her swimsuit straight out at arm's length from her body, like it was filth.

Leon took it and then had her move her robe back from her shoulders. He photographed her shoulders and back scratches. "I'm going to softly roll a few cotton swabs on the scratches for possible bacteria or the assailant's skin cells or scales that came free."

"No problem; be hard if you must. I've felt it before. I don't bruise easily," she stoically answered. "I've done radio commercials; comedic and dramatic roles are my specialties."

164

"I highly recommend going to St. Augustine Emergency Center to be examined," said Doc. "Also, I would recommend not trying to get pregnant this cycle because of all the known risks, like infection and the question of paternity if you do become pregnant."

"Oh really … ?" She hesitated. "Oh! I could get an infection from that stinky assailant? And who would be the father if I did get pregnant?" realized Mrs. Kimberly. "I'll go to the hospital when my husband gets back later today. Could be soon," she quietly answered.

"Call this number." Leon handed her two business cards: a card for the CSI team and one for the closest hospital emergency department. "Call Tara Coltan from the CSI team; she'll meet you at the hospital and perform an internal examination on you and collect pertinent evidence to the crime."

"If you feel pain or nausea, we could call for an ambulance now to take you to the E.C.," Doc MacGrath offered.

"No, I'm O.K. I can wait for my husband."

"Here's my card if your husband wants to speak with me," offered Sheriff Gary.

Just then, Tara arrived at the Oaks Gardens State Park. "I felt that you needed to meet with Tara as soon as possible, since your husband is still not here. The two of you could talk somewhere in private. You may feel more comfortable speaking with a woman on your ship," offered Doc.

"Hi, I'm Tara, Assistant CSI examiner with this group of professionals. This is a beautiful boat … ship.

"Cruiser or yacht," Mrs. Kimberly corrected.

"Thank you! Cruiser …" Tara looked around as they walked through the cabins and talked. "How long is this anyway?"

"This vessel is a 2016 Princess S65 Sportbridge; it's really only sixty-four feet," Mrs. Kimberly stated matter-a-fact.

"I've never been on such a large sh … cruiser," said Tara in awe.

"It was a dream of my husband's. He bought it on our honeymoon. We can use this cabin, and please call me Kimmy, O.K.?"

They both sat in overstuffed upholstered chairs.

"The guys at the station always talk about horsepower."

"It's 2800 horsepower, but no matter how fast we go, this baby never planes off."

"You seem to know a lot about cruisers."

"My husband said to me, after I accepted his proposal, 'Find us a yacht that can cruise the Intracoastal and still let us feel safe out in the ocean. It will be our honeymoon gift to each other.'"

"Impressive how you took on the challenge."

"Men look at me and I'm nothing more than this." Kimmy outlined her body with both hands.

"Well, I think of you as much more, said Tara, giving a short laugh.

"Oh Tara, you must have the same problem. You are a beautiful young woman." Kimmy put a hand on her shoulder and slowly ran it down her arm and gently grasped her hand.

Tara paused while looking to the floor. "Sorry for being distracted from our real purpose of this meeting today. Kimmy, is there anything you'd like to talk about concerning this unfortunate and ugly assault?

"The men didn't respond to my mentioning of my assailant's member. I was bent over as I mentioned it to the men. I looked from the floor up his left leg and ..." She started to tear. "Sorry, please continue when you're ready." Tara handed Kimmy a tissue. "I saw a flap in his front groin open and a rigid, white rod appeared. I felt it enter my private part ... vagina." She stopped. "I don't know how long it was in me, but he slipped it out, still very rigid and wet with green slime or cum dripping off it. It disappeared behind the groin flap."

"This may seem impersonal, but I need to ask. How long was his member?" Tara looked at Kimmy's face.

"It was long, because I felt it deep and at times it was uncomfortable," said a demoralized Kimmy, looking back at Tara. "For sure it was longer than most men ... well, those men I've been with."

"Did you receive thigh scratches or have vaginal bleeding after?"

"No, just a smelly green liquid dripping out after. What I call his 'exit splash.'"

Tara pulled out some swabs, test tubes and small clear plastic bags from the orange evidence bag she'd brought.

"Here, you can look for yourself." Kimmy opened her robe and leaned back in the chair, spread her legs and holding her knees.

"Wouldn't you be more comfortable at the hospital or an urgent care facility, which the police department has arranged for in such situational examinations? We even have a private exam room at the station."

"No, that's O.K. I feel very comfortable and I like you, Tara. There are always a lot of people I don't know in a hospital, just standing around in the room." Kimmy then brought her knees and ankles further back to her shoulders. "Actually, I'm quite shy and get nervous in front of strangers. When there are men around, I need my husband present to feel safe."

Tara moved a stool to sit in front of Kimmy. She collected multiple swab samples from her bare bottom and thighs and internally from all three orifices: urethra, vagina and anus.

"These internal swabs are quite moist. Hopefully, they'll contain live sperm and DNA of the perpetrator," Tara explained. "Do you easily get yeast infections after antibiotics?"

"No, I don't. Why?"

"Have you ever contracted genital herpes?"

"I never have!"

"I recommend prophylactic antibiotics, since we know nothing about your assailant. Also, I took cultures for any aberrant or abnormal bacteria or viruses that may have been introduced by the perpetrator."

"What about the morning after pills to prevent pregnancy?"

"You'd have to discuss that with a gynecologist. I can give you a referral card."

Kimmy nodded and reluctantly took the card.

"I was a 'living model' for medical school students before I got married," said Kimmy, blank-faced.

Tara sat and listened.

The woman started wiggling her legs as she still held her knees. "I'm getting stiff."

"We're done with the exam."

"No actual finger internal exam?" She sounded disappointed.

"That would need to be with Doctor Ian MacGrath or a gynecologist. Because you were assaulted, you could elect to see an emergency room doctor," explained Tara.

Kimmy let her legs down and sat up in a cross-legged position on the upholstered chair.

Tara placed the stool back to where she found it. "How did you get into modeling?"

"Oh, my mom was a model for Frederick's of Hollywood's mail catalogue. She got me face-to-full-body framed posed photos taken at an agency and they got me to Victoria's Secret. My success there got me to a dedicated agent who found some auditions. Pornography was where the quick cash ... money ... was, but I wanted to be legit. Finally, I got small roles in B movies."

"And you were?" Tara sat forward in her stuffed chair.

"I took acting lessons. I was excited, yet I never got any big roles, never got discovered."

"But look where you are now." Tara put her hands in the air.

"It's not from me. This is from my husband's money ... and I really enjoy when he's here."

The woman closed her robe and wrapped the strap around her waist as she stood up. Tara stood up with her.

"Thank you for listening to me; you're a wonderful listener and so understanding," she said as her face became sad. She hugged Tara. "You know more about me than my own husband ever cared to know," she briefly cried. "I'll call the shuttle boat captain at the shore to come pick up you and your team for transport."

Tara collected her items, checked the evidence bag and closed it.

Tara and the four men all climbed aboard the *Ride Me Easy II* dingy, a 1934 barrel back Chris Craft and rejoined the awaiting Officers Brett and Brenner.

Tara looked back to the cruiser and saw Kimmy standing by the ship's starboard rail, watching her leave, and they both gave a disheartened wave.

The five investigators collected next to their vehicles in Washington Oaks' parking lot.

"I hate to say it, Sheriff, but this fits our weird Matanzas Monster," said Deputy Keith.

"Those scratches on her shoulders, back and thighs look very similar to Yuma's armpit scratches," added Tara.

"And the three deceased women's scratches," added Doc.

"I don't believe the perpetrator is a masked, wet-suited, claw gloves and flipper-wearing *Creature from the Black Lagoon* impostor," stated Tara.

"This victim, being pre-ovulatory, presents the interesting possibility of the predator having nasal and oral pheromone receptors. She may have been releasing olfactory detected pheromones, which this unorthodox perpetrator with an unnaturally, highly sensitive nose or olfactory organ detected," considered Doc MacGrath. He looked at the confused looking faces of the others, except for Leon and Tara, who nodded their heads. "Pheromones are smelled or tasted excretions signaling a nearby female is receptive for mating. Many female animals mark their territory when they're available for mating. Insects, like moths and butterflies and snakes, amphibians and lizards also mark their territories. Mammals such as cows and horses use their urine pheromones as the signal," informed Doc.

"By the way, the blood arsenic level were found in the victim at the 206 Bridge was at low levels, according to Rick. These levels are consistent with long-term exposure. She worked handling lumber for years. Cuts and slivers could be the common way the wood's arsenic was introduced into her circulation," relayed Officer Brett.

"Thank you, Officer Brett, for following up on her occupation," Doc injected.

"Back to the pheromones," Doc MacGrath was on one of his mini-lectures as the other three looked at each other and then away.

"Martha McClintock of the University of Chicago did a whiff-sniff study in 1971, where the perspiration of women at different times in their menstrual cycles was collected. Other women would smell these perspired odors. Within three months or less, all the women were having their menstrual cycles in synchrony. This showed how powerful these different pheromones could be. Pre-ovulatory pheromones are one of the strongest odors, supporting our perpetrator's reason for his timed attacks." MacGrath caught his breath, knowing he was losing his audience's interest.

Sheriff Gary had politely waited for the Doc to be done. "Now we have eight related crimes, maybe up to twelve in all, on the Matanzas River. All could have a seven-to-eight-foot, ugly or masked perpetrator, with scratchy skin or wetsuit and claws with webbed feet or flippers."

"Don't forget he or it has sexual urges that need to be relieved," Keith added.

Sheriff Gary walked over to the deputy and whispered, "Good job keeping your pecker in your pocket on the *Ride Me Ea*sy yacht."

"Just being professional," Keith responded, bobbing his head like a rooster.

They both laughed with mutual back slaps.

"Anything the rest of us should hear?" questioned Doc.

"No, Moving on. Because of the pharmacies and fertility center robberies for medication, he or it seems to have reproduction on this monster's mind," added Leon.

"She surely was dramatically entertaining," laughed the deputy.

"That would be labeled 'Status Dramaticus," added Ian.

"Again ... nobody leaks this info to the media. Only Director Leon or I will speak with the press. It will only add to the media frenzy for a Matanzas Monster. Unfortunately, we've got to get back to the arrogant Mr. Maxwell."

# Chapter 34

## *Manipulation*

**Max led** the small tour group across A1A. Alisa continued trying to place herself between Max and Patti. Blaze joyfully changed positions from in front of the group to behind it, like an exploring hound dog.

"This part of MAAW is all about research. Here we explore macro and micro marine life, old and new life." The professor turned and slightly smiled at Patti. Their eyes locked momentarily, until Alisa's face appeared in front of Max's. "Before we can continue, I must ask all of you to give a vow, a pledge, to guarantee that what you see or hear today or subsequent days, will not be repeated orally, photographed, or written out to anyone beyond the four of us," Professor Maxwell sternly said. "Do you know what that means, Blaze?"

"I do, Max. That I cannot talk about this place to anyone, except all of us. I do promise. I cross my heart on it." Blaze shook Max's hand and lingered before hugging him. The two women said "I do" and also shook Max's hand.

"Should we also hug you, Professor?" Alisa asked as she pulled herself close to Max.

A smiling Max responded, "Only if you want to" The bundle of four friends formed a caring bear hug of trust. "Your word is a strong enough bond for me."

The three watched as Max put in a multi-numbered code sequence and then used a third fingerprint, a palm print, and retinal eye scan recognition. Finally, Max pulled out a fob and pushed two keys separately, followed by pushing them together. "Once we in this windowless building, the door will automatically lock behind us. If you have claustrophobia, you may want to wait for the rest of us across the street." Everyone walked in.

Blaze asked his mom in a whisper, "What's claus-two-phob?"

"And what exciting frontiers have we crossed, Professor ... ventured into?" Alisa asked.

"I'm glad you asked, Alisa," he said as he smiled at Alisa and Patti. "But that story will have to wait until later."

They entered the first of several attached rooms. Blaze flashed passed them all.

"No running, Blaze," Patti called after him.

"And no touching," followed Max's volley. His eyes caught Patti's as she looked back at him. Alisa frowned as she passed Max, seemingly unnoticed.

"Normally, no visitors are allowed in this research facility. However, since I'm the Director of Marine Animal Aquatic World and the visiting director for the last twelve years and counting"—Maxwell raised his hands upward and spun around—"the official name of this place and my creation."

The entourage followed the professor into the next room. "Here the investigators work in the micro world of life." He pointed to individuals seated at multiple tables with microscopes and assorted paraphernalia next to them. "They are all sworn to and signed off on legal and scientific secrecy."

Several assistants said "Hello, Professor" as the group walked by.

"Remember, no matter how shocking, whatever you may see, you are all sworn to secrecy."

"Yes," smiled Patti.

"Always, whatever you need," said Alisa as she crossed her heart over her left breast. Max's eyes showed reflexive pupillary dilatation! Alisa knew it was a common response when someone sees something pleasurable. They grinned at each other like naughty children.

Alisa saw Max's eye looking at Patti. His pupils were now small and normal size.

"Blaze, let's do a special handshake of trust." Max shook Blaze's hands and then each slid their open hand up and grasped each other's elbow. "Now bounce your grasped arm up and down three times saying, 'I do, you do, and we do.'" Finally, they released each other's arm, did a fist bump and showed the thumbs-up gesture.

"Now we are observing how different micro-organisms reproduce. We perform single gene manipulation and see what effects occur in these organisms with a missing or added gene. From single cell protozoa to billion celled animals, gene manipulation is done. Interestingly, the first protozoa were discovered in 1818. The cell was named by a German paleontologist and zoologist named George August Goldfuss." Max looked at the blank faces. "The reason I tell you this is that I am related to this creative investigator, G.A. Goldfuss. His protozoa were later recognized as animals."

"How can you call protozoa animals?" quizzed Alisa. She knew the professor liked to be asked questions. This way Alisa kept Max's attention on her.

"This unicellular organism is an animal because, by definition, it can spontaneously move. It responds to stimuli, is heterotrophic, meaning it eats things outside of itself, reproduces and usually is a predator. The beginning of the survival of the fittest." Max paused. "That is why our facility started gene manipulation with this simplest animal. This is a eukaryotic cell, meaning it has a membrane surrounding its nucleus holding in at least three linear chromosomes. We followed Goldfuss' work to try to create new life. By the way, if the single cell has no membrane around its nucleus, it has a single circular chromosome. This would be bacteria called a prokaryotic cell. Eukaryotic cell linear chromosomes are easier to use than a prokaryotic circular chromosome."

They moved to the next series of rooms. "Here gene manipulation on insects occurs."

"Like houseflies?" Patti asked.

"At one time that was true. We needed to get our feet wet, so to speak. The already established gene site identification and gene manipulation techniques needed to be learned. Our facility then forged into the unknown.

Using moths, butterflies, wasps, bees and dragonflies, we expanded our new discoveries onto their gene sites. There are no foolish questions."

Blaze then blurted out, "Does that mean you crossed them all and got a winged flying man who could sting you?"

Max and the two women chuckled.

"What? Was that a stupid question?" Blaze asked.

"Oh no, Blaze, that was actually quite a smart question. It is ingenious of you to come up with such a clever conclusion," Max replied. "We found the genes that gave each insect its unique and desired trait."

"Example, Professor?" asked Patti before Alisa could speak. Patti smiled "Please, Max."

"Sure. For an example, the nocturnal tiger moth is hunted by bats that use echolocation rather than sight to find their prey."

"Is it the same echolocation as dolphins and whales use?" Alisa slammed out her question before Patti could get a sound out of her mouth.

"It's the same idea, just not the same mechanism of making the sound waves and detecting them. A survival trait was the evolutionary genetic change leading to some species of tiger moths having an abdominal auditory organ that detected the bats'presence. A second gene trait these moths developed was to produce ultrasonic clicking to jam the bats' sonar and mimic the clicking of another unpalatable species, thus avoiding the bats' attacks completely. This is like the viceroy butterfly mimicking the colors of its cousin, the toxic monarch." The professor hesitated for dramatic effect. "We have those gene sites identified."

"And how do you use this info?" asked Alisa, again moving to be in Max's face.

"We transferred these genes to other insects to see what effect there would be on the next generation carrying the transferred genes. Would it be a new insect species?"

All of them listened, intensely waiting for Max's next words.

"Let us move on to the next—"

"May we see any of these resultant new or genetically manipulated species?" asked Patti.

Max's cell phone's ringtone played "Smoke on the Water." "Excuse me," he said as he answered and walked away.

Blaze started to wander through the many lab cubicles.

"I'm sorry. It seems I have some visitors at the Marinescape front desk. We will continue our tour at another time."

Patti called out for Blaze.

"Alisa, I'll meet you at the front desk," said Max.

"Patti, may I speak with you for just a moment?" Max asked as he led her toward the research laboratory front door. "I'd like to ask what you think you could do at the fertility clinic that would facilitate the progress here at the research facility," whispered Max.

"Mom, you got to see—"

"Blaze, we're leaving. The professor has an important meeting."

"Nurse Patti, please consider what I asked."

"You really mean what can I personally do for you?" Patti snapped.

# Chapter 35

## *Revisited*

**Sheriff Gary,** Doctor MacGrath, and Assistant CSI Tara talked among themselves as Professor Maxwell and his Assistant manager Alisa LaFavour, approached them. The five made the customary greetings and proceeded to a small conference room on the second floor.

"Mr. Maxwell, I'd like you to again revisit your thoughts about the media's Matanzas Monster, if you would," Sheriff Gary politely asked.

"A true conundrum surrounds the beast, creature or media monster. All media watchers and readers will feed on whatever the media gives them. Once said and if repeated enough, it becomes the 'fact and true.'" Maxwell spoke as he wandered around the room.

"But Prof—"

"Yet..." restarted the professor's monologue, "this consists of confusion and desperation among the individuals most responsible for explaining and reporting the recent past events concerning the creature. What the media has created, a Gill Man, would be an evolutionary extreme rarity, basically a miracle of nature, one in billions, who really knows?" the professor calmly stated.

"I did encounter my own interesting and confusing rarity of nature." The sheriff tried to mimic the professor's words, phrasing and cadence. "I performed my own surveillance in a small boat along the Matanzas

River. This was in the early hours when most of the crimes and sightings occurred."

"Where all the crimes occurred," corrected Doc MacGrath.

"And the emergency room examination of one of our sexually assaulted victims, who survived, revealed similar findings to all the previously sexually assaulted victims," added Tara.

Max and Alisa listened and remained mute.

After a long silence, Gary spoke. "I actually had two encounters with an unknown entity." He looked straight at the professor and waited for a response.

Again, Maxwell remained silent as he exchanged glances with Alisa. She was going to speak, but the professor touched her hand and she stopped.

"I saw a long figure in the water several feet below the surface, swimming as fast as my motorized Boston Whaler" Gary hesitated again and stared at the professor. "This swimmer I estimated was about seven feet long, compared to my nine-foot boat. It rose close to the surface next to the moving boat and revealed its shimmering green, scaly entity, with a larger than expected head for its body width. It ended our encounter by diving deep and away into the river's dark depths." He now stared at Alisa, who just stared back without blinking.

"I ran the length of the Matanzas River twice. My second encounter occurred when a green-colored, large-scaled, five-fingered claw grabbed the side of my boat—while it was moving. It pulled several times, trying to capsize the boat. The clawed hand incidentally had an opposable fifth clawed finger, like a thumb."

"Interesting, an opposable thumb, like a gloved human hand," stated the professor, staring back at the sheriff.

"What are the Emergency Center's findings, Assistant Tara?" asked the sheriff.

"There are five out of the nine crime scenes with four or five parallel scratch injuries. The spacing between the scratch lines matched in all the victims. All had large scale fragments in or around the scratches," answered Tara. "Three of the deceased women and three survivors had the exact same foreign fluid in their vaginal vaults or thighs.

"Also, four victims had microscopic blood samples found in their wounds with non-blood typeable, non-human blood cells," chimed in Doc MacGrath.

"All victims' scratch wounds and all the foreign vaginal fluids cultured out salmonella bongori, commonly found on cold-blooded animals like frogs, toads, amphibians and reptiles, as reported by our lab assistant Rick LaGrande," relayed Tara. "Oh, did anyone mention, Professor, that all the female victims who'd been penetrated were pre-ovulatory? We think the perpetrator was able to sense their positive hormonal status by smelling their pheromones and then decided to proceed with vaginal entry—correction, attempted rape and deposition of his or its ejaculated fluids."

"One victim was menopausal, with her dog trying to bite the attacker," added Sheriff Gary.

"The person or thing first pulled her into the Matanzas River by lifting her by the shoulders. Then, surprisingly, it brought her back to the water's surface, not sexually assaulted and placed her on the river's bank," continued Tara. "She told me that she didn't see her attacker. The next day, the front page of several newspapers had quoted her account of the attack with her vivid description of him."

"And what was that?" asked Alisa.

"Headline was…

### 'Eight-foot green 'Gill Man'
### Spared lives of woman and her dog!
### Matanzas Monster reveals it has a heart!'

"Yes, I see your point and understand how these findings from the specimens, the observations and media accounts have led to your conclusions," Max calmly responded.

"But can you explain it, Professor?"

All eyes went back on the distinguished, multi-educational degree-laden Professor Rory Fergus Hamish Lachlan Maxwell. He slowly stood up and walked over to a chalkboard and looked at the group. Holding a piece of white chalk in his right hand, he turned to the board and started to write as he spoke. "The Carboniferous Period is where we start. This is from 310 million years to 248 million years ago. This era is divided into—"

"Excuse me, Professor, but why do we care about all this?" interrupted Gary.

Professor Max stopped writing and looked to the sheriff. "You wanted my opinion and possible explanation, did you not, Sheriff?"

"Yes."

"So let me explain in a fashion that will help all persons present to understand where my conclusions are coming from." Max continued to stare at the sheriff.

Alisa felt there was an ego or power struggle starting to brew between the two.

"Again, the Carboniferous Period was from 310 to 248 million years ago. The amphibian evolved gills, like your Gill Man. Gills appeared during this time. Then from gilled amphibians came the quadruped reptiles, which means moving on four legs on land. The oldest and largest reptile that still lives today is the crocodile, which appeared around 250 million years ago. Its cousin, the alligator, soon followed. These reptiles developed thick, rough, scaly skin—again like your Gill Man. Then some of these reptiles developed the ability to be bipedal for short distances. Bipedal means moving on its two hind legs, as the infamous Gill Man. Other reptiles evolved into the popular large bipedal dinosaurs."

"Like T. Rex?" a smiling Tara spoke up. The sheriff and Doc turned to look disapprovingly at her.

"Exactly right, CSI Assistant Tara," excitedly responded the professor, "the Tyrannosaurus rex, which is a genus of coelurosaurian theropod dinosaurs. We are now in the Mesozoic Era, which includes the Triassic Period, 248 to 206 million years ago, where most dinosaurs and mammals evolved. The Jurassic Period, 206 to 144 million years ago, saw birds evolve. Finally, we have the Cretaceous Period, 144 to 65 million years ago, when the dinosaurs began becoming extinct. Important for us is that it includes all ... I repeat, all ... biped reptiles. We live in the Cenozoic era, 65 million years ago to present day. Only a sliver of time represents human or Homo sapiens existence and evolution."

"So Professor, you're saying we have a gilled, green, scaly-skinned and biped reptile evolving hundreds of millions of years ago," summarized

Doc MacGrath. "Then our Gill Man, along the way, had to survive the Carboniferous Period, through the dinosaur extinction, several ice ages, hunting humans and at the same time evolve into a man-like walking creature to present day. This creature would have to survive from prehistoric time until present time? Do I have it right, Professor?"

"It would have had to survive all these periods and eras. You can draw your own conclusions. I just wanted to give you information to base your conclusions on and on how I came to my conclusion," nodded Max.

"Native Americans have a legend of a half-fish, half-snake, half-man, who avenges the Great Spirit's anger over man's disrespect for what makes up nature," injected Sheriff Gary.

"I think there are too many halves. I do get the Native American's unverified myth of a fish-snake-human. That is similar to Greek mythology—a chimera that lived on the sea bottom and ate crustaceans and humans. There is the mythical human body and fish face called an Atargatis. One has the female mermaid and male merman. Also the Jengu or water spirit—"

"I get it, Mr. Maxwell."

The room became silent. The three on one side stared at the two on the other side.

The sheriff started again with the questioning. "Mr. Maxwell, let us all assume there's an unknown perpetrator, a monster, a man-amphibian or reptile. Seeing as you're an educated person, head swollen with knowledge and multiple degrees up the ... what would you call this thing?"

The group waited for the scientific, all-knowing Professor Maxwell to give his sanctimonious reply.

"There is no denying there is a presence on or in the Matanzas River," agreed the professor.

"I saw the water beast when I personally explored the river because of the media's frenzy," spontaneously spoke Alisa.

The surprised professor expressed his emotion for the first time. His head quickly turned to Alisa with a very disapproving face.

"Well, Professor," spoke up Gary, "taking the described encounters of the present individuals today ..." The sheriff paused at Maxwell's piercing-eye look at his recently appointed assistant.

"With the described characteristics of gilled, large, green-scaled, water-and-land living man-like lizard, I would label this mythical creature as Branchiam Subaqueanus Sapienosaurur."

"That's your scientific name for the Gilled Underwater Man-Lizard?" Sheriff spoke to Professor Maxwell rather defiantly.

Max stood up as he grabbed Alisa by the arm and dragged her out of the room with him.

"Professor, this monster is not my creation," Sheriff Gary stated as the conference room door slammed shut after the professor's exit.

"What are you doing?" Max angrily shook Alisa with both his hands.

"What? What's wrong? What did I do?" the shocked Alisa asked. "Did I say too much?"

"Never go out on the river without me!" sternly spoke Max. His eyes seemed to be a flaming red, followed by a trace of tears.

"O.K., I'm so sorry. I won't." She saw his tears. "Oh, you care about me," Alisa smiled.

"Ah, I just do not want any injuries to befall you," he said as he turned away.

Alisa stepped up to Max and wrapped her arms around him from behind.

Max wiped his eyes and cleared his throat. "You're just too critical. Your work at MAAW and Marinescape—you are too important to me." Max's voice waned off. "I'm going to the research lab."

"Professor, you need to go back into the conference room to end the meeting." Alisa turned him around to face her. She straightened his lab coat collar and nodded to him. "You're ready."

The sheriff, Doctor MacGrath and Tara were still seated in the conference room.

"Well, thank you very much, Maxwell," smiled Gary in jest to the professor's empty seat just as Maxwell walked in.

"The meeting is over," The professor turned and started to walk out.

"I like Branchiam Subaqueanus Sapienosaurur," said the doc.

Max stopped and turned, smiling, then left the room.

"The professor is more complex than I thought," smiled Tara.

"Yes, but his armor has a chink in it," smiled Sheriff Gary. "Tara, you and the rest of our team need to fish around under the surface and pull out all the furtive facts about Maxwell and his assistant Alisa."

"Exemplary expression of your elocution was quite impressive, Sheriff Gary T. Sellack."

"Whatever you said, Doctor Ian MacGrath, Medical Examiner," replied Gary.

"What did you say to them, Max?" asked Alisa.

"Are we done, lady and gentlemen?" Max embellished and also deleted most of his encounter endings. "The Sheriff said 'We'll return if there is a reason to continue the questioning.'"

In the Marinescape lobby, the five crossed paths.

"Shall I call you Professor, or should I call you Doctor?" Sheriff Gary smirked at Maxwell. "Where did you say you received—got all those degrees, titles—what college did you attend?"

"I didn't. You all came and questioned me and asked me for my expert opinion based on my reputation and choose me from a list of local universities, colleges and governmental sources," the professor answered.

"Well, sir ... I think I can address you as sir?" Gary continued.

"Our extensive CSI database, Florida Law Enforcement Agency resources and the FBI resources of CODIS (Combined DNA Index System) and AFIS (Automated Fingerprint Identification System) resources were unable to find any record of you, Mr. Maxwell, before twelve years ago."

Maxwell stood mute with his arms crossed.

"Unfortunately for you, a disgruntled female employee was able to obtain your fingerprints for comparison and a rooted hair sample for DNA analysis. There is no record or evidence that you exist." The sheriff pulled out a couple of pieces of paper from his back pocket and unfolded them. "Your DNA results are even more unbelievable. It says you're a human chimera ... whatever that is." A frustrated Gary paused.

"I'm aware of my oddity, but it is of no concern for your 'Gill Man/ monster investigation," Maxwell said, cutting the sheriff off.

"Also referencing the 5,300 colleges and universities in the United States against degrees awarded and your name, results were ... zero." Gary looked up at Maxwell.

"I was performing research in South America for ten years before I came to the States at the request of Marinescape and Marine Animal Aquatic World. All you had to do was respectfully ask me outright," Maxwell calmly replied. "Concerning my education, I received all my degrees and titles from the UFAM, when translated from Portuguese is the Universidade Federal do Amazonas—the Federal University of the Amazonas located in Manaus, state of Amazonas, Brazil," Professor Maxwell proudly related. "For the sheriff's edification, the university has 645 ongoing research groups and programs and 65 graduate programs. Now all of you can appreciate why I don't need to waste a lot of time explaining my educational background. The meeting is over."

The various individuals nodded as they exited the room with its walls full of pictures of Marinescape and Dolphin Family Fun activity options. The room was normally used to explain the facilities tours. As Sheriff Gary and Professor Maxwell came to the doorway, Gary grabbed Max's hand and pulled him in close. "You are quite polished in how you present yourself. But you're not fooling me. I also have special skills ... and I know"—Gary yanked Max's hand downward—"that you're definitely hiding something ... something very big."

The professor pulled his hand away. "Sherriff, you're like an old dog: blind, deaf and can't control its bodily functions."

"Max, say whatever lets you feel more secure. This old hound dog has great smell and I smell a water rat. I'm fast with big teeth and locking jaws."

The professor walked away and the sheriff yelled after him, "I never give up until all secrets and sins are revealed, Mr. 'Doctor of Atrocities." Sheriff Gary immediately got on his cell phone. "Hello, Mr. Angel of the *Palatka National & Local News*? This is Sheriff Gary. I have some front page news for you."

"May I record this conversation, Sheriff Gary?" asked reporter Angel.

After Gary had relayed the totally suspicious facts concerning Professor Maxwell, Angell replied, "Thanks to you, Sheriff Gary, I will be presenting this as an ongoing biopic in a daily series. Thanks for trusting me."

"And the same goes for you, Mr. R.W. Angel," Gary stated. "No exaggerating or fictional sensationalizing of the facts."

# Chapter 36

---

# *Misunderstandings*

**As Tara followed** the other two out of the conference room, she saw Alisa looking out over the Marinescape's peripheral wall. "Is the tide in or out?"

"It's in," answered Alisa without turning to look at Tara.

Tara was waist-high at the white wall as she stood next to Alisa. They both rested their arms on the wall and leaned forward to stare out.

"What does 'in' mean?"

"The surf is in," Alisa answered. "Today the surf is apathetic and shows no emotion."

Tara turned to eye Alisa tearing up. "Kind of like men." placed a hand on Alisa's hand.

They both remained quiet for a long time as they listened to the surf.

"You must have found the professor someone special to take his actions and words to be so hurtful. It seems to be a male characteristic."

"Yes, I do care about ... I mean, for him," slightly smiled Alisa.

"I can understand how that could happen. He's so knowledgeable. He takes an interest in everything he touches." Tara looked upward. "He's so personable. And physically fit. I noticed he appears strikingly interesting, whatever he wears. He makes the clothes look good, like a men's *GQ* model. I bet he can wear anything and ..." Tara stopped when she noticed how Alisa was looking at her.

"You like him, don't you? I can't believe you're playing off my emotions for him. Tara, you're such a bitch." Alisa started to walk away.

"Wait a minute, Alisa. Yes, I admire him. Who wouldn't?" Tara interrupted.

"You're like that fertility nurse, Patti. She wants a piece of him too," exclaimed Alisa with her eyes tearing up again.

Tara tried to put a calming hand on Alisa's shoulder but she shook it off and walked away.

As Tara and Alisa split, Tara saw Max walking over to sit by Patti, who was by the dolphin aquarium. As they sat together on one side of an open air aquarium, a boy walked back and forth by the white cement wall. He was following some movement across the ocean surface.

"Hey, Mom, watch the three dolphins jump together."

Max remained seated next to a smiling Patti. "I'm very interested in your work with in vitro fertilization. Here at MAAW research facilities, we do, as you might remember, a lot of genetic manipulation on insects and small aquatic animals," Max explained. "We are set up to perform insemination of animal sperm and IVF with manipulated sperm and egg."

"I find IVF exciting and personally rewarding, especially when a couple has the resultant pregnancy," widely grinned Patti with a special glow on her face. She placed her hand on Max's mid-thigh to accentuate her emotions for IVF … and Max? Alisa had been watching the two of them from afar. Patti's action was just too much for Alisa to watch, so she left.

Tara had been watching all three adults and the excited boy. She decided to leave after Alisa had left.

"I was wondering if you would consider …" Max started to ask.

Blaze came up to Max and stood there holding his hands.

"What is going on? Have a question?"

"When did dolphins first appear in the ocean?"

"About 13 million years ago, in what is called the Miocene Epoch."

"Then what's the difference between dolphins and porpoises again?"

"Let us go over to the side of the aquarium. One important difference is their behavior. Dolphins live in large groups and show no fear of humans. They will often interact with humans and swim alongside all sizes of boats or ships. Up to a dozen may swim together and they like to play in the wakes of boats and ocean waves," Max explained.

"Like those three needle nose dolphins jumping together?" pointed out Blaze.

"On the other hand, the porpoise lives in small pods of two, three or maybe four members. Rarely do they come near boats. And they only come to the surface to breathe."

"Is that one near the bottom swimming over there?" Blaze asked.

"You are right. They are so shy, we cannot use them in aqua shows," Max stated.

Blaze ran off to the far end of the Oceanarium.

Max went back to Patti again to sit with her. "Biological anthropologists suggest that the porpoise's life expectancy is only fifteen to maybe twenty years, compared to a dolphin's fifty years or more."

"So a porpoise's reproductive capacity matures earlier than a dolphin's?"

"Patti, you are correct. Thus, the porpoise's body ages and wears out faster."

They both watched Blaze meander around the pool as Patti remained silent.

"That gives a reason for trying to control reproduction," he added.

Still there was no verbal acknowledgement by Patti.

"That's why I was going to ask if you would consider being part of our research team," the professor quickly continued. "I know you have a full-time job and are raising Blaze, so if you could at least act as a consultant."

"I'd be concerned that …" Patti hesitated. "That it would conflict with my moral beliefs."

"And that's exactly why we want someone like you to be involved in this research. I wouldn't expect you to be part of any questionable activities if you felt it was wrong for you."

"So you say," said Patti as she walked away.

# Chapter 37

*Facts*

---

**"So what dirt** has the team kicked up about Maxwell and Alisa?" quizzed Gary as he stood in the small conference room in the county annex. The team sat in front of him.

"Officer Cerilla Brett, what do you have?" asked CSI Director Leon.

"Professor Rory Fergus Hamish Lachlan Maxwell is well educated as a medical and veterinarian doctor, marine biologist, ichthyologist, biological anthropologist, environmental evolutionist, animal reproductive endocrinologist and animal physiologist, as demonstrated by a whopping number of published articles involving frontline research," reported Brett.

"And Sheriff, you already informed the team that Maxwell received his professorship and doctorate in Brazil."

"Boring," snapped Gary. "Dirt, we need dirt."

"Wait for it," Brett interrupted. "Surprisingly, the professor doesn't have an American degree in any of those areas that I mentioned. Not a single degree. Only a general Bachelor of Science Degree in Zoology and a Ph.D. in the same."

"I knew it. He's a liar." Gary slapped his hands and rubbed them together. "Patrolman John Brenner, what do you have?"

"We still find no evidence of Rory F.H.L. Maxwell the IV in the United States or its territories," he sadly reported. "That could be explained by his undocumented presence in Brazil, except for his name

'Maxwell' in Manaus, Amazonas, Brazil. The Maxwell research papers are simultaneously attached to another name, Aikana Massaka on the Amazon River, at multiple sites on this 3,999-mile-long river."

The room was silent.

"Tara, what have you found?" Director Leon looked at her.

"Not as dramatic, but Miss Alisa Favour from Michigan has a history of obtaining college degrees at several universities and colleges, with only a Bachelor of Arts in Sociology and an Associate's Degree in Environment Science. Oh, multiple state warrants for her arrest for speeding tickets and a warrant for her arrest in Michigan for multiple unpaid parking tickets."

"Just to shake up the professor, I wonder if we could arrest her and send her back to Michigan," Deputy Sheriff Keith sneered.

Sheriff Gary shook his head. "I doubt there would be a strong enough case for extradition papers. I believe the State of Michigan would have to send the paperwork to us. We could call the Sheriff's Department from each county where the citations were issued. They would contact the State Attorney General's office ..." Gary looked for Dispatcher Mary Jane. "What do you think about that, Mary Jane?"

"I could help MJ with the paperwork on Alisa," volunteered Keith.

Gary looked at Mary Jane's displeased face.

"We' just put that idea on the back burners," said Gary as Mary Jane smiled at him. "We need to concentrate on Maxwell. Where did he come from, who are his parents, his birth records? I need deeper probing. Get more facts. I've never trusted someone with three or more names. They're always guilty of something."

"I already have the records on Maxwell's start twelve years ago when he showed up to be a consultant at Marinescape. He redesigned the old Marinescape Aquatic World after the hurricane damage," added Brett. "Still I found his social security number was issued with the help of Marinescape."

"What does he do at night? Does he have some recreational activities, hobbies? Everybody has some kind of vice. Come on, team, find his bad side. Where does he hide his deepest secrets? What's with those turtleneck shirts when it's so damn hot?" Gary carried on.

"I've staked out Marinescape thinking I'd pull him over for a moving violation, but he never leaves the facility," added John. "I don't even know if he drives or owns a car."

"To be complete, we need to consult another reptile specialist," Gary brought up the idea.

"There's a close facility called St. Augustine Alligator Farm," added John Brenner. "It's just up A1A, before the Bridge of Lions in St. Augustine."

"Why don't you and Tara visit the farm and find out if they have anything to offer us concerning the Gill Man story," ordered the sheriff.

"I have some experience around alligators," interjected Keith. "I could go with them."

"We can only spare two personnel at this time."

"I've visited the farm with a friend, as I believe John has with a relative," added Tara.

"The St. Augustine Alligator Farm is also a zoological park and has every species of alligator, crocodile, caiman and gharial," John relayed.

"I even saw a Komodo dragon and saltwater lizards," Tara expressed with some excitement.

"The two of you need to remember you're there to gather potential useful information. You are not on a pleasure trip or mini-vacation," reminded Gary.

# Chapter 38

## *Exploring*

**Max had his entourage** again re-collect: Patti, her son and Alisa.

"We are now in the back group of rooms of the research facility nearest the Matanzas River. This is where more complex attempts for inter-species crossbreeding with different insects and other small animals are created."

"What insects are the best ..." Patti and Alisa asked at the same time.

"For crossbreeding ... ?" Max finished their question. "We found that the dragonfly has the most desirable traits for us to begin with."

"Let me guess what traits," requested Blaze. "They've got the greatest vision, like they can see all around them."

"However, they cannot see a small area directly behind their head. Next?"

"They can fly like a helicopter, hover and fly straight up, down, back and forth." Blaze acted out the actions with his arms.

"That's number two," Max said, looking at a smiling Patti.

"Flying is essential for dragonflies. If they can't fly, they'll starve. They only eat their captured prey in mid-flight. They even mate mid-flight," Blaze proudly expounded.

"Where did you learn about dragonflies?" asked Max.

"My mom got me the entire *Compton's Encyclopedia* set, so from the 'D' volume."

"Did dragonflies live with dinosaurs?" asked Max.

"Yes, they were as big as birds, like hawks."

"Actually, dragonflies appeared around 300 million years ago, at least 50 million years before the dinosaurs. They were the first winged insects to evolve. Today, you see dragonflies with a maximum wing span at five inches. When they first appeared on earth, the air had very high oxygen levels, allowing for monstrous dragonfly size; wingspans of almost three feet were found in fossils," added the professor. "These are just two important traits identified to possibly use for gene site manipulate."

Alisa raised her hand and Max nodded. "There are over five thousand known species of dragonflies, so the third important trait would be finding the gene trait that determines if the dragonfly will live three weeks or one a year."

"And maybe longer," added Max.

"How do you use this gene site information?" Patti asked.

"To make a better insect," seriously answered Max.

Patti acted uncomfortable.

"And it is a way to perfect the gene manipulation technique for future more complex animals," he added, looking at Patti.

"That's a wonderful idea, Max," professed Alisa. "Don't surgeons practice surgical procedures on sedated and then euthanized animals before moving to human surgeries?"

"I am going to complete the biopic of the very unique qualities of the dragonfly, unless you all are tired of this insect chronicle?" Max said.

Blaze and Alisa answered, "Don't stop! It's so, so interesting." Patti did not respond.

"This insect has three main body segments and six legs. However, unlike other insects, the dragonfly relies entirely on flight for its movement, not using its legs to walk. Its legs are for holding on to foliage while resting and observing. Otherwise, its legs are used in flight for grasping a mate and copulating or for grasping prey for eating."

"What is copandlate?" shyly asked Blaze.

"Cop–u–lation is the activity to reproduce their species," Patti softly spoke.

"I would actually like to give the gene to get dragonflies to walk," smiled Maxwell. "Let us look deeper into its eyes, wings, flight speed and maneuverability during flight," he continued. "First, the eyes consist of 28,000 individual telescoping lenses called ommatidia or compound eyes. The large eyes appear out of proportion to the rest of the head and body. They cover most of the head and come together at the top. The many lenses of the eye provide more of a color spectrum beyond humans seeing red, green and blue. The dragonfly can see these three colors and ultraviolet colors.

"It is still an enigma how the two eyes come together in front and see a mosaic picture of these colors while detecting high speed motion all integrated into its brain. Next, the dragonfly has two sets of front edge-notched wings. The front pairs are smaller than the back pair. They function independently to give the dragonfly speed and obtain different heights during flight, but it cannot fold its wings against its body. The dragonfly characteristically extends its wings horizontally or perpendicular when at rest.

"Third, the dragonfly's flight is amazing." Max paused. "Its sets of wings operate independently, so its flight consists of hovering in one place for up to a minute. It can fly backward, sideways and change directions instantly. Its speed of flight is unbelievable, like some kind of superhero. Backward speed is three body lengths per second; forward flight speed attains up to one hundred body lengths per second. Questions or comments … ? Well, let's move to the outside tank next to the Matanzas River."

The group silently walked in line to the tank side.

"Blaze, why do we think dolphins are intelligent?"

"Is it because they're so friendly with people?"

"True, but many animals are friendly toward humans. We consider the dolphin one of the most intelligent animals compared to us. So I need a more specific trait."

"They talk to us?"

"Yes, they use sounds to communicate with other dolphins and humans using whistles, clicks and chirps," Max continued. "Amazingly, dolphins do not have vocal cords to speak like us."

"Don't you mean, not yet?" smiled Alisa.

Max added, "In the world of artificial gene manipulation anything is possible."

A frowning Patti crossed her arms.

"So how does a dolphin make its sound?" Blaze asked.

"They produce sounds using special nasal passage lips. When the dolphin pushes air through these lips, the tissues vibrate, producing sound at various frequencies, like humans push air through their vocal cords to speak words. Dolphins will whistle, squeak, click, chirp and moan. Their language consists of different noises in patterns, like humans do to make words."

"Well, how does a dolphin recognize another dolphin?" Patti asked.

"Just like you have your own unique voice, every dolphin has a signature whistle or a blowhole-a-zation that is unique to them."

"I see dolphins doing funny things to each other," laughed Blaze.

"Just as we humans play without speaking, so do dolphins. They give each other visual cues, like shaking their heads, clapping their jaws, caressing fins and snouts, slapping, poking each other and blowing bubbles when keeping directly in physical contact."

"So do I when playing and pushing without speaking to a friend," Blaze nodded.

"Why did you say this specific dolphin was isolated in this outdoor research pool versus being with the dolphins in Marinescape and Dolphin Family Fun pools?" asked Alisa.

"I did not say," Professor Max replied. He pointed out how the dolphin named Brutus behaved. "See how it chases fish in the tank, even head-butts the slow swimming turtle."

"An angry dolphin?" asked Blaze.

"We use positive and negative reinforcement methods to alter its behavior. Divers have been butted by Brutus, even when underwater hand feeding."

Alisa and Blaze noticed scars on Brutus. "What you mean, Max, is that's why he's so mean and aggressive. I would be too if someone kept hurting me," Blaze said sadly.

"MAAW rescued Brutus from another water park that used electric prods to teach him tricks," relayed Max.

# Chapter 39

## *Gator*

**The two investigators arrived** at one of Florida's oldest continuously-running attractions, since 1893, in the oldest continuously-occupied city in America, since 1565, St. Augustine Alligator Farm Zoological Park of St. Augustine. Once CSI Investagator Tara Coltan and Patrolman John Brenner identified themselves, they were directed to the park's management.

"May I welcome the two of you to our Park? How can I help you?" asked Eduardo.

"We're from the St. Johns Crime Scene Investigation team," answered Tara. "We have a few questions concerning alligators and crocodiles."

Eduardo looked around and became quite uneasy. "Please step into my office. I assure you we have committed no illegal activities here. We belong to the AZA, Association of Zoos and Aquariums." Eduardo faked a smiled. "We follow all their—"

"We're not here for that reason, sir," said Patrolman John. "We're here on a fact-finding mission concerning reptiles."

"Oh, excuse my misunderstanding." He tapped on his desk intercom. "Could you please send for Maska Manta; he is probably working with a gator burgher," explained Eduardo as he folded his hands, like he was praying with a real smile.

John and Tara looked at each with questioning faces.

"Gator burgher,' the prior owner was British, so that was his word for each animal enclosure, a borough and the inhabitant alligator is the burgher. And here is Mr. Maska Manta." Eduardo motioned to the two guests. "Brenner and Tara, Mr. Manta."

"Well hello, Tara." The grinning Maska grasped her arm and shook her hand.

"Have we met before?" Tara asked as she slightly stepped back. "Should I know you?"

"My older brother has spoken of you many times. His face glows like the morning sun whenever he speaks your name."

"Yuma is an acquaintance, a professional relationship," Tara said shyly.

"We are here to ask you about reptiles, sir," interrupted Brenner.

"It will be my pleasure." The junior Mr. Manta still looked at Tara.

"We are specifically interested in alligators and crocodiles." John stepped in front of Tara. "How do they move?"

"You will see that alligators move on their bellies in a slithering action," Maska answered. "Or they can do a high walk and run with their belly off the ground, even jump forward."

"Really?" Tara acted surprised.

"Now crocodiles are more limber. They can stand on their rear legs for a few seconds when it involves getting food." Maska raised his arms and moved a few small steps forward, making a hissing sound. "Now, imagine a creature seven or more feet high stepping toward you."

"Quite a monster move, Mr. Manta," Tara chuckled. "Why do they hissing?"

"When they're startled, threatened or eating on land, they exhale through their nostrils or constricted glottis and palate." Maska exhaled slowly. "Other sounds have been heard, like clicking, growling, roaring and moaning, especially during mating."

"Do they have gills?'

"No, they get air through their lungs."

"How fast can an alligator or crocodile move?"

"On land they can sprint up to five hundred feet at over thirty miles an hour. In the water, they may swim over twenty knots per hour or twenty-three miles per hour for a longer time." Maska Manta stood with his arms out in front, as a swimmer does when preparing to dive.

"One more question," Tara asked, "does the animal's skin ever come off?"

"Yes, when the animal is in a tussle with another gator, when pursuing prey, when under stress or just mating." He smiled at her. "Its skin, consisting of scales, may shed in patches. The scales range from very large to small, like on fish."

"Thank you, Mr. Maska Manta, for your time. This has been quite informative." Patrolman John Brenner shook his hand. Tara only nodded thanks from afar.

"Wait, Mr. Manta, any way you could give us a couple of alligator or crocodile scales?"

"No problem, Miss Tara, just follow me."

The three walked to the alligator borough. Maska grabbed a noose on a pole. He stepped next to the closest gator and harnessed the snout and mouth in one motion, followed by a quick flipping of the animal onto its back. "O.K., Tara, come on over with a gloved hand and rub its belly. It's O.K." Maska waved her closer. "This is one of the docile ones. The scales release off its body easiest from here."

Tara very reluctantly walked to the beast and knelt down beside it and Maska. She waved her hand over its abdomen several times, slowly getting to the point of touching it.

"You need to press harder and with smaller circles," said Manta, slower and quieter.

Suddenly, a flap on its lower abdomen opened and a white, rigid, right-angled, four-to-five-inch penis appeared. It ejaculated immediately several tablespoons of white gel-like fluid. The penis then disappeared and the flap snapped shut as fast as it had opened.

"Congratulations, he likes you," Maska laughed.

"Either your massaging of his lower abdomen turned him on or he smelled your body odor, which he interpreted as you being in estrus, midcycle, or ovulating."

Tara didn't respond as she started to shake her right hand.

"Wait, Tara, put the fluid in this." John handed her a cup.

Tara followed his smart suggestion. She went to wipe off her hand and wrist.

"Put that cloth also in this bag."

"You'll find your alligator scales in that gator whack," reported Maska. "Thanks for coming."

***

**The next afternoon**, Rick reported live sperm in the ejaculate, which was also positive for salmonella growth on the initial culture media and individual scales.

"On the one hand, you got it," smiled Rick, "and on the other hand?"

"You were born a standup comedian, Rick," a serious Tara responded.

"The scales off your glove revealed large scales, like those recovered at the crime scene." Rick stepped from one foot to the other with one arm upward, like a jovial puppet on strings.

"I'm not rubbing your belly," grinned Tara.

"Tara, you have a phone call on line one," relayed Mary Jane.

"Hello, I was just calling to see if you're O.K.?" asked Maska Manta. "You know who to call if you need gator whack product for female gator insemination or whatever."

"Very funny, I'll keep it in mind if I need another job, Mr. Manta."

"Tara, I have another phone call for you on hold, line two," Mary Jane giggled. "Sheriff Gary is telling me to tell you not to tie up the police department's lines with personal business."

"Hello, this is Tara."

"I was just calling to make sure you weren't getting infatuated with my baby, immature, foolish and not as good-looking brother," Yuma Manta said. "Don't forget, we still have an upcoming date. All we need to do is pick a day and set a time."

"As I told your brother, I'm fine and I still have no extra time for socializing."

***

**Sherriff** Gary was going through his mail and came across a copy of the *Palatka National & Local News and Entertainment*. He read the front-page headings and story:

*Renowned Professor Explains 'No Monster' Exists*
*Local Marine Biologist has Questionable Credentials and History*

First part in a series of related fact finding stories by R.W. Angel

Gary showed Leon and Doc the story and then called for another interview. "I believe this confirms that our perpetrator is of reptilian origin." Moving in closer, Gary said, "We now know one of Tara's specialties."

"What did you say, Sheriff?" Deputy Keith asked as he came in the office. "Did you mention Tara's name and me?"

# Chapter 40

## *Tempest*

**Wind blew in from the east.** The curtains on the open window moved inward with the warm, moist breeze. On the white-sheeted bed lay Alisa, spread eagle and nude. She relished the breeze across her body. She occasionally performed snow angels while watching the ceiling fan rotate with its rhythmic hum. "I wonder what Alistair is doing right now." She grabbed a soft pillow to her chest and started rocking side to side. "What's Max doing right now?" She squeezed her legs together and flipped onto her stomach. Grabbing her remote, she turned her TV set on mute to Foxy Local News with the scrolling text on the bottom of the TV screen.

*Winds will increase in speed over the next twelve hours. Build-up of atmospheric pressure should continue pumping in warm air flow with risk of a tropical storm moving into mid and northeastern Florida coastline Weather updates as they become available.*

"Let's see WCN… depressing news from storm central … no weather updates."

The Weather Channel showed a heavy rain going into northeast Florida. Alisa turned off the TV.

"I'm not going to let anything dampen my day. This is going to be a *great* day for me and for him."

***

**Wind** blew through the open windows of the Expedition. Sheriff Gary was reclined in the driver's front seat. He felt the air circulating in the front of the SUV seats and whistle out the open rear windows. Gary had parked on the southbound traffic lane shoulder where the A1A spanned the Matanzas River Inlet. "That wind feels like it's in a counterclockwise spin. Is a hurricane coming?"

The "NO Parking, NO fishing From Bridge" signs vibrated. He watched the river's wind waves and the ocean waves battling to engulf each other in the mixing bowl of the inlet. Gary tried to reach forward to turn his commercial station radio on, but ... the sheriff dozed off.

"The wind must have blown me into the water. There she is.—"

The blue mermaid sweeps by in a blanket of effervescent bubbles. As the turbulent water clears, I see blurred images of cylindrical objects tethered to the river bottom. I walk toward the non-moving images with the cross currents pushing me backward toward the ocean. I lean forward, bent at the waist, eventually making progress.

"Oh my ... this can't be true." The underwater tethered objects are one ... two ... three naked and decaying women. "Not again—the victims of the Matanzas River reptile monster."

Suddenly, I see a fast-approaching shadow, moving with no difficultly, coming straight for me. It appears larger and larger with distinct arms and now a large ugly head with rapidly kicking legs. A skin diver is in a green wetsuit? A woman in a blue and yellow bikini is now next to him. "Claws," I gurgle.

I place my right hand on my hip, but no firearm. I try walk backward, but the current is too strong to escape.

"I'll swim to the surface and then to the river shore." As I turn my back, I feel one ... two hands with sharp knives burning into my back, arms and armpits. I squeeze my eyes shut and try to scream.

A crash and a clap are followed by rolling thunder and a scorching bright bolt of lightning.

***

**Wind** howled outside as Mary Jane sat behind her dispatcher desk. With her left arm supporting her head, she started daydreaming about Deputy Sheriff Keith's whispered words to her.

"Until we can have time together..." Or was it, "until we can meet to be together"? Or "until we meet again, together time ... or time will"?

She was interrupted by a crash and a clap of thunder. A startled Mary Jane sat straight up, only to hear another clap and see a bolt of lightning brightening the dark, cloudy morning skies.

"He's just a flirt and tries to make it with anything in a skirt. I do like the nickname MJ, though. "Then there's Gary. He talks with me, asks my opinion and treats me with respect. Yet all —Gary thinks about is that darn green, slimy and murdering monster. Office rumor says he's an alcoholic, divorced and a mean ass-kicking son of a bitch when out on the streets of Jacksonville. I think he likes me ... if only he wasn't a cop." Mary Jane laid her head on her desk. In the distance, she heard rolling thunder and a deluge of rattling window panes' percussion, playing the accompaniment of a rain-orchestrated, modern symphonic overture. Her body shivered one time down her spine waiting for the electrifying bolt of light, which never came. "What's the use? I need to get away from work to meet someone, my kindred spirit. Wait, what about Rick LaGrande, who seems quite grand and always makes eye contact, smiles, hesitates, but never says a word to me, just a head nod? Can I crack his shell and find a pearl of a person waiting for me?"

***

**Wind** blew through Rory Maxwell's hair, which did not move. Max stood looking up and down the Matanzas River behind the research building. A twelve-foot-wide black underground tube went a short distance from the river to the back of the research building. The tube wasn't noticeable from above, since it was covered by green, grassy sod. The river view revealed only a sliver of an opening, seen by only the most astute passing observer and only on wavy days. Max knew it was there, since he had previously swum through its barnacle-covered inner surfaces and had originally designed it. Thunder and lightning seemed not to bother this wetsuit-covered man as rain started to pellet him from all sides. His green scuba diving suit and flippers flexed as he rocked back and forth impatiently. The river's surface was covered with patterns of water whirls with four-to-six-inch waterspouts briefly forming. Max looked to the disturbing sky as sheets of horizontal rain continued to assault his face. "Definitely a tropical storm is brushing by Marinescape. The Greek god Anemoi sent us a warm zephyr; now it has become a tempest which the two of us can tolerate."

***

**Wind** slapped Deputy Keith's outside window shutters as he had his morning coffee. He considered his prospects. "This must be like being the master of a harem," he laughed. "So many choices," he mentally collected a list of candidates. He got another regular Keurig K-Cup of Dunkin Donuts Original Blend.

"My prime 'AA' selection is Miss CSI Assistant of the Year, Tara, who can assist me anytime, anywhere, doing my wishes. Next is Mrs. Kimberly, the only 'AAA' selection, doing her thing in each of the cruiser's cabins and wearing her teeny-weeny multicolored bikini, bouncing, acting and posing only for me." He readjusted his clothing for comfort.

"The 'A' candidates are MJ talking dirty to me and then Officer Brett, wearing her shining black boots and creased tight blouse with handcuffs on her belt, acting naughty.

He felt a stirring, which led to him seeking some private pleasure time. After a few minutes, he was able to look out his kitchen windows as the rain deflected off the three panes like bullets off body armor. Thunder and lightning bolts reminded Keith of a battlefield, though he had never been in such a situation. The deputy had actually never fired his weapon or been fired upon. He sipped his third cup of coffee, originally called Open Kettle, then Dunkies, Dunkins and Dunk in 1950, soon to be renamed Dunkin' Donuts.

"I like to drink with a brand endorsed by winners, like the Boston Red Sox, the New England Patriots, and the Olympic gold medalists, like spark plug gymnast Mary Lou Retton, whose height was perfect for many activities." Keith smiled. "Oh, who can't forget the blonde figure skater Aliona Savchenko or tennis star Maria Sharapova or the greatest Olympic medal winner—Michael Phelps at twenty-eight! All of them can melt my Popsicle, except not Michael. I don't discriminate among women ... American, German or Russian.

Overhead thunder and immediate lightning explosions electrified Keith with sexual enthusiasm. "I feel the winner's mojo spreading in me. I even feel charitable." He wiped his hand dry, followed by a vigorous buttock slap.

"I would even let either dog woman of the Matanzas River crime scenes experience my charms. Their facial attributes make them candidates." He felt stirring again.

The Greek gods above continued to rumble their displeasure at all human arrogance.

***

**Wind** blew up SR A1A on Anastasia Island, rattling Patti's home plantation shutters. "Mom, is our house going to blow away, like the big bad wolf trying to get the three little pigs?" Blaze asked from under his bed.

"No, son, it's just a rainstorm passing through. Eventually this wind will move the storm out of here faster." Patti knelt down by his head.

Blaze squirmed out from under his bed and sat on it and Patti joined him.

"Kids at school are talking about a hurricane coming. What will we do?"

"You'll have a few days off school and we'll drive inland to your grandparents' place."

"What about the animals at Marinescape and Alisa, Max, the research building and—"

"They have their own evacuation plans if a hurricane does come."

Patti thought about the endearing Professor Maxwell and wondered if he did have a safe haven. For a moment, she considered asking him if he'd like to go with them inland, but then there was Alisa. They must have their own plans for Marinescape and MAAW employees.

By afternoon, the wind became less threatening, the hard rain became showers. Maxwell had retreated into the research building and changed into the MAAW's usual professional garb. He went through room to room. A finger impression and retinal recognition with a keypad code opened the metallic green door. Once inside, he walked over to a bench by a built-in floor pool leading under the west building wall. Maxwell picked up a microphone that had a wire running underwater into the pool. He clicked three fast, three slow and again three slow clicks. The professor reclined on the bench and waited.

# Chapter 41

# Revealed

**The wind and rain ended** within two days and was followed by a brilliant blue sky. Only minimal repairs were required to reopen Dolphin Family Fun and Marinescape and to use Marine Animal Aquatic World.

Max continued the trio's research facility tour. "If I remember correctly, we were in the insect room. Many insects have been investigated for desirable gene characteristics: the crawling insects with legs, such as the cockroach and scorpion and then the flying insects, such as the grasshopper, the housefly, the bee, the dragonfly and the wasp, which are all considered arthropods because they have jointed body parts. We looked at the earthworm and ringworm, which have segmented bodies without joints. Then we looked at snails, clams, octopi, squids, starfishes, jellyfish, crabs and lobsters. All of these are invertebrates," lectured the professor. "I went through this list of animals on which we performed DNA analysis to illustrate my team's journey."

"Which did you find the most useful?" Alisa queried.

"Without question, the most intriguing are the butterfly species and the rainforest dragonfly." Max smiled at her. "The first candidate chosen was the monarch butterfly for gene and particle chromosome transfer. Unfortunately, after the transfer, the butterfly did not acquire the traits we hoped for. The biggest disappointment was that the monarch didn't become predictable in its action; it did not learn and remember key human word instructions."

The group followed Max to another room with small clear, multi-holed cubicles and a cage.

"Now the rainforest dragonfly has resulted in a truly scientific miracle." Professor Rory Maxwell glowed.

Patti and Alisa stood by the back wall. Blaze stood close to the professor. Max opened one of the cubicles and placed his index finger in and Blaze watched a dragonfly fly out to Max's shoulder. "Blaze, don't make any quick or jerking moves," said Max. "Do you trust me?"

Blaze slowly nodded.

"Are you afraid?" He looked to Alisa's smiling face. Patti looked tentative.

"Now I want you to pucker your lips. I'll show you. Remember, no abrupt movements."

Blaze watched the four-inch-long dragonfly with a five-inch-wingspan turn around on Max's shoulder. The other two stood frozen and held their breath.

"Are you ready, Blaze? Extend your arm; this is the sound to make one time only: 'Pop!'" Max looked to Blaze and the dragonfly flew to Max's other shoulder. Max nodded slowly and pointed to Blaze.

"Pop!" Blaze watched the blue and black flying arthropod land on his extended forearm.

"Don't move your arm; don't breathe on it," instructed the professor.

Patti covered her mouth with a hand and Alisa enlarged her already big smile to a Cheshire cat at grin while slowly nodding her head.

"Now the dragonfly can see what we see and ultraviolet light frequencies that humans cannot see. The dragonfly uses its senses to remember your ultralight and heat aura patterns, which each individual possesses. It has taste, touch and smell senses on its leg hairs and its extended antenna and mouth. It hears you and where you are by a tympanic membrane on its abdomen." Max again looked to the women. "Your identification has been established by the dragonfly. Now 'pop' your puckered lips three times," Maxwell excitedly stated. "The dragonfly will remember you for the rest of its lifetime."

"How cool is this?" The dragonfly did a vertical lift off Blaze's arm and remained aloft and then flew away somewhere in the closed room.

"Where did Speedy go, Max?" Blaze lamented.

"You've named the dragonfly Speedy? It must have sensed extreme emotional change occurring in you so it departed for safety," explained Max. "If the dragonfly is on your body and senses danger, it will take flight and circle the threatening object, thing or person."

"Such an extraordinary creature is only possible with gene manipulation. Well, at least in one generation," Max answered. "Natural evolutionary selection started all these gene-controlled traits to be passed on over millions of years. The two-and-a-half-foot-wingspan dragonfly has been identified in fossil findings from 300 million years ago."

"How do you justify your actions?" Patti interjected. "What possible purpose can it serve?"

Alisa responded, "It's for the betterment of all mankind. Such manipulation will most likely lead to gene manipulation or therapy to fight diseases like cancer and diabetes."

"Where will it stop? Who will control and monitor such work?"

Max stepped between the two women with hands up. "I understand both your viewpoints."

"Blaze, we need to leave," angrily pressed Patti.

Blaze "popped" his lips and the dragonfly appeared from somewhere in the room, like a hummingbird from its hidden perch in a tree. Blaze held out his arm as a landing dock. "I can't leave now. Speedy needs me," a red-eyed Blaze insisted.

Speedy hovered over Patti and then circled over Blaze as his mom grasped his hand.

"I'll let the two of you out the entrance," Max said sadly.

Alisa remained behind, looking around and saw a closed green door on the wall facing the river. She tried to open it, but it was locked. Alisa turned and made a "pop" sound.

"Patti, the techniques of gene manipulation and specific gene isolation has been remarkable," Professor explained. "These insects and other invertebrate animals I mentioned are models for more complex gene goals. My team is very close to managing cancer cells, stimulating pancreatic cells to grow for diabetes reversal and isolating inherited gene diseases like

Huntington's chorea Disease without medications, maybe defeating these single and multiple gene diseases."

Patti stopped with Blaze in hand. "So you're not doing these things just to prove you can?"

"Definitely not ... I and the team are committed to finding genetic sources for human ailments and hoping to provide successful gene therapy without radical irradiation or chemotherapies. My discussion with you concerning fertility is to increase the chances for normal embryos, resulting in normal, healthy and long life for offspring with productive lives." Max withdrew his hands from the high security steps of opening the front door. "And how will you accomplish a person achieving a longer life, Professor?"

"Let us consider two twisted helical DNA strands in each chromosome." He crossed his two index fingers. "At the end of each strand is a telomere, like an aglet made of plastic or metal at the end of one's shoelaces. This end piece, the telomere, allows the chromosome to duplicate itself with each new cell division. Some of our body's cells die every day and need to be replaced," he enthusiastically explained, having captured Patti's attention. "Unfortunately, each time the telomere replicates, it gets a little shorter. When it becomes too short, the DNA cannot replicate and the cell line dies, called apoptosis, or imperfectly-formed cells may become a cancer cell."

"Thank you, Professor, but I still need to rethink your claims and my possible involvement with you and your secluded research team. May we leave, Professor?"

"Of course, you have my private number. Please feel free to call me anytime with questions or thoughts to discuss." Max stood in the doorway of the research building's front door. "Remember, Patti, evolution as we know it is not optional in this ever-changing world."

He watched the pair approach SR-A1A. "Change is inevitable. Is it is not better to direct it than just respond to it?" Maxwell yelled to them as they crossed the road to the Marinescape parking lot. Blaze looked back and waved.

\*\*\*

**The professor** went back inside where he found Alisa strolling around the insect room. He watched her try to open the non-windowed green door, walk away and try again. When Max walked in next to her, she shook and stepped slightly backward, like a child being caught doing something naughty. They smiled at each other.

"I have complete belief in and support of your mission," Alisa said as she gently held his hand.

"I feel our relationship is to a point of full trust between us," Maxwell whispered in her left ear, even though they were alone. "It is time I show you something nobody, I mean no one, has ever seen or could imagine." Max went to the green door and unlocked it. With a slow swing open, he turned his head and nodded. Alisa slowly walked in, like a parading royal princess or a prisoner going into a previously unseen room with heavy trepidation. Maxwell followed her and then the door automatically closed and locked.

He proceeded directly to a green-tiled elongated pool. The square ceiling opening was covered, which allowed sunlight but wasn't visible to those looking in. Alisa stepped around the three accessible pool sides and returned to sit on a bench on a wall.

"Well, what is your assessment, Miss Assistant Manage?" Max asked.

"There is only one door, which is secure and soundproof. I'm assuming the Matanzas River is on the other side of that wall, since I see slight water movement back and forth."

"Correct."

"The sided pool with a … I'll call it a waterway, under the wall going to the river? The waterway's pool front has a gradual ramp into the water. Its underwater surface is rough to make the transition easier from shallow to deep water. Finally, I see these artificial surroundings requiring no maintenance and an open ceiling covered with striated glass block or plastic, allowing natural light without inner detail being revealed. All these factors would make a visitor feel comfortable and safe." Alisa turned to Max, who immediately grabbed and hugged her with such enthusiasm that Alisa exhaled loudly.

"Oh, I am sorry, I am just so amazed by your observational and inductive reasoning powers," he said before releasing her.

Alisa looked to him. "I'm pleased more than you can image." She hugged him again.

"You have left out one critical factor, my dear. What or who, is this room for?" the professor questioned. "How is your deductive reasoning ability?"

Alisa only heard the words "my dear" and nothing further. Max's mouth was moving with nothing coming out. Her cloud of silence was broken when Max gently kissed her left cheek.

"What did you say? What did you ask?" a dazed Alisa squeaked out.

"I was wondering who or what you thought this room was for?"

"Something very special," spoke Alisa in a normal voice. She stared at Max's face with a cocked head.

Their mouths were zooming in, wanting that forever desired for an almost kiss. And then they both heard a splash and turned toward the sound.

# Chapter 42

## *Imagine*

**Outside the research building** along the Matanzas River and Oceanside was a flurry of activity. The river was filled with boats. These vessels were armed with depth finders, water microphones, submerged movie cameras, ultrasound and ultraviolet underwater detectors. Military style drones with infrared thermography cameras filled the air above the river's length. The search area now included Anastasia Island, Fort Matanzas National Monument Park, Marinescape and Marine Animal Aquatic World, down river to Washington Oaks Gardens State Park. At least fifty land vehicles, including a TV station truck labeled "Breaking News," had parked along A1A. Several private helicopters, two TV copters and a Coast Guard helicopter also patrolled just off the ocean shoreline and the Matanzas River.

Back at the station, Sheriff Gary sat at his desk flipping between several newspapers. His reporter acquaintance, R.W. Angel, had kept his word and sent the sheriff copies of any stories involving information obtained from him. A series of six day supplements had been running in the *Palatka National & Local News* and had been picked up statewide. All of these news supplements had been about Professor Rory Fergus Hamish Lachlan Maxwell and the mystery surrounding him and the suspected Matanzas Monster. Sheriff Gary smiled while reclining in his chair.

"Well hello, Mr. Angel," Gary said out loud and sat up.

"The *Orlando Sentinel* and the *Palatka National & Local News* both are offering a ten-thousand-dollar reward for the first photos of the Matanzas Monster," he read out loud, bringing Mary Jane and Doctor MacGrath to his office.

The dispatcher's phone rang, so Mary Jane stepped back to her desk. "Hello, Sheriff's office, Mary Jane speaking. No problem, he's right here."

Gary took the phone and the person on the other end of the line was almost screaming.

"I'm so excited and it's all thanks to you. The *Orlando Sentinel* says that the paper with my series might be nominated for a Pulitzer Prize for Public Service as an example of meritorious public service!" yelled R.W. Angel. "The *Orlando Sentinel* received this award in 1993."

"Congratulations, Mr. Angel, keep it going," complimented Sheriff Gary. "And thanks for almost doubling the Crescent Beach population with your award-winning series," Gary said sarcastically.

"It's the price of success," Angel laughed.

***

**Deputy Keith** reported from out on the war zone. "Sheriff, the land, river, ocean and air are infiltrated with money-hungry, fame-seeking, self-absorbed, inconsiderate men and women. The circus continues with news media interviewing individuals who claim personal encounters with the creature, the monster of the Matanzas River. Psychics who claim they can feel the thing's presence know where it is and what it yearns for." The deputy was getting swept up in the outdoor hysteria. "If I may say, this atmosphere of confusion is quite titillating for me."

"Space Cadet Keith, it's time to come back to earth and reality," retorted Gary.

"Yes, sir, I'm back on track. 'Protect and Serve,' Sheriff. There's even a pregnant womaan emphatically saying to whoever will listen, that she is with the creature's child. She was trying to convince the TV media that her skin is getting thicker, scaly and green and her nails are growing very fast on both hands and feet and she wants to be in water all the time."

"Remember, we only get involved if there is violence, attacks on individuals, destruction of personal property and the occurrence of injuries," the sheriff reinforced.

"Did you ask her how, when and where she conceived?" Tara asked after walking into the office and hearing the conversation. Are you sure it's not your baby, Deputy Keith?"

Some in the room smiled and the sheriff laughed out loud.

"Very funny, your humor is wasted on me, I'm like a submerged in water alligator sprayed with a water hose or being rained on." Deputy Sheriff Keith responded. "Whoever she is, she is quite attractive for a pregnant woman."

Tara picked up the phone. "Hello, yes, he's here. She's looking for a real man to date?"

Keith moved to grab the phone, but stopped. "I'm deeply hurt by how you think of me."

"That's one of the things I like about you being resilient, a man in the suit of armor."

***

**Max** and Alisa still heard moving water in front of them. Above was a blurred dome with a shadow of a hovering helicopter. It passed off to the south. "I see the ceiling barrier works."

"O.K., you've seen the secluded green door pool room, so time for us to go." A rippling water pattern appeared like a surfacing submarine from the depth. Or was it more like a dunked ball underwater waiting to emerge? They waited for … and nothing?

"Hey, that was almost exciting," laughed Alisa with relief and disappointment. Max placed a hand on her shoulder. She responded by turning back to Max's staring face. "Ah," Alisa barely gasped.

A dark green, bumpy-surfaced, half globe gradually rose out of the pool near the river side wall. The two then watched. Rising slowly out of the water, two red shiny lights appeared or gleamed, at the two viewers.

"Is it real?" Alisa asked quietly. She tried not to move. "Max, is it?"

Max's phone rang once. He put it on vibrate.

"It does exist, he … it … whatever is right here, in front of us, ready to leave the water. "Alisa looked to Max and then looked back in anticipation of seeing more of whatever, but it was gone. She saw no ripples from its submergence. She quickly scanned the room. It was nowhere to be

212

found. Not relaxing on the bench. Not playing hide-n-seek in between the vegetation. Max was on his phone.

"We have to go," Max frowned. "The organization's CEO wants to speak with me."

"Is that a bad thing?"

"Since I've never seen or spoken with this individual, I'll guess it is bad."

"I think I saw red eyes. But why red?" she questioned.

"An alligator or crocodile can have red or yellow eyes. They have an exceptional sense of sight with sensitivity to the slightest movement. It almost has 360-degree peripheral vision because the eyes are on the sides of its head. It actually can visually track several prey at one time. The reason for its excellent night vision is because behind its retina is the tapetum lucidum, Latin for 'bright tapestry.' It's a layer that reflects back light through the retina to markedly intensify any received light and so the red eye color."

Alisa nodded. "Was that a crocodile or alligator?" she asked.

Max gave no direct answer. "So our friend saw us in the dim light, heard my phone ring and disappeared because it felt uncomfortable." He opened the front door but held Alisa back as he viewed the chaos in front of them. "Let's go back in and take a secret, secured underground passageway to the main Marinescape building's lowest level. Once I finish my meeting with the Big Cheese, I'll find you on your maintenance rounds."

\*\*\*

**Maxwell** sat outside with a secretary in a section of the complex he had never been to before. The CEO's sentry secretary was quite smiley, dressed in a blue and white dress with a cresting wave pattern across her top and bottom. "I've heard so much about you, Professor Maxwell. It's nice to finally meet you," said the short, curly-haired blonde, middle-aged woman.

Maxwell stood up and leaned over her desk to shake her hand. "It is just as much a pleasure for me to meet you." He kept eye contact throughout the exchange.

"I'm Miss Siggins. I have to admit, you're not what I expected— with all those degrees, awards, trail of published papers — and the serial newspaper stories and the notoriety they've brought you. You're much younger and no ring, which—"

"Thank you for coming at such short notice," interrupted a white-bearded man at his doorway. He waved Maxwell to enter. "What do you prefer, Doctor or Professor Maxwell?"

"Whatever makes you comfortable or just Max?"

"You're not what I expected. So clean cut in appearance and young. This coverage of you in different types of media, which is not that complimentary, is quite inflammatory and degrading and it questions every aspect of your life, education, achievements in science and your actual existence." The CEO flipped through multiple newspapers, magazines and printed out internet articles on the table between them.

Maxwell didn't handle or even look at any of them. "I'm not aware of any confusion concerning my reputation or presence in the world."

Max glanced over to the secretary still standing in the open doorway. "Yes, Mrs. Siggins?"

"I have another story on the professor and it mentions his association with us at Dolphin Family Fun, Marinescape and Marine Animal Aquatic World, sir." She covered her ring finger and kept her eyes in contact with Max's until her twirl and two-step dance departure. "If you need anything else, you know where I am." She looked back and saw Max watching her.

"Thank you, Mrs. Siggins, please close the door behind you." The CEO never looked up.

Maxwell remained unmoved. The CEO did not look at the article.

"It seems the media wants to show their collective power over an individual and create a circus atmosphere with me being their freak for complete humiliation and destruction," the professor calmly stated. Max stood up. "I will move on to another marine facility and—"

"Max, Max, please sit down. I just want you to appreciate my predicament."

"Which is what, sir?"

"Our admission sales increased twice in just three days of the publications coming out— unprecedented for the life of this organization." He paused and tapped his pencil. "Now, after five days of media coverage, our sales have quadrupled. They all want a chance to see you, hear you and be in the presence of this renegade marine biologist." The CEO stood up.

"Who knows what will happen this weekend?" Grabbing the professor's arms, he said, "So of course I can't fire you. I need to give you a raise."

The CEO was so loud, the secretary came in.

"Will Mrs. Siggins be giving me my paychecks?" Max asked as he smiled at her.

"Of course not, that will be payroll, as always."

"I'll be happy with whatever you decide," Maxwell said as he exited the office. "I'm going back to work, if that is O.K." Not waiting for an answer, he left and closed the door.

"Professor Maxwell, I wanted to make sure you knew my offer to assist you in any, any way is clear and not just imagined." Miss Siggins smiled with her striking blue eyes.

"I thought I saw you were wearing a wedding ring?"

"Oh, that worthless thing, it's only a formality; pay no attention to that. I wear it to keep salesmen from hitting on me." She paused and wiped her hair behind her ears. "I get off work at 5:00 p.m. Monday through Friday," she smiled. "On the weekends, I just drive around with no real destination. I'm very willing to change if someone gives me a reason." She slipped a small piece of paper from her palm to his with a lingering hand caress and finger wiggle.

# Chapter 43

## Unfulfilled

**Sheriff Gary and Deputy Sheriff Keith** drove together down SR-A1A.

"Wouldn't you expect something to be discovered by now?" complained Gary.

"Now Sheriff, let's not discount the two deadhead underwater logs, a sunken boat, several river caves and fish that have been found by all the high-tech equipment being used," smiled Keith.

"Where the hell can this green, seven-foot, four-limbed, walking freakish creature or reptile called the Matanzas Monster who desires to get women pregnant?" Gary asked in frustration as they drove by three TV station trucks positioned at Marinescape.

"We did stir the pot and made the waters around Mr. Maxwell very murky," said Gary.

"I agree with you, Sheriff. You're a great mixer of people's lives. The balloon-headed, arrogant, self-righteous, self-absorbed and pretentious wanker called Max."

"Oh, now you speak with British colloquialisms?" They both laughed.

When Washington Oaks Gardens State Park was reached, they turned back north.

"The yacht *I'm Riding Easy* is gone," Gary commented.

"Did you mean *Ride Me Easy*, sir? Oh, that Mrs. Kimberly ... wasn't she every man's dream girl?" Keith stared at the horizon with a slight drool at the corners of his mouth.

"Deputy Sheriff Keith, you are in a position to reflect to society respect and authority," stated Gary. "Don't you think you need to curtail your remarks about women around women?"

"I do, but right now it's just us guys." He put up a hand for a high five, but none was given.

"Hey, there's the irritating chump," Gary said as he saw Max cross A1A toward the research building in front of them. Gary did a U-turn behind Maxwell and pulled up next to him. Max stopped.

"Good morning, Professor," Gary said as he put his fist in front of his mouth and coughed.

"Why do you have such animosity toward me, Sheriff Gary?"

"Oh, I don't know." Gary turned his face away from Max and then snapped his head back like a flipping restaurant kitchen door. "Could it be you're lying and hiding important information from us concerning the supposed monster apprehension?"

"Thank you so much, Sheriff, for admitting that this monster is of supposed existence and conjecture and that you are the one who has fed the growing media frenzy," Maxwell calmly stated in his usual fashion.

"That's not what I said ... what I meant. You're a sneaky wordsmith of dubious character," Gary said as his voice became louder. "You can't keep the lid on this boiling pot of the truth."

"Sheriff, we should go," said Keith as he laid a hand on his shoulder. "We have no cause."

Sheriff Gary shrugged Deputy Sheriff Keith's hand off.

"Be on your way and don't think we're done with this. All liars trip over their own words." The sheriff spun his vehicle's wheels turning it back northbound on A1A. "Damn sheep shit."

"Well, that was a pleasant encounter. You put the professor in his place."

"Stick it; stick it real deep." Gary slammed the accelerator down and flipped the vehicle's siren and tumbling red and blue lights on. "We have to find something to squeeze this fruit dry until he tells us what he knows and about his illegal doings."

Later that day, Gary and Keith sat in their own police vehicles, side by side and facing opposite directions, with the windows down.

"All is quiet on the home front," Deputy Keith observed. "No overhead air traffic. No boats motoring on the river. No road traffic or parked vehicles along A1A."

"This is my favorite time of day." Sheriff Gary started to day-evening dream. "A blanket of tranquil darkness is being pulled from the ocean over the landscape. A ribbon of red in the western horizon sealing the night sky shut. Just a few screeching owls mashed with honking cranes bantering off each other. Serenity is complete with the sounds of nature."

"When did you become such a bird lover, Sheriff?"

"I do love those Eastern Screech and Great Horned owls' vocal exchanges. Listening to them communicates, I feel I'm included and get invigorated. They help me develop insightfulness."

"I also feel invigorated by Mrs. Kimberly, Miss Tara, Miss Mary Jane, Officer Brett, and that pregnant—"

"I get it, Mr. Johnny Wad Holmes," interrupted the sheriff.

"I'll take that as a compliment, Gary, you're the—"

"Wait, I do get it," the sheriff interrupted Keith again. "Where is the liar always going to and always coming from when we call on him?"

"—he comes the research building?"

"Exactly," Gary sat up at attention in his SUV seat. "That's where we need to interrogate Professor Bubble Head. This is the building we need to get a search warrant for."

The two sat speechless as they waited for the first car to pass them in the dark. The two vehicles were partially hidden in the tree-lined entrance to the Fort Matanzas National Monument Park, off the west side Oceanshore Boulevard, as SR-A1A is known in Crescent Beach proper.

"Well, no dispensing tickets tonight," Keith broke the silence.

Sheriff Gary mumbled something about a search warrant tomorrow.

"I got to learn to let loose. Let these women know I'm available." Keith continued to ruminate over his female fantasies, "maybe if I were to lower my female expectations?"

Gary fell away in his own dreamland—

I know you're in there, you evasive mole, Gary yelled as he pounded on the front door entrance to the research building. He gave it one last fist slam. Well, hello. Gary slowly opened the door and stepped into a poorly lit room. He looked around and heard gurgling or gibberish sounds emitting from a very dark corner. Hello, anyone there? This is Sheriff Gary of the St. Johns Law Enforcement Agency. Gary walked forward and noticed he was only wearing a blue and white bikini bottom. He patted his bare chest—no uniform, no weapon, no star. The gibberish sound got louder and swirled around him as he walked through a growing oval pathway. The opening shriveled up behind him. Gary … Sheriff, help me … ha, ha … we are glad you're here. Fuzzy figures large and small moved in front of Gary.

I see you, whoever you are. The images cleared in their form.

We are happy you have finally found us, a male voice said from above him.

It has been hard for us to contain ourselves, a female voice added.

Gary slowly stepped closer in the now lighting up dark space. "Who are—? The Sheriff moved nearer to the very tall, appearing dark-green-skinned figure and a short white figure. He stopped. The man or something stood before Gary in a dark green wetsuit with flippers on its feet. It had a rigid, bumpy hooded mask with outcropped ears, scuba breathing gear going into both sides of its neck and gapping mouth with red lips on a green-colored lizard face. The white female figure with folded arms stepped closer to Gary and she appeared familiar.

Sheriff Gary, this is our family. She opened her arms, revealing her bare breasts, from each nipple hung a mini green scuba diver, but no creature. Help me, Sheriff! Mary Jane ran around the periphery of the circular room being chased by … Deputy Sheriff Keith.

This is our family of several generations spoke the breast-bearing blonde woman.

Gary looked back at the tall, green figure and its head popped out of the wetsuit like a Jack-in-the-box. It was the Professor Maxwell!

This is our family of several generations, now completed in millions of years, the professor stated.

Mini lizards, alligators, green scuba figures and mini creatures surrounded Gary and jumped up onto his ankles. Gary felt them scratching his skin.

You see, Sheriff, these generations have completed their development in only months, the woman said. Gary now recognized her as Alisa!

The hanging nipple mini-creature had now grown to the magnitude of a normal newborn human-creature. The two were still breastfeeding with Alisa's arms under each, caressing and bouncing them.

Sheriff, help us! Now Mary Jane and Tara ran in smaller and smaller circles around him. Gary saw Keith running behind them, laughing.

Alisa was now very close to him. Sheriff, please take one. Now you know our secret. Alisa smiled and offered a creature for him to hold.

The sheriff now had burning up to his knees. He looked down to see scratches in groups of four from his bare knees up to mid-thighs.

Louder and louder the voices grew, the calls for help, the breast suckling creatures, the gurgling, the laughter became one deafening sound of an oscillating roar like crashing monstrous waves on an ocean shoreline. "I got to get out," Gary started to mumble. "I got to go," he yelled out.

***

"What, Sheriff? What did you say?" a voice asked.

"I'm tired of this," the sheriff's rant continued. "I have to go, go, go …"

Gary felt a hand shaking his shoulder more and more vigorously. "What? What's going on?" As Gary opened his eyes, he saw Keith standing at his open vehicle door.

"You were saying that you had to go. Go where?" questioned Keith.

"Oh … oh, I was saying I have to go home to sleep," Gary replied. "There's nothing for us out here; let's go home."

"I always wondered why you drive a Ford Expedition and I drive a Ford Bronco."

"Let's think about that. You're a deputy sheriff and I'm a sheriff." Gary stared at Keith.

He just nodded and looked southward where the Matanzas Inlet would be visible in daylight. "You know, I can sleep with my eyes open." Keith smiled as he got back into his vehicle.

"Man, Gary, I was surrounded by women running by me," Keith laughed. "That's one of my faults. I can't just choose one."

Sheriff Gary drove away on northbound A1A.

Deputy Sheriff Keith flipped his headlights on and saw something step out of the roadside vegetation. He flipped on the high beams. "What was that?" Keith asked out loud and leaned into the windshield. Reflexively, he kept steering the vehicle toward the river. He saw nothing. Once his Bronco was in gear, Keith accelerated into the West River parking lot to light up the inlet and shoreline. For only a moment, Keith thought of calling Gary. "Damn. Nothing"

# Chapter 44

## Survival

**The sheriff tried** to decide if he wanted to stay awake or fall asleep and be haunted by dreams that seemed to be associated with his conscious conflicts and fears. "I'm not going to sleep." He turned on his fifty-inch TV and fell asleep within minutes—

Water had become a common backdrop to his dreams. This one would be different. Gary heard pouring water. His ankles felt wet and cold. The water level now had slowly crept up to his knees. He tried to focus his eyes, but all was a poorly lit blur. Gary looked around but couldn't see anything clearly, just darkness to infinity. The cold water had reached his groin as he stood on his tip-toes trying to spare his package from going under. Gary's feet moved around to find something to stand on and elevate himself. He looked straight up and saw a small opening dispersing light he could see what seemed to be a domed ceiling. He tried to reach it.

"Oh damn, so close." His two hands waved in the air above him. The water had progressed to his armpits and the nape of his neck soon followed.

"I'll dog paddle"—he spat out the cold salt water—"until I float to what I pray is a lid or cover of this tank that I can punch out." He started to float and kicked his legs and his arms, mimicking the breaststroke. He noticed how heavy his boots were. "Need to untie these stones and wiggle my feet free." The boots sank to nowhere land below.

"The hero always gets out of the death defying situation." Gary's fingertips finally felt a furrowed metal surface with a seam all around the top's edges. "I must think clearly. Yes, you are Sheriff Gary. It's a lid. James Bond always escapes. I'm just as cleaver as him." His head flexed backward to keep breathing above the rising water level.

"You got a problem, Sheriff? Can you hear me, Sheriff Gary?"

A short silence followed on the sheriff's intercom.

"Sheriff Gary, should I call Deputy Sheriff Keith?"

"Get me out," Mary Jane heard. "I'm getting out," Gary yelled as his eyes opened.

"What did you say, sir?"

"Nothing, nothing it's nothing at all. It's not important, Mary Jane." He wiped sweat from his face. He sat up and saw his sweat-saturated bed sheet.

"Several residents have reported hearing gun shots."

"Call Officer Brett and the EMS to the location."

"Already done, but Officer Brett and Deputy Sheriff Keith responded to an alleged domestic abuse. They say it's resolved. They're both going to the address on July Lane, about half way between the Matanzas Inlet and Marinescape, on south Rattlesnake Island, off A1A, Matanzas River side."

When Sheriff Gary arrived, Deputy Keith and Officer Brett were standing outside the Ford Bronco parked on the river's shoreline.

"What do you have here?" the sheriff queried.

"This fisherman claims to have shot the monster while motoring down the Matanzas River," spoke the deputy.

"I was boating down the river watching my awesome depth gauge with sonar when—" The hyped up fisherman was interrupted.

"Did you discharge a firearm into the Matanzas River, sir?" Sheriff Gary asked.

"Well, yeah," the surprised man responded, "my entire clip. I'm sure I hit the thing."

"We have secured a 9 mm and an empty clip," Officer Brett reported. "We also have seized his twenty-one-foot whaler with a mounted depth gauge. It's moored on the shoreline."

"And what were you using this crystalline material in an unmarked plastic jar for?"

"I don't know. I found it in the boat when I rented it." The fisherman looked away.

"So is it possibly an illegal substance, not to be used in public waters?" Deputy Keith pressed on the top, which easily opened. The deputy put it up to the fisherman's face.

"Hey, be careful, it's poison!" The fisherman stepped back.

Doctor MacGrath pulled up to the shoreline. "Anyone hurt?" he asked.

"No visible injuries. We sent the paramedics away," Officer Brett stated.

"Explain your encounter again."

"I was using my excellent color images, when something swam perpendicular and under my vessel. I immediately turned my craft to follow it. This thing was a fast swimmer. I clocked it at twenty-five to twenty-eight knots per hour. I kept right on top of it, even though it moved in a serpentine manner. Quickly I identified four limbs with two webbed feet. Its head turned from side to side with each swimming stroke and flipped on its back. It swam the backstroke underwater without slowing down. That's when I visualized the whole body. I knew it was what the media described as the 'Monster.'"

"Where were you on the river?"

"About one mile south of the inlet is where I snatched my gun and started firing at it. It started to swim back and forth, so I dumped the poison in its repetitive path."

Doc was visually examining the crystalline substance. "Did the creature slow down?"

"No, not even after hitting it, but as you see, a lot of fish came to the water's surface."

"What do you think, Doc?"

"This is most likely a pesticide or piscicide."

"Doc, isn't this creature an invasive water species, a parasite on human society?" Keith asked. Doc looked to Sheriff Gary. "Keith is right." They both nodded their heads.

"Sir, I'll need to take you in for fingerprinting. You'll need to stand before the judge and be sentenced for discharging a firearm and spreading a toxic substance in a public area," said Sheriff Gary as Deputy Keith cuffed the fisherman.

"You all should thank me for at least wounding this monster," the fisherman whined. "I could have killed it. It's probably on the river bottom. You guys need to find it before it's swept out into the ocean. Make sure the newspapers know I'm the one who shot it.

"We'll also confiscate the weapon, boat and the container of crystalline substance."

"I'm telling you, I'm sure I hit the thing several times. It was only ten feet below me," the man said as he squirmed. "I bet the poison affected it, maybe finished it off!"

"Last questions: Did it bleed and did it attack you?"

"No bleeding. Well, no attack."

# Chapter 45

## Friendship

**Maxwell had convinced Patti** that the research facility was a good place for them to renegotiate in a "valley of seeing, hearing or touching no evil." They sat at a small table by a wall that was covered by a mural of the Matanzas River. Patti looked around and realized they were in a room without a ceiling, within another larger room with slightly higher walls and with an opening at its ceiling and finally the largest room and walls with a closed ceiling over all the rooms. The walls had several open doors.

"Do you need any water, tea, coffee or pastry?" Max asked.

"Like you have pastries?" Patti ribbed Max. "The table is fine." She didn't look at the professor. "Why did you hang this enormous picture on the wall?"

"It makes this room more alive, light and fresh feeling," Max smiled.

"Are these multiple ceilings a mind game for visitors?" she snidely asked as Blaze ran by. "Walk, Blaze, with respect, young man."

"First, Patti, there are very, very few visitors like yourself and Blaze." Max was still smiling at her. "Patti, you are an honored guest and peer."

"Charmed," Patti said. "And I'm not your peer. You'll have to pay for your own sins."

Blaze walked by them sideways, pointing to the mural. "Very cool, I see myself right there."

They sat in silence. Off to the side, Alisa was watching them, unbeknown to the couple. She stood at the slightly open green door, left open as Max rushed to be with Patti.

"There goes Blaze again, briskly walking through the doors of the ceiling-less rooms," Max hiccupped with a laugh. "I hear his rapid pitter patter even when we can't see him."

"I'm sure he's running behind those walls." Patti finally looked at the still smiling professor.

Blaze ran past an open door with small cages. He circled back and looked in. "Hey, I don't see no one, so I'll just walk in." With some perusal, Blaze spotted his buddy, Speedy. He looked around again. With a flick of his wrist, the dragonfly was exiting the cage and soaring with joy.

Speedy, you're so majestic," Blaze praised.

As Blaze moved slowly from room to room, Speedy would fly straight up, sometimes turning in mid-air and soaring straight down onto Blaze's shoulder, top of his head or extended arm. Blaze made sure he stayed out of the mural room where his mom and Max still sat mumbling something. Max's right hand was now on Patti's.

"Do you think they made up, Speedy?" Blaze asked hopefully. "Are they serious friends? Are we going to eat together and spend evenings together?"

When Alisa saw the professor place his hand on Patti's hand, she just couldn't watch anymore. She slid sideways into the pool room and sat on the wall bench. Her face fell into her open palms, buried. Within less than a minute, Alisa heard a faint splash and looked up. "Ah!" She reflexively closed and covered her mouth.

In the mid pool, a green irregular dome emerged. Alisa stood up, still covering most of her face, except the parted fingers allowing her to see.

The watery dome continued to elevate, exposing scrawny remnants of ears on the side of its head. Water dripped off the ears, followed by … red glowing eyes! Alisa slowly edged her way toward the still slightly open green door. The creature moved slightly to the back wall and Alisa stopped. They stared at each other as his sparkling ruby-red eyes seemed to hypnotize her. The creature continued to retreat, yet it slowly rose to expose its neck and shoulders, with arms by its sides and then a narrow but very bumpy waistline. Alisa started to walk toward it.

"So, Patricia, are you willing to walk back into a different room, the pool room?"

"No, not really, Professor. I'm comfortable right here."

The creature slowly submerged back to its observation spot. Alisa heard voices, so she rushed to the vegetative wall of plants. Using her hands, she separated the plants to find a hideout. The water ripples had dissipated. Alisa felt secure in her camouflage of green, brown and pale white covering of fake jungle around her. Her brown Bermuda shorts, brown gym shoes, pale white blouse and hair wrapped up in a bun behind her head were lost in the vegetation.

Yet instead of Alisa's loathed couple prancing in, a dragonfly flew in first followed by a quietly-stepping Blaze. Alisa watched them undetected, as proven by Blaze and the dragonfly showing her no attention.

"Speedy, this is our room of fun," rambled on Blaze as he spoke away from Alisa, so she was unable to hear all his conversation with Speedy. The dragonfly sat and flew from Blaze's shoulder, like a parrot on a pirate's shoulder. It flew close to the damp floor and then high to the semi-permeable, well-lit central ceiling, which created shadows for the dragonfly to play among.

"Speedy, why have you stopped?" asked Blaze as he started walking to the vegetative wall and bench. "What are you staring at from mid-air?" Blaze was now directly under Speedy. With scrutinizing eyes, he scanned the vegetative covered wall. Blaze moved in so close his face was flush and then submerged within the fake plant leaves, like pushing one's face into pooled water to improve one's vision. All he found were multiple irregular light brown squares applied on the back wall. Alisa held her breath.

"Now with that explanation, will you please step into the decorated pool room with me," Max asked Patti as he held her hand.

Blaze leaped to the back wall within the rustling vegetation and turned toward the room. The couple stepped back and forth with hesitation between the two rooms. When they faced the other room, Blaze put his arm straight out from the wall of plants. As he expected, Speedy lowered down and landed on his upturned forearm. The arm slowly retreated with the dragonfly into the jungle and disappeared.

The couple finally entered and sat on the single wall bench in front of the concealing vegetative plant-covered wall. "Mankind is riddled with communicable and genetic-based diseases, toxic substance exposures causing human ailments and accidents resulting in deformities and dysfunction. These are the issues this facility is working to resolve, correct, prevent and bring to an end," Professor Maxwell expounded while continually watching Patti's face. "By using small animals, we are very close to being able to flip a person's fate in their favor."

"And this was accomplished by you playing Jesus or God?" Patti sternly asked.

"Do you think God would be upset with me if I found a way to re-grow islet cells that began reproducing insulin in a juvenile diabetic's own pancreas, within their own abdomen, so the person no longer had to give themselves insulin shots?" Max asked Patti. "By taking an insect's genetic material, putting it with a salamander's insulin growth factor gene, we can extend the telomeres on the ends of select chromosomes. Give the individual a vaccine, like a subQ shot, one time and this material may be carried as an inactivated viral vehicle which automatically goes to the pancreas to repopulate its insulin producing glands."

"I'm not sure," she sighed.

"A person has degenerative neurological nerve demyelinating disease, which results in their ability to do less and less and finally have no body movement."

"Why do I, an infertility specialty nurse, need to hear this?" she asked, perturbed.

"Then let me just illustrate with this last example of how God has given me the drive and learned ability to help others." Patti did not reply. "An individual has a horse-riding accident in which they're thrown from the horse and sever half their spinal cord," Max softly spoke.

"It's very tragic for the person and their family," Patti grimaced.

"Now there are several animals that can regenerate limbs with tissue, blood vessels and nerves." Max looked into her eyes to see if he was wasting his breath.

"Please continue before I must leave," Patti threatened Max's desire for her to stay.

"Spiders can re-grow a missing leg and its function. The multi-segmented planarians or flatworms can re-grow their bodies and function with just one body segment remaining. Lizards can re-grow their tails and sometimes a leg with full function."

Patti watched Max closely.

"All these remarkable re-growths are genetically controlled, so we isolate the gene sites involved, extract the said genes and apply them to injured animals and then humans." Max stood upright with excitement.

Patti stood up and started walking to the green door.

"Patti, please, let's sit back down," he pleaded as the two stood by the open green door.

In the vegetative wall, Blaze wiggled a little. "Oh Mom, please leave," Blaze whispered. "I got to get out of here." He wiggled again.

On the other hand, Alisa was quite comfortable, with Blaze still unaware of her presence.

The talking couple was even unaware of the two human wall fixtures.

"Professor, I don't want to seem rude, but what do you actually want from me?"

"Please excuse my professional rudeness, Patti. Let us go back to the wall bench and I will explain my situation."

"I prefer to keep walking to the front exit and I'll listen," Patti politely stated. "And where is Blaze?"

"Could we just sit on this next room's bench for a minute?" Max implored.

Patti loudly exhaled.

"I'm sure we will find Blaze quickly or he'll walk on by us since this multi-ceiling room seems to be his favorite room."

She walked over and plopped down on the bench. "You are quite a persuasive, persistent and charismatic man, Professor Rory Fergus Hamish Lachlan Maxwell the IV."

***

**Back in** the pool room, Blaze moved his arm and Speedy flew to mid-room. He struggled free of the vegetation, which seemed to have grown around him. "How can these fake plants grow?" A plant branch or sucker had stuck to his bare leg. He shook his left leg with no success of release. He then grabbed the plant sucker attached to his leg and pulled. He heard a suction cup release sound.

"Mucky ... snot ... goo..." Blaze wiped off clear, mucus like, slimy gunk from his skin. "It slimed me. I feel so funky." He looked around, no one. "Who put this on my other leg?" Blaze pulled harder, wiggled it ... and it snapped off. "Ouch!" he cried out. "That hurt, but the sucker head is still there." Finally, the sucker head fell off with his scratching and pinching it. From the attachment site, some blood started to ooze, like when someone removes a lake leech. He stepped his leg onto the bench and examined the battle wound. "No big deal." He took out a tissue paper his mom always put in his pockets for emergencies, usually nose blowing. Pressing the tissue over it, the oozing quickly stopped. He folded it and returned it to his pocket.

All this time, Alisa had watched Blaze. She almost came out when she saw the blood.

Speedy returned to Blaze's right shoulder when he stood upright. "One more assignment has been successfully completed," he laughed.

Blaze peeked out the green door, seeing if he could make a break back to Speedy's cage.

"A slow walk behind a few walls unnoticed and Speedy, you will be home."

Blaze went out the door, but Speedy didn't follow. Instead, he flew around the pool.

"Hey, Speedy, what's the excitement?"

Speedy set his hover between Blaze and the pool. Blaze looked toward the pool and saw a few concentric wave circles going to the pool's shallow east edge. "That's different." He watched as a green bumpy dome started rising out of the pool's front west edge. Speedy landed on Blaze's left shoulder, which was farthest from the pool.

"You're the creature, aren't you, Mr. Creature?" Blaze asked as he saw the thing extend its body upward to its knees. "I guess you like shallow water."

The two stared at each other ... well, the three stared at each other, as Speedy had lifted and slowly flew toward the creature's bright ruby-red eyes. Actually, the fourth person staring was Alisa. She slowly untangled herself from the growing wall. The other three turned to watch her.

"Sorry I didn't let you know, Blaze, that I was in the vegetation with you."

"I'm so glad to see you." Blaze started to come toward her.

"Stop, no sudden or quick moves, Blaze."

Alisa had several suckers on her body and branches wrapped around her legs, arms and waist. She moved forward and all the branches revealed elasticity, like rubber bands. With the other three still watching her, she pulled a pair of scissors from one of her Bermuda shorts' pockets.

"Blaze, I'll come to you." Alisa stepped away from the vegetative wall and more plant suckers appeared. She snapped the branches and then snipped the suckers close to their attachments on her clothes and skin. Efficiently, she cut three from her legs, one from each arm, five from the front of her blouse, which included both breasts and a few from her Bermuda shorts' buttocks and from her groin. Alisa methodically approached Blaze and the creature.

Speedy flew within inches of the creature's face and sparkling eyes. The creature raised an arm and extended its arm. Speedy flew and sat on its wrist. Alisa saw the creature retract its claws.

She hugged Blaze's shoulders after getting to him. Alisa and Blaze watched Speedy fly up and down in front of the creature. Then the dragonfly glided acrobatically around the creature's head, shoulders and chest.

"Aaee," they heard.

"Was that from the …?" the two asked each other.

Even Speedy stopped cruising and looked at the creature. Unbelievably, the creature raised both arms with palms upward, expressing some emotion of friendship or maybe asking "What?"

"The creature understands us," Blaze excitedly stated.

"Aaee," the creature again emitted.

"We can't keep calling it creature," Blaze said. "What do you want us to call you, your name?" I'm Blaze; she is Alisa," he said as he pointed to her.

It looked at Blaze and then Alisa and then back and forth a couple of times. "Yau …Yao," it said as it moved its head and neck forward.

# Chapter 46

## *Understanding*

**"Patti, I believe we can** come to a compromise that will make both of us emotionally, professionally and personally comfortable and happy with each other."

"Max, just come out and state your case of what you want from me."

"I started with small goals involving plants, then insects to fish, amphibians and ending with reptiles," the professor professed. "These animal manipulations brought them healthier and longer lives. Each achievement led to greater knowledge obtained from the previous building blocks." The bio-geneticist placed one hand above the other, going up an imaginary ladder. "Simple cross species breeding led to simple single gene insertion."

Doctor Maxwell paused for Patti to interject any questions. None came.

"A single gene became multiple gene insertions to partial chromosome insertion, finally leading to attempting different animal egg fertilizations with the same and different species sperm. I am now proficient with the intracytoplasmic sperm injection, ICSI, microscopic techniques."

"Congratulations, Professor, Doctor of human and veterinarian medicine, bio-geneticist, researcher, experimenter or what should I call you?" Patti sighed.

"I would like you to address me as your co-worker, associate, colleague or simply or limited partner." Patti smiled back. She stood up, turned away and then sat back down.

"I will be willing to work with you on your new goal."

***

**This is what** we've learned so far," Blaze said as the creature still stood knee-high in water. "Is your name Yau or is it Yao?" Blaze waited for a response. None, he turned to Alisa. "Is it a boy or girl?"

"Definitely boy, I just know," she smiled at the creature. "'Aaee' is happy or like. 'Yaa' is yes, 'yoo' is no and 'Eaa' is eat. With retracted claws, there are one, two, three or four fingers, with an opposable thumb," added Alisa. "Why did you pick Yao over Yau, Blaze?"

"Well, the creature is seven-and-a-half feet tall with large hands, like the famous pro basketball player, versus the name Yau, for the well-known, short-statured mathematician?" Alisa chuckled.

"I did say Yao ... Yao," argued Blaze.

Alisa looked down at herself and saw the cut sucker stems had finally fallen off her skin and clothes. Since cutting them, she had stood next to Blaze by the pool. She glanced back to the vegetative wall. The branch stems she cut were now in different locations. The suckers didn't shrivel up. It was like they were alive and migrating home to their source.

"Blaze ... did you see any of those sucker fragments moving?"

***

"Tell me of your new goal, Max. I'm still leery and vacillating if I want to be your partner in science," Patti softly spoke.

"I've accomplished amazing results with manipulation and directing the outcome of already existing animals. I am starting to see new, better and longer living animals."

"I understand and that's wonderful but what about me?" Patti pointed to her chest.

"You have valuable fertility nurse skills and knowledge. I have special skills. If we put us together, we'll start with a completely clean slate.

We can create things new to this world ... life, Patti, maybe better than humanity itself." Max stopped and stared at Patti's face.

"Would you be killing already existing life?"

"Definitely not, this would be improving the older basis of life and possibly be creating brand-new life or species."

Patti squirmed and then stood up; she turned to Max and placed her two hands on her hips.

"No eye has seen.

Nor ear heard,

Nor the heart of man conceived,

What God has prepared ...

1 Corinthian 2:9"

Patti now preached with crossed arms.

"Everything I have done, achieved, my mind's eye has seen, dreamt of, imagined, I've heard around me, has been with God's direction as felt in my heart," Max revealed to Patti. "God has given all of us the right to choose, may it be good or bad. Society labels our actions as right or wrong, good or evil. How something is used or thought of is left for us to set forth to the masses," Max now preached.

"What would be my part if I were part of your team?"

"You mean as my partner," interjected Max.

"The amount of my participation is yet to be determined, Max."

Max moved in closer to Patti. "I first need donor eggs, fresh or frozen," he whispered.

# Chapter 47

## Gotcha

**"We will solve these** Monster murders or I'm going to retire and go fishing," Sheriff Gary proclaimed to his team. "I want to know what, where, why and with whom our list of people under suspicion fit in this puzzle. Get an infrared thermography unit on the Coast Guard helicopter to run the coastline, the Matanzas National Monument Park, the inlet, down the river and Marinescape to the Friends of Washington Gardens State Park."

"Why would the Coast Guard agree to do that for us?" asked Keith as he smiled at Tara.

"Because these unsolved crimes are as much their responsibility to solve as ours. The US Coast Guard has eleven responsibilities or missions, one of which is PWCS, meaning port, waterways and coastal security. Included in this mission platform is protecting the US domain and its residents.

Oh, also let them know we have their scandalous recording of the naked woman's breasts," smiled Gary. "Should you have at least one early morning or early evening or both, infrared river scanning?" asked Doc MacGrath.

"You are right on, Doc. Both, since that's when the perpetrator is roaming."

\*\*\*

**Patti,** I will need donor eggs for a patient of mine in Brazil. I will purchase a travel cryopreservation tank for the transport and storage of the eggs in the research building," Maxwell explained. "I will pay the ten thousand dollars for the six frozen human eggs."

"I'll tell my clinic doctors that—" Patti started.

"The donor eggs will be stored here until transport to Manaus, Brazil."

"I have to get Blaze home."

Max kissed Patti's hand. "Thank you, Patti." He then hugged her. Face to face Max hesitated and their eyes met while still in the midst of his hug. Max kissed Patti on her right cheek and resealed his hug.

In the pool room, they all heard, through the partially open green door, Patti's statement of getting Blaze. All faces were toward the door. Speedy flew above Blaze and Alisa motioned Yao to leave.

"Oyo?" Yao questioned.

"Yes, Yao, Oyo," Alisa reiterated.

"Oyo, Oyo," Blaze also said in a panic.

Yao slowly sank in the water as it walked backward. Blaze peeked out the door and saw his mom and Max still talking with their backs to him. Blaze waved slowly for Speedy to follow. The two went out and then through another open doorway and were out of sight. Quickly, Blaze was in front of the correct cage. At first, Speedy playfully flew around like a puppy not wanting to come to its owner. Finally, he came to rest on Blaze's wrist and then slowly moved into his cage.

Blaze heard moving voices in another room. He quietly closed the cage door. When Blaze found where the voices came from, he turned around and walked backward into their room.

"Blaze, how nice it is of you to return to your mother."

"Yes, how fortunate the timing of your return, Blaze," stated Max. Max asked Blaze to walk to the side of the room with him. "You should know I have exceptional hearing and sight. I would consider it respectful to ask first before taking Speedy out of its cage for a cruise."

Blaze looked at the floor.

"Professor Maxwell is everything all right between the two of you?" questioned Patti.

"We're just discussing our secret."

Alisa looked around the room. No waves in the pool. The sucker stems had all made their way back to the mother plant. She readjusted her clothes, especially her wrinkled blouse. She discreetly slipped out, letting the door touch its framework but not lock.

The group said their goodbyes as Officer Brett watched Patti and Blake cross A1A to their parked white Cadillac. Max remained inside and locked the front door.

"How was your meeting with Nurse Patti, romantic?" Alisa asked as she walked to him.

Max held up a hand. "I hear a helicopter hover somewhere. Do you think all that interaction between Patti and I was about dating?"

"Well, I saw you holding her hand gently, like getting ready to kiss and propose to her."

Max smiled, then, erupted into laughter. "We were negotiating a future fertility issue."

"Why have you never negotiated like that with me, Max?"

Max led her to sit sideways on the same bench he'd sat on with Patti. He took both her hands and placed them on his shoulders. He placed his hands inside her arms on either side of her face. "Alisa, I apologize for not recently expressing how important you are to MAAW, Marinescape, to the animals and especially to me," Max gently squeezed her face between his hands, touching her lips with his thumbs. He studied her lips, cheeks and eyes. Alisa's eyes flashed back and forth between his eyes and face. "Alisa," Max kissed her right cheek. "Alisa," he kisses her left cheek. He was still touching her lips when Alisa pulled his face in and locked her lips on his. Several lingering kisses led to both becoming naked, except for Max's turtle neck. They melted their naked bodies into one. After riding the pony, she fell on top of Max as a human sandwich lay flat on the bench.

"Need I say more?" Max said as they both laughed. "I want you to make me a promise."

Alisa raised herself up on her elbows.

"Never go back in the pool room without me."

"How did you know?"

Max did not answer her directly, but instead said, "This creature you and Blaze call Yao has instincts for self-survival, food and reproductive sex. Primal, reflexive sex …"

Alisa fell back on him with a slapping sound, like a wet piece of meat on a cutting block.

\*\*\*

"**Sheriff**, you have a call from the Coast Guard," buzzed in Mary Jane, "saying they have a seven-and-a-half-foot-long swimming thermo image by the MAAW building.

"Where is it going?"

"They said it's just staying right there in the vicinity of the MAAW's research building."

"See if the Coast Guard armed vessel is close enough to go south from the inlet and I'll call my friend with a fifty-foot fishing yacht to come from the Washington Gardens State Park and go north for a 'pickle' or 'hotbox' play." The Sheriff started to get excited. "Mary Jane, call the local Florida State Police divers with their weapons to get to the research building and I will meet them there. Tell the team that whoever is available should go and I'll meet them there."

\*\*\*

"**It was about** twenty years ago, I was studying and started all my research projects from deep on the northwest Amazon River, University of Manaus, right where the Rio Negro River meets the Amazon River. It's a beautiful location surrounded by two million square miles of Amazon rainforest, at least when I was there."

"Where did you come from?"

"The people along my journey were most informative. Rio de Janeiro was about four hours and 1,500 miles by plane. Or you could drive fifty-nine hours by car or bus for 2,688 miles to Manaus. You'd go almost directly north from Rio, meeting several different indigenous inhabitants."

"How did you communicate with them, Max?"

"Most spoke Portuguese, which was not their native tongue. One of the friendliest and most westernized was the Tikuna indigenous inhabitants or

Natives Indians. They didn't really care how you referred to them," stated Maxwell. "I did learn some Portuguese."

"Didn't the natives have first names?" Alisa asked.

"Oh, they picked up Portuguese or Spanish names, like Paulo, Carlos and Joao."

"Where did Brazil get its name?"

"It came from Europeans harvesting Brazilwood from its coastline. They called it 'river of Brazil' or 'terra do Brazil daleem do mar Ociano,' land of Brazil beyond the ocean sea," smiled Max.

"One last personal question, Max, why do you wear turtlenecks?"

"I thought you wanted to know more about my many projects on the Amazon River?"

"I do want to know and understand your work," said Alisa as she lay flat on his chest.

He sat her up and studied her face. "Do you really want to know about me, the turtlenecks?" Alisa slightly smiled and nodded. Max slowly removed his turtleneck. Alisa saw two one-inch long, vertical scars. They were on each side of his neck. The edges of the scars curved inward, giving the scars depth. Alisa took her index finger and gently touched the groove. "Does it hurt?"

He shook his head.

She placed both her palms on his scarred neck.

Max hugged her and got up. "I am cold," he said and got dressed.

Alisa did the same.

***

"**From the natives,** I heard two very intriguing oral legends. The first was about the Mapinguary, a large, hairy man-like thing that harvested and ate many plants and animals. The natives could not do their harvesting until after the Mapinguary came through. If they did not wait, the Mapinguary would harvest native women for sex and then eat them alive."

"I think the legend is quite disgusting. It sounds like a warm air, sea level hashing up of the cold air, high attitude Abdominal Snowman myth," Alisa interjected.

***

240

"**Mr. R.W. Angel**, I wanted to give you heads up on the creature sting operation and anticipated capture, which is about to occur in the next thirty minutes," informed Sheriff Gary.

"Where is this going to happen?" the Palatka journalist asked.

"Have you gotten your Pulitzer award yet, Mr. Angel?"

"I'm getting closer with each exposé I write, Sheriff."

"The acquisition of this monster is going to occur near the Marine Animal Aqua World research building off SR-A1A. See you there."

***

"**The second oral** legend is folklore again from the Amazonian Natives along the northwest Amazon River. This fanciful creature, called the Botodolphin, could have multiple transformations. If it wanted respect, it would kill a male Native. This was the sign for the Natives to have all the virgin girls brought to line up on the Amazon River banks, where a naturally occurring blowhole existed. The Botodolphin appeared in a very masculine, tattooed human form, with a white hat, to stroll by the impressionable young virgins to seduce and impregnate one. He was able to determine who was receptive for pregnancy."

"Is that like the media Matanzas Monster?"

Max looked toward the pool and seemed not to have heard the question. The two were now sitting in the pool room on the vegetative wall bench.

"These plants aren't plastic, are they?"

"No, they are not, Alisa. They feel and look like plastic, but they are genetically altered with the traits of living plants," the professor proudly stated. "My path of creating plant longevity and regeneration started in Brazil."

"I knew it when Blaze and I had them attach to us."

"I thought I told you never to be in this pool room without me. And how did Blaze get in?"

They both looked up to a blurry image of a loud helicopter as it flew over the room's dome.

"Blaze came in this room with Speedy. I was already in the room."

"And what did you see?" Max sternly asked.

"We both saw Yao come out of the pool."

"Yao?"

"That's what he called himself, his name," Alisa still speaking apologetically.

"So it speaks, does it?" a surprised Max asked.

"Oh yeah, it said its name. He also has words for yes, no, eat, go, happy and the numbers one, two, three, four," Alisa excitedly said. "We learned those words in a very short amount of time."

"The reason I told you not to be alone in the pool room was that the Creature—Yao—has extremely sensitive hearing, smelling and vision. So when a woman is near ovulation, Yao will react violently with its primal urge to mate, with no regard to the recipient's safety."

"I've read the newspapers and heard the TV reports and what was said at the media's interrogations of the police," Alisa explained. "I suspected Yao was very sensitive to female pheromones being released midcycle. What you didn't know about me is that I don't ovulate, because I'm on the birth control pill."

Max gently held her head between his hands and kissed her ears, forehead and checks, ending on her lips with lingering contact. Alisa placed her hands on each side of his neck and strummed Max's horizontal neck scars with her thumbs.

"I was born with thin open neck slits concealed within a water-air membrane. As I got older, they scarred closed."

"So they were gills? What did your mother say about it?"

"Never knew her. I remember as a boy tagging along and helping a Scottish Amazonian River explorer, who adopted me, educated me about the world and society, fed me and named me after a famous Scottish scientist, James Clerk Maxwell, a mathematician and physicist and himself, Andrew Rory Fergus Russell Wallace. He told me I was destined for greatness with such a name." Max started speaking softly. "Rory was a world explorer and discoverer of rarities. Maxwell was the formulator of the classic theory of electromagnetic radiation."

"So where were you born ... in Brazil?" Alisa asked.

"Somewhere up the Amazon River; that is why I have such a love of the Amazonian Basin, which is mostly covered by the Amazon Rain Forest," Max embarrassedly answered. "That is why I have an accent."

"A sexy very accent and that is why you are uncomfortable using word contractions," Alisa smiled

"We both know a secret about each other," Alisa said as she hugged Max.

"Just one more secret to tell you but — that helicopter will not stop buzzing this building," Max responded quite annoyed.

"Isn't that also the sound of a large boat or cruiser?" Alisa added.

\*\*\*

**"Gentlemen**, today I expect you will capture the mythical and infamous long-talked-about Matanzas Monster," explained the Sheriff Gary to the two police divers.

"You'll want to take your underwater defensive weapons, since this creature won't be captured peacefully. This will give you the opportunity to kill or unlikely, capture alive this monster from the Matanzas River!" Sheriff Gary also instructed them to stretch an underwater Kevlar mesh along the MAAW shoreline, because infrared helicopter scanning had identified warm water outflow coming from the building's back wall.

Deputy Sheriff Keith saw Professor Maxwell and Alisa exit the research building's front door. He approached them.

"Professor, you'll be happy to know that the impossible, improbable and murderous mythical dinosaur is about to be captured or if necessary, killed."

Maxwell looked to Alisa, who had grabbed his arm. The two hurried to the river side of the building.

"Oh Professor, do you remember the on-ship rape by the monster at Washington Gardens Park," the sheriff yelled after the two. "The victim got pregnant, but she had a miscarriage."

Maxwell stopped and turned toward the sheriff.

"The woman's miscarriage started with bleeding," Doctor Ian MacGrath added. "The bleeding became a hemorrhage and her doctor was forced to do a dilatation and curettage, a D&C, after a vaginal ultrasound revealed no fetal heartbeat.

Professor Maxwell was going to ask Doctor MacGrath a question as he walked toward the doc.

"No, Professor, the pathology report noted nothing beyond tissue fragments, as usual," MacGrath expounded. "She was only seven weeks."

"And no hydropic placental degenerative tissue found in the mix?" Professor Maxwell asked Doctor MacGrath.

Doc MacGrath nodded.

"You do know your pathology, Professor."

"Chromosome studies to be done on the products of conception?"

"Sorry, Professor, none were ordered by the surgeon performing the D&C. However, I retained a few fragments for my own study. What do you think I found?"

"I'll bet you my Jaguar sitting over there that there were abnormal chromosomes and abnormal total chromosome numbers."

The doc looked straight-faced at the professor. "Do you have a ride to get home?" Doc asked.

The professor waited and then they both laughed,

"You are correct, Professor. You still have yourself a Jaguar."

When the professor, Doc and Alisa got behind the research building, they saw the top of a black net stretched across the shore by the building.

"Is it over the canal?" Alisa attempted to ask.

Max coughed loudly to prevent the doc from hearing her question.

The three saw the hovering Coast Guard Sikorsky helicopter and two large ships, one being a Coast Guard vessel with a bow-mounted water cannon. Along both river shorelines were surrounding armed community police officers and State Police. The sheriff walked over to the shocked couple and Doc.

"Well, Mr. Maxwell, you're about to have your limited dinosaur knowledge expanded." A journalist stood behind Gary. "Let me introduce Mr. R.W. Angel from the *Palatka National & Local News*, in case you want to make any statements or give an interview to the journalist who has made you famous … or is that infamous?"

Maxwell gave no comment and squeezed Alisa's arm to stop her from speaking.

The trapping occurred quickly from that point onward. The two vessels turned sideways with hanging metal gillnetting down to the river bottom, blocking the Matanzas River north and southward. The helicopter called down on its public address system that the thermography image was still swimming in the confined area, mostly in a circular fashion. The helicopter swooped low and dropped a net directly on the thermography image. The creature tried to swim away from the sinking net above it.

The helicopter, unfortunately for the creature, dragged one end of the net, following the creature until it became entangled in the snaring mesh.

"We have it," the announcement came over the copter's PA system.

The tired creature tried to get untangled and swim toward the research building's undetected canal. It stopped when it saw another net stretched across its hidden safe haven. The helicopter had a lead line, which lifted the monster out and above the Matanzas River's surface as it squirmed in the net.

"Well, Prof, we captured the mythical monster alive," Sheriff Gary announced the obvious. "What we didn't think about is where it can be held secure in a prison cage and still be able to survive."

"Until you do, this reptile looking animal cannot be out of water for any period of time," Professor Rory Maxwell forcefully recommended. "The reptile needs to be in water, either fresh or salt water, the flowing river, ocean or brackish water to use its gills and not suffocate."

Everyone gawked at the dangling remnant dinosaur monstrosity.

As Alisa looked up, she reflexively put her arms up as if to reach it, "Yao," she yelled. The creature seemed to look down and stopped wiggling. Mr. Angel started to write on a notepad.

# Chapter 48

## *Captured*

**Sheriff Gary stared** at the professor of marine animal biology, herpetology and disliked mendacious liar, fabricator and elegant speaker.

Maxwell studied Sheriff Gary's face. *Was he actually asking me for advice or trying to snare me in some ploy and capture me, just like he did with Yao?*

"Well, what are you thinking, Prof? Are you astonished with these recent events? Are you just going to synthesis another lie?" said Sheriff Gary.

Maxwell slightly turned his head, still unsure of the sheriff's motive. "Astonishment suggests one being bewildered or perplexed," the professor said as he stared upward. "On the other hand, a Pseudologia fantasica and mythomania describe it as a personality disorder. I am neither." The professor continued looking at the sheriff. "I'm not exactly sure what you want from me, Sheriff?"

"I want your opinion on what to do with this animal anachronism."

Maxwell rolled through multiple scenarios of the sheriff catching him in some incriminating statement and being prosecuted as an accessory to Yao's crimes of violence and death. Max looked to Alisa, who leaned to Max's left ear.

"You know where Yao could be safe, secure and still be under our care," she whispered.

Maxwell looked around and saw that a group of familiar people had collected: the crime scene *investigators (Are they gloating that they caught me in a lie? Yet it is not really perjury. I just gave my educated professional opinion … no liability in that.).* The sheriff, Leon and Alisa stared at Maxwell. Deputy Sheriff Keith stared at Tara. Tara was staring at Patrolman John Brenner. Officer Brett was staring at the deputy. Doctor Ian MacGrath was staring at the dangling Yao, still called the Matanzas Monster.

"Sheriff Gary, I am in the position to ask the board of directors of Dolphin Family Fun, Marinescape and Marine Animal Aquatic World to use their specially designed facility for aberrant aquatic animals. You would need to ask the County Sheriff's Department of Affairs if they would be willing to rent the facility's most secure water contained marine cage," said the professor and director of the facilities.

Sheriff Gary now studied Maxwell with squinting eyes.

"Until you decide, you must drop the reptile periodically back into the river water."

"Go ask your appropriate people right after you show me and my CSI team the water enclosed cage."

As the law enforcement team followed Maxwell and Alisa across Oceanshore Blvd, A1A, they all saw the massive parking lot of vehicles and vehicles on both sides of the road as far as the eye could see north and south.

As Maxwell and Alisa reached A1A, they were swarmed by the media, newspaper reporters and TV and radio interviewer personnel. Reporter Angel was still stuck to Sheriff Gary, asking for comments on the developing situation.

"Alisa, take the sheriff and his team to the restricted area and I join you shortly," the professor directed.

On returning to the CSI team, the professor stated, "The directors of the facilities said they are happy to accommodate law enforcement at no additional charge to the Sheriff's Department. Their two conditions include paying for daily water and creature maintenance and that the caged creature is open for public viewing."

As he walked around with the CSI team, the professor explained the above aquarium restrains, the underwater viewing portholes, the thirty-thousand-pound stainless steel netting across the top with electrification if needed and the four-foot-thick aquarium walls of concrete with very high PSI or pounds per square inch.

"This electrified metal mesh is the same used by the Florida Prison Department of Corrections," continued Maxwell. "The high strength concrete is made by lowering the water-cement ratio to lower than 0.35, giving an extremely strong compressive strength of the highest class."

"O.K., I'll give you a written approval to place the monster in this containment aquarium," agreed Sheriff Gary. "Deputy Sheriff Keith, call the copter to bring the thing here and drop it in this body of water."

"Alisa and I will keep it healthy and alive," Maxwell stated.

"The St. Johns County Sheriff's Department and/or the State Police, Florida Department of Law Enforcement, will hire security guards, each armed with a Taser and firearms to watch, guard and contain the monster," Sheriff Gary informed and warned the professor and Alisa.

"Remember, this monster has committed capital crimes. If engaged, these special police Tasers can be dialed up to five-million-volt charges, one hundred times more powerful than the average fifty-thousand volt local police use. If this thing tries to escape or cause harm to another human, lethal force will be used at the security guard's discretion."

"Thank you, Sheriff, for your concern of this minimal brain capacity, genetically determined, primal reflective animal for food, reproduction and its survival," Professor Rory Maxwell sympathetically stated.

Within two hours, the very short-breathed Matanzas Monster was imprisoned in its new home in the secured back lot of Marinescape-Marine Animal Aquatic World. Officer Brett and Patrolman John Brenner were stationed to guard and observer the monster until security guards were found and positioned to replace them. Both struck up conversations with Maxwell and Alisa.

"You must have an interesting job here at the Marinescape facilities?" asked John.

"Professor Maxwell has been very educational and compassionate concerning my career here, which has led to promotion to a higher position of responsibility. It's also quite rewarding work at MAAW, at least for me," answered Alisa with a smile as they both watched the monster swim in a figure eight pattern.

"No disrespect, but do all marine biologist use so many words to answer a question?" asked an also smiling Patrolman John.

"Ah, I guess that's a compliment," shyly answered Alisa. "I'm not an official marine biologist myself, as of yet."

Patrolman John looked to Officer Brett.

"I know the feeling," Brett revealed.

"I've known of your presence here at Dolphin Family Fun, Marinescape and Marine Animal Aquatic World," Officer Brett said as he moved in closer to Maxwell. "You're quite a controversial entity in the media, especially the *Palatka National & Local News*."

"Why thank you for noticing, Officer Cerillia Brett. May I address you as Officer or is Brett respectful enough?" the professor asked her.

"Brett is fine, as long as Maxwell is respectful enough for you."

"Max is fine for me. Now that we have been formally introduced," Max said as he used a two-handed shake with Brett, which Alisa immediately noticed.

Alisa took John's hand and led him to a corner of the secured aquarium in full view of Max.

"John we call this—"

"Patrolman John Brenner, please."

"Isn't John good, since we'll be spending some time together." Alisa now held both his hands to keep him facing her as she spoke. John nodded.

"This is called once-in-a-lifetime aquatic animal find in all of human history around the world, to find a live reptile hundreds of millions of years old. We call it Yao ... I mean, we shall call it Yao," Alisa proudly announced.

"You mean like Yao Ming, the Chinese professional basketball player?"

"Well, the reptile actually named—"

"It must be, because this reptile is seven-feet-six-inches long, the same height as Ming," John excitedly stated. "Yao played for the Houston Rockets of the National Basketball Association. He played center, number 11, eight times NBA All-Star first team."

"Let me—" Again Alisa was interrupted.

"I almost forgot. Yao was the only player to lead the NBA in all-star votes from outside the United States," John finished his speel, out of breath.

Alisa decided not to reveal that the name Yao actually came from the reptile itself, to avoid more confusion.

"John, the reptile and your hero's names just are coincidently the same," Alisa stated as she let go of the patrolman's hands. "You sure know your basketball."

"I must admit, I first saw and heard you when I brought my nephew here to Dolphin Family Fun. You were our very exciting, informative and attractive tour guide. My nephew was so infatuated by you, he said, "I want to be like her, to be with her," John laughed.

"Thank you for sharing that with me," said Alisa shyly. "Do you have children, John?"

"No children … divorced for three years. My ex couldn't take the stress of worrying about me."

"Let me show you the lower viewing area." Alisa took John's hand again.

Max saw them going to the lower level and had Brett do the same with him. Brett had turned out to be quite a chatterbox. Her monologue started with a complimentary review of all she knew about the professor, to be peppered occasionally with not-so-well-disguised criticism and partially hidden accusations of perjury concerning the reptile monster. The two stopped next to Alisa and John at one of the portholes. The professor interrupted her continuous train of words, which were now about her life.

"How do you like this view, Officer Brett?" he asked as he peered through the circular magnifying bubble glass. "You will agree this helpless and confused primitive reptile has only one thought, as any trapped animal would—thoughts of escape."

She nodded but still progressed without pause to a waterfall of mixed words discussing her goals for her career. Her rapid-fire word slinging revealed partial and entire word reversal dyslexia. However, this didn't hinder Officer Brett's parade of words and expressed thoughts. Professor Maxwell finally stopped her wordy montage.

"Officer Brett, your career goals are admirable," Maxwell complimented her. "Maybe if you built a case against me, say for collusion and murder with this pea-brain reptile, it would project you to Detective, Deputy Sheriff, Senior or Chief Deputy Sheriff. Once you're recognized for being a sleuthhound with your organizational skills, 'Sheriff Brett,' that would lead to your own county municipality," Professor Maxwell expounded in an accelerating mode, mimicking Brett's vocal diarrheal example.

Officer Brett stopped speaking and turned away from the porthole to the professor. She put both hands on her hips. "I wasn't insinuating any criminal activity on your part, Professor." The officer looked at him with a smile. "I do like your description of my escalation in law enforcement to sheriff. You're a great motivational advisor." She lightly touched the professor's arm.

Alisa and Patrolman John were still exchanging idle chatter.

"Alisa, I do see you as having an interesting occupation."

"I don't know if I'd call it an occupation," Alisa replied as she stared at Yao swimming.

Patrolman John moved in close to Alisa. Yao stopped swimming and slowly approached Alisa's viewing porthole. "Would you consider having a beverage or meal with me so we could become more familiar with each other?" John asked in a friendly, non-intimidating law enforcement vocal tone.

"I'm open to that invitation." Alisa smiled and moved in closer to John.

Yao was now pressing its face against the porthole glass, which magnified his ruby-red glaring eyes. Neither of the humans noticed. Yao put its hand on the glass and extended its five finger claws. Still there was no notice by the two of them. Yao then started to thump its hand on the porthole. A muffled gurgling and underwater roar or growl was noticed by them as they watched Yao actually scratch four lines in the glass.

"Alisa, we should all go, since the reptile seems quite agitated for some reason," requested Max.

As the four moved toward the exit staircase, Yao followed them, one porthole to the next. They came to the aquarium's open-air surface and saw Yao rapidly swim in circles, causing water to splash out of the aquarium. Then Yao jumped up and grasped the net with all four limbs, like a spider springing on its prey. Its face pressed against the confining network so hard that it raised the wire slightly out of the water. A gurgling sound loudly projected from Yao's mouth.

"Yoo, Oyo, yoo, Oyo," over and over.

When no response came, it started to violently shake the suspended stainless-steel net.

"Professor, should you electrify the wire mesh?" asked Patrolman John.

"I agree, Professor, electrify the mesh to teach the monster some restraint and respect and that it isn't the one in charge," loudly spoke out Officer Brett.

The group watched for a moment as Yao continued its attempt to snap the mesh or pull it off the wall with the repetitive shaking.

"Patrolmen Brenner, would you please step off to the other side of the entrance door so the reptile cannot see you?" Maxwell asked.

"But I'm supposed to watch—"

"Officer Brett and I will still be right here with it. Alisa, walk over to the aquarium's edge."

Once the patrolman was out of Yao's sight, the reptile released the mesh with its webbed feet and just hung with its clawed hands and pressed upward with its face, so Alisa saw its glowing ruby-red eyes. As she stood at the water's edge alone, Yao released the mesh completely and its face submerged so only she could still see it swimming in place and looking up to her. She was also the only one who understood Yao's request.

"Yoo, Oyo, yoo, Oyo … no, go, no, go." Alisa watched Yao and slightly smiled to herself.

The water's surface became calm.

"Well, Professor, you are also a social anthropologist," remarked Officer Brett. "The monster also has feelings and expresses its emotion."

"That is probably true," responded the professor. "However, I think those reptile expressions actually cover up its primal instincts of territorialism and desire for reproduction."

Brett turned and looked directly at the professor's face. "What I think is we got off on the wrong foot concerning each other, Max." Her eyes opened wider, eyebrows went up and her pupils dilated, as if asking "Can I call you Max? I expressed myself poorly, Max. I meant to say how much I admire all your accomplishments and especially what you've done here at Marinescape and Marine Animal Aquatic World." Officer Brett moved in next to Max and started to whisper.

Alisa had noticed their increasing intimacy with growing anxiety. "Professor Max, would you come over here?" she asked with a brazen voice. "Look at Yao as it floats at the surface." Alisa pulled Max in close to her and pointed. "Please scrutinize Yao's surface, right there is lacking scales, right there." She put her extended arm in front of his face, with her ear kissing his.

"Those less thick and smooth areas are lacking scale grow from the reptile's superficial epidermis, called alpha and beta-keratin. Single scales may be lost or even shed and then replaced within a couple weeks with a new layer of scales as the reptile grows older and larger," the professor commented.

"Maybe those are wounds caused by a firearm that left smooth spots on Yao," said Alisa.

"That must be from the fisherman firing his hand gun into the river trying to kill Yao. He did claim he hit the reptile several times," agreed Max. "However, as I said, as the reptile grows older, it will also grow a thicker and more durable external plate, overlaid growth from a deeper dermis layer, like a turtle shell, called a scute, Latin for shield."

"Is there any animal fact you don't know about, Max?" Alisa gave Max a hip-to-hip hug.

As she made body contact with him, Alisa glanced over to Officer Brett, who just gave Alisa a fake smile.

# Chapter 49

## Secret

---

**Patrolman Brenner peeked** around the soon to-be exhibit's entrance and saw the professor wave him to return to this secured aquarium area.

"Alisa, we should leave so Yao doesn't get upset again by seeing Patrolman Brenner and you together."

Max moved Alisa toward the entrance. He then turned and walked over to Officer Brett and said a few words that made her smile and she shook his hand.

"What was that all about?" Alisa asked in a suspicious manner, like a wife would do.

"No big deal. I told her the reptile's name was Yao."

"What did she say?"

"I know, like the Chinese pro basketball player. Patrolman Brenner had told her and that he can't keep a secret," Brett smiled and shook Max's hand." Max smiled and put his left arm around Alisa's shoulders. The two walked toward the Dolphin Family Fun Center. Mr. Wells rushed out of his office upon seeing them. "You will not believe this." He drooled as he spoke rapidly. "This is a secret, so don't tell the other Marinescape employees, O.K.?" Without waiting for an answer, he started babbling in almost unintelligible speech. "Your buddy, R.W. Angel ... you know, the journalist who writes about you every day ... gave you a lot of credit for confining the Matanzas Monster here at Marinescape." Wells laughed.

"Thank you very much, Professor. This morning's edition of the Palatka Newspaper was texted to me by Angel. He'll be featuring an entire special edition all about you and the Matanzas Monster."

"You are very welcome, sir," the professor smiled at him. Max wondered how Sheriff Gary would take the upcoming news release.

"Mr. Angel sent me a synopsis of the breaking special edition."

### The Secret Is Out
### Matanzas Monster Real,
### Alive, Confined at Marinescape
Once in a Life time, Must See to Believe!

"The board of directors had an emergency meeting and we're extending the park's visiting hours. It will expand as visitor demand increases. Of course, Professor Maxwell, this will require you to expand your hours with the Monster and your fast growing public."

Maxwell only nodded without a word.

"Oh, we can't forget the other part of Mr. Angel's story about the monster's love interest.

### The woman who tames the Beast ...

Alisa and Max looked quickly to each other.

"You know, like in the *King Kong* classic story ... the Beauty who tamed the Beast."

"I'm not wearing any special costume," Alisa immediately refused emphatically.

"Professor, we need you to come up with a scientifically based name or official sounding name for the facility to display to the visiting public and give the media."

Once Wells was finished talking at the two dumbstruck individuals, he scurried off and disappeared, as any rodent would have.

"You notice that he didn't mention that this increase in hours for us will be associated with an appropriate pay increase," Alisa now disgustedly stated.

"The administrator expressed no concern or interest in Yao's welfare," Max said, showing disappointment.

"You have a place in your heart for Yao. I can tell."

"I've had a long-term relationship with Yao." Max looked skyward. "Don't say that in front of Sheriff Gary or his staff. We might end up in his county jail or worse."

Alisa turned Max to her and placed her right index finger to his lips. Max pursed his lips then sucked her fingertip into his mouth. Alisa grinned and spread her open hand onto his face.

"Let's go somewhere private to talk and express our emotions. The pool room would be nice," Alisa said as she pulled her finger out of his mouth and grabbed his right arm to pull him toward the outside and across A1A. "The pool room brings back fond memories of us, together."

"I'm also drawn to the pool room for seclusion," Max agreed.

After locking down the facility and pool room door, the two sat down on the vegetation wall bench. "I was amazed with you, that after I spent years with Yao, you learned more about Yao than me in only five minutes."

"Actually, Blaze and I together discovered Yao's ability to speak," Alisa explained. "We had Yao respond to a few words. Yao actually reacted to English words with his gurgling and guttural sounds. I think all Yao's words are made up of only vowels."

"So you really have no secret method of communicating with Yao?"

"Yao told Blaze its name first by Blaze pointing to himself and saying his name." Alisa demonstrated by pointing to herself. "Yao pointed to itself and said 'Y … a … u … Y … a … o' repetitively until Blaze spoke its name out loud."

"I do have a secret to completely reveal to you alone," Max said as he turned on the bench.

"You already know I spent time in Manaus, Brazil and ventured up the Amazon chasing oral legends and long-time myths. One such commonly unveiled native oral history and fear was the ille lacertos, the man-lizard."

"Ille lacertos?" repeated Alisa.

"I became obsessed with finding and at least photographing ille lacertos. I never expected more than just those river and inland explorations." Maxwell stopped talking.

Alisa was riveted for his real-life adventure to be continued. "Don't stop now, Max." She grasped his forearms and shook them, as if to wake him from a dream.

"On that fateful forty-ninth trip, led by a Native Indian guide who promised this would be our myth-busting trip, I saw it." Again Max did a dramatic pause. Alisa started to unbutton his shirt. "Not much is going to happen beyond this point until you tell me more." She ran her hands up and down his chest, never losing eye contact.

"As I waded through dragonfly-sized-mosquito-infested jungle, mud, snakes and leeches filled my boots. I saw an upright, scaled man or reptile slowly walking away from me, shaded by trees. I turned back to my guide, who had disappeared. As I turned back to where he or it was, I now saw movement back down at the Amazon River. Damn, the canoe I came in was gone!"

"You must have been scared shitless," Alisa spat out onto Max's chest. "Sorry."

Alisa undid his belt and trousers. "You captured that moment perfectly." An excited Alisa kissed his nipples.

"As I slowly and quietly turned back, a seven-foot-plus standing reptile, definitely not a man, had moved one hundred feet to ten feet within just seconds." Max started to sweat and clear his throat. "As I describe the situation to you, I feel as if it is happening to me right now. We stood motionless. I looked at its red glowing eyes. Neither of us blinked. It breathed loudly; I held my breath. It brought both arms up with extended claws. I slowly brought both my arms up and extended and spread my fingers. I arrived at the point that I had to exhale and breathe heavily with gulps of air."

Alisa had completely removed his shirt and used it to wipe sweat off his face and chest.

"Again we stared at each other. I was mesmerized by its red laser-like eyes and it's unbelievable presence. The reptile lowered its left arm and retracted its claws. I lowered my right arm at the same time. Both our respiration rates slowed down together. After what seemed like a couple of days, we stood relaxed and I wanted to shake its hand ... not."

"How could you get away, alive and unharmed?" Alisa kissed his moist cheeks.

"My secret of surviving the Amazon wildlife is about to be revealed, my dear."

Alisa immediately removed her blouse and bra and performed a bear hug, pressing their chests into one, and repeating his spoken phrase, "my dear," in his ear.

"With my hands touching my Bermuda shorts pockets, I felt a lump on my left side. I reached in and brought out a few M&M peanuts, not melted, which the reptile's extremely sensitive nose detected. With my survival and panic mode taking over, I extended my open left hand of M&M peanuts. That is my secret of survival, just mini ball-shaped M&M peanuts. The reptile extended its right hand, palm up, retracted claws. So I emptied my hand's treat into its. It rolled the candy around in its hand, smelled them and finally ate one at a time. It showed remarkable hand and finger dexterity. During this time, I slowly walked backward and finally turned away from it to walk faster. When I got to the Amazon River shore, I reluctantly turned back around. Oh, what a relief, the reptile was gone. As I bent forward with my hands on my knees, I exhaled a long sigh of relief. Then I remembered I did not get any photographs.

"Oh no, no proof of its existence," I said out loud. I slapped my right leg, then left, then right again in an act of flagellation. I peered up and down the river for my canoe. The guide obviously took it. Looking for anybody, for any signs of human life, I sat on a partially burned-out log. A log a Native meant to carve and burn out into a canoe. While I waited for something or someone to help me, I saw glowing red eyes under the water's surface. The reptile ———I gave up all hope and just sat there. I watched as its head slowly emerged from the slowly flowing river water."

Alisa had Maxwell stand up and she pulled down his pants. "I think you will think more clearly with your britches off," she giggled.

"May I sit down?"

"No, I want you to be as exposed as you felt you were in front of Yao." Alisa continued to giggle through her words. "Wait, is this reptile Yao?"

"Yes, it is. I don't know how or why I thought Yao understood me and wouldn't maul me to death … or eat me. As we again stared at each other, I pointed to myself and then down the river, repeating the action several times. I looked around the river. Yao had disappeared."

Alisa placed her hands on both sides of his tented up, green vertical-striped boxers.

"On the opposite side of the river, I saw Yao's head pop up."

"Yes, Max, you have popped up," Alisa said as she slowly navigated his shorts to his knees. "Hello!" she said as Max's member twanged. Alisa gave it a quick "Hello," with puckered lips and then did a US military salute. She pulled his shorts back up and again slowly pulled them down again.

"Well, to make this long story short, Yao had slowly navigated a canoe from the other shoreline to me. I made it back to Manaus. I made several trips back up the river and Yao miraculously found me each time as I presented my 'secret' gift of treats as a sign that I came in peace."

Alisa made the first significant move, which stopped all talking. They used the bench for sitting as they were one, lying as one and then the mammalian natural position of both facing forward. Exhausted after all this, Alisa squirmed out and sat on top of Max. "I've always wanted to ride a dolphin like a cowboy, cowgirl," she said as she raised a free arm and rocked back and forth.

"Continue with your story of how you and Yao ended up at Marinescape and Marine Animal Aquatic World."

"I had sent my bio to several aquatic parks, made up of my works in a list form and summaries and abstracts of each study. I described my interests, degrees of accomplishments and future goal," Max stated a matter-of-factly. "Of the replying institutions, I chose here for their enthusiastic interest in me and willingness to let me go unrestrained in aquatic animal research and rebuilding of the research building after the hurricane's destruction. But how did the two of you actually leave the Amazon and get to the east coast of Florida?" She got off Max and both sat next to each other. They were still sweating and short of breath.

"I obtained a ten-foot water transport cylinder with a small hose connection for fresh and salt water replacement, two semi-clear viewing windows and an installed inside adjustable light source."

"And Yao trusted you?"

"Since Yao got in the tube with me every three hours for regular feedings, I would say Yao trusted me."

"And the type of transport was by …?"

"I wanted St. Augustine as my original destination. My choices were by air, so commercial freight in eighteen hours, or by water private freighter at approximately four weeks, plus or minus a week, to cover several thousand miles."

"You chose air?"

"Yao was quite comfortable in the air—no air sickness, no claustrophobia—and I felt the airplane's engine droning sound would put him to sleep. We landed at the Jacksonville International Airport. I rented a truck for a less than three hour drive to Marinescape and Yao slid out of the tank into the Matanzas River behind the recently built research building."

"They built this entire building for you, Max?"

He nodded and at the same time kissed her bare chest all over.

"How did you ever get through customs and quarantine regulations here in the US?" Alisa asked as she massaged Max's thigh and other nearby areas.

"I stated that this was a specially designed transport container designed in Brazil. It had a fresh air valve, salt and fresh-water circulation and a temperature-controlled environment for possible marine animal pickup in America."

"And that worked?"

"I was supported by Marinescape documentation for my entry into the country with my supplies. They didn't seem to care since they never opened the container, just looked in the two non-lit tank windows," Max pulled Alisa onto his lap.

"That's all the US customs did, you smuggler?"

"They did scan, with difficulty, the two-layered metal skins container, which showed it empty. They did have two DEA dogs sniff it out with no interest, except for a German shepherd urinating on the tank's side. As I said, I offered to open one end. They choose to just look in the two dark windows. Of course, I did not offer to turn on the inner light.

"What is the purpose of your visit, Mr. Maxwell? the customs officer had asked."

"And you said to take back an aquatic animal to Brazil," Alisa answered in broken words as she bounced.

"The custom officer added that I would be visited by a law enforcement agent and the US Fish and Wildlife Authority." Max hugged Alisa until she said "That's good, ah … that's enough… Uncle," she laughed.

"They didn't stop my tank hauling truck before the airport exit or visit me later at Marinescape's empty tank," Max finished as he and Alisa lay down on the fake wood floor.

# Chapter 50

## Crowds

**The next day**, the news was out and the crowds were in. The administrator found Professor Maxwell on the second floor looking up and down A1A.

"Do you see the masses of people almost fighting to get in to see the main attraction?" Mr. Wells drooled and wiped his mouth on a handkerchief from his suit chest pocket. "Professor, we need a name for the Matanzas Monster, the creature or this reptile. We can't use those mentioned names, as they were the media's concoctions. We'd like a more exotic name, a scientifically based name or a hit in the face name they'll repeat because it is fun to say. Repeating the name over and over and telling their friends about it!"

The professor smiled as he placed his right hand on the Wells' shoulder. "Alisa, come on over here, please. Tell us which name you like the most as the approaching and excited crowds of tourists enter the park?"

"You mean a Dinosaur, like 'the million-year-old Man-Reptilus? Here are some other choices: Aquae Vitiae (life from water); Serpentium, the Reptile; Corcodillus Singula Hominid, Single Crocodile Man; Lacertos, Lizard or finally, Corcodillus Singula Vivens, the One Lizard or Crocodile of Death,"

"I like the 'death' on any of the other names," Wells interrupted.

"Why not just use Yao?" Alisa suggested.

"And who's Yao? Oh, like the basketball player Yao Ming?"

"Yes, we just named the reptile, which is seven-and-a-half feet long or tall," quickly answered Professor Maxwell.

"I get it, Ming is seven-and-a-half feet tall," smiled the administrator.

"Yao, Corcodillus Singula Vivens, the one Crocodile of Death," said Maxwell. "I choose this name, since Yao looks more like a crocodile than a lizard."

"Yao has caused at least three deaths," Wells added. "What a theatrical air to the exhibit."

"Allegedly committed," Alisa also added. "I'm sorry, sir, you never introduced yourself," she inserted as she put a hand out.

"Professor Maxwell knows me, Missy. I'm Director Walker Wren Wells." He grinned widely and shook her hand with both of his.

"I'm just Alisa, no prefix of Missy, Director."

"Oh, we're all friends now; no more Mr. Director, please. Use one of my other names you like. Whatever you choose is fine by me."

Alisa nodded.

"I see a wonderful opportunity for our facility, a probable financial windfall." Walker got excited and started to drool again. "This is how I see the Yao exhibit being scheduled. There are two levels and the upper open-air aquarium will be a less expensive ticket, with Alisa as the narrator and answering questions," Wells said as he continued to smile at Alisa. "The lower level with the viewing portholes has Professor Maxwell as the biological marine anthropologist explaining how such a creature still exists in the present day." Wells looked at Maxwell. "Make sure, Professor, that you use the ascribed name of Corcodillus Singula Vivens, the one Crocodile of Death. Of course, these tickets will be more expensive. Some time limit should also be set. Dawn to dusk?"

"We're doing this all day?" asked a concerned Alisa. "Who will do our normal daily animal maintenance rounds?"

"Your replacements can be easily found, especially if I give them a title. And the two of you will have an appropriate pay increase."

"How about at three or four o'clock, visitors get half price tickets with no narrators until dusk?" Alisa asked sternly and getting in Wells' face.

"Look out at that traffic line that has formed before opening time. Wait, wait, I just had an epiphany. What if we had someone from the local sheriff's department? They could once a day relive their tracking down and capturing of the creature—Yao."

"That's a great idea. Why don't you do that? It is your idea, so you should get the credit and pass that idea by Sheriff Gary yourself," half-smiled Max.

After Wells left, a panicked Alisa placed herself right in front of Max. "I can't narrate about Yao. What do I really know?"

Max led her into an unused room and closed the door. "I will do the first few open-air narrations with you by my side. You will quickly pick up the knowledge and eventually you'll speak first with me behind you and only adding remarks if you happen to lapse about some information. I know you're a fast learner." He brought Alisa in close and started to kiss across her face and neck.

Alisa grabbed his waistline and pulled her groin in tightly against his. "I feel you have responded to my alarm for action." They scooted together to move and flipped the door lock.

"We seem to be on the same cerebral frequency, Alisa."

After a half an hour of exploring, fumbling and gasping for air, they got off the floor, dressed and left, going in different directions.

Several days of the schedule for the professor and Alisa became weeks and a month. The sheriff's department did send a different law enforcement representative three times a week for a stipend, which went into the local policeman's general support funds.

The irony of St. Johns Law Enforcement's involvement was that the Marinescape, Dolphin Family Fun, and MAAW properties were partially in Flagler County. However, since the original crime scenes and murders occurred in Sheriff Gary's jurisdiction, his team continued to follow through until Yao's capture. The State of Florida had agreed to pay the Marinescape for Yao's maintenance, food, and 24/7 security personnel.

"It's so sad that the original investors from the Vanderbilt Estates and Ilya Andreyevich Tolsoy—yes, the grandson of the Russian Leo Tolstoy—sold off their shares during the early Marine Park's continued growth," exclaimed Wells to the passing professor and Alisa. "In the 1970s, the yearly attendance topped at 900,000. Then we lost our allure to other built attractions in Florida. The almost demise and then phoenix rebirth of Marinescape occurred after hurricanes Floyd and Irene in late 1990s."

"And why are you giving me this history lesson, Mr. Wells?" asked Max.

"Professor Maxwell, if the attendance for this first month continues, we will top off attendance at four million because of Yao. Profit projections for Marinescape will be sky high."

"If you care, Yao's physical health is fine, but its mental status has been declining," Alisa interjected as she walked with the other two.

"How do you know a reptile's mental status?" asked Wells.

"Don't you get it? Yao is no ordinary aquatic animal. It has evolved into a part-time terrestrial, upright and walking creation of natural selection gone astray. This occurs once in a billion years of Earth's history continuum of life before and after the dinosaur's demise," emphatically stated Alisa.

"Oh, I like that. We can use that on our web page and media blitz." Walker Wren Wells pulled out a pen and paper and started to write. He looked up at the professor and Alisa. "So I'm a heartless soul, but I'm the one who has kept this facility alive."

Max and Alisa started to leave.

"All right, Miss Animal Psychologist, suggestions to make Yao mentally healthier?"

"I have seen Yao respond to hearing its name being said. Yao has excellent smell, hearing and sight, many times better than a human. I wouldn't be surprised if Yao can read lips," Alisa explained. "Yao acts like there will be an action of friendship when mentioning its name. With no response from us, it has become more and more demoralized in its confined space. I recommend we use another name or reference word for Yao, like Matanzas Dinosaur."

"Brilliant, I love it," said Wells.

"Then you will love that 'dinosaur' is from the Greek, deinos, meaning fearfully terrible and sauros, meaning lizard," added Professor Maxwell, "another catch phrase for you, Mr. Wells."

"So now what is this reptile's official new logo going to be?" a resistant and stymied Mr. Wells asked.

"*Dinosaur Crocodilles Hominid*, terrible crocodile man, I believe is appropriate," answered Professor Rory Fergus Hamish Lachlan Maxwell the IV.

After 4:00 p.m., Max and Alisa were standing on the second floor watching the pushing and excited masses enter the park.

"Hey, there is Patti and Blaze," said Max and he went down to make sure they got a free entry.

Alisa followed like a dog with its tail between its legs. Max walked through the entrance into the crowd and found his two friends. Alisa waited at the entrance.

"Hi, I have missed you both," Max said as he hugged Patti and shook Blaze's hand with their secret handshake. They met up with Alisa.

"How nice to see you, Blaze."

"I've a … been just a counting a … the days … a … to see you again," Blaze bashfully stuttered and shook Alisa's hand.

"I can tell you've been thinking about what you were going to say when we met. That is quite mature of you. Come over here, my assistant marine biologist." Alisa hugged Blaze.

"O.K., Blaze, that's good, good enough." She tapped him on his back as Blaze remained holding on tight. "All right now, time for us to break."

"Professor Maxwell, it is nice to see you again."

"I have missed you, Patti, so much," said Max as he slowly gathered her up into his arms. Once he released her, she returned the sentiment with a bear hug of her own. "How has life been for you and Blaze?"

"I've had the fertility clinic work with greater than a 71 percent overall pregnancy rate. Blaze has blazed through school. He definitely missed your male mentor presence," smiled Patti.

Max hugged both women together. "Let us all go over to the Dinosaur Crocodilles Hominid exhibit."

They walked in pairs. Blaze, acting as a mature eleven-year-old, imagined how a man would behave with as a woman's escort. Patti and Max made small talk. The four passed under a gilded archway announcing the "Land of the Prehistoric Matanzas Dinosaur Aquatic Arena." This circus atmosphere was brought on by signage, moving reptiles in evolutionary stages, Hollywood style sound effects and underwater lion roars, gurgling and bubbling sounds from multiple speakers.

"Wow, this is great! It excites me," Blaze yelled out and ran to one of the animated standing crocodiles with forward groping hands. Alisa followed. The animations changed from crawling to forward leg raised position to a standing creature.

"These animated amphibians, reptiles and dinosaurs have several anatomical errors," noted Max. "The Marinescape designers never consulted me about what you see or hear at this exhibit."

The open-air aquarium was completely surrounded by five people thick.

"Oh Max, is there a live animal in that pool?" sadly asked Patti.

Max nodded.

"Who is that man standing over there with a side arm?"

"There are two armed security guards, one up here and one at the lower viewing area. "Actually, they both have a handgun and Taser set at nonlethal defense tool."

"Don't you think this water cage is excessively cruel to the animal?"

"I do feel it is cruel, but the reptile is not under my or the Aquatic Park's control. Yao is a prisoner of the county for several alleged murders. Sheriff Gary, under my recommendation, has Yao confined here within these thick concrete walls and if needed, this covering metal net, which could be electrified," an unhappy Max explained.

Blaze came back with Alisa in hand.

"Can we get closer to Yao, Max?"

"We will get close once the park is closed," said Max.

Patti stood next to Blaze. Alisa slightly smiled at Patti.

"The park closes at dusk, but Professor Maxwell told me the powers that be are probably going to install above ground lighting to extend visitor hours," stated Alisa.

"It will be terrible for Yao if they do install underwater lighting around its confinement aquarium," Max stated. "That would definitely contribute to mental stress and confusion. Add disruption of the reptile's circadian rhythm and metabolism, all these factors would lead to irritability, resistance to instruction and unprovoked violence."

"Can we go eat?" asked Blaze, bright-eyed.

The other three all laughed and agreed.

Later that day, the swarming people throughout Marinescape, Dolphin Family Fun and The Prehistoric Matanzas Dinosaur exhibit scurried off like ants into their holes. There was only one security guard left once the visitors left the exhibit.

"This was another record day for this exhibit, Professor," remarked Alisa. "This is according to Director Wells, who I'm sure is stalking me, his 'Missy.'"

The foursome walked up to the open-air aquarium and immediately saw Yao hanging on the net closest to where they all stood. Blaze pulled out a partially eaten cinnamon roll from his pocket. "Is it O.K. for Yao to eat this, Max?"

"Yes, Yao will eat sweets and most human food."

Blaze placed the roll on the inside edge of the pool.

"Wow, what happened? I never saw Yao take it," giggled Blaze.

"Beyond Yao's super hypersensitive senses, it has frightfully fast reflexes. Not the typical awkwardly slow stalking as shown in the monster movies." as the three watched, Blaze slowly walked, stooped over, with sideways extended crooked arms and hands.

"Exactly, Blaze," laughed Max and the others.

"Eaa ... Yaa ... Eio, Yaa?' came the sounds from Yao.

"I think Yao wants more," responded Alisa.

"Yoo ... sorry, Yao," said Blaze.

"How are you able to communicate with it ... Yao?" a surprised Patti asked.

"Mom, do you remember when you and Max sat alone in the multiple ceiling room? That's when Alisa and I first saw Yao. It gave us its name and a few words within minutes," explained Blaze, mimicking the professor's phraseology and stance.

"I was very impressed, since I had no idea Yao spoke," Max smiled back at Blaze.

"Does Yao only speak in vowels?"

"Mom, that's all we know—"

"And have heard from Yao," interrupted Alisa.

"I'm sorry for Yao; he has no friends. I'm sure Yao would really like to see Speedy."

"Yaa, Yaa, Yaa," voiced Yao.

"Does Yao understand everything we say?" suspiciously asked Patti. "Must it be confined and treated like this?"

"Unfortunately, there is not much I can do about Yao's present situation. Yao is a prisoner of Sheriff Gary, the St. Johns County and the

Law Enforcement Agency of Florida. It is unknown how long they will keep Yao ... alive," answered Max.

"Hey, where's Yao?" Blaze yelled out.

"Oh, that is how Yao acts when it is mad." Max placed a hand on Blaze's shoulder.

"Can we go downstairs?"

The four looked through two portholes. Yao was at the opposite wall of the aquarium. They moved around to the next portholes and the next. Yao kept moving to the farthest point away from them.

"The typical response of a child," commented Professor Maxwell.

Patti looked to Blaze. Max looked to Alisa.

The four split up at the park entrance, Patti and Blaze heading to their car. Alisa and Max waved.

"Max ... Max, we have to do something about Yao's situation," pleaded Alisa while clinging to Max's side.

# Chapter 51

## *Nemesis*

**They both sat** with their feet on the sheriff's desk, facing each other. They both had their right hand on their hip holsters.

"You're up, Deputy Sheriff Keith."

During a long stare down, neither man moved.

"Ding," went the large black badge on the deputy's chest.

"Got yea, that's seven for me, zero for you." Gary looked to a tally display box on his desk.

"Are we done, sir?" complained Keith.

"Oh, you're no fun. Well, shoot until one of us reaches ten."

"I'll surrender to you now."

"Good morning, guys. Why is Deputy Keith surrendering?" asked Dispatcher Mary Jane.

"Oh, I was just giving Sheriff Gary the lead so he'd play," said Keith as he pulled out his Laser Tag gun. "Ding! That's one point for me," Keith said as he smiled at Mary Jane, who was dressed in a tight blue pinstriped blouse and above-the-knee wrap around dark blue skirt.

Gary pulled his gun and sho, "Eight to one."

Keith responded with a rapid fire, "Two, three, and four."

Gary ended the competition with, "Nine and ten. That's it, ten to four."

"Well, gentlemen, this is quite mature, making the law enforcement agency proud," said Mary Jane with her hands on her hips. She made two consecutive hip shifts as she waited.

"Actually, there are 'walk through' shooting competitions at police training grounds with moving friend and foe targets. One uses live, deadly fire," dramatically presented Deputy Keith.

"All right then, I'll leave you to your police business." She turned around slowly, performing a Marilyn Monroe hip waddle away from them. At the doorway, she swiveled her head part way back to see if they were watching. They were.

"Marilyn Monroe's waddle was unnatural," spontaneously spouted Deputy Keith.

Sheriff Gary waited for the cinephile to spread his knowledge. On the other hand, Gary had become a wordsmith of his own, using two Greek original words combined together, as the word above, called a portmanteau.

"Metro Goldwyn Mayer Studios decided to cut her heels unevenly to create a sexy walk as viewed from behind," Keith stated and then pounded his chest with closed fists.

"I do understand you a little better with the recognizable ape gesture," nodded Gary.

Both were sitting up in their swivel chairs and looking around the sheriff's office, which was an example of minimalism decor.

"You know, life has become quite boring without us tracking down the Matanzas Monster," complained Gary. "In fact, we haven't had any calls reporting suspected crime or complaints," added Keith. "No assaults, robberies, speeding, trespassing, vandalisms, not even a peeping tom. I miss seeing the CSI team out every day, even Director Leon's dry humor and Doc's trivia. Oh yeah, Tara and I had a hot streak going for a while," Keith remorsefully said. "Are the prosecutors moving on the monster's crimes?"

"Not that I know of, saying not enough evidence. They've deferred to Fish and Wildlife, Animal Control and such," said Gary, walking into the front office with Keith following. Keith bee-lined directly to the dispatcher's desk.

"From my still friendly law enforcement agency's gossip line," spoke Mary Jane in a quiet voice, "the county and state administers aren't moving for action, since both are getting a financial cut from Marinescape's 'Golden Goose' Matanzas Monster exhibit. Don't the county and state pay Marinescape for keeping the monster?"

"That is true, but Marinescape pays an entertainment tax to the county and state. Naturally, we get no credit from the upper brass for tracking down and capturing the thing alive."

During this time Deputy Keith was leaning over Mary Jane's shoulder, whispering.

"Any calls, Miss Dispatcher Mary Jane?" asked Sheriff Gary.

"Oh, yes, Miss MJ, any calls?" Keith reverberated.

"Just the same calls from neighbors up and down Oceanshore Boulevard about the mayhem from the massive amount of visitor traffic looking for parking around Marinescape," mentioned Mary Jane.

"Deputy Sheriff Keith, call Officer Brett and Patrolman Brenner and have them accompany you to monitor and control the A1A situation. At least the neighborhoods will see your presence," the tired Sheriff Gary slowly spoke. "Mary Jane, please call the towing companies to be on alert.

*** 

**Because A1A** was congested north and south of Marinescape, the local residents had petitioned the Florida Highway Commission for a traffic light at the Marinescape parking lot entrance. They also petitioned the FAC, Federal Aviation Commission, to allow amphibian aircraft to have a secure landing at the bays by the Willy-Marine Laboratory and the University of Florida annex facilities, both in the town of Marinescape. It was a bay off the Matanzas River-Intracostal Waterway. That would involve the US Army Corps of Engineers' input.

The sheriff and the rest of the law enforcement team left in separate vehicles. As they approached the road cluster, which looked like a beehive, Gary pulled over and his caravan followed.

"What should we do now about this myriad mess of cars on both sides of A1A as far as our eyes can 'sea'?" asked Keith. "We could just start ticketing every illegally parked vehicle. We would make a lot of money for the county. We'd set a County record. We'd be heroes."

"Any other ideas?" asked Sheriff Gary.

"We could ticket only those vehicles obstructing flow of normal A1A traffic?" volunteered Officer Brett.

"We could give warning parking tickets with future tickets and tow away?" opted Patrolman John Brenner.

"What a waste of time and paper," criticized Keith.

"O.K., this is what we'll do today. Any obstructive vehicles to safe traffic flow, you will ticket on the spot," explained Gary. "Do we have any 'NO Parking' yellow tape?"

"No, but we do have 'DO NOT CROSS Police Crime Scene' tape," stated Deputy Keith.

"Get the tape and stakes and post them. North of the Marinescape park entrance, we'll post it on the northbound side of A1A, the same south of the Marinescape entrance, on the southbound side," continued Sheriff Gary. "Have Mary Jane put in an emergency order for 'NO Parking' tape or signs. She should also get an emergency order from the highway commission for an automated traffic light for the Marinescape entrance off A1A."

"Patrolman Brenner, that will be your duty. Post the yellow tape we have today and replace the tape when the order comes in," commanded the deputy.

The team started down A1A. Sheriff Gary drove up to the park's walking visitor entrance and parked in a posted 'NO Parking' area. "May I speak with the day manager on site?"

"Sheriff, how may I help you today?"

"I'm here to give you fair warning that as of tomorrow, the Sheriff's Department will be ticketing illegally parked vehicles. Those vehicles that actually obstruct safe traffic flow will be towed away. I suggest that the Marinescape authorities open the park's properties for additional parking spaces for your patrons."

"Thank you so much, Sheriff, for the heads up."

The next day, Deputy Keith sat on the corner of Dispatcher Mary Jane's desk. "Good morning, good looking. Do you have the tally of today's issuing of tickets, MJ?" he asked with a wink. "I did summarize the tickets issued, as the sheriff asked for," she said while she waded through a pile of papers on her desk. "The listing is by total numbers per officer. The most tickets were issued by Deputy Sheriff Keith, at 114."

"Yes!" Keith did a closed fist pull down pump. "Oh, sorry, please continue MJ."

"Officer Brett issued five tickets. Patrolman John Brenner issued four and Sheriff Gary issued one ticket, which will be voided if they present their vehicle registration at the County courthouse within ten days; otherwise, a fine of fifteen dollars will be issued."

"I don't want to be critical of the sheriff, but the fifteen dollars won't even cover the cost of the registrar's time, paperwork and the filing of the ticket," Deputy Keith plainly stated.

Mary Jane looked up at Keith with disapproving eyes but no verbal comment.

"Oh MJ, let's move on. How would you like to go out to dinner tonight with the department's winner? I'll pay," he offered as he winked twice.

"Oh, gee whiz, I have a double shift today and night."

Just then Tara came up to Mary Jane's desk. "Is the sheriff in?"

"You can go right in, Tara."

Deputy Keith immediately jumped off MJ's desk and followed Tara.

"Hey, Miss Beautiful, wait up for your date for tonight. Did you hear the latest big news?"

"Sheriff, I just received a text from one of the security guards watching your prisoner at Marinescape," said Tara as she looked back over her shoulder at Keith. He stood directly behind her as she bent forward over Gary's desk. "I'll read it to you." She moved to the side of Gary's desk and stood upright. "He wrote that he heard Professor Maxwell and his crony, Alisa, talking. The professor said to her that the monster was a long-term friend of his."

With a startling and thunderous awakening of the office, the sheriff stood up and slammed his hands on his desk.

"I knew all along that the titled bastard was lying to me. I will nail his ass right into prison and execute that murderous Matanzas Monster!" angrily shouted Gary.

"Wait, Sheriff, it gets better," Tara smiled.

"The professor and Alisa were heard talking about some plan to free the monster."

Sheriff Gary was truly conflicted. A few months ago, he was the center of attention in the media—locally, statewide and sometimes nationwide. Gary also had the attention of the State of Florida Law Enforcement Agency. In both arenas, the daily attention might fluctuate from him being thought of as a brilliant Sherlock Holmes-like figure or a clownish buffoon character. He had to admit, at least to himself, that he enjoyed being in the limelight—the same limelight he ran away from twelve years ago in Jacksonville to end up in small town Florida. Yet the monster's escape defiantly would bring back his internal and external 24/7 strife.

"Well, Sheriff, how shall we proceed?"

"In good conscience, I'll ask for more security guard surveillance."

Deputy Sheriff Keith and CSI Assistant Tara glanced at each other, wondering why the sheriff had said 'in good conscience.' Every great societal hero needs an irrefutable evil nemesis.

# Chapter 52

## Rights

**While the three sat** in the sheriff's office, more than a Marinescape parking problem was brewing.

Dispatcher Mary Jane interrupted the collection of three silent contemplators. "Sheriff, am I interrupting something important?" The three reflexively shook their heads

"The day manager of Marinescape called complaining of some kind of demonstration or sit-in at the park's entrance. He's fearful of violence breaking out."

"Did he say how many people were suspected of being involved?"

"No, he did not, sir. However, I did hear dogs barking in the background."

"It feels like a screenplay for a Western to me," Gary said as he stood and placed a hand on his hip holstered firearm and his other hand on his Taser. "The sheriff rides into town to foil the disrupters of the peace. Mount up, giddyup and let's ride on, my posse. We are going to restore and preserve the public peace." Gary waved the team onward. "Tara, let Director Leon know we're going. Ask him if he's interested in joining us."

When the three law enforcement vehicles tried to enter Marinescape's parking lot, they met cars in utter confusion trying to enter and leave and being blocked in by sign-holding demonstrators.

Sheriff Gary had not forgotten his media connection and notified R.W. Angel of the Palatka Newspaper about a developing story. Even though he'd been nominated for the one-hundred-year-old Pulitzer Prize, Mr. Angel still would do daily and local stories for the paper.

Sheriff Gary turned on his light rollers and siren, but nothing changed. The other vehicles following did the same. Gary was thinking he might have more of an effect by getting out of his Ford Expedition, but he wisely waited. The demonstrators' banners slowly opened like the biblical Red Sea. As the three police vehicles crept along screeching with flashing lights, Gary read the banners, written in blood red, green, brown and feathered black letters like fur. Several signs had symbols of crossbones, poison emblems and circles with lines through them.

"Animals have Rights," "Sin & Crime," "Be Humane to Animals," "Animals are Our Friends," "No Animal Experimentation," "Stop Animal Cruelty," "Friends Not Skins," "No Hides, No Furs," "Neglect is Animal Cruelty," "American Humane Society" and "Rights For Animals" were all slogans being displayed on signs and T-shirt-wearing demonstrators.

"I'm so relieved you're here," said the three-pieced-suited Mr. Wells of Marinescape. He was leaning over and acting exhausted. "I didn't expect this kind of stress when I took this job."

"Yes, sir, I understand your situation," Sheriff Gary tried to calm the manager. "My team and I will start by asking the demonstrators to exit your private property. If necessary, we will proceed to arrest the most violent and resistant demonstrators."

"Has there been any vandalism of the park property?" Deputy Keith asked.

"Have there been any personal threats toward you or any of the personnel?" asked Brett.

"Have any demonstrators touched or put you in a position where you feared for your safety or life?" asked Patrolman Brenner of Mr. Wells and several Marinescape employees who had gathered around the officers.

After all the questions were answered, Sheriff Gary said, "Let's get to it."

Additional officers had arrived from St. Augustine, Palm Valley, Hastings, Flagler Beach, Palm Coast of Flagler County and as far away as Putnam County's East Palatka, Crescent City, Melrose and Lake Como.

Dispatcher Mary Jane had sent a call for additional manpower to control a "massive" demonstration at Marinescape as ordered by Sheriff Gary once he arrived.

"Sheriff Gary, how are you doing?" Mary Jane called out. "I also sent out your manifest of orders for the officers who were able to respond."

"The situation is seemingly getting under control with minimal violence and no arrests.

"I was asking about your stress level, Sheriff. Your situational stress there may be relieved by coming to the office. I'll be ready if you need anything, sir, anything at all from me,"

"I'll keep that in mind."

"The response for assistance is phenomenal," Tara called back to Mary Jane. "Sheriff Gary is proving himself to be a ringmaster of this circus."

By early afternoon, over four thousand demonstrators had collected, as estimated by helicopter computer photo counting. About fifty officers had trickled in to help. They slowly moved the unwanted and vocal visitors off the premises. Of course, this resulted in masses of people on local beaches and lining Ocean Boulevard.

"Our next priority is to re-establish safe and normal traffic flow on State Road A1A," the sheriff announced on the police frequency band. This main artery of the East Coast north-south travel had been detoured to Federal Highway 1 since earlier that morning for an unknown duration. (Foot note U.S. Highway 1)

"No warning tickets today," exclaimed Deputy Keith. "I see the tow truck services have lined up for action."

Over a portable public address system, Gary announced sternly, "All vehicles blocking the Marinescape entrance or blocking A1A traffic will be towed away. I repeat, all blocking vehicles will be towed away under St. Johns County and State of Florida law ordinances. Any individual or group of individuals obstructing any visitor entry to the private Marinescape premises will be arrested. I ask all people for their cooperation."

Once police presence decreased, demonstrators slowly oozed back to Marinescape's parking lot periphery. By next morning, the parking lot had refilled with a demonstrator sit-in.

***

**From one** of Professor Maxwell's favorite office viewing areas on the second story of the administration wing of Marinescape, he and Alisa watched the demonstrators' confusion and disruption of daily Marinescape activities. Alisa pulled in tight to Max like a barnacle on a ship's underside hull.

"Is this a good time?" asked Alisa, looking up to Max's thoughtful face.

"You are absolutely correct," he replied. "During all this distraction, this would be the perfect time to break out Yao."

Alisa released Max like a sucking leach burned with a cigarette. Yet Max didn't release one of her hands. With an allemande turn of their bodies, as in the common German dance or American square dancing, Max kept them together.

"Oh yes, my dear," Max reeled her back to his side like in a Scottish country dance move. This brought them face to face to French kiss each other deeply until gasping for air. They appreciated their international courting moves. The couple's passion led to them using the entire conference room arena as if they were in a skating, gymnastic or dance competition. They exaggerated their moves as if at the Olympics. From a table top to the overstuffed chair, the couch, the wall side chair rail and ending with a fused body roll under a mid-room table.

"You know ... you know how to take a girl around the world, Max."

"We took each other on that pleasurable Love Boat fantasy," he whispered in her ear, sealed with a slobbering lick. "You are my goddess Aphrodite."

"How can you compare me to a mythical Greek goddess? You are an adorable big fool?" Alisa whispered back. "And I mean not too big, just right for me."

"You have the perfect Grecian head sphere and face." Max took her head gently between his hands. "Your most striking goddess feature is the Aphrodite-like cheek folds."

"I'm sorry," she said as she sat up. "You're saying what?"

"You are beautifully symmetrical and alluring folds from your upper check bones to the outer corners of your moist and succulent soft, full-lip trimmed mouth."

Alisa stared at Max and snorted through her nose. "Is that an attractive goddess trait?"

"That reminds me of your aquatic dolphin-like part … it completes you. You are my goddess of sensual love and desire with your Grecian face and sweaty body, my Eros of love and the Roman Cupid of desire," Max orated as Alisa buried her head into his chest and lower. "You are the true embodiment of the emotional confusion brought on by love and its mystical beginnings."

"May we stay like this, melted into one, forever?" Alisa mumbled and gasped for air.

The couple's dream state was broken by boisterous yelling from outside.

Their simmering, sweaty bodies peeked out the room's front window to see and hear the demonstrators back in full force at the park's visitor entrance, chanting in harmony.

"Today I feel sorry for Sheriff Gary, though he doesn't like or respect me," said Max.

Alisa nodded in agreement. "TV cameras have a way of clarifying or stirring up the haziness of confusion into riotous actions and spewing hatred. Hey, let's go down to the cafeteria for a bite, like a dolphin sandwich … dolphin the fish." Alisa swirled her tongue around her mouth and swallowed. She jumped up and bounced her free hanging parts. She even bounced as she dressed with a multitude of dance steps.

"Your doggie is at your beckoning, my lady."

The demonstrators, vocal protestors and a few spectators re-collected over the next few days. The mixing of animal rights activists, the members of the Animal Liberation Front (ALF), and the Anti-Vivisection Coalition (AVC) had all gathered at Marinescape. Each group felt they had something special and different to offer as they wrestled for frontline breaking news and live TV coverage.

Patti and Blaze arrived on the second day of perturbation. The two threaded their path back and forth between tightly held together and repetitive banners and T-shirts. Patti and Blaze stayed close to each other.

"I see Alisa and Max!" Blaze started pulling his mom. "Alisa, we found you," he exclaimed as he hugged her. "Are you guys going to help Yao out of this mess and get it free again?"

"It's hard to know if Yao's ultimate fate is affected more by its caged environment or the self-interest of protestors. What is more harmful for the reptile?" Patti asked.

Max motioned the three to follow him rather than to try to call out over the hostile-sounding chants. He found an unused second floor tour group gathering-administration room.

"This looks familiar," grinned Alisa.

***

**Riding south** from Jacksonville Airport, a group of men and women listened to the megaphone-holding speaker at the front of the unmarked bus.

"Your purpose today and probably for the next several days is to add to, disrupt, confuse and frustrate the animal people, Marinescape employees, law enforcement and to make a media spectacle. There will be bonus money for those who actually get on TV, any questions?"

A few hands went up and were answered.

"Yes, you will be paid $100 dollars each twelve-hour day, with cash or American Express cash cards. You may do as many twelve-hour shifts you like."

"What are the tactics to use?" yelled out one of the T-shirt wearing, sign-carrying demonstrators. "Push tightly-packed people forward and look backward and call out 'Don't push!' You'll carry easily-breakable and twist-tied balloons of animal urine or blood. Throw them forward into the crowd, on the sides of buildings with Marinescape advertising posters or Marinescape employees trying to speak to the crowd. Even better would be a turned-away policeman, but just don't get caught. Also, if you're by a demonstrator handing out paper flyers, bump into them so they drop and litter the area. Every little bit adds to the chaos we're trying to create."

The bus driver saw the line of cars and informed the speaker. "As you leave the bus, you'll pick up your balloons. We'll be letting off a few people about a quarter of a mile from the Marinescape entrance, a few more of you at the entrance and the last group of people past the park. This maneuver will ensure an adequate separation of your arrivals. It's a beautiful day, so have fun and be mean."

***

**After each expressed** their concerns for Yao, no actual solution was agreed upon by the four. Blaze ran to the window to watch the pandemonium.

"I have an unusual and very bizarre proposal for you two women," Professor Maxwell said as he scanned between their surprised faces. He cleared his throat and held Alisa's and Patti's hands.

"Yao, unfortunately, in following his primal, genetically controlled instinct to reproduce, did commit attempted rape with the inadvertent death of three innocent young women."

The two women turned toward each other in shock.

"Despicable, disgusting, deplorable, disgraceful, awful, unacceptable, unforgiveable, wretched, vile —" Patti and Alisa volleyed the words back and forth.

"As I may want to help Yao to bolt to freedom, nothing has changed. It will repeat its actions until recaptured or put down by the police or a bounty hunter."

"So what the hell do you want from us?" Patti angrily asked.

"The small upside to this once-in-a-billion chance of evolutionary creation—the 300,000,000 years of natural selection piece of work—is Yao, among other things, is able to sense one of its own."

"I don't get it. Where are you going with this?" asked Alisa, who was just as mad as Patti.

"So if Yao had an offspring, it would most likely be satisfied," softly spoke Max.

"Most likely, that's not enough reassurance! Still unacceptable," stated the two women.

"I'm giving my very best assessment for a never before encountered situation in an already unbelievable occurrence in nature and the history of humankind," the professor explained.

"So just come out with it," an irritated Patti bellowed.

"Before the two of you get up and walk out, please … please hear my entire proposal."

They both sat with crossed legs and arms and pursed lips of disgust.

"All right, here I go." He took a deep breath. "We would obtain several sperm specimens from Yao, which I will explain later. I have already started Yao's treatment for a known salmonella infection. It is easily treated with a high dose oral ciprofloxacin. An adult human's high dose is 750 mg. thrice a day. Taking into account Yao's seven-and-a-half-foot height and five-to-six-hundred pounds in weight, I'm giving him 1500 mg. thrice a day in his food. The loading dose was 3,000 mg. Its semen specimens will prove this infection has been eradicated. I also will test and culture for other unpredicted bacteria and conduct blood tests for human sexually transmitted diseases or STDs." The Professor was happy they were still present and listening.

Patti glared at Professor Max. "I know where you're going with this," she snarled.

"How do you draw blood on such a large animal as Yao?" Alisa asked thoughtfully. "Better yet, how do you expect to get sperm from Yao?"

"I'll explain all that after I have completed my proposal for the two of you."

Blaze came back from the window. "I get all the sign waving and yelling outside. They want to help Yao have its rights protected. Yao does have rights, right?" Blaze asked.

"Blaze, the question is and what all the fuss is about." Patti got up and went over to him. "Do animals have the same rights as we do? Do they have any rights?"

Max got up and proceeded to the window and looked out for a while. The other three watched him walk around the room, tracking along the perimeter like a caged animal, until he came back to the table and chairs. He pointed to the chairs with an open hand. Blaze shrugged his shoulders. "Whatever," he said as he went back to the window.

The cast of three were seated again.

"To get to the point, I would like you, Patti, to use a washed, sterile and concentrated Yao's sperm specimen for intrauterine insemination, IUI." Max then turned to Alisa. "And inseminate you, Alisa, to hopefully carry Yao's offspring."

The room became the imagined silence of outer space. Patti stood, knocking her chair over.

"Blaze, we are going home, now!" Without looking at Max or Alisa, they left without a word, slamming the office door behind them.

Alisa sat in shock, seemingly not breathing and staring but not seeing. Max moved to sit next to her. He slowly caressed her cold, limp hand. They sat lifeless for what seemed to be an eternity.

"Was this your plan all along? I'm thought of only as your reptile whore? You'll never know how deeply you cut open my heart and soul, throwing them away." Alisa stood up slowly. "I quit. You are dead to me." She made her exit from the room, Marinescape and Max's life.

***

**Max** brought a folding beach chair and sat next to the netted pool. He watched Yao swim near the surface back and forth, occasionally stopping in front of him. He reviewed his life and his goals. He noticed the two security guards were nowhere to be found, so he decided to confide in Yao.

"I took my fairy tale perfect life and shit all over it. My earth-shattering discoveries and potential Nobel Prize in three categories: medicine, chemistry and a new category of genetics, now mean nothing without Alisa. All my knowledge, reputation and degrees are of no solace to me now, since I dn't care about anything."

"Yaa, aee," came from a gurgling Yao. Max reiterated, "Yao's yes and no? Yao, you have been such an important part of my life. What do I do now? Oyo ... Oyo," it replied.

Max translated, "go ... go. I want to let Yao Oyo, but ..."

The exhibit had been closed to the public since the demonstrators came on the Marinescape campus. The admissions had dropped from a ten-time-high record-setting pace to one-tenth of normal and the worst attendance at Marinescape's history. The Dolphin Family Fun owners, in Georgia, also saw attendance suffer terribly. The Georgia people advised getting rid of the Matanzas Monster, which would rid the park of the protestors.

***

**As Max sat** there in a corner, he dozed off ... and snored.

"Max, Max, where are you?"

"I'm right here," he mumbled.

"I thought we were life partners. We fit together so well. Are we getting married?"

"Yes, I want ..."

"Max ..."

"Blaze loves, admires and looks up to you like a father, which I thought you would be."

"Yes, I could …"

"We thought you were the 'wunderkind' for Marinescape, for Marine Animal Aquatic World," smiled a man in a three-piece suit.

"Oh Mr. Maxwell, blah, blah, blah, blah … you're being arrested as an accessory to capital murder; you're looking at the end of your life," smiled Sheriff Gary as he started laughing.

"And for the first time in the Nobel Prize history, three awards are being presented to one individual … but wait, you did what?"

"It's all so dark. I'm falling, help!" Max fell out of his folding beach chair and landed on cold, hard concrete. "Where am I? What the …?" He opened his eyes to see a clear, dark sky filled with sparkling stars. "Life is good. I will rectify my wrongs. I can correct my mistakes … and make amends."

# Chapter 53

## Quotable

**"As a protestor**, what do you hope to accomplish here?" asked Mr. Angel.

"Animals have rights, like us. I'm bringing this crime being committed here to the people's consciousness. Give us freedom!"

"Have you actually seen this Matanzas Monster?"

"No, but I feel I have a moral obligation to this animal. Stop animal cruelty!"

Other protesters gathered around Mr. Angel, shouting "Stop animal cruelty! Stop animal cruelty! Stop animal cruelty!" R.W. Angel was forced to give way to more protesters as he was supplanted by a TV crew moving next to him. Once Mr. R.W. Angel was free, he approached a young woman wearing a T-shirt which read "Would you wear a human foot for good luck?"

"Why are you here today?"

"I want the masses to be remorseful for how animals have been tortured and killed. We need to cut off the money mongers. Let's cut their skin off and wear it like a fur, a belt, a shoe, a hat, a key chain. Stick it to the Man!"

Again the protestors gathered around Mr. Angel. "Stop animal torture! Free all caged animals! No more experimentation, Liberation is the only way! Animals are all God's creatures! Animals feel pain! End animal barbarism!"

Angel looked behind him and saw why the protesters had flocked to him. It was again live TV coverage. Everyone wants to be on TV.

Angel had made it to the park's visitor entrance; he turned back to take in the turbulent, angry sea of people. He met a Marinescape security guard. Angel showed him his press pass.

"Can you find a Marinescape spokesperson to give a comment?"

While he waited, an aqua-colored muumuu Hawaiian dressed woman with pigtails came forward. She apparently wanted to cover her large abdomen.

"Hi, I'm Wendy. I'm carrying the monster's baby." She proudly smiled and held both hands under her swollen abdomen.

"Wow. Tell my readers how this happened to you." He offered her a hand to sit on a nearby low wall. "What's your full name?"

"I'm Wilma Wyanetta Williamson. People call me Wendy, O.K.?" Sam nodded. "I was walking along the river, the Matanzas River and I felt my backside becoming wet. I turned and saw a sad man, like alligator face."

"Were you not scared?"

"I had a warm rush of peacefulness come over me as his rough-skin hands gently grasped me at my waist and turned me to the rising sun."

"Did you resist?"

"Not initially. I don't know why I didn't." Wendy shrugged her shoulders and tilted her head to one side, which flipped both her black pigtails to the side. "He walked backward as he gripped me tighter and moved into the river. Then I did become panicked and stiffened my body."

"Did you think you were going to drown, Wendy?"

"Hell yes! I squirmed like when a hand grabs a bunny rabbit. He slightly relaxed his grip and slowly laid back into the river water. I heard sounds like 'Yaa, Yaa,' which became muffled gurgling.

"Did he tear your clothing off?"

"No need, since my short dress floated up and I had no underwear. He liked when my pigtails kept going back and forth in front of his face. He then gave a pitiful moan and started panting, like he was trying to get air."

"And then what?"

"He released me and submerged while I floated on the surface, feeling warm all over."

"You could breathe?"

"Oh yeah, no problem, most of my head was above the water, with my arms out and legs straight together forming a cross."

There was a moment of silence as she looked skyward, smiling.

"What are you thinking of?"

"The pleasure I felt as I lay supported in the water while my stretchable shorts and underwear slid down and—"

"I thought you said you were wearing a dress and no underwear?"

"Does it matter?" She seemed to zone out looking to the clear sky.

"What happened then, Wendy? Don't leave me … I mean, don't leave the readers hanging."

"A filling, fulfilling feeling in my female fuzzy area." Her right hand grabbed her groin. "I had an orgasm. Can I say that? I think It also had one, might have been only a few seconds, accompanied again with different singing of guttural moans, groans and a flow of repetitive vowels," exhaled Wendy loudly. "To me, it felt like hours of post orgasmic bliss."

"Excuse me, but you said before—"

"He then gave another pitiful vibrating moan."

"Really, does it matter?" Again she drifted off looking into the blue sky.

"Well, could you tell me how your encounter ended, Wendy?"

"He released me and sank away into the river. I floated a bit and had to swim a few feet until I realized I could walk. A car went by and honked its horn. I then realized my shorts were still at my knees. I corrected that quickly."

"I thought you said you wore no … How far along are you?"

"That's a funny thing. As best I can remember, I should be about nine, ten weeks at the most. But the doctor's exam and ultrasound says I'm twenty weeks." She looked to the ground.

"What's wrong, Miss Wendy?" R.W. Angel bent down to look at her teary eyes.

"The doctor said the ultrasound had some unusual findings. He didn't know what they were. He called U of Florida and made an appointment for me to be seen by a specialist, a perinatiest …just?"

"It was probably a Perinatologist, maternal-fetal medicine specialist."

Wendy looked up with a puzzled face.

"Specialists take care of you and your baby before and during the baby's delivery. That's a good thing," Angel said as Wendy smiled. "So when is the appointment? I'd like to be there with you."

"I can't really remember what date they told me," she answered with an unreadable face.

"Here's my card and personal number. Call me when you remember and I—"

"I have your card, thanks." Wendy got up with Angel's help and waddled away.

*She doesn't look or act as a woman who's first trimester pregnant. She sits with her legs wide-spread, she has trouble getting up and the abdomen already protrudes like a third trimester,* he thought.

***

**The day manager** appeared fifteen minutes after Wendy had submerged into the sea of people.

"Yes, Mr."—the manager read his chest press badge—"Mr. R.W. Angel. I'm Director Wallace Wren Wells of Marinescape. I have a few important statements to make."

Angel and Wells were joined by Sheriff Gary and Tara.

Gary acknowledged them. "I reviewed your situation, Mr. Wells, at Marinescape properties," said the sheriff. "There are several signage options:

No Loitering at Any Time.

Marinescape Patrons Only.

Violators to be Removed from Premises or Arrested.

No Littering Fine (amount$).

"Signs would be enforced by your security force. One more suggestion— have paid parking. All vehicles need a day parking pass," summed up the sheriff.

Manager Wells thought for a moment. "But then Marinescape is the 'bad guy,' as seen by the public and probably the media."

Gary tapped Tara on her shoulder. "Let's go."

"Sheriff Gary, why is law enforcement taking on all this chaos?" Tara asked.

"We're here at the request of Marinescape officials to ensure the public's safety, maintain order along Oceanshore Boulevard, as it abuts Marinescape properties and ticket or arrest individuals in any act of violence toward persons or public or private property.

"For updates on the monster's status, you should call the Sheriff Department's office in Jacksonville. For Marinescape protestor status, call my office, Mr. Angel." Gary blended into a slightly parting sea of people.

"And you would be?"

"Tara, Crime Scene Investigation's Assistant to St. Johns County Law Enforcement Agency, at your and the public's service." She extended her hand. "You must be Mr. Angel, Pulitzer Prize winner from the Palatka newspaper?"

"Yes, I am R.W. Angel from the *Palatka National & Local News*. No, I haven't won the Pulitzer Prize, at least not yet. I've just been nominated. I hope you don't mind me asking, but would you like to go sit at the South Beach Grill? I haven't eaten all day." He gave her a friendly grin.

Tara studied his face for a hidden agenda. "Sure. You do realize I'll only be able to tell you what is on public record, as I'm sure the sheriff already told you."

"Great and I completely understand."

They arrived in separate cars. Idle conversation occurred until they were seated.

"Do you like their fish dip, Tara? O.K., we'll start with that, diet soda, and unsweetened ice tea, thanks. So Tara, tell me what you know about the Matanzas Monster's future, according to Sheriff Gary. Since the sheriff captured it, I'm assuming he will be controlling its fate."

"The sheriff has instructed us about what we can speak about, so I'll start with your assumption, which is incorrect. Sheriff Gary and the Chief of St. Johns County Law Enforcement Agency are not the animal's controllers."

"May I record our conversation?"

"Sure. The ultimate decision of life or death for the monster is given to the Chief of the Florida State Police.

"Tara, do you remember when I did the Weekly Feature Magazine for the paper on 'Yao, the Matanzas Monster? May I use the monster's name, Yao? The amazing millions-of-years-old dinosaur: it is trainable. It will respond to common visual and spoken commands and most fantastical (he paused for effect) it is able to communicate back with vowel-based words!"

"So the feature was written to help you secure the Pulitzer?"

"No, it was to build a popular movement for saving this truly remarkable ancient creature."

"So you caused the Marinescape demonstrations?"

"Again no, these animal rights organizations were already planning to come before the feature hit the presses."

Tara just sat there and acknowledged him with one head bob.

"I'm doing my job and what I'm good at, just like you're doing your job, which you do very well, exceedingly, remarkably, exquisitely well," the reporter spoke confidently to her face.

Tara's face slowly became one large smile.

"May we two professionals get back on track and discuss Yao's fate of life or death?"

"Would you like to order a meal?" asked the gum-chewing waitress with pinned-back black hair and a pencil behind her ear.

Tara looked at the laminated menu. "I'll have the fresh baby spinach salad with shrimp."

"Grilled or blackened? Grilled it will be. And you, sir?"

"I'll parlay the pasta salad with grilled chicken. If it's good, I'll have a dessert to follow."

The waitress stopped writing and shook her head. "So you want me to stake an order for pasta salad topped with grilled chicken which may win me an opportunity and privilege to order you a later prepared dessert, sir?"

Angel smiled at the wise-ass waiting waitress. "That is quite impressive, ma'am."

"It comes from years at the dog track, sir." She left with her own smile.

"You are quite interesting, for a man," said the still smiling Tara. "I'm going to need to investigate you, just on principle. I have my ways of finding out what you're hiding. I have years of experience handling bodies, probing for their secrets."

"I like the probing part. I have years of experience with law enforcement. I know it's best to not resist their probing and be right up front and out with what I got and want." Angel's eyebrows went up. "I really, really want to continue this social intercourse later, in a more private atmosphere, but sadly, for now, may we return to the life-or-death question?"

Tara looked around to see if anyone was listening to their conversation. "The State Police want to just euthanize the creature. But a public relations person brought it to the governor's attention that this 'issue' is politically a hot potato that could affect emotionally-charged voters. The governor is now interested. Behind the scenes are the closed-mouthed FBI and invisible CIA."

"Oh man, this is so hot, it's going to burn the readers' hands, power surge the radio to silence and make TV screens become black!" He nodded and licked his lips.

Tara saw his watering mouth. "Save that saliva for later." Both had a short giggle.

"I would walk very, very lightly, Mr. Angel," Tara said, looking around again. "The FBI is interested because of the three capital murder case investigations. The CIA is interested in the professor and his South American, Brazilian connection to Yao. Did the professor bring this reptile illegally into the country? The FBI somehow knows about the professor's possible illegal genetic engineering on animals. They may keep the CIA up to date on some issues. That collaboration between the two agencies seems mythical to me, knowing their rocky history together. Remember, the CIA is always thinking about using something for black ops."

Tara saw a blonde woman leave her solo table and stand next to theirs."May I sit down?" Alisa asked. "Working at the Marinescape and Marine Animal Aquatic World, I've developed my brain's ability to separate sounds. My ears perked up when you mentioned the professor, Professor Rory Maxwell and that woke me from my dumfounded depressive mood."

"I thought the two of you—"

I quit my relationship with the cold-blooded fish Maxwell. I quit my job there, severed all ties with anyone at Marinescape," she said as her eyes misted up.

Tara offered her a paper napkin. As Alisa dabbed her eyes, she started asking them questions. "Mr. Angel, how about giving me a newspaper reporter's summary concerning Max and Yao? I can take it."

"Professor Maxwell is on the verge of being prosecuted by the State of Florida and/or the FBI and the invisible CIA for his assumed actions.

Yao's fate is rocking on the fence between being forever caged, but not at the complaining Marinescape or executed by electrocution, a gunshot to the head or lethal injection with a Ketamine cocktail of high dose insulin, high dose narcotic or potassium chloride—maybe all of them, considering Yao's size, weight and reptilian-dinosaur origin."

"That was quite concise and shocking." Tara took in a deep breath and slowly exhaled.

Alisa said nothing but looked out into the ocean.

"I didn't get to tell the two of you that I met a pregnant woman at the Marinescape protest. She claims Yao is the father."

"And you believed her?" asked the surprised Tara.

"I'm no obstetrician, but she described a very detailed encounter with Yao. She claimed to be ten weeks. She directed my hand to feel her growing pregnancy. The womb was at her belly button. Isn't that five months? I felt violent and rapid movement."

Alisa got up and left without a word.

Tara thought for a moment. "Was it an earlier conception with a human boyfriend?"

"Well, I have to get to press," Reporter Angel relayed. "May I call you if dinner is an option?"

Tara grasped his hand as he stood by her. He opened his hand to see her card. He smiled.

"You know I'm all about following up hunches?" Angel said as he put it in his shirt pocket.

"If too much time passes, a hunch may dissipate into thin air," remarked Tara. She walked out into the parking lot and spotted Alisa sitting in her white and black convertible Beetle.

"Alisa, can I sit with you?"

No reply came as Tara opened the passenger door and plopped down next to Alisa.

"Is there something I can do for you?" Tara asked while Alisa watched the seagulls hover.

"You left before Mr. Angel made a ridiculous statement."

Alisa showed no interest.

"He said that she was pregnant, proclaimed Yao was the father. Can you believe that?"

Alisa started crying. "The professor wanted me to get pregnant with …" She struggled with the words could not cover her flow of wet emotions. "…by Yao!"

"I thought the two of you were a thing?"

"He wants me to get pregnant, but not with his … Please get out of my car, please."

Tara stood outside Alisa's car. "Here's my business card." Tara reached through the car window. "If you have the need to talk …."

Tara watched Alisa leave the restaurant's sandy parking lot and lay rubber as her car tires hit the pavement. Tara approached her own Ford SUV, where she saw a handsome man standing at a nearby vehicle. She sat down in hers.

"Tara?" She looked up as he appeared next to her car door. "What are the chances?" he smiled.

"Yuma, Yuma Manta?" responded a surprised Tara. "Here I am, as previously promised. I'm a perennial admirer, Tara." Yuma put a hand on the roof of the SUV. "How is your life without me?"

"Good, good, keeping busy," she answered.

"Are you O.K. with the imprisonment of el Lagarto or is it a she, la Lagartija?"

"It's a male named Yao. I do feel conflicted with the treatment of Yao, yet it's a serial rapist and killer," smartly answered Tara.

"I like how it's named after the giant pro basketball player," Yuma nodded. "I've seen its barbaric exhibit. Yao is contained in a bath covered by an enormous basketball hoop net, the irony."

*Um, that is a great metaphor or is it a simile?* Tara asked herself.

"We're going through a magical metamorphosis with this serendipitous meeting. Oh, I sense it, the collision of unearthly worlds. Take in the ether of outer space."

Tara waved her hands in front of her nose.

"Yes, I also sense the Great Spirit moving his hands above us to bring together two endlessly searching souls to be one." Yuma looked up with upwardly pointed hands. "I'm getting another feeling, that we should return to the South Beach Grill to refresh our auras."

Tara opened her car door.

"Wait, let me check my schedule. Let's go. It says I'm available 24/7 for CSI Assistant Investigator Tara, who saved my life."

They walked the short parking lot distance to the Grill.

"I didn't really save your life," Tara corrected him.

Yuma placed an arm around her shoulders and turned her into the offshore breeze. He watched her hair flare back with closed eyes and upturned face.

"Nature has a way of revitalizing us when we are in the right place with the right person," Yuma said as he also assumed her position.

# Chapter 54

---

## *Pressure*

**A day later**, Alisa phoned Tara.

"Sorry for calling. Have you or the sheriff seen or heard anything about the professor?"

"I don't know about Sheriff Gary, but I haven't seen or heard. All our department personnel are overwhelmed by animal rights protesters," complained Tara. "We're lucky the sheriff called for help and so many law enforcement officers responded."

The line was silent.

"Hello, Alisa, you still there?"

"I have a big favor, Tara?"

"Sure, name it."

"Could you, would you, call me with Yao's baby updates?" Alisa sniffled.

"Every OB doctor update I get from my sources, you're the first I'll call."

Later that same day at twilight, Doctor MacGrath received an urgent call from the dispatch.

"Doctor, Sheriff Gary called. He explained that an incident occurred in the Marinescape parking lot," anxiously relayed Mary Jane.

"Are the paramedics there?"

"They're on the way."

"And so am I."

"Sheriff, there's nothing we can do," the paramedic said as they cleaned up their supplies and left.

Deputy Sheriff Keith helped Officer Brett set up the yellow police "Crime Scene" tape. Tara slipped into her Arrowhead Proguard breathable hazard suit, then did the routine numbering, photographing, identifying of evidence, sealing, dating and signing the evidence bags. Patrolman John tried to control the gathering gawkers.

When Doc MacGrath arrived, he was aghast by all the blood on site. *Was it too much blood for one body?* Doc questioned himself. He knelt by a woman whose legs were sprawled wide apart. Her abdomen was split wide open up the middle to her mid-lower breastbone, the xyphoid process. Her naked body below her breasts was completely covered in blood. Between her legs was an indiscernible, ill-shaped mound of multicolored red, green and brown tissues.

"Are those organs and limbs in that mass of goo?" asked Sheriff Gary as the rest of the CSI team collected around to observe, got nauseated and some even threw up.

Director Leon squinted. "Did something move?"

"I saw it move, I think," gasped Officer Brett. "Yes, it was that brown scaly part."

"O.K., let's wrap up the body and separately scrape up the heterogeneous blob ... yes, like the movie," MacGrath crudely joked.

No one moved.

"It was only a joke, it's not really from outer space." Doc stood with his hands on his hips. "Or is it?"

Officer Brett stepped backward.

"She told me that she was ten weeks pregnant but felt more like twenty or more weeks," said a woman gawker. "She looked five months or more to me, especially since she claimed it was a very active baby. I saw her abdominal wall move like a turbulent ocean. I was afraid to touch her."

"Did anyone see what happened?" Deputy Keith asked the surrounding crowd. "Anyone, I know there are no TV cameras, as of yet, but I need the information now." He heard a man's voice. "Her name was Wendy. She yelled 'its coming' and squatted down. Green fluid sprayed out on her dress and ground like a fire hose. She yelled 'I can't take it… the pain … I can't' and laid out on the ground. I think she passed out or something."

"Thank you, sir," Deputy Keith said as he started to leave.

"I'm not done. Then she was surrounded and covered with bubbling red and green blood. A gurgling, then growling, followed by a horrible tearing sound came from under her dress as her legs split 180 degrees and then a loud pop and plop, maybe onto the ground. That's when her dress tore up the middle."

Ian thought back to the previous century and the horrible images of the crimes committed by Jack the Ripper.

Tara attempted to call Alisa several times but hung up. Then Tara's phone rang.

"Hello … yes, I tried to call you … well, I have sad news." Tara heard Alisa start crying.

"Would you rather meet? No. O.K., the supposed Yao's pregnant lady had a miscarriage and neither survived." There was more sobbing, coughing and mumbling about Professor Maxwell.

"Doctor Ian MacGrath will perform the autopsy … yes, lots of blood," Tara finished with Alisa hanging up on her.

Alisa had no trouble getting back into Marinescape without her security pass. Everyone recognized her and liked her for her hard work ethic, wanting to teach, lack of gossip and trustworthiness. Alisa greeted one and all as she perused the park. She was trying to decide if her next walk would be to the Yao exhibit or the research building. "The exhibit must be closer," she said, as if having a conversation with someone. She entered the once most popular animal exhibit, now deserted and closed by management mandate. As Alisa took in the sight of the pool, Yao became excited. It swam the entire length of the pool, back and forth, gurgling "Ah'isa, Ah'isa."

"Yao, you know my name!"

At the farthest end of the pool away from her, Alisa saw a bent over human form.

"Hello there, are you O.K.?" Alisa yelled as she quickly approached the form.

The person slowly waved a hand as if to signal "Go away."

When she was within several feet, she recognized a large unshaven face of the man in very wrinkled clothing.

"Oh my ... Jesus Christ, Professor, is that the once proud, confident man I knew, now shriveled, filthy, slumped over in a deformed way in a small beach chair?"

"Thanks for the kindly worded obituary. May I quote you? You shouldn't say the Lord's name in vain, young lady," said the now sitting up man.

"I was saying a little prayer for this wretched man before me. I can't believe that your appearance is ... so revolting to me, Professor."

"Maybe if you sang "Amazing Grace" I would magically appear as I once was?"

His hand before his face went partly skyward. "You see before you a man once living the perfect professional career, filled with accomplishments and with the perfect love life. Take this God-fearing man, in love with the Greek goddess Aphrodite, who loved this man with unimaginable fervor. Then slowly the man transformed to become a thoughtless, heartless, soulless cadaver. All this happening with one careless thought being spoken out in words, sending a grenade's exploding shrapnel into all his closely gathered loved ones."

Alisa helped the professor up and held the elbow of his bent over figure, as if he might fall. They settled on a large bench and watched a net-clinging Yao. Time passed with only thinking unknown thoughts between them and the mumbled partially unintelligible vowel-studded words from Yao. The one security guard passed them several times. Alisa broke the ice.

"Is there now only one security guard?"

"I guess they don't think of Yao as a threat anymore."

"Oh, the police are still very aware of Yao's threat risk and are considering its fate," Alisa relayed. "Actually, that's why I'm here."

"Can you ever, somewhere in my remaining life, ever—"

"I don't know, Max. You assaulted me with the most painful and deadliest of hits. It went deep into my loving heart and drained out all the love I had for you. All the compassion, understanding, caring and forgiveness I had for you."

"I've been visited by the hateful gods of the underworld … despair, fear and death," the teary-eyed professor pleaded to Alisa to reconsider their relationship.

"I can't, because my love history with you has been wiped clean from my brain. I only think of you as one of my thoughtless employers, boys and men in my lifetime."

Max got up and stood over the pool and the swimming Yao. "I have been very selfish. From my first hearing of the oral cultural tales of the Amazon River to finding, befriending, transporting, caring for, studying and using this mythical, fantastical and mind-stimulating creature, reptile, monster and finally, as named by you, Alisa, Yao," Max recalled.

"Now this trusting, hearing, seeing, thinking, speaking and bright-eyed animal has been betrayed, like you, Alisa, by this anthropological skinless, soulless, narcissistic, hollow, modern man, Homo sapiens, no, homo rudolfensis, homo erectus, farther back, homo neanderthalensis, homo habilis, Australopithecus, who evolved from Pan, the chimpanzee. There is where I belong as a monkey. Thank you, Mr. Scopes. Well, that was the reverse taxonomical lineage of humans and the despicable Rory Fergus Hamish Lachlan Maxwell the IV."

"While you wallow in your own self pity, Yao's life is on the line. The authorities are considering executing Yao. Also, I heard they may prosecute you as an accomplice to three capital murders and rape with Yao."

The professor's eyes jumped from Alisa's face to past the security guard to look to Yao clinging on to the overlying pool net.

"So I now feel the pressure … the urgent need. I must help Yao escape," Max mumbled.

Thoughtlessly, Max, emotionless and cruelly, said to Alisa, "Oh, before I forget, there was a woman who claimed to have Yao's baby. Unfortunately for her, she died during her miscarriage. Tara said Doctor MacGrath was going to perform the woman's autopsy and that of the blob of something she delivered." Maxwell turned to Alisa to hold her hands, but she stepped away.

"We already both know how selfish I am. Is there any way you could call Tara to get the autopsy results?"

"Yes, we do know how self-centered you are. You just can't stop using people." She turned and walked out of the exhibit.

300

"Will you, Alisa?" Max called after her.

"What do you think?" Alisa called back with a raised extended middle finger. She exited without losing a step.

*** 

**A cleaned up** and shaven Professor Maxwell showed up at the sheriff's office and asked Dispatcher Mary Jane if CSI Assistant Tara was in.

"I'll call into the lab for you, Professor Maxwell," Mary Jane widely smiled. She rose from her desk and leaned forward in her sleeveless, loose fitting V-neck blouse.

"May I give you something?" she asked as she blushed. "Something like water or coffee?" She held her position while trying to slip her heels on. "How about something to nibble on, like a donut?"

"I believe I can give you something," he offered as he knelt and slipped each of her shoes onto her hose-covered feet. Mary Jane stayed hovering over his head.

"I feel like Cinderella, waiting for—"

"Professor, was there something I could do for you?" Tara asked with both hands on her hips. "Unless I'm interrupting the two—

"Oh, no, thank you, Miss Mary Jane O'Corcrain, for calling Miss Tara Coltan."

She placed a hand on his shoulder to regain her stature. "No, Professor," Mary Jane said as she sat down behind her desk, "Thank you."

"Let's go into the sheriff's office, Professor Maxwell." Tara held a hand out and pointed the specific office. Tara followed him in and closed the door. She waved Professor Maxwell to a chair in front of the sheriff's desk. "I hope our conversation today is more pleasant for the two of us than our last official grill fest at Marinescape." Tara wearing a mid-thigh skirt and sat on the desk edge, in front of Maxwell, with one foot on the floor, the other dangling.

"This is the first time I've seen you in regular street clothes."

"Today is a paper catch up workday for me." She started to rock her free leg slightly toward the professor. "May I address you as Max?"

"Only if I may undress you, sorry, I mean, address you as Tara."

They both smiled.

"My dyslexia has been revealed. I meant no disrespect, Tara."

"None was taken." Tara started to rock her leg faster and actually slid forward on the desk, causing her dress to move up her pale, bare legs.

Max and Tara both glanced at Tara's extended thigh and made eye contact. Max repositioned his legs and pants in his chair. "So how did you find your way to be sitting in front of my desk?" she asked as she kicked off her shoe from her rocking leg into Max's lap. "Oh no, I'm so sorry; that's so rude and clumsy of me."

Max palmed the black heeled shoe, knelt and softly slid it onto her bare foot. "Well, this is unusual for me, twice in one day. Maybe I'm bad luck for shoes," They both laughed. "On a more serious note, I came to ask a very large favor."

Tara stopped rocking her leg and sat forward with both arms supporting her. "Should you whisper it to me?" she said in a jovial tone.

Max didn't move. "I heard a woman had a miscarriage and died at the Marinescape demonstrations and that Doctor MacGrath was performing an autopsy on her."

Tara slid off the desk, walked around and sat behind it. "Let's say an unrelated person to the deceased was to ask me for such information. Only the doctor, the sheriff or Director Leon is authorized to release it. I'd be obliged to report such a request to the sheriff. Knowing said person had a special interest in the case and he might also be a suspect in capital crime and rape cases—"

"I understand and accept your sworn duties and my risk. I'm not denying my interest in this awful incident occurring on Marinescape property, where I am the biologist and it could involve Yao's actions." Max never broke eye contact with Tara.

"Please wait here. I'll see what I can do." As she passed, she slightly rubbed the seated professor's shoulder.

Doc MacGrath returned with Tara following.

"You know how this makes you look?" the doc asked.

"You're a scientist. You must understand why I need to know, Doctor MacGrath."

Doc read the final autopsy report to the professor. "She bled to death from severed and ruptured pelvic iliac, uterine, hypo-gastric and aortic vessels," the doc detailed. "The most likely cause for the major blood vessels rupturing was the delivery of a total mass equal to a full term, ten-pound pregnancy. She claimed to a bystander she was ten weeks and the father was Yao." MacGrath cleared his throat. "This was not a ten-week pregnancy and not a human fetus. I found scale-covered skin and green blood mixed with the woman's red blood. It had a partial amphibian or reptilian tail, a three-chambered heart of two atria and one partially split ventricle that would mix oxygenated and deoxygenated blood. As you know, human's have a four chambered heart with complete separation of oxygenated and deoxygenated blood."

"Crocodiles have a four-chambered heart," added the professor. "Maybe it was in the embryonic stage of cardiac development?"

"As I mentioned, the blood was green, the hemoglobin was forty-two grams per deciliter; remember, a human's average hemoglobin is twelve to fifteen. The karyotype contained four types of diploid chromosome numbers, meaning two chromosomes in a pair. There was a twenty-three-paired human, a thirty pair, a thirty-two pair and a thirty-four pair. This included male and female lines of X and Y as well." Doc stared at Professor Maxwell. "Oh, one more thing about the delivered mass—it was a growing monster. A mass of disorganized organ systems, skin, scales, intestine, cartilage, bone, nerves, six eyes, et cetera. The best description would be spaghetti and meatballs, red, green and yellow vegetables all mixed together with a lower alligator clawed hand, which actually twitched."

Behind Tara, Sheriff Gary and Deputy Sheriff Keith came into the doorway to the office, followed by Officer Brett and Patrolman Brenner.

# Chapter 55

## *Coupling*

**Alisa and Tara** sat at the South Beach Grill. "How are you doing," asked Tara.

"I haven't really had anything to do with him. He made some truly distasteful requests of me and another woman." Alisa stared out into the ocean. "He wanted me … to get Yao's sperm … carry Yao's …" Alisa stopped talking.

"I'm sorry. But I do have a funny story about sperm." She looked at Alisa and got no reaction. "Well, I'll make a long story short. A case concerning a suspected victim of Yao's attacks has been stalking me. There's an alligator farm north of us that I went to because I needed info about alligators and their habits. I went and took a private tour with this special attendant who happened to be the brother of the stalker. I was about to leave and he said 'Watch this' as he flipped the gator on its back. He said, 'They really like having their belly rubbed.' He told me to go ahead and try rubbing a spot he pointed to.

"Of course, I'm reluctant." Tara looked again at Alisa, who was now listening. "Yes, I was afraid. I placed my hand over its lower abdomen and starting with an air wave. I slowly got down to its scales and touched on and off. The brother told me to put on constant pressure." Tara paused and Alisa looked up. "Wham, a lower abdominal flap opened and a white rocket popped out and shot white-green sticky fluid all over my hand and lower arm."

"What did you do?" an interested Alisa asked.

"I wanted to fling its cum at the instructing brother, but it was too adherent to my skin. I then was going to wipe it off, but the brother told me to collect it in the container he gave me."

They both broke out in loud laughter.

"Yuck! It quickly was becoming stringy, like gooey melted white cheese."

Alisa and Tara had another chuckle and held hands to bond over the gross and embarrassing situation.

\*\*\*

**Sheriff Gary** came into the office before leaving. Dispatcher Mary Jane was the only one there.

"Hard and long day, Sheriff?" asked Mary Jane.

"Do I look that bad?" he asked as he sat down in front of her desk. "And please call me Gary, Mary Jane."

"Please call me Jane." She walked behind him and started massaging his shoulders.

"Oh yeah, that is so … so good!"

Still behind him, Jane moved her hands down the front of his chest, with her breasts slightly pressing and swaying on his neck and back of his head. "Gary, I've always admired you from afar," Jane spoke into his left ear.

"I need you to call Deputy Keith and tell him that he's on call from right now, but don't stop what you're doing, I beg." Gary looked at her upside-down face. "Whose house is closest?" He placed his hands on both sides of her head and wiggled his upper body to kiss her lips.

\*\*\*

**Alisa sat** alone thinking about obtaining reptile seed. *Would that work on Yao?* She wondered.

She put her VW's top down and turned south on Oceanshore Boulevard, heading to Marinescape to talk with the despicable Max.

Suddenly, a red Cadillac XTS convertible going north honked several times and did a high-speed 180-degree turn and sped up to catch her.

"Is that an undercover cop with some warrant for my arrest?" Alisa yelled out to no one. "Is this guy crazy? He's pulling up next to me in the oncoming traffic lane." Alisa slowed down and looked to her left. "Can't be? It is Alistair Crowley."

He signaled Alisa to pull over and then followed. He popped out of his Cadillac to her Beetle's driver side window.

"It's great to see you," he said as he leaned into the car and hugged her almost out of her seat. "I hope you don't mind me kissing you all over." He smacked his lips on her neck, face, arms, exposed upper chest and then ended on her thighs. He kicked off his Croc shoes while leaning deeply into the driver seat. His head landed in her soft Bermuda-shorts-covered lap.

"You're going to have to get out of your situation by yourself," Alisa laughed.

He rolled his whole body across her into the passenger front seat. "I'm lucky you don't have a stick."

After a little fidgeting, his one hand was under her buttocks and his face was buried in her shorts. "It's good to be home," Alistair said as Alisa ran her fingers through his crown hair.

***

**Tara was** back in the CSI lab. "Hey Rick, what's your hottest and newest test for us to use?"

"I've been checking out a newer VMD, vacuum metal deposition, using gold and zinc for latent fingerprints on non-absorbent surfaces like thick paper. Regular fingerprints are detectable on absorbent surfaces for twenty-four hours or less. The fingerprint impression is from sweat made of mostly water, fatty acids, triglycerides, amino acids and chlorides, which easily wash away. With this nanotechnology, the long-lasting fatty acid components are preserved, which will make a negative of the fingerprint."

"Oh Rick, keep talking dirty to me." Tara ran her fingers on his sideburns, down his jaw, his chest and stopped at his trouser belt. "Don't stop talking, Ricky."

"I'm comparing this technique to iodine fuming, super glue vaporization fuming and positive chemical reactions with ninhydrin, which turns blue or diazafluorenone, which turns yellow."

Tara had Rick's belt unfastened and his trousers dropped to his ankles.

"Yeah, ah, I'm including the use of the old dirty method of just dusting with black ferric oxide powder, other trace metals and rosin, talcum, cornstarch or cocoa powder to detect fingerprints," Rick stated with enthusiasm and heavy breathing.

"Let's test something … if I can leave my fingerprints on this." Tara rubbed her hands together like rolling soft bread dough into a firm, long breadstick.

***

**Deputy Keith** received his text concerning his new work shift starting immediately. As he walked through the department offices, no one was to be found. He texted MJ, Tara and a protestor he'd met at the demonstration. No Twitter, Instagram, text message responses or cell phone calls picked up.

"Well," he said as he tapped his chin, "I know I can depend on her to answer. Hello, Officer Brett. I know your detective examination is very close. I was thinking of you. We should get together." He waited for her answer of "yes." "Great, I'll meet you at the Salty Cowboy's Doggy, the intracostal waterway restaurant. It will be my treat," Keith happily answered.

"I think you mean the Salt Water Cowboys, north off A1A? I will meet you there and be ready for a full menu of questions," Brett replied.

***

**"Excuse me;** I was looking for Alisa Favour. She works here?" Patti asked of a girl with a name tag "Jennifer" behind the admission counters to Marinescape. "Any idea when she's working today or where I might find her?"

"Alisa and I are really close friends," Blaze said, acting a little hyper. "She and the professor gave me a special pass to Marinescape and Marine Animal Aquatic World."

307

"Nope, she's not here." A man walked up to Patti and Blaze. "Hello, I'm Mr. Walker Wren Wells, the administrator of these facilities. Miss Favour resigned for no apparent reason. She left no forwarding address. That was a while ago with no explanation. Now Professor Maxwell has been taken into police custody. It's something to do with our very successful Yao, the Matanzas Monster exhibit." He watched their happy faces turn to surprise.

Patti nodded thanks as she and Blaze left. By the time Patti reached her Cadillac, Jennifer had run out to her.

"Alisa did say to me that she was going home after a last meal at the South Beach Grill."

"Thanks so much, Jennifer Lynne Longing." They shook hands as Patti read the name tag.

"You might still catch her there."

*** 

**Mr. Manta** causally walked into the police substation and toward the woman behind a desk with piles of folders and four microphones in front of her.

"I'm hoping you might help me." Yuma leaned forward on her desk. "I'm mystified by all these microphones you're responsible for. You must be the spinal cord of this station."

"Well, I can communicate with all officers and staff when necessary," the substitute dispatcher answered, acting a little panicked.

"I'm amazed how you can stay so friendly during all these days of stresses and still be such a strikingly beauty and calm-voiced dispatcher, Mary Jane."

"Oh, I'm not Mary Jane. I'm just covering until she comes back. I'm Madeline."

"Oh Madeline, 'When I dream at nigh … I see you walking.'"

Madeline blushed as she looked down to her desk.

"A song I remember called Madeline."

"And what is your name, Mr.—"

"Mr. Yuma Manta. Please, just Yuma. I hoped to have brunch or is it now lunchtime? I was with Tara, but business called her away, just a bit ago, Temp Dispatcher Madeline. Maybe you remember my voice? I was recently on the phone asking for directions to this location," Yuma spoke softly.

"I do remember a Mr. Manta calling here from the Alligator Farm Park in St. Augustine."

"Oh, that wasn't me. What did my slithering brother want?"

"Sorry, sir, I can't divulge information about other callers. But I can follow up on your request, Mr. Yuma Manta."

"Yuma, just Yuma."

Madeline smiled with a nod. "And what did you say you were here for, Mr. Yuma?"

"I was involved in a crime involving the Matanzas Monster. It attacked me and a CSI assistant Tara processed me. She also took me through those difficult times." Yuma became verbally more dramatic and sad about the attack. He lifted his arms and pointed to his armpits.

"I'm so sorry for you, that you had to go through such trauma."

"The sunny side of that cloud of gloom is that I met Tara. So I'm here to thank her in person," he said, continuing to smile.

"Let me call around to see if she's here," Madeline responded. She placed her hand on his hand, which was still on her desk. He responded by caressing her hand with both of his.

"I'll need to use this," she said as she withdrew one hand. "Hi, it's the dispatch desk. I have a man asking to see Tara." This request was followed by a couple of minutes wait.

Tara called back on another phone to the dispatcher. "Say I'm not here. He's been stalking me."

"O.K., I understand and no one has seen her today? Thanks."

"Sorry, Mr. Manta, she's nowhere to be found."

"I'll leave a note."

"Probably won't help, but if you like, I'll take a written message for Tara."

Yuma borrowed a pen and paper and wrote with no hesitation.

*Tara, tomorrow is another day.*
*I will look to the sky and ask*
*The Great Spirit to guide me on my quest,*
*for my womanly love… for my life purpose.*
*So far, all signs lead back to you.*
*Sincerely with the Sun, the Wind and Water,*
*The scarred and grateful Yuma*

\*\*\*

**Brunette and red-haired** girls came up behind Patrolman Brenner.

"Sergeant, what's happening here?" the brunette asked.

"Yeah, Sergeant, what's happening here?" the red-haired girl repeated.

Patrolman John Brenner turned around with his right hand covering his sidearm.

"Ladies, I am Patrolman John Brenner of the Saint Johns County Law Enforcement Agency. How may I help you?"

"Wait, is this county yours?" one asked. "Or named after you?" the other asked. "You should be like a general or higher."

"No, I am a patrolman here to try to keep the protestors civil in their actions respectful of private property and other people."

"Wow, that's a lot on your shoulders. I'm Brandy; she's Candy."

"Yeah, I'm Candy; she's Brandy. Can we follow you around?"

"No, I'm on official business here. I'm on duty and not a tour guide."

"I understand and I'm O.K. with that," said the brunette Brandy.

"I'm O.K. too and I understand that too," said the red-haired Candy.

Patrolman Brenner started to walk away.

"Sergeant ... Patrolman, is that your cop car with the bubble lights on top? We've always wanted to do a ride along in one of those cars," smiled Brandy, rocking back and forth as she squeezed together her shoulders to reveal more from her low-cut blouse.

"Yeah, we've always wanted ... what Brandy said." She also mimicked Brandy's pose and pressed her breasts together and up.

"That would be a code violation and—"

"Please, we always wanted to be with a real cop. Pretty please, pretty double please?"

John shook his head and gave a small grin. "When my shift is over and if the two of you are still here, I might consider giving you girls a ride."

The two jumped up and down, clapping their hands with the energy of jumping beans with bouncing breasts.

"Hello, Dispatch, I'm signing off from the animal rights demonstration at Marinescape. All has been quiet the last three hours. I definitely noticed that the number of protestors has diminished by at least half. I deduce it is secondary to the TV media left for the next breaking news story."

John walked tiredly to his patrol car.

"Surprise, we're still here for that ride."

"Surprise, we are here, you know, for our ride."

"That is so cool to hear you speak cop talk," Brandy excitedly said.

"Yea, so cool, the cop talk," head bopping Candy agreed.

"Right, where do you girls want to go? You know the ride is in the back seat, in the cage?"

"That's even cooler!"

"Yeah, even cooler!"

"We have a special place we want to take you, like Alice in Wonderland kind of stuff," they said as they smiled before jumping into the back seat.

"I've been a bad girl," Brandy giggled.

"Yeah, I've been a bad, bad girl too," giggled Candy. "I'm bad, bad, bad girl."

"I'm that and twice that," claimed Brandy. The girls went back and forth with this banter.

"Where to, ladies?" asked John.

"We need the lights rolling, a start up siren and we'll give you directions." They both pressed their faces and breasts against the perforated Plexiglas between them and Patrolman Brenner. "It's the directions to the Stairway to Heaven, dear one, dear you, dear me and you, Patrolman and us." Brandy and Candy licked their lips.

\*\*\*

**At a nearby** private home, the CSI Director Leon played several piano compositions. Some he played from memory, others by reading sheet music. His wife was surfing on the internet and occasionally looked out to the Atlantic Ocean's breaking waves. As Leon finished one classical, modern or jazz piece, his wife complimented him on his progress in key timing and auditory expression.

\*\*\*

**"Look**, there's Alisa's convertible white Beetle." Blaze jumped out of the Cadillac and ran to the restaurant's front door. Patti told the hostess that she saw her friend already seated.

"I see my son has found you and successfully convinced you to stay."

"He is quite persistent. Blaze and I have made many fond memories." Alisa put a hand on Blaze's shoulder.

Patti sat next to Alisa and wasted no time on small talk.

"Professor Maxwell has been placed in county jail because he has admitted to some kind of association with Yao. The Governor of Florida has been put in the position to decide if Yao should be prosecuted for capital murders, rapes and assaults." Patti watched Alisa's face as she explained the urgency to help the professor.

"How can I help a person I trusted completely but who tried to use me like one of his genetically altered animal's whore?" Alisa started strong but ended her sentence with tears.

"I empathize with you fully, since he also made me feel cheap and experimentally expendable." Patti placed her arm around Alisa and they both became teary-eyed in sync.

"I want to help Max, Yao and Speedy," said Blaze, standing up at the table and taking a Mr. Atlas pose as if he were holding up the Earth.

Patti and Alisa both broke out into laughter.

"I'll call the county jail to see if Max is eligible for bail," said Patti, pulling out her cell phone.

"What? Professor Maxwell is out where? Do you know where ... oh, you don't know?"

"Where do you think Max went?" Patti and Alisa looked to Blaze.

"Let's go to Yao at Marinescape," exclaimed Blaze.

The two cars headed south, with Blaze riding with Alisa.

"Boy, I ... I mean girl, I really love riding in a convertible ... with you, Alisa." Blaze shyly glanced over at the driver.

The threesome had no problem parking two cars, since many of the non-committed or unpaid protestors had left. The avid animal rights believers still followed them to the park's admission entrance.

"Badge, badge, badge ... go right in." The three turned left and headed straight to the exhibit.

"Sir, have you seen —never mind." Alisa left the security guard and went to the seated professor, who was watching Yao.

Yao immediately swam to Alisa's side of the pool, having heard her voice. Blaze ran around the pool to Max and jumped on his back. Max swung Blaze around on to his lap as the two laughed. Max, holding Blaze's hand, walked over to the women.

"I am so happy to see all three of you again, to reunite the four of us."

Alisa remained silent and kept her distance.

"We're still missing Speedy," said Blaze in a high-pitched voice.

"I thought you had been arrested," Patti said as she hugged Max.

"I was detained. I know Sheriff Gary was drooling to lock me up forever," Max smiled. "The scenario of a wild reptile being accused of capitol murders, rapes and assaults. Animal rights groups locally, nationally and internationally had taken an interest. Public sentiment swayed in favor of the reptile because of its display at Marinescape. No prosecutor wants to be involved. The state attorney general has bumped it to the governor to decide what to do."

"So what's the bottom line?" Alisa broke in.

"At this point, it has led to a Grand Jury having been called in to decide if I should be taken to trial for collusion. Now I just wait."

"What does it mean 'you just wait' for the Grand Jury?" Blaze inquired.

"In my case," Max explained, "the county prosecutor has decided that since an animal, Yao, is the one who committed the supposed crimes and I am suspected of being a collaborator with the said Yao, a Grand Jury is set up to review and decide if there is enough evidence to take me to trial. However, the County decided to bump the case up to a Federal Grand Jury out of Jacksonville's federal court system. Until the Grand Jury occurs and makes a decision, I am free to go as I like, as long as I stay in the State of Florida."

"But what is a Grand Jury, Max … Alisa … Mom, anybody?" complained Blaze.

"A Federal Grand Jury is a group of twenty-three randomly picked people empowered by law to act as jurors to examine the validity of the accusations made against a person. They decide if there is enough evidence to take the person to trial."

"Max, you heard about the pregnant woman claiming to be carrying Yao's baby?" presented Alisa.

"Yes, and her miscarriage and her following tragic death," answered the professor. "That's how I was corralled by Sheriff Gary when I reviewed the autopsy reports with Doctor MacGrath."

"And what were your conclusions, Professor?" asked Patti.

"It was Yao's conception. Its offspring was physically a severely deformed collection of organs. The offspring had at least four sets of different chromosomes, called tetraploidy."

"Why did the woman die?" Alisa asked, shooting eye darts into Max.

"The pregnancy grew two to four times faster than a normal human pregnancy, which resulted in the woman's uterine rupture. The deformed pregnancy still grew in her abdominal cavity after rupture, with the placental blood vessel attaching to her pelvic blood vessels, including the aorta, the pelvic walls, intestine, bladder and her diaphragm."

"She must have been scared shitless! Sorry, Blaze," Alisa apologized.

"At such a fast growth rate, the pregnancy did not allow her body to adapt. The rupture of multiple organ systems at the same time probably brought on rapid internal and then external blood loss, causing her to lose consciousness and die in one minute or less," explained Max.

"So she felt—" Alisa was going to ask.

"Very little or no pain—she experienced a very brief time of awareness before her expiration," Max answered her question.

"So what are the plans for Yao?"

# Chapter 56

## *Together*

**The four gathered** together to form a closed group while Yao, the reptile, iterated a string of vowels near them. It was a reunion of a lovin' human hug. Alisa purposely did not touch Max. As their hugs dissipated, they lingered around separately while the security guard went for a restroom and food break.

Once the guard was out of hearing range, the foursome started throwing out their suggestions to the others as a plot was formulated to free Yao and Speedy.

"Let us consider this animal's future and set our differences, personal dislikes and anger issues aside for now." Max looked at the stone-faced Alisa and Patti. We should only consider freeing Yao if we can control its urges. That would be to create and give Yao an offspring," suggested Max, "thus turning off its primal urge to mate. I have been treating Yao with a mixture of antibiotics. Interestingly, many turtles, amphibians, lizards and reptiles have a blood-based immune system that naturally kills environmental microbial invaders. Yao has inherited some genetic tolerances by natural selection, which takes advantage of its green blood. Human blood has hemoglobin, which makes our blood red. When hemoglobin starts to break down, it becomes biliverdin and bilirubin. Excessive levels may be deadly to humans. Yao has green blood from high levels of hemoglobin degraded to biliverdin, which kills many of the more than 170 malaria species. Only four will infect humans. Yao's immunity protects it from salmonella enterica and typhimurium and others, E. coli or Escherichia coli, staphylococcus aureus and streptococcus group B. Not willing to take any chances, I got Yao's blood—"

"How in heaven, did you get a five-hundred-pound, seven-and-a-half-foot long, angry reptile to let you draw its blood? And from where?" Patti asked, shaking her head.

"After sedating Yao through his food, I swam in the pool to the bottom and drew blood from its midline head behind the eyes."

"Weren't you afraid of Yao waking up while you were in the pool?" a scared Blaze asked.

"Well, by proper medication measurement, based on weight and height or just being lucky, Yao did not die from an overdose and did not wake up prematurely. I was watching its gill respiration rate, not wanting it to stop or accelerate." As usual, Max explained the situation calmly. "I cultured for all the bacteria and parasites I mentioned. I included culturing and microscopic slide inspection for viruses like Human Immunodeficiency Virus and the herpes family of viruses."

"And your results, Professor?" still stone-face Alisa asked.

"All the results were negative for invasive organisms."

"Did you do its karyotype?" followed up Patti.

"Yes, I did; in fact, several cells, which revealed Yao is a genetic chimera. Yao's cells have three genotypes or three chromosome sets of base pairs. Mix these genotypes with a fourth cell line from human chromosomes and there is genetic and phenotypic or outward appearance that Doctor MacGrath found at autopsy of the confusing blob."

"So that was the monstrosity the woman delivered at her death?" stated Alisa loudly.

Maxwell nodded.

"Patti, are you willing to sell me twelve human donor eggs through your fertility clinic?"

"I've struggled with the morality of this situation."

"I am a M.D. board certified doctor in Obstetrics and Gynecology, with one of my subspecialties in reproductive endocrinology and infertility and reproductive female surgery," said Max.

"And what would you say to our clinic's R.E.I. for him to let you purchase the donor eggs from an egg repository in Atlanta, Georgia?" Patti quizzed Max.

"I would list my credentials, with the wish to help my client achieve a pregnancy."

"Why request so many eggs? The normal number would be six."

"My client has a genetic disorder requiring PGT, pre-implantation genetic testing, before the embryo transfer or ET. My client had at least two genetically established miscarriages, probably more."

"Oh, Doctor Maxwell, you are good, very good," smiled Alisa.

"You will need your own nitrogen freezing transfer canister for the purchased eggs."

"Doesn't your clinic rent such containers, Patti?"

"Yes, but then the R.E.I doctor will know more about you, like your address, past SART pregnancy rates."

"SART, is that 'search and rescue transponder,' which emits radar to ease the search for a ship or life raft in distress?" volunteered Alisa.

"Sorry, it's the Society of Artificial Reproductive Technology, a scientific organization to document IVF success for fertility clinics who are willing to submit their pregnancy rate," corrected Patti with a smile at Alisa.

"My next step for a Yao-based pregnancy is to obtain its sperm, ladies."

"Well, Patti is the head fertility nurse, isn't that right, Patti?" encouraged Alisa.

"No, I think Alisa is the perfect candidate to procure the reptile's seed, being the marine animal assistant at Marinescape with an associate's degree in zoology. Alisa, you do have a special knowledge you have attained at Marinescape," encouraged Max.

"I don't know about that," Alisa shook her head. "Really, I don't think so."

"The next step is preparing Yao's sperm," interrupted Max. "Some reptiles and amphibians respond to their habitat temperature to determine if their created fertilized egg's sex is to become male or female. Yao has survived and self adapted millions of years and still its sexual genetic-carrying sperm are able to fertilize, as proven by the autopsy of the unfortunate Marinescape pregnancy loss of lives. Yao's sex selection has evolved to be now sperm deterring the sex of the offspring.

"So the environmental water temperature for reptiles influence if male Y carrying chromosome or female X carrying chromosome sperm will be created. Thus we need multiple sperm samples at different temperatures from Yao."

"What does that mean to a person obtaining Yao's sperm?" Alisa asked, almost in a whisper.

"Excellent question," Max said as Alisa smiled at Patti. "There are three suspected temperature ranges to consider. If the water temperature is warmer, like greater than 93.2 degree Fahrenheit, all the sperm are carrying genetic males. If the water temperature is cooler, like less than 86 degree Fahrenheit, all the sperm are genetically females. If the temperature is being 86 to 93.2 degree Fahrenheit, the sperm maybe either genetic sex.

"So I will need three sperm specimens, one from each temperature range. Several techniques are used to separate the Y and X sperm," Professor Maxwell continued. "First, each specimen will be centrifuged in a tube. The X-containing chromosome is heavier than the smaller and lighter Y-chromosome-containing sperm. This spinning will leave the lighter sperm on top to be siphon off. Next, since all matter has some kind of electrical charge, the Y sperm will have drawn to one electromagnetic pole, separating out only the Y-carrying sperm for male offspring. Another consideration is that lighter Y-carrying sperm are faster than X-carrying sperm. So place the sperm in a column with progressively thicker albumin and those sperm going the farthest are Y-carrying sperm. The remaining sperm in all the above procedures will have a greater chance for a female offspring."

"I don't think I can do the Yao thing," pleaded Alisa again.

"I am going to change Yao's water temperature. It will take twelve to twenty- four hours to have an effect on its sperm, if any affect happens at all," planned Max.

"In humans, don't you need three to six months to see a change in absolute human sperm numbers, quality, motility and viability or its time of survival?" Patti asked.

"True, Patti, but with this reptile, sperm quality is probably much more environmentally affected and produced so much faster than humans," the professor answered.

***

"O. K., Alisa, we are ready to have you get the first specimen."

"Max, I'm being truthful, I can't do this," complained Alisa.

"Now, I know Tara told you of her surprising experience. She didn't say it was a bad or unsafe experience," coached Max. "I will be right next to you. The security guard is sleeping behind his newspaper."

"I believe in you Alisa," encouraged Blaze.

"Blaze, I want you to stand over in that corner, away from all this, which I do not want you to see," instructed Patti.

Max led Alisa to the pool's edge. Yao was already there from hearing her voice.

"Now just swish your hand in the water."

Reluctantly, she stuck her finger tips in and flicked the surface water.

"Here, do this." Max placed his whole hand in the water and swished back and forth to make small waves. "Yao won't bite or grab your hand."

Alisa followed Max's example and Yao rolled on his back, holding the metal mesh with his hands and feet.

"Go ahead and rub Yao's lower abdomen, Alisa."

She did a few circling motions. She looked at Max. He showed his open hand, palm down and going lower into the water. Alisa took in a loud, deep inhale and submerged her hand until she felt its scales.

"Press more firmly in smaller circles," Max smiled and continued slow nods.

Patti slightly smiled, nodded and motioned her hand in small loops.

In a super-fast moment, they could hear the sound of a water slap as Yao's abdominal flap opened and an approximately ten-inch white, curved rod flashed out.

"Here, Alisa." Max quickly placed a clear medical cup in her left hand to capture the airborne stream of white-yellow goo that shot up and toward her left hand. Max held her hand to prevent her from withdrawing. Some white sticky goo hit her forearm, with most of it going into the cup. In probably five seconds, the ejaculation was done spurting from the rod,

319

which was back under the abdominal flap. It slapped closed, spraying pool water on Alisa's left forearm and shoulder.

"Oh shi … damn, Yao," She looked to Max. "Yucky, slimy, disgusting, revolting, repulsive physically and psychologically sickening," Alisa cried out and became tearful.

Max poured a powder into the sperm cup and stored the cup in a metal cooling container. Then Max, Patti and Blaze came to Alisa's side as she frantically wiped and re-wiped her arm, shoulder and clothes.

"How do you feel now, Alisa, now that it over?" comforted Max and the other two with rubbing hands and side hugs.

"I'm done, retiring from this job … never again," lamented Alisa as she left.

At the end of the day, Max had processed, examined for adequate sperm and froze it. Max changed Yao's water to a mid-range temperature. That night, he called Tara. Professor Maxwell had just gotten off the cell phone with Tara when Patti rang him to say his prepaid order for donor eggs had arrived and were in his nitrogen freezing container he'd purchased.

"Patti, thank you so much. Any chance you could bring the container to MAAW?"

"Of course... May I bring Blaze?"

"It is about time he gave Speedy some free air time." They both chuckled.

*** 

**Max** let the two in the secure MAAW building. Patti, wearing a summer dress, handed the metal nitrogen-filled canister to him, which was immediately put away.

"How about you do us a big favor, Blaze?"

He nodded eagerly.

"Go and exercise Speedy for a while."

Blaze started to run and slowed to a walk as he looked back to see his mom watching him. "I know Mom, no running." He waved over his shoulder.

They sat on a familiar bench in the multiple ceilings room. Patti and Max felt their thighs touch. "Very pretty flower print dress, Nurse Patti."

She swung her touching thigh over his nearest leg. "I see you're wearing the loose-fitting brown exercise shorts you like, Professor Rory Maxwell." Rory pulled her entire body over onto his lap.

They looked around while listening for Blaze.

"He must be pretty far away," Rory said as he scooted himself directly under Patti's hips and maneuvered his shorts down to his mid-thigh.

"I barely hear Blaze," Patti agreed as she fluffed her dress to completely cover both their hips.

"I must mention, we are having a bare union, wouldn't that be the correct word description? I have a strong feeling we are going to be one," Max commented. The two shifted hips until they slowly exhaled, "Ah … it's so nice to be so close to you," smiled Patti.

Like a car's pistons at idle, their time became most climactic, a perfect humming together harmony.

"It's getting late and Blaze has school tomorrow." Patti pulled out a few Kleenex and reached under her sun dress.

"Thank you, my dear," smiled Max.

"Yes, we're now quite refreshed," smiled Patti at Max. After each adjusted their apparel, they both stood up.

"I think you need to relax a bit longer," Patti said, and both heads looked down.

"I believe nature is revealing the chance for another … opportunity for our pleasure?"

Patti and Max's eyes locked.

"Ah, I've got to get Blaze home."

Max readjusted his clothes again, showing only normal loose brown shorts. He found Blaze and Speedy. The abnormally growing dragonfly flew into its new larger cage with no reluctance.

"Patti, if you like, you could come back. I will be performing ICSI on two donor eggs."

"Oh, I can bare … ly wait," she commented as she touched his lips with several of her fingers.

# Chapter 57

## *Fertilization*

**The next day**, Patti and Alisa were present for the ICSI with Max.

Three rolling chairs were at a table with a dual lens microscope. The scope was attached to a video camera. The camera not only recorded the procedures to follow, but also fed to a forty-inch TV monitor to easily watch.

"Since the ICSI pipette manipulator is on my right hand, I will have one of you assisting me with the ICSI of a donor egg each. We're doing a total of two eggs. Who would like to be first?"

Neither woman volunteered as they sat with eyes cast at the other woman, so Max chose Patti to be first, since she had some familiarity with gamete manipulation at the fertility clinic.

"Alisa, you'll become more confident watching the procedure done on the monitor."

Sliding a small petri dish under the microscope, the three saw live, swimming, normal head, mid piece and flagellating tailed sperm.

"Now Patti, this will be a little like a video game. All these sperm are good to use for ICSI. Your objective, if you accept the mission"—Max smiled at Patti—"is to suck one, just one, sperm into the very narrow pipette. That sperm will be injected, ICSI, into one donor egg." *Appendix ICSI*

After twenty one attempts, Patti captured a single sperm.

Max pushed the sperm out of the pipette into another petri dish. He broke the sperm's tail and re-aspirated the immobile sperm into the pipette. Now Max moved the sperm dish to the side and replaced it with the egg dish under the microscope.

"Did you know the human egg is the largest cell in the human body, of either sex?" said Max.

"Well, Max, you're out of the running for the biggest … human cell," smiled Alisa. All three laughed.

"The two of you can watch the intracytoplasmic sperm injection procedure."

The TV monitor was filled with an egg being held by a pipette at the egg nine o'clock position. "Now from the three o'clock position on the egg, we see the sperm-carrying pipette come into view. There is the sperm at this pipette tip. We puncture the egg cell wall. The pipette tip is now in the egg's thick liquid part called the cytoplasm. We inject or deposit the sperm next to the egg's nucleus. The cell's nucleus has a protective membrane around the cell's DNA. I have activated the egg pre-ICSI to dissolve its nuclear membrane to allow the egg's DNA to be released. Breaking the sperm's tail activates the sperm's DNA to be released and for the two DNA mix." Professor Maxwell finished his dissertation.

"All right, Alisa, it your chance to play capture a sperm."

With the tact of a proficient sperm catcher, the pipette sucked in one aggressive sperm and was ready for delivery. "Alisa, you are the star attraction for capturing high quality sperm in only one attempt."

Alisa's right arm went up and did the Queen's' hand roll wave as she looked to an imaginary surrounding crowd.

Max repeated the petri dish exchange and egg piercing with sperm without difficulty.

"In humans, fertilization begins with the sperm dissolving completely and releasing one single strand of DNA next to the egg's single strand of DNA. These two strands of DNA mix and then recombine the chromosomal material into two new chromosomes. This interaction of egg and sperm occurs within sixteen to twenty hours, called Day Zero. I consider this a miracle in itself," expounded the professor.

"Day one is fertilization of the single cell beginning to separate into two cells.

Day two you see two cells of the embryo becoming four cells. Day three is now a six to eight cell embryo growth. No viewing of the embryo on day four. By day five, there are two hundred to five hundred cells, now called a blastocyst, the usual day for embryo transfer, ET or freezing of the extra blastocysts," still lectured Professor Max.

"But you are going to check each blastocyst for all its chromosomes, right Max?" asked a worried Alisa, who spoke before Patti.

"You are again correct." Max placed a hand on Alisa's shoulder. "After PGT-A or Preimplantation genetic testing for Aneuploidy on the blastocysts, they are then frozen. Aneuploidy is a chromosomal abnormal embryo. In humans, you wait one or months for the female endometrium or her uterine lining to be in sync for the best time for ET. I have been able to bypass this last step."

***

**Alisa walked** into Yao's exhibit and immediately saw Max speaking with Tara.

"What's going on here?"

"I asked Tara, in her non-official and secret capacity, to be here to give you encouragement for Yao's second sperm collection," Max said as his hand went around Tara's shoulder.

Alisa stopped walking. "I thought I told you I couldn't do that thing again."

"I thought with your distinguished sperm service yesterday you would like to try again?" smiled Max as he walked toward Alisa.

Tara walked over to the pool.

Alisa then walked out of the pool area and stopped at the front admission desk. "Tell them I quit!" Alisa ran out of the Marinescape entrance. Max ran to the parking lot looking for her. He saw Alisa's white Beetle, with its black convertible top still up, spray gravel from its tires until hitting A1A. The partially-spinning and side-stepping Volkswagen with a front engine placement since 1997 faded northbound into the strong ocean breeze and to the sounds of breaking ocean waves.

When Professor Maxwell returned to the pool, he found Yao hanging by all four limbs. It saw Tara standing poolside with a collection container in hand.

"Thank you, Tara. I owe you one for helping me today," Max said as he walked over to Tara. She smiled with an accented eye wink. They both knelt. Tara held the collection container in her left hand and placed her right hand in the water to massage Yao's belly. The flap opened, a white erection appeared and its specimen was completely received in the cup while Yao moaned, gurgled and vocalized vowel sounds.

The sperm was prepared and placed in a nitrogen freezing portable metal container. Max then turned up the temperature to greater than ninety-four degrees Fahrenheit for the last day of sperm harvesting.

"I have time for a break before I'm due at work," whispered Tara into Max's ear. They both looked at the security guard, who had a watchful eye on them.

"I'll leave first and meet you outside the exhibit."

Tara agreed. Once they walked down a hallway, Max turned into a room with a door sign: Marine Biologist. "It's a small office, which I rarely use. But it does have a lock on the door." As the door closed and locked, the two intertwined into one writhing, sitting, rolling bundle of joy and pleasure.

"What about that sperm?" she asked and they looked to the small metal container the size of a home grille's propane tank.

"I think we have time for one more sperm catch and release."

\*\*\*

**Meanwhile**, Alisa slowed her car down to forty-five miles an hour, wiping away her tears. About three miles north on A1A, just past the Fort Matanzas National Monument Park parking area, a southbound convertible Cadillac whizzed by Alisa, honking its horn.

"Oh no, is that Alistair again?" said a panicked Alisa. The honking vehicle did a U-turn, spraying dirt up and pulling in behind her. Suddenly, he was driving next to her.

"He's doing it again."

"Alisa, pull over, pull over, honey," shouted the driver.

"Alistair, have you not learned to drive?"

"Please pull over." Alistair then went back behind Alisa.

An opposing southbound car honked and passed both of them.

Once Alisa was on the road's shoulder, Alistair followed and pulled in tight behind. He jumped out from his car and hung into her narrow open passenger side window. Even with the car's top still up, Alistair leaned way into the window, wiggling his whole body in with his head falling face-up into her lap.

"I'm home!" He turned his face downward with a nuzzling nose into Alisa's Bermuda shorts' crotch.

"Are you doing this again?" smiled Alisa.

"Are you finally going to join the adventure I'm on?" he replied with a muffled voice.

*** 

**Max and Patti** studied the two embryos' development.

"Here is ICSI egg number one. It has fertilized and is an embryo." They both watched the TV monitor of the focused petri dish.

"The multi-cell embryo is more three dimensional than a single sperm we used for ICSI. Sperm is very small, about 0.002 inches or 0.05 millimeters. The unaided human eye with normal 20/20 visual acuity can see about twice that size, about 0.004 inches or 0.1 millimeters, which happens to be the size of our donor ovum, Latin for egg or egg cell."

"Do you call this a day one, since the fertilization led to a dividing embryo?" asked Nurse Patti.

"Yes, it is two cells, each starting to divide again, soon to be a four cellular embryo. It's right on schedule."

"O.K., ICSI egg number two is fertilized and has amazingly become a blastocyst," gasped Professor Max. "Of two hundred to three hundred cells, it is way ahead of a normal embryo growth. I will need to do PGT-A today for the genetic makeup. I will take two PGS samples and run a twenty-four chromosome testing. The second sample I will send off for PGT–SR, chromosomal structural rearrangements detection," summed up Max.

"I thought we humans had twenty-three chromosomes pairs?" Patti asked.

"You are right."

Max hugged Patti and went to kiss her left cheek. She quickly turned her head to bring a solid lip kiss between them. Her hands held his head to face hers to guarantee a moist, cemented, long labial locking love fusion for lasting effect. Max responded with his roaming hands forging under her blouse and separating to roam the twin peaks. Their rolling chairs eventually turned toward each other.

As a caterpillar slithers down a tree, so did their bodies slowly make the downward road to pleasure and satisfaction. Time passed slower than maple sugar dripped from a tree tap.

"Is performing PGT-A as much fun as we just experienced, Max?"

A kiss covering Patti's mouth answered her question.

"It's time for me to go pick up Blaze from school. Will there be time for Blaze to play with Speedy? I did notice that the dragonfly is still growing."

"Answering your two questions … yes and yes," Max smiled. "Oh, if convenient, wear your long, loose and fluffy flower print dress again."

Time flew by, as did Speedy with Blaze below.

"Shall we rest on the 'volup' bench?"

Patti grinned without a word.

"Since you asked … not …volup is short for the Latin word voluptatem, meaning pleasure."

"I'm all for mounting the volup bench," Patti smiled back, holding his hands.

\*\*\*

**"Professor Maxwell**, there are some police to see you. Can you come to the front desk?" squawked the intercom call from the Marinescape front desk. Within seventeen minutes, Max stood before Sheriff Gary and several other officers. Patti and Blaze were in the back of a crowd of people who had collected.

"Rory Fergus Hamish Lachlan Maxwell, you are under arrest for your participation in capital crimes committed by the reptile called 'Yao' as determined by the Grand Jury."

With handcuffed wrists behind him, Max was paraded through the long way out of the Marinescape lobby, through the parking lot and into the lit-up backseat of a St. Johns County Sheriff's patrol vehicle. Many shocked faces watched Rory Maxwell pass in silence.

\*\*\*

**Alisa looked** to the floating clouds as she sat next to Alistair in his convertible. The stop for Alistair's work eventually would be Daytona Beach. He told Alisa she could use his Cadillac anytime. So the mentally stressed, confused and depressed Alisa agreed to sell her Beetle at Palm Coast Used Cars. They ended up spending the night at the Ritz-Carlton Grande Lakes, Orlando. She thought, *It's nice to have someone take care of me. I don't need to work or have a career. Lifelong dreams can change.*

The next day, the twosome was driving again after a twin naked body circus fest in the multiple rooms of their fabulous suite.

As they drove to the next stop, Alistair pointed to his lap and said, "Hey, babe, how about taking care of this?"

"Oh, come on, as it is, I got no sleep last night doing your fantasies."

"I'm under a lot of work stress; I need a release." Alisa succumbed to his pressuring and his guiding hand.

"Here we are, the Hilton Daytona."

Once their bags were brought to the room, Alistair pulled down the security latch and started to undress.

"What are you doing, Alistair?" asked an exhausted Alisa.

"I got two-and-a-half hours until my seminar presentation, so snap it up and get undressed and on the bed."

Again, Alisa gave in. After their private parts session, he opened his briefcase and reviewed his cursive written outlines and notes.

"Baby, you can order food for the room or dine in their restaurant while I dazzle the audience for two to three hours."

After the seminar, Alistair came into the hotel room and found Alisa sleeping in front of the TV, which was showing the movie *Enchanted* with Amy Adams and Patrick Dempsey. Alistair dropped his pants and boxer shorts in front of her closed eyes pulled the blankets back and climbed in bed behind her.

"Alistair, I'm too tired and I'm trying to ... uh, uh."

"I'll be done soon," he said between his deep grunts.

The next morning, the couple was off, back to the Ritz-Carlton Grande Lakes, Orlando.

"Babe, take this room key and I'll meet you there before my final and most important seminar of the month. I'm going down to the lobby to get some important clients greased up with lip service shit."

Soon after his monologue to Alisa and visit downstairs, the door opened as Alistair was starting to undress.

"Hey, why are you not yet undressed? Chop, chop … woman."

She was dressing and stopped. She sat down in a lounge chair.

"What the hell get undressed," Alistair demanded.

"I feel like you're just using me, that you don't really care about me as a person … for me," spoke Alisa, starting to tear up.

"You bitch! I was giving you a big break to be with an upwardly mobile male star. You're just a cheap whore. I can get any woman at these conferences who would beg to be in your situation. Get up!" He grabbed her arm and shoved her into the hall. The door slammed shut and locked behind her.

"You can't do this, the rest of my clothes, my night bag? Where's the money from the sale of my car?"

"You should have thought out your desertion plan a little better," laughed Alistair through the door. "It's too late for begging, you slut, you bitch, you whore," he yelled behind the door.

Alisa was now in a torrential downpour of tears.

"How could I be so naïve, stupid … stupid … stupid," Alisa repeated through her tears.

She went down to the ice machine room to get some water to drink or at least an ice cube to suck on. Alisa looked at her arm, which had become discolored and decided to apply ice to the enlarging bruise. Down the hall she heard a door open and slam shut. She looked around the corner and saw Alistair going for the elevators.

"If only I had …" She slapped her thigh and felt a room key in her pant pocket.

In a moment, Alistair's room door was closed and locked again after Alisa.

"There's my luggage, makeup bag and…" Alisa saw Alistair's briefcase. "Let's look inside. Notes, outlines, list of jokes … his professional life." She closed it up and carried it with her bag and suitcase out of the room after looking down the hallway. She walked over to the staircase, down to the first floor and out a side door and into a parking lot. At the end of the building were several open green "Waste Management" corrugated metal bins.

"I'll just throw some papers in this one, these in this one and the briefcase in this really stinky one."

Alisa went back to the side door and through the hallway to the registration desk. She sat on a front lobby couch, placing her two bags behind a nearby chair and looked out a window. "Who can I call?" She called Max. No answer. She tried Blaze at home, but again there was no answer, just an answering machine. Finally, she called Patti at work.

"One moment, please. Hello, this is Nurse Patti."

"Patti, I'm in a terrible situation and—"

"Who is this?"

"I'm so sorry; this is Alisa, Alisa from Marinescape and MAAW."

"Oh, right your Blaze's friend. I apologize I didn't recognize your voice. I'm working."

"I'm stranded and need a ride back to Marinescape this morning if at all possible, please," a desperate Alisa asked.

"Where are you exactly?"

"Orlando, I think. Yes, at The Ritz-Carlton." She waited with a hopeful exhale.

"Don't you have a car?"

"It was sold."

"You can't use Uber or a Greyhound bus?"

"No money, I have no money." Alisa again became tearful.

"Oh, I'm at least two or three hours away, going the speed limit. I'll get there as soon as I can and then you can explain it all."

"Patti, I have to hang up."

"You fuc*king bitch, where is my briefcase?" an irate Alistair screamed. He hovered over Alisa within inches of her face.

The Ritz-Carlton manager immediately came over to them. "Sir, would you please keep your voice down?"

"Screw you, this mother fuc*kering bitch stole my briefcase with all my papers!"

The manager waved over a security guard. The bell captain also came over.

"Sir, sir, look at me. If you don't keep your voice down, we'll have to remove you from the premises until you can control yourself."

Alistair grabbed Alisa's arm and pulled her off the couch. The security guard grabbed Alistair's arm and pulled it up and behind his back. While being walked out, Alistair screamed obscenities at Alisa, who sat back down on the window couch.

"I apologize, ma'am, for the disturbance. Do you know that man?"

"No, he came over and called me a different woman's name, unknown to me. I'm just waiting for my ride," Alisa answered.

She watched through the hotel's large front window. Alistair wrestled with three men in the canopied car turnaround. The four men continued wrestling toward the hotel landscaped water fountain. While Alistair resisted the security guards, he stepped into the water fountain's base pool and slipped. Alisa watched with delight the event in slow motion. Alistair's rear end, legs and arms followed in his warlock-like water ballet to become completely wet.

"Life does bring laughter after sadness," Alisa giggled. A warm rush of satisfaction went from face to ankles. Her anger with Alistair and herself that had been a flaming forest fire was now just a simmering pile of ash.

\*\*\*

**Patti pulled up** in her Cadillac and Alisa ran out with her luggage and threw it into the back seat. "Drive, drive." While driving south on I-95, Alisa explained how she'd become bewitched and entwined with Alistair's good looks, sexual prowess, charm and web of promises.

"This all lured me to physical, emotional and financial dependency on him, ending in disaster, all at the same time, not to mention complete, thorough loss of my self esteem."

"What happened to your Beetle?" Patti sadly asked.

"Alistair sold it saying I could drive his new Cadillac anytime. Then he literally dumped me in the hotel hallway and kept my car money."

"Where's your receipt?'

"I had no receipt or money." She became teary-eyed.

"Yes, you definitely hit bottom," consoled Patti.

As they approached Marinescape, Patti asked, "Where do you want to go, Alisa?"

"I'll call Max to see if he can put me up and give me my Marinescape, Dolphin Family Fun, Yao, the Matanzas Monster exhibit tours back to me."

"I'm sorry to tell you, but Max has been arrested for collusion with Yao for capital crimes."

"What about MAAW and his sensitive work and experiments there?" asked a shocked Alisa, becoming teary again.

"I guess you have a lot of reasons to be sad. You can stay with me and Blaze. But we need to find which jail Max has been taken to," Patti anxiously stated.

# Chapter 58

## Confinement

**Patti called** the local sheriff's office and found out that Maxwell had been taken to the Florida Department of Corrections, JSO, at the Jacksonville Sheriff's Office, Jacksonville, Florida, for those who need extra personal security.

"So we're going, right?" asked Patti.

The two were directed to the John E. Goode Pre-Trial Detention Facility, which was on the correction facility's main campus.

After Patti and Alisa had their purses searched, their bodies scanned, selective pat downs, and a signing in, a tall and muscular guard led them to a room with one small high-in-the-door window. They stepped in and the door closed and locked. Looking around the room, they saw a bolted down metal table with handcuffs attached to its side facing the door. Three metal chairs were at the table. The women chose the two away from the cuffs.

"Boy, I feel like I'm the prisoner," Alisa said, looking around. "I couldn't make it in a place like this."

"As they say, you do what you got to do to survive," non-emotional Patti recited.

"Why do the pat down? They'd already used a metal detector and a body scanner on us. Why feel up my body?" Alisa complained.

"They patted both of us to not appear discriminatory," nodded Patti. "They really only wanted to get their hands on you, Alisa."

"No, come on."

More small talk continued, but nothing actually important, about themselves or Max or their relationships with him.

After an inexcusable amount of time in polite societal talk, the same guard brought in a handcuffed Max. They both stood up. He sat down. "Ladies, please sit down and relax," calmly stated Max.

The guard changed Max's cuffs from his to the table-attached ones. The guard then stood against the door with the window behind him.

"It is so wonderful to see the two of you, together ... and civil," grinned Max.

"How are—" they asked in unison.

"I have no symptoms of Incarceritis," Max interrupted. "I have limited time today, so I would like to review the next steps until my release."

"What—"

"Ladies, please, I deeply appreciate your concerns. The third day specimen needs to be obtained and placed in the nitrogen container. Then turn the temperature down to seventy-five degrees Fahrenheit. You know 'it' will become less active and aggressive. See if the Detroit PGT-SR has come in."

After fifteen minutes, they were told it was time to go as the guard changed the cuffs back to behind Max.

"Make sure the MAAW is—"

The door closed behind him and the women remained standing in the relocked room. All was silent. They saw the guard's face peering through the room's small window. The door unlocked and he led them back to the original waiting room.

***

**The Cadillac ride** back was quiet. The exhausted Alisa fell asleep.

"Alisa!" The front door opened and Blaze jumped in. "Great to see you," he said as he hugged her, snuggly-tight to her body in the front seat. Alisa noticed a little more pressing with his shoulder, arm and elbow. She stopped his inward moving hands.

"Keep your hands to yourself," said Alisa as she tried to move away. "Would you please give me some space?"

"Blaze, behave yourself and put on your seat belt."

"I think we should go directly to the MAAW, get the cryo-genetic nitrogen tank and then see Yao for the third specimen," suggested Patti. She looked to Alisa who acted like a beaten dog. "Alisa, why don't you call Tara, since now you two are friends? Ask her to come over to Yao's pool."

"She's really not—O.K., I will." Alisa backed off from crying.

***

Tara walked into Yao's closed exhibit and found Alisa, Blaze and Patti standing by the net-hanging Yao.

"Blaze, it's time for you to go watch Dolphin Family Fun and people with the aquatic mammals. Don't give me that look, go," Patti insisted.

The three women looked to each other as Patti held the specimen receptacle in an outstretched arm. Yao looked at them also, with its abdomen pressed up to the net, gurgling.

"Alisa, are you ready to do the deed? Yao definitely likes you the best," Patti suggested, offering her the prized container.

"Who made you the boss?" Alisa spewed angry words.

Patti put one hand on her hips

"I'll be right next to you, Alisa," encouraged Tara.

Patti handed the receptacle to Alisa.

"Horse breeders use a very similar receptacle, like you have in your hand, at least once a week," added Tara.

All three women knelt by Yao. Patti looked to the guard, who seemed to be sleeping. Alisa put her hand above Yao's scaled lower abdomen, the receptacle in the other hand.

"Here we go." Tara placed her hand on Alisa's and pressed down. Tara's other hand steadied Alisa's receptacle hand by holding her arm.

"Wham!" The flap slapped open, the white rocket went up and out and the liquid package flew and was delivered in its entirety without a spilled drop. It was all over in four seconds with Yao's cascade of vowels and groans.

Tara stood up, Alisa remained kneeling, and Patti reached and took the receptacle from Alisa. Both Patti and Tara said, "Good job, you did it."

Alisa sat down cross-legged with an enormous smile on her face. "Yes, yes, yes!" She yelled, with both her arms up with fisted hands.

The guard awoke, sat up and looked around like he'd missed something. Patti went down the stairs to drop the pool temperature.

"Ladies, let me take this container to MAAW facility and I'm buying lunch," Patti said as she helped Alisa stand up. The three ladies left together, spreading stories and making jokes about the morning's events, to become future friends.

All three sat in the Cadillac's front bench seat thinking of their accomplishments as they approached the World Famous Oasis Restaurant on north bound A1A.

*The professor will be proud of my taking command and getting his check list done. Oh, check on the PGT test results*, thought Patti.

*How did Patti know the MAAW front door security codes? Oh well, I did it. Max will be so proud of me*, thought Alisa.

*Right now, I'd like to be obtaining the professor's private specimen, several times, in different ways*, thought Tara as she contained her Cheshire cat smile.

\*\*\*

**Sheriff Gary** was in his usual morning position, sitting at his desk, his feet propped up on the desk's corner and reading several newspapers. Deputy Sheriff Keith was also in his usual morning position with his legs propped up on a different corner of the sheriff's desk. Instead of newspapers, he read or reviewed explicit pictures, which made him smile, clear his throat and occasionally readjust his pants.

"Good morning, Officers," greeted Dispatcher Mary Jane.

Deputy Sheriff Keith held a vanilla-colored folder with his choice magazines within. He flipped to the front of his magazine folder.

"Oh, reading *Road & Track* this morning, are you?" joked Mary Jane while she looked at the sheriff.

"Why shouldn't I look at things that can show off what they got by revving up their horsepower on my demand?" Keith replied.

"Are your coffees O.K. or do you need refills?" Mary Jane winked at Gary. Both men nodded, "Yes, ma'am."

"Listen to this." The sheriff sat up. "The governor has announced that two organizations are bidding for custody of the homicidal reptile. It should be put down like any rabid animal. It should have happened when the creature was first captured by me, I mean by the team, Coast Guard and assisting law enforcement agencies."

"What organizations?" asked Patrolman John, who walked in.

"The Smithsonian National Zoologic Park research department and the Howard Hughes Medical Institute have both made proposals to the Florida Governor's office. The governor has checked with the Florida State Attorney General, who claimed the governor has the power to make such a decision for the betterment and safety of the general Florida populous and possibly the national public at large. This is a pile of smelly, soft bullshit!" Gary threw the newspaper on the floor.

Patrolman John picked it up. "The Smithsonian National Zoo states it would build a safe, humane and public viewing area. This area would mimic the reptile's natural habitat. The HHMI, Howard Hughes Medical Institute, has developed a special interest division headed by two well recognized world-renowned individuals. Professor—"

"Damn, not another professor," swore the sheriff.

"You have a problem with professors, Gary?" asked Keith.

"My limited exposure to multi-degree holding people, who act like their title entitles them to do and say whatever they want, irrespective of the law, is near my boiling point," Gary growled. "That's my problem."

"Sheriff Gary, here's the article in the *Palatka National & Local News* that was mentioned by your buddy, R.W. Angel. I printed this from Mr. Angel's international internet news reference." Mary Jane softly placed the printed reference page on his desk.

"John, finish reading from the newspaper before I explode," grinned Sheriff Gary.

"Continuing: The HHMI has created a new department labeled 'Live Prehistoric Animals, LPA. This HHMI division would be able to build a habitat, manage and study the reptile called 'Yao.' The division has studied the species of jellyfish that has survived 650 million years, the 500-million-year-old Nautilus, the 400-million-year-old imperial scorpion, the 300-million-year-old tadpole shrimp and the 130-million-year-old purple frog. Two American-based scientists would be co-directors of LPA. Professor Amy Anastasia Alla Adamoffski, PhD. She is an evolutionary genetic paleobiologist. The doctor recently was on the team who evaluated the Kennewick Man. This was the prehistoric Paleoamerican skeleton found in the banks of the Columbia River by Kennewick, Washington, United States. The professor confirmed the found remains of an almost perfectly preserved specimen belonged to an 8,900-year-old human. From description, media photo and video, Professor Adamoffski would estimate Yao's age between 250 million and 300 million years old. 'Really, once in a lifetime, once in recorded Humankind finding which should not be lost,' stated the professor," Patrolman Brenner stopped reading.

"Let me continue reading," sprang up Deputy Sheriff Keith, grabbing the newspaper. "The second respected co-director is a well-known philanthropist Mr. Costtufner. He is known for his commitment to repopulating animals on the endangered species list. Mr. Costtufner has helped bring the North American Bison to the public's interest. From 40 million wild bison numbers in the fifteen-hundreds, up to near extinction by 1889 with only 1,091 in the wild. He has today brought their population back to over 500,000 live bison across North America. These two individuals of science are teaming up and expect to find advancements in mankind's knowledge and secrets to expand future health care and longer life spans."

"What is this world coming to where animals that kill humans becomes a popular icon and people worry more about an animal's welfare than about unemployed, homeless people, starving and dying children and … and forget about the murdered people's rights," spoke Sheriff Gary on his soapbox.

# Chapter 59

## *Justice*

**The next day**, Dispatcher Mary Jane started rubbing the shoulders of the sheriff while he slept with his head on his desk.

"Did you sleep in that chair all night?" she asked as Gary mouthed back something.

"Did you happen to see the German newspaper article referenced in R.W. Angel's editorial? I marked it for you."

Gary pulled her hands down to his crotch as he kissed her bare arms. This led to the soft caressing of her breasts by the man saying, "I want more of you, MJ."

"Not here, not now, Sheriff, you're on duty," whispered Mary Jane.

The dispatcher left while the sheriff read Angel's editorial.

"Call Patrolman John Brenner into my office, please," asked the sheriff.

"Yes, Sheriff," John came in and stood at attention.

"Relax, John. I have some detective work for you. You do want to become a detective, don't you?"

"Yes, sir."

"I need you to find or get someone to translate this article about Yao. You can start with Editor R.W. Angel."

"Sheriff, I heard you talking about yesterday's news," remarked Mary Jane. "Here's today's *St. Augustine Record*."

**Nationally known reptile to be moved?**
*Marinescape's renowned reptile, called Yao,*
*will be managed by HHMI-LPA.*
*This is America's second largest philanthropic medical institution. As a*
*consequence, the professor accused of multiple crimes is to be released.*

Sheriff Gary crumpled the newspaper in silence as Mary Jane stood in his office's doorway.

*** 

**Patrolman** John Brenner started this quest by contacting the writer, Editor Angel. He referred John to his librarian acquaintance in St. Augustine. Patrolman John moved on to the St. Johns County Public Library's main branch.

Finally, John found Erica, Angel's reference person. After their introductions, the sought-after newspaper would soon be discovered.

"Erica, I have some research to do, finding an article that was referenced right here. It will need some translation," smiled John. He fondly remembered their very first meeting quite clearly. The woman with glossy black hair parted in the middle and curling down to her shoulders as she sat behind the library information desk of the stacks. Her face was beautiful and radiated happiness.

"May I help you, Officer?"

"Nice to meet you … Erica," he said as he read her nicely placed cursive written name badge at the bottom of her bulging blouse's V neck. "I wondered if you could find this German publication?" he smiled.

"I believe I can do that for you, sir."

As she came from behind the desk, he noticed that Erica held her right arm across the front of her body and walked with a slight limp.

"What happened that you …" As she turned toward John, he decided not to ask. "What happened that you wanted to be a librarian?"

"I enjoy learning. Here I can be a perpetual student. Every request has the potential for me to learn something new," Erica gleefully responded. "Here we are … the German journals in alphabetical order. Yours is the most recent one.

*Deutshe Wertlos Aktuelle Ereignisse Um die Welt*

"… meaning 'German Worthless Current Events around the World,'" translated Erica. Patrolman John stood smiling in amazement. "So you translate German?"

"German, Spanish, French, Russian, and Mandarin, if that might help you in the future," smiled back Erica, unabashed at John's closeness.

John held the newspaper in anticipation of turning pages for her to translate. Their hands met and he refused to part his hand from hers. Their eyes looked up from the paper and met with a passionate stare, a stare seeming to look deeper into each other's being. John's hand slowly crept onto her wrist.

"Shall I translate the article about Yao? It was referenced from a column by R.W. Angel in the *St. Augustine Record*—"

"Actually, I only need just the excerpt about Professor Maxwell and Yao, if you would, Erica."

They moved to a table with a pad of paper. Sitting next to each other, they turned to see the other's face. The unblinking stare began again.

"I will be your scribe," said an open-mouthed John.

It seemed like hours but was only nine minutes. Erica began:

As recorded by the court room stenographer. A prosecutor for the State of Florida began the questioning.

Prosecutor: *Please state your name.*

Maxwell: *Professor Rory Fergus Hamish Lachlan Maxwell the IV, M.D., Ph.D., DVM, ARAV,*

*B.S, B.A., Marine Biologist, ABMGG, OB/GYN, Evolutionary Biologist, Bio*

*Anthropologist, Professor of Zoology, Aquatic Ecology—*

Prosecutor: *Thank you, that is all we need at this time. Is the address of the professor on record sufficient?*

Maxwell nodded.

Prosecutor: *For the record, that was a yes. Professor, what are your associations or affiliation with the reptile called Yao?*

Maxwell: *Would you like me to describe each stated degree and how it could apply?*

Prosecutor: *No, thank you, not at this time. Could you answer my question?*

Maxwell: *First, I would like to thank this court's judge, the prosecutor and the State of Florida's legal system for allowing me the opportunity to answer questions in pursuit of truth and justice concerning my past, present and future.* He nodded to the judge, the prosecutor and the assembled members of the Grand Jury, which is used in the United States legal system when needed.

Prosecutor: *Professor, you do realize that this is a trial. The people here are members of the jury, not the Grand Jury, who are the people who already decided there was sufficient evidence to have you retained for this courtroom trial? Here is the seated Honorable Judge Jugo Jugalin on this trial.* The prosecutor pointed to the judge with open hand.

Maxwell: *If you please forgive me, Honorable Judge Jugalin.*

Prosecutor: *Do you understand, Professor?*

Maxwell: *Yes, I do, because I trust what you tell me is truthful.*

Prosecutor: *Can you answer the posed question, Professor Maxwell?* He scanned the jury for their reactions. *Professor, I'll rephrase the question for you. Would you tell us all you know about the reptile, what you did, experienced and your concerns about the prehistoric reptile that is called Yao?*

Maxwell: *I would like to tell you of what you ask, but I need you to refresh my memory of what you want me to speak of. As of right now, my recollection seems to fail me. The reminisce of what you ask, I will need you to provide some key words, phrases or points so as to help me recall of what you want me to answer what you ask of me.*

Prosecutor: *Do you know Yao?*

Maxwell: *Yes, I have heard the name Yao many times during this hearing, trial, I mean cross examination by you, others today, before today, and several others have said this name prior to this occasion and in this courtroom.*

Prosecutor: *Professor Maxwell, do you understand you already had a Grand Jury and they decided you should go to trial? Today ... right now is that trial for determining if you are guilty or innocent of said accusations of multiple crimes.*

Maxwell: *I do understand you, but do you understand I need you to repeat what you think I should now say to you in front of the jury in response to your original question, today ... right now?*

The court room gallery laughed.

"Should I go on, Patrolman John?" asked Erica.

They made eye contact with matching smiles.

"I think this is almost all I need. These are enough wasted words that my Chief Sheriff Gary could tolerate and hopefully not boil over." John slowly shook his head.

"So what more do you need to fulfill your visit today ... right now?"

They both laughed as John placed his left hand under her right hand, which was against her body and grasped her left with his right hand.

"What is your full name?"

"I am actually Eva Eirkr Elisson. My father was Norwegian and my mother was Jewish, but most people call me Erika"

"What I need and gracefully ask, Eva ... would you like to go out to dinner?"

# Chapter 60

## *Life-Force*

---

**"Mr. Angel?** This is Sheriff Gary. We are from Crescent Beach," introduced Mary Jane.

"Of course, Sheriff Gary, we've met before. You've been quite informative, truthful and helpful to my career, sir," answered Mr. Angel. "In addition to my contributions to the *Palatka National & Local News*, I've secured a daily column in the *St. Augustine Record*, thanks to your allowing me first dibs at breaking stories about Yao and the Professor Ma—"

Sheriff Gary interrupted. "And that is why I'm calling. Do you have any breaking news concerning Maxwell?"

"Matter of fact, I do. The professor is being released today and acquitted of all alleged crimes and supposed associations with Yao's capital crimes," Angel said with some excitement. "Mr. Angel, I know in my investigational gut with over two decades of solving such heinous crimes, I detected illegal activities, Maxwell is guilty of all the allegations and even more than what he was accused of."

"You know, Sheriff, just like you, I need facts. I also know, but it's not verified, that HHMI-LPA, the Living Prehistoric Animals department, has won the approval of the Florida Governor to hand over Yao to their organization for care and scientific investigation." Angel waited for the sheriff's response, but there was none. "And to your disapproval, I'm sure,

Professor Maxwell will be asked, as a paid consultant, to take over the management of Yao."

"The professor's life just keeps going his way. I know in my gut that this alphabet soup national organization is hiding some truth."

***

**Patrolman John** walked into the sheriff's office.

"I have your German newspaper article translated for you to read."

"Well, good morning to you, sleepy eyes. Have a hard night, did you?"

"Sheriff Gary, I—"

"Did you have time to shower, comb your hair, press your uniform and shine your shoes?"

The patrolman stood erect, mute and looking straight ahead.

"O.K. John, thanks. Just set it on my desk, a challenging job well done."

"Is there a problem?" asked John.

"It's just that I'm at the end of my rope; time to move on and accept failure on this one." The sheriff rotated his head up, around and away from John.

John stood across his desk, looking now at the back of his head.

"Sheriff, you need to read this translation; you owe it to yourself."

Gary turned back around and picked the single spaced, typed out, single sheet of paper.

"I hand-wrote the translation, but Eva typed it out for you, sir."

Gary looked up to John's grinning face, "Eva?"

"That's the librarian who actually did the translation. She knows at least five languages. We kind of got along." John looked upward to the ceiling.

"Did you now," Gary smiled and snorted.

"Sheriff, the typed paper..." John straightened up to attention.

The sheriff sat with slumped shoulders as he glanced at the paper. "Ha, how funny. This is the jerk I know and hate ... what bullshit. Oh, I can't believe this." Gary carefully laid the page down and stood up. "Mary Jane, I'd like you to frame this testimony. When I get discouraged, I'll read this and get fired up again." Then he laughed. "Oh, as I've said before, this guy is definitely guilty. I'm probably the only one who can ... who will catch him again, yes again and make the charges stick! I'll make his life's luck run out and turn the luck my way." Sheriff Gary stood behind his desk and slammed his fists on it.

"Yes, sir," John accented the sheriff's claims of action.

\*\*\*

**Patti** and Alisa again drove north on I-95 to see Max. As they drove on the Jacksonville State Police campus and passed many State Police cars and County Sheriff vehicles, Alisa complained and began to sweat, remembering her prior law enforcement encounters.

They were in the same style of room with one small window, table and chairs, and a tall guard who brought Max in without handcuffs.

"Ladies, how fortuitous that you have arrived today, this afternoon and specifically within this hour," Maxwell gleamed.

"Where are the cuffs?" asked a standing Alisa.

Max motioned her to sit down, as he also did, while Patti was already seated. "I am being released. They are processing my papers as we sit. You will be able to take me with you to Marinescape."

"How is this possible?" Patti asked while leaning toward Max.

"I am not sure. I went to trial for half a day. I testified in a vague and masterful fashion, I thought. The defense attorney asked for a meeting in the very pleasant Judge Jugalin's chambers. They came out of her chambers and the judge announced that all charges against me were dropped, case dismissed. I am now on a fast track for discharge."

Within minutes, the guard re-entered and led Maxwell out of the room. The ladies had to remain behind.

"I tell you again, Patti, I couldn't survive even half a day in here."

In a short time, the two were back in the waiting room.

"Surprise, I'm waiting for the two of you. I got through like something not wanted, like shit through a goose," he joked.

No laughs from the women.

"Life is good!" Max grinned and tilted his head back to let the wind rush over his face as the car raced down the road.

While the trio sat in the front seat, southbound and down, the ladies related the events that took place during his absence.

"Believe it, Alisa obtained the third and last Yao sperm without difficulty," related Patti.

Max was seated between the ladies. He turned and gave Alisa a wet kiss on her left cheek.

"The sperm was processed and frozen."

Max planted a similar kiss on Patti's right cheek.

Alisa looked at Patti. "When did you learn to freeze sperm?"

"At the fertility clinic … remember, I work at one," snapped Patti.

"You don't have to be a bitch about it," Alisa snapped back.

"Ladies, please, what about the embryo growth?" Max tried to calm the two sirens.

"Both embryos grew greater in cell number and total size."

Max went to kiss Patti on her right cheek again. Patti quickly turned her head enough for Max to kiss her lips inadvertently. A token, very brief kiss, since she was driving.

Max put an arm around both their shoulders, "I knew I could depend on my two most favorite, lovely and loving girls." All became quiet and copasetic.

When they approached Marinescape and Marine Animal Aquatic World, Max stated he hoped they would come inside the MAAW facility to evaluate the embryos, PGT results and a surprise Max had for them.

Patti looked to her watch, "I have two hours before I need to pick up Blaze."

Alisa stared out the car's front windshield. "I have no car, nowhere to sleep, no job, so I guess I have all the time in the world."

Max smiled and hugged her. "I get it."

Patti asked, "Get what?"

"Blaze would be getting it," remarked Alisa. "It's a movie title quote by James Bond."

They walked from the Marinescape parking lot through the MAAW front door and all sat in front of the microscope attached to the large video screen camera feed.

"Embryo number one has nine becoming ten cells, this being day four to five. This is not very encouraging, because the growth is behind," summarized Max.

"Now embryo two: wow, with so many cells, it can't be counted."

"What's with that ring of cells with some mass within it?" posed Alisa.

"Patti, what do you think?" asked Max.

"The inner cell mass will become the actual living fetus and all the other outer cells will be the grouping, the—"

"The just as fast growing placenta and fetus's surrounding membranes," stated Alisa.

"You are both correct."

They both looked to Max for the next step, each with a hand on his upper thigh.

"The first embryo is behind a normal growth pattern; the second embryo is way beyond the normal time for embryo transfer time to the uterus," he said, looking back and forth at the women.

"Let's review the two PGT, Preimplantation genetic testing. The testing by the Detroit based PGT-SR with structural rearrangements shows embryo two is a genetic chimera. That means two different chromosome chains, in this case a twenty-three pairs, probably human, from the donor egg and a thirty-four pairs from the reptile's sperm."

"Is that compatible with life, surviving birth and a surviving woman?" Alisa sniffled.

"Alisa and Patti, fear not. Follow me for my surprise."

The three walked through the green door into the pool room with the vegetative wall. In a corner stood a machine on a wheeled cart, with gauges, tubes and a computer. It was the size of a washing machine.

"You know this pool is connected to the Matanzas River?" Max walked knee-deep into the pool dragging a green, plant-covered cube-shaped object on a separate wheeled cart.

"Well, what do you think of this domus vita?"

Two blank faces looked back at Professor Maxwell.

"This domus vita in Latin means 'house of life.' It is an artificial uterus for the two growing embryos."

"How can this plant be alive and produce nutrients to pass to a growing embryo?" a puzzled Patti asked.

"So I don't have to carry the embryo?" asked a smiling Alisa.

Max pointed to the octopus-looking machine. "Roll that heart-lung device over here, please."

The two astonished women pushed and pulled the alien-looking object to Max. As he connected several tubes to the domus, he explained. "These pink bladders you see are the artificial lungs I created. They will use room air to oxygenate the flowing red blood cells through the domus. The red blood cells origin is from me. The lower solid region of this machine contains the rhythmic pumping artificial heart to force the lung's oxygenated blood to the domus to be used by the embryo. Then this tube will soon become blue, returning deoxygenated blood to be pumped back to the lungs to be re-oxygenated. It is pretty simple? Alisa, my dear, you do not have to worry. I will not ask you to carry the embryos." Max was hugged by Alisa.

"Patti, look to the wall with all the vegetation growing on it. Let's go and sit on that wall's bench."

"This is a nice place to sit and relax," Patti said.

Alisa stood by with a smile.

"What the ... this wall's plants are trying to grow on ... both of us." Patti exclaimed.

"These plants have been genetically enhanced to monitor and respond to different environmental stimuli, like pressure from our seated weight on the plants, the sound of our voices, exhaled $CO_2$ or carbon dioxide from our breathing, our heart beats and our body heat."

"How is this possible?" asked Patti as she easily removed plant suckers from over her chest's heartbeat, moving chest wall and pulsating wrists' arteries.

"I used the genetic sites I found, which guided stem cells to injured areas within our bodies' organ systems."

"But plants don't have circulatory systems," Alisa insisted.

"Most people believe or have never thought about your statement," said Professor Maxwell as he stepped up on his imaginary lectern and started his monologue. "Vascular plants, like trees, have xylem and phloem to be the transportation systems to move water, sugar, nutrients and minerals in them. Xylem is made of tubules like our vascular blood vessel system. Phloem are cells that sit end to end like sponges, which transfer sugar and other molecules made by the plant to supply every cell with energy, including in the roots. The xylem dies every year, leaving trunk rings. The phloem lives year-round. Taking the xylem and phloem plant genetic-based characteristics and the genetic ability of stem cells to heal ... the ultimate result is an artificial genetically created uterus. This uterus will supply the embryo with nutrients to grow and for the eventual delivery of hopefully live offspring. Thus we have the domus vita. Fully functional once it is attached to the H-L machine," Max proudly displayed. "This is the first time ever seen by anyone, besides me. What do you think?"

"You should be the recipient of the Nobel Award in Physiology or Medicine! They should give you two awards, one for each category," stated Patti.

"I'm just blown away." Alisa smiled so large it took over her entire face. "I've never known or been in the presence of such a genius."

"Genius is a relative concept, which everyone has the potential to have revealed. Genius is a state a mind composed of patience, observation beyond the ordinary, thinking out of the paradigm, pursuing a dream until it became reality, persisting beyond repeated failure, learning from one's mistakes and believing in yourself, even if others do not." Max paused with a face of resolve.

"We need to run the heart-lung machine for at least an hour. Then check its gauges so that the oxygen level of 97 percent or greater, the carbon dioxide level stays at 5 percent or less, fasting glucose of 85 to 104 mg/dL and the electrolytes of sodium, potassium, chloride and bicarbonate are all in the normal range in the circulating serum. I have added low levels of biliverdin and bilirubin, which are normal in the makeup of Yao's reptile green blood."

"Mentioning Yao, are we going to help it escape before HHMI-LPA take it away?"

Alisa and Patti looked to Max who said "Don't forget Blaze, who would vote for an escape plan."

# Chapter 61

## *Domus*

**"What is your plan** from this point, Max?" Alisa asked.

"I want to show you the two collapsible chambers in the domus. In humans, day five after fertilization or conception is the best time for embryo transfer, because the endometrial lining in a uterus would be most receptive for attachment with the best absorption of nutrients. When compared to the petri dish fluid nutrients, which by day five are no longer sufficient for adequate embryo growth and if no implantation has occurred, the embryo begins rapid demise. It needs to send cells to invade a lining with has blood vessels to sustain life and growth."

"So what have you done to mimic and meet this demand?" Patti questioned.

"The domus has the vegetative vascular plant system of the xylem and phloem I have mentioned. To go to the system, I open a flap to enter each chamber. Instead of passing a catheter through a woman's cervix, which is the entrance to the uterus from the vagina, I just separate the walls of the chamber and place the embryo within and close the flap. I'm going to place the two embryos in separate chambers so their growth curves will continue and not affect the other."

Patti looked to her watch. "I have to go pick up Blaze. I'll call back to check on your progress, Professor." She gave him a peck on his check.

Max reviewed the gas and nutrient gauge levels on the H-L machine. "All is ready." He waved Alisa over and they looked at the TV monitor together at the embryos to be transferred.

"I have butterflies in my stomach with excitement," said Alisa, holding her breath.

"Not real butterflies?" he laughed.

"Oh, I feel something, something good is going to happen today," said a grinning Alisa.

The two embryos were ready and the domus placements went without any difficulties.

The two smiling friends removed their shoes and pushed the domus vita under water. The heart-lung machine remained dry on the side of the pool.

"The time has come for the domus to prove its worth," said Max prophetically.

Alisa wrapped her arms around him. "It's time for you to prove yourself worthy one more time."

They slowly wiggled to shore while pulling their clothing off and bonded their bodies to be one.

"I feel I'm in a movie scene from *On the Waterfront*," said Max as he succumbed.

"Let's see if your vita can find my domus, Rory."

Their writhing, naked bodies rolled into the pool and created their own water turbulence. With gasping breaths and sounds of mutual pleasure an orchestral climax by Pyotr Illyich Tchaikovsky's *1812 Solemn Overture, in Op. 49, in E b major* brought both to exhaustion. They lay on their backs motionless, looking up at the domed ceiling.

"I see your own twins do float."

"I see the tip of your periscope peering above the water's surface," spoke Alisa, still catching her breath. "I think your package is looking for more." She mounted on his steed for another shoreline ride. The slapping shoreline waves began again.

***

**"Excuse me, Miss."**

The young lady behind the counter turned to face the handsome man in a dark blue suit.

"Ah, yes, I'm Jennifer. How may I help you today, sir?"

"I was hoping to speak with Professor Rory Maxwell."

"Let me see," she licked her lips, staring at him.

"Are you able to page, text or call him?" the man smiled back.

"Why yes, right on." Jennifer pushed four numbers and typed in a message.

Alisa heard Max's pager vibrate and then they both heard a ringtone play "Smoke on the Water" next to his wallet. Alisa started to gallop quickly to finish her ride and then fell off next to Max.

Max answered his text, stood and got dressed. "Hello, this is Professor Maxwell. How may I help you? May we meet at the Yao, Matanzas River Monster's exhibit?"

He left Alisa lying in a calm body of warm water.

Max met the visitor in the Marinescape lobby. "Let us go to Yao's exhibit."

"Are you Professor Rory Maxwell? I am Theodor Kedzorkovic. I represent HHMI-LPA, the Howard Hughes Medical Institute and department of the Live Prehistoric Animals division. We met during your short term confinement and trial." Mr. Kedzorkovic saw the security guard sitting in a corner. He walked over and looked down at Yao, who looked up and started to rapidly swim back and forth. "Is there an area where we may speak in private, like a conference room?"

The professor and Mr. Kedzorkovic sat opposite each other at a table in the second-floor conference room, which was quite familiar to Max.

"Off the record?"

The professor nodded.

"You agreed to be part of the Yao management team in exchange for several favors, which brought your trial to a speedy termination and your release from jail. Here is the contract you signed. Is that your signature?"

Max flipped through the typed multipage document. "Yes, that is my signature, also a witness's signature and your signature and dates by each name."

"In seven to ten days, we will text you an exact day and time. A limo will retrieve you to take you to the St. Augustine Airport. An HHMI marked Gulfstream Jet will transport you to our national headquarters in Chevy Chase, Maryland, to design the holding facility and requirements to keep Yao alive, healthy and safe. Of course, its confinement needs to be safe for all our surrounding personnel."

"Will I be able to bring my assistant marine biologist with me?"

"Yes, you may. I am reminding you, out of common courtesy, that if for whatever reason you negate your part of this signed agreement, we will have legal grounds to pursue some form of punishment," spoke Mr. Kedzorkovic. "Our legal department may resort to have all … all your hard-earned degrees declared null and void, charge you with unethical practices and have malpractice proceedings started … while you wait back in prison."

"I will need to make arrangements with Marinescape, Dolphin Family Fun and Marine Animal Aquatic World for my short sabbatical," explained Professor Maxwell.

"That has already been taken care of. Your facility will continue to pay you and hold your position for you. HHMI-LPA will also pay you our usual consultant fee and your housing and food stipend while you're with us. Necessary daily transportation to and from will be provided. If you want your own vehicle, that's at your expense. Are there any questions, Professor?"

He shook his head, shook the lawyer's hand and took his copy of the work contract.

Max went back to the green door pool room to find Alisa standing only in her underwear and watching the H-L machine's gauges slightly changing.

"You always look good, no matter what you wear or don't wear," complimented Max.

She hugged him and rolled her body back and forth against his.

"We'll unveil my periscope in a moment. Are you able to come with me in a few days to the Washington, D.C. area?"

"I'd be thrilled, as long as you're there and don't abandon me."

"What do you mean? Whatever, you can stay at my place until you get your own again. You can use my Jaguar until you replace your 'missing' car." Max talked slower and slower.

Alisa manipulated his growing predicament to ensure he would be in the best working order, by whatever method she needed. One method made Max steel-like. He lifted and carried Alisa to the vegetative wall bench, which already was stained by their prior sweat, etc.

"My responses are yes, thank you and thank you," replied Alisa. They began their aerobic positioning in earnest.

***

**The next day**, the foursome collected in the multi-ceiling room before going to the pool room.

"Let us see what progress Yao Unus or one and Yao Duo or two embryos are doing."

Max pulled the domus halfway out of the pool. They were now asymmetrical, with one flap bulging like a Mickey Mouse ear. "A normal pregnancy would just be giving a positive serum or blood pregnancy test now. The serum level detected today would be ten to fifty mIU/mL or milli International Units per milliliter. The hormone would be of HCG or human chorionic Gonadotropin. Maybe a positive urine pregnancy test would also occur. Both the domus HCG chamber levels are much higher."

"A human's normal pregnancy heartbeat is seen at six weeks, maybe five-and-a-half weeks, with the average office vaginal ultrasound probe, which I have brought here today," stated Reproductive Nurse Patti with a professional air.

"We will gently press the probe into the domus right over the entrance flap, which was used for the embryo transfer," instructed Professor Maxwell.

The four held their breath.

"Let's look at Yao Unus. Where are you? Hello, there is the pregnancy sac number one. "Max moved the probe very slowly back and forth to find if any fetal parts had developed. The embryonic primitive two chamber beating heart was at 135 beats per minutes as counted by the ultrasound's computer. The average normal human fetus has 80 to 120 bpm if greater than five-and-a-half weeks this early in the pregnancy. This pregnancy was barely four weeks.

"There's also something else … two pulsing ultrasonic gray and white spots next to each other. Does that mean twin pregnancies from two embryos?" Alisa questioned.

"If anything, it would be one embryo that divided into two," corrected Patti.

Max said nothing as he studied the Yao Unus images.

"Time for Yao's Duo's ultrasound visualization," Max announced as he laid the ultrasound probe gently on the domus second flap. "Oh, I felt a bump or a throbbing." He lifted the probe off the vegetative flap. His face expressed excitement and fear.

Alisa, Patti and Blaze looked to Max for an explanation.

Professor Maxwell replaced the probe firmly and directly on the flap. An inward force pushed the probe to the side of the flap. He again lifted the probe off the flap.

"May I feel for myself?" Max nodded to Alisa.

"I'd describe it as a deep rumbling, punching or fighting?"

Patti followed with two hands completely covering the bulge. "It seems obvious to me its fetal movement, arms … legs?"

Max tried with both hands to position the probe. After unsuccessful attempts to forcefully move the probe, the movement diminished, finally becoming still. They all crowded around the small portable ultrasound machine's screen.

"This fetus is equal to a ten to twelve week fetus in human growth terms, but one would not expect detectable externally felt movement!"

The two women gasped and Blaze said "Cool."

"A human-shaped head, gill slits, four limbs with digits, a short tail, a primitive nervous system or notochord, four chambered heart and … two major chest-to-abdomen throbbing blood flows. This fetus has two aortas!" Max vocally listed his visual interpretations of its structures.

"Are those four eye sockets?" asked Blaze.

"We will have to wait and see, Blaze." Max patted him on his back.

A crackling sound again came from a wall-mounted intercom.

"Professor Maxwell, this is Jennifer. I'm your and Alisa's assistant from the front desk."

"Hello, Jennifer, I'm sure we must have worked together in the past," Maxwell sarcastically answered the two-way intercom.

"I moved up to Oceanarium maintenance when Alisa originally left us un-expectantly."

"Great, Jennifer, what do you need from me?"

"I watch Yao throughout the day. The security guard called me and he said the reptile was getting anxious and—"

"I'll be right over."

Maxwell immediately left and his three Musketeers decided to come with him, adding Jennifer to the posse.

At the poolside, Professor Maxwell saw Yao hanging from the metal net. Its movements suggested that he was mad, frustrated or wanted out of his caged structure.

"Sir, how did all this start?" Professor Maxwell asked the guard.

"I was sitting and eating my fish sandwich peacefully. I had a half left, so I walked over to poolside and waved the half a fish over the pool. Well, that reptile was all excited and swam by a couple of times." The overweight man wiped his brow. "It grabbed the net with all four and started shaking the net violently."

"What did you do then?"

"Well, I did the reasonable thing. I put the fish back in the sandwich and ate it."

All five individuals looked at each other and then to the guard, who was wiping his mouth.

"I knew I shouldn't feed the creature bread and condiments."

"Thank you for the information. Please, in the future, don't feed anything to or tease Yao." Max turned to see Yao calmly hanging from only its two front claws while watching Alisa.

Blaze tried to walk over to Alisa, but Patti held him back by his shoulder.

"Should we go back, Max?" asked Patti.

"Yes, please do, so I may show you what to do each day if I have to leave for south Washington, D.C."

As the group prepared to cross A1A, he looked back at a sun-highlighted Jennifer standing alone in the parking lot. The professor walked back to her.

"Jennifer, maybe in the future you will become part of this closed circle of Yao's faithful."

"I will do whatever it takes to prove where my loyalties lay, Professor Maxwell. You'll soon see I can be trusted and eager to perform with and for you, sir," smiled Jennifer.

They shook hands. Jennifer used a two hand clasp. The top hand softly rubbed his. Her other lower hand twitched a finger rubbing his palm. Was it to tickle?

"Call me Max," he nodded and squeezed her hand.

\*\*\*

**After the four** re-collected at the green room pool, Max was ready to list their daily duties.

"Blaze, please be sure to pay attention. You will be the ladies' monitor to ensure that they don't miss any steps concerning the domus and heart-lung machine. Does anyone notice anything different since we left?" asked Max.

All three spoke. "The domus is out of the water."

"The domus must, I stress, must always be underwater except when visualizing the fetuses. Check that all the H-L machine levels are normal. On the side of the machine are listed the normal ranges. You all must ultrasound the two fetuses every day, since their growths are so rapid and unpredictable. And, of course, document everything."

"What if there are weird and fearful changes suggesting early delivery time?" asked Alisa.

"Where are the deliveries to occur and by whom? Do we need a pediatrician present?" a worried Patti asked.

"I hope to be here or return from Washington to do the underwater deliveries. These underwater offspring should be able to fend for themselves after delivery. You forget I am a certified ARAV specialist—Association of Reptilian and Amphibian Veterinarian. However, there will be a short time period of maternal activity in which you two will need to partake." Max looked to Patti and Alisa. "Blaze, you may help as instructed by your mother and Alisa."

# Chapter 62

## Dating?

**"So we will be done** with this pain in the ass professor and his reptile freak?" smiled Deputy Keith.

"That sounds like we've said this before." Sheriff Gary tapped his pencil.

"I know that melody you're tapping out," Keith bragged. "Almost, close, I got … no, here we go … no don't have it. I give up."

Gary looked at a staring Keith and shook his head. "It's the code we all know, Keith. You must know. It's S.O.S. in Morse code." Gary loudly rapped his knuckles to the code on his desk.

"Sheriff, you will be as amazed, I think, as we are," spoke Tara as Rick and Mary Jane following her in.

"Shall I call in all available personnel, Sheriff?" Mary Jane asked.

"We were unable to use a common dating isotope, Strontium 80, since it only appeared worldwide after 1945." Tara handed a report to Sheriff Gary.

He glanced at it and handed back to Tara as Deputy Keith tried to grasp the paper. Detective Brett and CSI Director Leon walked in.

"Tara, please read your recently received report," instructed Gary.

"When I first found a scale of the criminal perpetrator of murders and assaults, I took a chance it could be used to date Yao's life span. I sent the scale to the University of Arizona, College of Science, for an accelerator mass spectrometry or AMS, for radiocarbon dating." Tara looked out at the staring faces of Rick and Leon. "Radiocarbon dating with carbon-14 depends on the decay of this radioactive element created by cosmic rays changing nitrogen-14 to C-14. Nitrogen is the most abundant element in the air. C-14 is used by plants, eaten by animals and becomes part of their cells. So an organic part of Yao can, in theory, be dated. Any questions? O.K., so here are the results of the AMS. Their disclaimer is that the maximum dating only goes back fifty thousand years, maybe as far back as seventy thousand years. Yao's scale, which came off its clawed hand, is greater than seventy-thousand-years-old!"

A few gasps, no remarks and no questions.

"Yao is more than a mutant alligator or crocodile," stated Tara.

******

**"While we** are still here together, there is a critical issue all of us need to address," Max seriously stated. "The HHMI-LPA will be removing Yao to an undisclosed location to do whatever they like, unmonitored. Do we accept this action?"

"No," blared out Blaze.

"What do you see our options are, Max?" questioned Patti.

"Simple, break Yao out to freedom," interrupted a hyperventilating Alisa.

All three turned their eyes on to the professor, the one with all the answers in the past.

The small group of mutineers gathered at poolside. "As I see it, number one is to loosen up the steel net attachments to the walls for Yao to make his own escape. Number two is to wait and see how Yao is treated, since I was told I would be part of Yao's management. Number three is to take no chances of broken promises and assist Yao with an escape by cutting the net and hope the authorities will think an animal rights protestor did the act." Max looked at the three nodding heads.

A man wearing a black vest walked into the Yao exhibit and stood next to the pool. Yao swam back and forth. "You killed my daughter," he said as he pulled out a gun. He seemed to aim and fire at Yao, but the revolver clicked empty several times.

The security guard woke up and slowly approached the man, who knelt down crying. The guard reached for the gun, which had been dropped through the mesh.

\*\*\*

"**Rick**, do you know of other ways to date objects," asked Tara. Rick was reading an article in the *Journal of Biochemistry* titled "The Scent of Disease: volatile organic compounds of the human body related to disease."

"Ricky?" as Tara started to wrap her arms around Rick's abdomen and squeeze. He laid the magazine down. "I wanted to make sure you heard my question."

"I know one can date with reference to a tree trunk's rings, reporting the climate changes. Dating of fossils can be done by testing for trace radioactive elements in bone. The farthest back in time dating is by testing for cosmically created radioactive isotopes in the atmosphere deposited on the earth's rock surfaces," finished groaning Rick. Tara started a search for his dangling participle. After a short time of personal recovery and redressing, they both started internet and journal searching for fossil dating.

"Now, if a fossil can't be used or isn't helpful for dating, the rock and sediment around the fossil will be used for dating," summed up Rick. "Why are you so interested, Tara?"

"I don't like not knowing something that is scientifically-based information," Tara answered. "Like the age of this Yao."

"Here's what I know about that. Radiometric dating involves the use of some isotope's decay rate over time compared to another isotope for dating. They use rubibium-strontium, thorium-lead, potassium-argon, argon-argon, and uranium-lead decay comparisons for dating. All have a very long half life, 0.7 to 48.6 billion years. Thus the relative proportions of the two isotopes can give good dating, if they are present in the sample. Only a nanogram or one billionth of a gram, equal to 0.0352 ounce of the sample, will be all that is needed."

"Just the other day, I watched a blackbird use a stone to crack open a sunflower seed," said Tara, looking to the ceiling.

Rick then spoke. "I saw a big mouse play with a little mouse."

"That is supposed to be a cat plays with a ... Rick, you are so abstract and still funny. I love you for being you."

"You said 'you being you.' Am I being a mouse or a cat?"

Tara pinched Rick's ear. "Are you listening to me?"

Rick went to grab Tara's left breast, but she moved away faster, followed with a hand slap.

"No, really, if a bird uses a stone, why can't we? This is what I'm thinking." Tara increased her speed of speech. "I noticed that as Yao hung from the metal mesh over its pool, it had solidified scales on its right waistline."

"When were you that close to the reptile?" questioned Rick.

"I went to see Yao at the Marinescape exhibit dedicated to Yao, the Matanzas Monster. More importantly, the solid area looked like some kind of rock. If I could get a small sample of that suspected rock on Yao—because that area has been with Yao since that injury, maybe hundreds of thousands of years ... maybe millions of years?"

"You think it could be from volcanic action?" Rick bobbed his head like a rooster.

"Now we're both on the same page," excitedly stated Tara, placing his hand on her breast.

"Then igneous rock is commonly mixed with hot lava, making a metamorphic rock." Rick also spoke faster. "O.K., we need the most common isotope used for igneous rock." He flipped through one reference book to another with his available hand.

"Here, on the internet, I found that the University of California performs isotope potassium 40 to isotope argon 40 assays, decay of one to the other comparison. This gives a dating range of 500,000 years to 4.6 billion years. If the date is hard to believe, then we'll do a confirmatory assay," said Tara.

"I found this in one of the reference manuals," added Rick. "If we need a confirmation, we'll use isotope uranium-238 to lead-206. The half life of the isotope is in the same range, with the dating range slightly narrower at 10 million years to 4.6 billion years."

I'm embarrassed to admit I don't know the difference between lava and magma," Tara said as she caressed his privates with her smiling face.

Rick's hands rubbed her back. She sat up, moving his head to her chest.

Later, another internet search revealed "magma is acidic, contains high silica levels becoming molten rock within the earth at 1,600 to 2,120 degrees Fahrenheit," read Tara.

"Lava, on the other hand, is when the magma comes out onto the earth's surface as molten lava at 1,165 degrees Fahrenheit and begins to cool down. When molten lava mixes with another rock, usually igneous rock, it is called metamorphic rock," finished Rick.

"So we hope this rock fragment burned and scarred on Yao's waistline scales."

***

**Mary Jane** interrupted Gary and Keith's "fastest draw" game. "Sheriff, the security guard Thyther at the Yao's Exhibit called saying there had been a shooting."

Once Gary and Brett arrived, they approached the guard standing over a crying, bent over man on a bench outside the Yao Exhibit entrance.

"Was there any resistance, Thyther?" asked Officer Brett.

"My baby girl is gone … it raped her and murdered her."

"Guard Thyther, where is the weapon?" the sheriff asked.

"I saw him drop a small 6-round Ruger, I think, on the covering mesh. The gun was then grabbed by the monster and both disappeared," anxiously explained the security guard.

"Smythe, did you unload several rounds into the damn creature yourself?" whispered Gary.

"What did you say, Sheriff?"

"Nothing," Gary said in a whisper. "Sir, what is your name?"

He shrugged his shoulders.

"Who is — was—your lost loved one, your daughter?"

He gave another shoulder shrug.

"Where is your firearm, sir?"

No response from the man.

"Officer Brett, take this uncooperative man to the station's holding room," ordered Gary.

As the two were leaving, the man said, "Wendy, poor Wendy."

***

363

**"So we all** agree, help get Yao free for a better life rather than to be a continuous experiment as a prisoner with little chance for friends," concluded Blaze. "How do we do that?"

"When is the security guard the least aware of Yao's activity?" posed Alisa.

"He goes to read the specials on the cafeteria menu. Unable to decide, he orders two meals, goes to the restroom, back to the cafeteria to read a newspaper and then back in line to order a dessert," smiles Patti.

"How do you know his routine, Patti?"

"Just being a mother; we'll leave it at that."

"Then he has a cerebral steal," added Max. "You all know the drowsiness that occurs after a big meal ... oxygen preferentially goes to the intestine. Tomorrow will be our action, A-day to act."

"I will short out the electrical network that was set up for electrocution in an extreme attempt to stop an escape," planned Max. "Then I will loosen one length of pool mesh with a rub cover wrench."

"I'll speak with Yao," stated Alisa. "It knows more than anyone would think it could actually understand."

"Quiet now, the security guard is coming," announced Max.

Three minutes later, the guard walked in eating a pastry.

"How did you know he was coming, Max?"

"I heard his mouth and jaw chopping. Hello," answered Max as his cell phone started to sing out "Smoke on ..."

"Let me look at my schedule. How about now?" he laughed. "We will continue this planning session later today. I have a supposedly urgent meeting with the Assistant CSI Tara, from the County Law Enforcement Agency."

\*\*\*

**Professor Maxwell** and Tara met at the Marinescape first-floor hallway. Tara spoke of two concerns. "Wendy, who claimed to be carrying Yao's pregnancy, died a horrendous death. Her father came to the Yao Exhibit and emptied his handgun toward Yao."

"Was Yao hit? Any green blood spilled in the pool? Did Yao stop moving and sank to the bottom of the pool?" asked Max.

"Well, no to all three," answered Tara.

"No problem. Let's walk over to the exhibit. What is the second concern?" Max listened to Tara's plan and her arguments to support her idea.

"Ah, I was hoping to do the abdominal massaging and you, Professor, perform a small biopsy," smiled Tara. She studied his face. "Max, we'll talk later, in a more private atmosphere, where you decide what I will owe you. But first I need you to perform the biopsy." Tara stood up and placed her hands on her hips and coyly tilted her head and hips.

"I'll gather what is needed. How much do you need for the dating?"

"No more than two grams, in case there will be two assays."

Within a half hour, the two accomplished the specimen retrieval for dating. The experience was seemingly painless for Yao, who enjoyed the rubbing with the expected happy ending.

"We will get together in a more conducive environment for our mutual settling up," the professor said as he shook Tara's lingering and squeezing hand. "Tara, you'll report Yao is status quo?"

Fortunately, unbeknown to the professor, Alisa, Patti and Blaze watched the entire preparation, biopsy process and Max's goodbye handshake, with nothing more personal.

"I should still have time to send off the specimen today," Tara said and then waved as she left.

"That was all about—" Patti stopped with Blaze and Alisa behind her.

"Obtaining a surface biopsy of Yao's scaly skin for dating its age," interrupted Max. "The guard is now off to dinner for at least an hour."

"The guard wasn't interested in you getting a biopsy?" asked Patti.

"I will just mention that any participation from this point on is probably a criminal act. I know it is for me, as far as the St. Johns Law Enforcement Agency, Marinescape and the Howard Hughes Medical Institute, with whom I signed an all-encompassing contract, are concerned. If I am caught releasing Yao, guaranteed prison time will be waiting for me," said Max matter-of-factly to the other three. "If I am caught, I will emphatically state that you were not involved and were unaware of my entire plan. You were misled by my words, actions and promised results."

"Max you are an amazing wordsmith. You don't need me as your public relations personnel," Alisa said as she hugged him. Blaze quickly became glued to them. Max smiled at Patti and nodded to join the group appreciation bonding fest. This was an affirmation that all were committed.

The guard acted as predicted—ate, re-ate and slept with a confirming snore. Max committed his part of the already-spoken crime. Alisa and Blaze spoke with Yao. Yao easily pulled the mesh out of its way. Patti, Alisa, Blaze and Max all pointed to the white outer wall for him to escape over. Once over, the four ran to the wall and watched Yao walk into the surf. In a thoughtful action, Yao stopped and looked back to the four viewers. Alisa and Blaze waved and Yao partially lifted a hand up. Tears started to flow; even Max had a salty tear collect and require a wipe. Alisa thought she saw Yao with teary eyes. The foursome quickly vanished.

# Chapter 63

## *Crime*

**I need to assess** the last twenty-four hours of growth in the domus," stated the professor.

"I'll come with you," added Alisa.

"I have to report to work," Patti regretted. "And you, young man, have school tomorrow."

"Mom, do I have to?"

They had their goodbye hugs.

"We should have enough time to evaluate the two fetal growths before the anticipated police interrogation begins."

***

"**W**ell, tell us what happened here, Mr. 'Loyalty Security' Guard Thyther?" Sheriff Gary read his shirt logo.

"When I left for dinner, the creature was swimming slowly back and forth, as usual. When I came back, I sat in my chair as usual. I noticed nothing peculiar, Sheriff."

"So what got you to call the police station, Thyther?"

"A little while later, I got up to relieve myself. That's when I noticed that part of the net was lower in the water. I walked over and noticed no creature in the pool. Of course, I released the Taser from my utility belt, did a quick search of the premises and found no creature and immediately called your station number on my speed dial."

"Then why did we find you lying on the exhibit floor when we first came in, Smythe?" asked Sheriff Gary.

He looked away. "I pulled it out of the holster and accidently Tasered my foot."

"So all you described was after you woke up?"

"Yes sir, Sheriff."

"Just call me Sheriff. You're lucky you had the Taser on normal charge and not at high lethal."

He nodded.

"Did you see any wet footprints? Did you see anything that might help the investigation?" asked Deputy Sheriff Keith.

The guard stood mute with a facial grimace.

"Sheriff, the security electrification of the metal net has been shorted out," reported Rick.

"What is your impression? Accidental or purposely shorted out?" asked Gary.

"Either is possible, can't say at this time. I'll have Tara photographic and fingerprint the site," responded Rick.

"Sheriff, a series of ratchet nuts on the wire net connections to the outer pool wall circuitry became loose and released," relayed Detective Brett. "There are tool markings on some nuts, but I can't tell if those marks were made on the original installation tightening, if it was a purposeful recent loosening or if the nuts just slowly worked their way free with Yao's repeat violent yanking and pulling on the mesh. But because of the salt water, most loosened nuts do have some rust, even though they are stainless steel, so they were probably loosened by Yao's actions."

"Have Tara and Rick seen if they have any tests or tricks to tell the difference," joined in CSI Director Leon.

"Sheriff, you'll want to see this," announced Patrolman John Brenner.

The two leaned over the outer Marinescape wall and saw large footprints in the sand leading to the ocean shoreline.

"Sheriff, I also found Wendy's father's firearm, a Ruger GP 100, on the pool bottom under a log with other paraphernalia thrown in by visitors."

"Anything interesting?" asked Gary.

"Coins, Timex watch still ticking with the correct time, a small flashlight and a diamond ring,"

"Get Tara to photograph and cast one of those footprints before the ocean waves wash them away and then have her photograph the creature's hidden stash," ordered the sheriff. Gary studied his face. "Then do that, John." Gary placed a hand on his shoulder and then turned to Keith.

"Deputy Sheriff Keith, you know who we need to question."

The deputy went to the front Marinescape desk.

"Good morning, Missy," greeted Keith with his devilish "cat ate a canary" smile, looking for another prey of a juicy mouse.

"Good morning. "What do you need, Officer?" replied Jennifer.

"I'd like to take you out for something to drink, eat or sometime else. I'm very flexible on hours," smiled the deputy."

"Ah, I'm working right now, I—"

"Would you happen to be looking for me, Deputy?" asked Max.

"You are a … yes, I am. I need to question you and your assistant, Alisa, about the reptile's escape sometime late last night or early this morning."

"I'm right here at your disposal, Deputy Sheriff Keith," said Alisa as she came up behind Max.

Jennifer mouthed "thank you" to the professor.

The three found the infamous or famous, conference room for verbal exchanges. Deputy Keith asked many questions of the two. There was a lot of sidestepping of the questionees, with no significant or useful answers given for the deputy to surmise any helpful conclusions. The deputy left angry and frustrated.

The professor and Alisa felt they weren't guilty of any criminal actions they could be levied against them. As the two left for the MAAW facility, Jennifer came over to Max.

"Thanks so much, Professor, for directing the officer's mind away from me. I owe you one." She touched Max's arm as he left.

Once they crossed A1A, Alisa asked, "What was that with that girl?"

"Oh, the deputy sheriff was being a predator."

The domus vita was half out of the water. Max checked all the H-L machine gauges, which were all in their normal ranges.

"Here is the ultrasound machine," offered Alisa.

"You can do the two fetal scans," Max confidently said and handed her the probe.

Alisa scanned chamber one with a large smile. "All the organs I can visualize appear normal to me; however, the heart rate is only ninety beats per minute by the built-in computer counter. Also, my measurements don't reveal much growth having occurred."

"Those things you mentioned are somewhat discouraging. We will be looking again in four days or sooner. Let us evaluate chamber number two."

Alisa reluctantly started looking at the much larger second fetus. They glanced at each other. "This guy's heart is at 161 beats per minute. It definitely has two aortas. It has ten fingers and toes. I see no claws. Do you agree, Max?"

"You are right so far."

"The notochord or spinal cord seems to be progressing as expected. The head is more human-shaped than Yao's. All the limbs are long by the measurements. One eye has disappeared. Now I see only three eyes."

"Anything else?"

"Its overall size equals a five-month pregnancy, not six weeks, as predicted by dates," Alisa summarized.

"And the skin appears—"

"Bumpy," interrupted Alisa.

"Finally, what is your prediction of its sex?" asked Max as he lightly elbowed Alisa.

\*\*\*

**A** man and woman came to the Marinescape's front counter.

"How may I help the two of you?" asked a smiling Jennifer.

"We would like to speak with your marine biologist, Rory Maxwell."

"No problem, I know he's still on campus." The front desk phone rang and Jennifer handed it to the woman without asking who it was.

"Professor Maxwell? This is Miss Amy Anastasia Alla Adamoffski from HHMI-LPA." Then the phone was handed to the man. "And I am Theodore Kedzorkovic, J.D. I'm the lawyer you met in jail previously when you signed the Yao maintenance contract. We would like to see you and Yao. Shall we meet at the Yao Matanzas Monster exhibit?"

Fifteen individuals eventually came to the exhibit. Alisa stood by the dismantled metal mesh speaking with Tara. Also present were Marinescape Administrator Mr. Walker Wren Wells, the attorney Ted Kedzorkovic, paleobiologist Amy Adamoffski, CSI Director Leon and Lab Assistant Rick. Professor Maxwell and the security guard stood behind them all, pretending to listen.

"Ladies and gentleman, how nice we could all meet today," announced Professor Maxwell.

"Professor Maxwell, this is no blithe seaside gathering for your amusement," staunchly spoke Kedzorkovic. "We have had a devastating situation occur here, with very serious consequences for you, Professor."

"Well, Mr. Kedzorkovic, I don't really see where the severe repercussions come back to me," answered Maxwell in his usual matter-of-fact way. "Oh, what a surprise, the late-comers from the downstairs viewing area, Sheriff Gary and Tonto ... no, I apologize, Deputy Sheriff Keith."

"The problem for you, Professor Maxwell, is that you signed a contract facilitating your jail release based on seeing Yao. I look around and do not see Yao," Kedzorkovic smirked. "Doctor Adamoffski, do you see the reptile Yao? Doctor, did you not make this trip to see this prehistoric reptile?"

She hesitantly nodded for the lawyer's charade.

"Does anyone? Sheriff Gary, Deputy Keith, CSI Director Leon? Oh, I apologize to the responsible party, Professor Rory Maxwell. Do you see Yao? Does anyone see Yao?"

Additional people showed up behind Tara and Alisa. There was Patti, who'd been called by Alisa, and the front desk attendant, Jennifer.

"Let me think." Maxwell tapped his index finger against his right temple. "I could be mistaken. On page sixteen, paragraph three, I remember reading that I would perform health management for Yao and set safety parameters for HHMI personnel working with and around Yao." Max paused and looked at Mr. Kedzorkovic. "You probable have the actual contract in your black briefcase in your left hand." Professor Maxwell looked to the briefcase. "Feel free to check. I may have used a little paraphrasing. I distinctly do not remember any language, legal or not, describing my responsibility to secure that Yao could or would not escape from the Marinescape exhibit pool. If it was moved to another location, that also would not be my responsibility." Maxwell put his hands out and palms up in a "What, me?" gesture.

"Sheriff Gary, have I, Professor Rory Maxwell, committed a crime?"

No response from the sheriff except a scorching stare.

"I believe the CSI team is done here," proclaimed Director Leon.

The law enforcement and CSI team made their exit, except for Tara and Sheriff Gary.

"Here is your termination paper and final checks," Gary said, handing them to the security guard.

"No bonus for the extra time I put in?" complained the guard. "Anyway, you can't fire me. The State Police Chief is the one who hired me and could let me go."

"Look at who signed the release papers," said the sheriff as he walked out of the exhibit.

"Oh," retracted the guard, verbally and physically.

The lawyer approached Mr. Wells. "The HHMI paid you in advance for the harboring of the reptile. We will expect the prepayment paid back in full within a week; otherwise, a 20 percent interest charge will be added every week."

"That is like extortion. But I will need more—" The attorney turned away.

The attorney and paleobiologist made their exit with no parting statements.

"Doctor Adamoffski, would you like to spend a few minutes reviewing what I know about Yao, the prehistoric reptile of interest?" asked the professor.

"I just need a few short comments with the attorney first. Yes, I would like that."

They made their way to the professor's small office.

"All wise-talking criminals will slip up ... and I'll be there to catch him," remarked Gary. "Give me five minutes alone with that slimy, prickly urchin and I'll get the guilty shark bait to confess," snarled Deputy Keith.

"To be able to do that, it needed to be before 1966," commented Gary.

"I'm not getting your point, Sheriff."

"In 1966, the US Supreme court decided in favor of Mr. Miranda in the case against the State of Arizona. So that is why we say, in his name, "You have the right to remain silent …""

Mr. Attorney Ted Kedzorkovic walked out mumbling messages into his hand-held recorder. The security guard went to eat. Alisa, Patti and Tara exchanged thoughts when Jennifer walked over to them.

"Wasn't that man just brilliant, just such a brilliant speech by the professor? He was so sexy," Jennifer gushed. "Seeing and hearing it live was like watching a TV episode of *Law and Order*."

Jennifer left, and the three remaining women casually fished around the other two's thoughts with indirect questions about how personally involved they had been with Max. As they left, each glanced at the stairway to the conference room.

"What's so fascinating about the room upstairs?" Patti asked as she walked upstairs.

The other two kept walking straight to the parking lot.

Tara saw Alisa climb into the convertible Jaguar. "Quite a spectacular car you're driving," commented Tara.

"Thanks. I lost my Beetle and Max said I could use his car anytime I needed to."

\*\*\*

**"Professor** Rory Maxwell, I was quite impressed with your resume and response to Mr. Kedzorkovic," Doctor Adamoffski stated as she touched Max's hand. "I haven't seen anyone handle him in such a way." She looked at Max's eyes with a smile.

They sat next to each other by his desk and filing cabinets.

"Nicely organized, tightly packed office, Professor Rory Maxwell," remarked Amy as she scanned the disheveled journals on his desk.

"Please call me Max."

"I will if you call me by my favorite name? Do you recall it?"

"I'm thinking most people call you Doctor Amy. I'm favoring Alla. Therefore, I suggest a reorganization of our names which seem to fit tighter together … Alla and Rory." Rory moved his chair closer to her chair and placed an arm on top her chair. She heard the door close and lock. Max slipped his arm off the chair to behind her back down to her waist.

"Was that the sound of a door locking? Professor, I think you and I have given each other the wrong impressions."

As he pulled her in tight to him, Doc Alla pushed Professor Max away and stood up. She extended an arm and the two lightly shook hands. Her other hand unlocked the door.

"Maybe we should leave some things for a future meeting ... or not," the Doctor Amy said as she turned and walked out and away from the office.

# Chapter 64

## Unexpected

**A month passed** with no one seeing or talking with Professor Maxwell. Alisa drove his car, so people assumed she knew where he was. "I'm staying at his condo and I haven't seen him since Yao's escaped."

"I and Blaze have been at the MAAW and the front door code has been changed," Patti relayed.

As the two women stood in the Marinescape parking lot, a St. Johns Sheriff vehicle passed them and did a sharp U-turn to get back to the parking lot entrance. "Hello ladies, I was looking for Professor Maxwell and Sheriff Gary," Tara asked through an open car window.

"Of course, you're looking for Max for yourself, aren't you?" smiled Alisa.

"Well, I heard through the grapevine you were living with him."

"I stay in his condo, but he hasn't been there for about a mouth."

Tara acted a little flustered. "If you see him, tell him, off the record, that the sheriff is planning to somehow capture him committing a crime," Tara relayed. "Also, the HHMI-LPA department has hired a group of professional human and animal trackers to find and recapture Yao." Tara closed her window, U-turned again, and headed north.

"I hope Max is O.K.," Alisa shouted out loud.

Tara drove back to the substation. *Oh no*, she thought, *my personal stalker is back.* He waved. She parked the vehicle and dropped her head to the steering wheel.

"Hi, Tara, do you remember me?" the black-haired ponytailed Native American said.

"Yes, I do, Mr. Manta."

"I heard the el lagarto or la Lagartija … depending on if it's male or female … has escaped. I'm here to help the police capture it." Yuma stood with his hands on his hips.

"The State of Florida Law Enforcement Agency has taken over that responsibility; they have usurped us locals again." Tara looked out her car window, avoiding his face.

"I'm sure you and your sheriff would like to usurp them by capturing or killing it."

Tara looked to his smiling face.

"See my red, rusted, bent up 1977 F-150 truck over there?" Yuma pointed, "The whole back bed is filled with bags of jicama," he proudly stated. "Mexican yam beans, Mexican turnip, legumes, Verbascum and Thapsus plants, which contain the aquatic fish and animal sedative. It is an old Native American fishing secret to always catch what an Indian wants."

"And what do you do, use them as bait because Yao loves to eat them?" Tara stepped out of her vehicle.

"Quite funny Tara, I will crush the gray bark, roots, stems, leaves and seeds to get the toxic powder. Then it goes in the waters where the creature is hiding. In a short time, the aquatic creature will float to the surface, and it is your turn to do what you must."

"What is the actual chemical extract?" she asked. "A sedative called Rotenone, which given in high enough doses will kill. This ignorant Indian knows it works by impairing the animal's oxygen consumption," Yuma answered with his sarcastic comment.

Tara hesitated and slowly answered. "Sounds quite admirable, Mr. Manta; however, as I said, our department branch is not involved with the Yao problem. I'll pretend you didn't tell me about your specific plans."

"Since I'm here, how about us going to your favorite restaurant for a bite?"

*** 

**Max listened** to daily helicopters flying slowly over the research facility.

"It has been a month and they still haven't found me." He scanned the first chamber. Max stood thigh-deep in the pool. "Here you are, Unus embryo, five days since the last scan and the heartbeat has stopped. The embryo has lost its definition and is now a nonviable pregnancy." Max looked toward his partner and they both silently grieved. It was the first time he had seen Yao with teary eyes.

Max opened the flap and reached into the number Unus chamber. The shriveling fetal sac, the size of a grape, easily peeled away into his hand. Max dropped it into a specimen jar with saline. "I will do a karyotyping, looking—" He looked to Yao.

It nodded its head. "Look fo bad?" Yao said.

Max was astonished. "That is right, determine chromosome numbers and for abnormalities to explain the fetal loss."

Yao seems to understand English speech and its vocal responses had markedly improved with its daily green room communication with Max. Yao had most likely evolved vocal cords from its normal primitive airway flaps found at the junction of its throat and main bronchus or airway.

Maxwell had deduced Yao would wait in its Matanzas River haven, the vegetative, sky-lit pool room. There was more of an animal attraction to its potential offspring than Max ever expected. Yao disappeared in the pool water as the sound of a helicopter approached.

Prior to Max performing his chamber duo domus vita ultrasound, he released Speedy within the research facility. All inner doors were open. Speedy could be heard but not seen outside the pool room's green door. While Max had locked himself away in the research facility, he had performed more artificial genetic engineering or manipulation. The first of the two "new and improved" animals was an insect named 88 Butterfly from Pantanal, Brazil. This area of Brazil was the largest tropical wetlands in the world. Pantanal was Portuguese for wetland or marsh. The butterfly's uniqueness and identifiable marking was by the number "88" on each wing. Max brought the 88 Butterfly frozen with him from Brazil in its very early developmental cocoon until now. He genetically manipulated the butterfly by injecting a viral particle, called a virion, with desired genes into the central cocoon undeveloped DNA mass. This gave the butterfly the same physical flying abilities of a dragonfly, like Speedy, but added vocal sound recognition by their wing sensors and two head antennae.

Again as Professor Maxwell prepared to scan chamber two of domus, he called out "anima mea?" Within moments, he heard the sounds of buzzing and wing flapping. Onto his head and left shoulder landed anima mea, the 88 Butterfly and Speedy.

"I see the two of you are still flying together." For whatever reason, Speedy bonded to anima mea. The big difference between the two was that anima mea came when called, like a dog. Speedy responded about 50 percent of the time. The second difference was that anima mea had a larger wing surface area, so it could just float as it hovered but still go up and down and backward with minimal wing movements. Thus, it had an advantage over the dragonfly Speedy.

The scan of chamber two definitely revealed active life, with violent kicking against the ultrasound probe. "Good morning, Mini Yao."

At that moment, big Yao's head appeared and approached the ultrasound's viewing screen.

"I called it your protégé Mini Yao. Is that O.K.?"

"Yaa," Yao saw the two companions.

"These are Speedy and anima mea. The dragonfly is for its speedy flight. The number 88 Butterfly winged insect is anima mea, meaning psyche or soul, named for its lofty, floating flight."

Yao appeared to be listening and concentrating on the words.

"Mini Yao will soon be ready for its live birthing into the pool, Yao. I want to include Patti and Alisa for assistance. They know of your existence, just not that this is your new home."

Yao became excited, with some water splashing and slapping the water's surface. Max was not sure if Yao was excited at hearing Alisa's name or the soon-to-be water birth offspring.

"Ali … aze … B … aze."

Max assumed it meant Alisa and Blaze.

"I think with the growth rate on Mini Yao, the birthing should be in another month," Max said to Yao's concerned looking face. Yao stood near Max with its arms out in a T shape. Speedy and anima mea flew and perched on each arm.

The second genetically manipulated new creature was a calico cat from the Humane Society near the time for its euthanasia. Professor Maxwell removed one of the cat's ovaries. He retrieved several eggs from the rescued female cat and then performed ICSI with veterinarian supplied cat sperm. Max created a carrier virion that would be adding DNA genes with desired characteristics. Once the fertilization occurred, the virion was injected into the egg's nucleus before cell division. The final step consisted of placing the embryo into one of the horns of the Calico cat's bicornuate uterus, which means two cavities like a Y, something many animals have. When the artificially created baby Calico was born, its birthing mother cat was extremely attentive.

There were several gene sites Professor Maxwell manipulated. As with Speedy and anima mea, Max introduced new genes to the creature's chromosomes. All three have excellent 20/2 vision. Normal human vision is 20/20 vision on the eye chart developed in 1862 by Herman Snellen. When someone has better vision than average, like 20/15, that means they can read at twenty feet what the normal person reads at fifteen feet. So these three creatures can see something clearly at twenty feet that a normal human could see clearly at two feet! The strongest natural vision in the animal kingdom is an eagle at 20/5.

All these creatures not only had tricolor (red, blue, green) vision but also ultraviolet range vision and excellent night vision. The cat's UV vision allowed it to see small urine droppings of rodents for tracking the animals. Finally, the cat's eyes were set at a thirty-degree angle outward to give up to a 340-degree visual field. Oh, the cat's eyes also could move independently, like an eagle's.

"Cali, Cali!" The cat came running to Max's feet as he walked out of the pool room. Speedy and anima mea followed Max by flight from Yao. Max turned back to see Yao's head become completely submerge.

***

**"It has been** almost two months and still no sign of the reptile or Maxwell," complained Gary.

"Well, thanks to that Indian Manta, we have lots of floating fish on the river," spoke up Deputy Sheriff Keith. "He said he used natural plants to hopefully poison the hombre el Lagarto. Of course, no Man Lizard surfaced. I gave him a fine for illegal fishing practices."

"Aren't the professionals for HHMI-LPA using a fish poison called Tricaine?" the sheriff asked.

"Yea, Tricaine mesylate, but I thought if I hassled them, I'd get myself into a probable legal shitstorm. You know, pick on the little, easy guy."

Down in the lab, Tara and Rick talked about the sheriff's dilemma.

"The sheriff is the one who actually caught that Yao. Now they tell him to stay out of the way," said Rick. "Maybe it's gone from our area or died?"

"I think Yao is much smarter than anyone gives it credit for." Tara kept looking through her microscope. "I wouldn't be surprised if Yao and Professor Maxwell have left together or he's sheltering Yao. I do wonder how Max is doing."

"I know you've always had a thing for him," Rick said, looking at Tara.

"Oh Ricky, you know you're my favorite. I've shown you that." She rolled her chair over to him and gave him sloppy kisses on his ear, face and finally his lips. "How is little Ricky doing?" Tara grasped his crouch. "Oh, I think big Ricky has arrived."

\*\*\*

**"I've asked** you to join me today for a joyous occasion." Max walked into the pool water.

"Blaze, you now have three friends to play within the multi-ceiling room."

The three were playful and compatible with each other and with now Blaze. In fact, as Blaze sat on the multi-ceiling room's bench, Speedy and anima mea sat on his two shoulders while Cali jumped up and sat purring in his lap. "Are all three friends from changed chromosomes?" asked Blaze.

"All three still have their natural chromosome number; I just added some genes," smiled Max. "There next to the bench is Cali's mother sleeping on a cushion."

"What is my chromosome number?" inquired Blaze.

"Well, boy, girl, mom and man are all forty-six-chromosome animals. Anima mea has twenty, Speedy has twenty-seven, and Cali has thirty-eight chromosomes. (*Appendix: Animal Chromosome Number*)

"If only there was a camera to capture this moment," mused Patti.

"I have good news and bad news," announced Max. "The bad news is embryo number Unus stopped growing and actually shriveled up. Its heartbeat slowed and then stopped over five days. The amniotic sac that should have grown around the fetus with fluid did not and shrank," Professor Maxwell explained. "Therefore, I removed the sac and removed the non-growing fetus with no heartbeat. The fetus had already become an amorphous mass. It was basically a grape that became a raisin."

"And what is the good news?" Alisa impatiently asked.

"That would be that fetus number two has grown tremendously fast. Instead of seven to nine weeks in size, our new member, whom I call Mini Yao ..." Max paused.

The two women laughed and clapped with enthusiasm and the watchful and excited Yao demonstrated its emotions with water surface slapping.

"I am pretty certain Mini Yao needs a water birth. Prehistoric aquatic reptiles and some dinosaurs birthed in the ocean or brine water. We will do that in this pool," the excited professor explained. "With other reptiles like the crocodilia class, the newborn break out of their shells and are completely independent of their mother and go on their own to survive. The new young then crawl into the water. In any case, we have these two scenarios covered."

"Is that why the domus vita is in the pool?" asked Alisa.

"Exactly, Alisa," answered Patti with a nervous smile. "In Mini Yao's case, we don't know what to expect." Max looked at the women. "No questions so far?" They all heard Blaze calling anima mea, Cali and Speedy.

"Now for general information, lizards, reptiles, amphibians and fish normally lay eggs and are cold-blooded. Yao is definitely not cold-blooded. A human's average body temperature is 98.6 degrees Fahrenheit, plus or minus a degree. Yao has thrived in 86 to 95 degree Fahrenheit on different occasions. It accepts its environmental water temperature but has always maintained being a warm-blooded animal."

"Like mammals do," interjected Patti.

"And why do we care? I mean how that will help Mini Yao's birth?" asked Alisa.

"I'll get there," smiled Max. "I suspect Yao's ancestry, the crocodilia, goes back to 150 to 250 million years ago. They always have been semi-aquatic and on land, like in the time of the dinosaurs, including the Triassic, 252 to 201 million years ago, Jurassic, 201 to 145 million years ago and Cretaceous, 145 to 65 million years, time periods. A gigantic marine lizard-reptile the size of a warm-blooded whale-sized mammal called a Mosasaur gave live births to their offspring swimming in water rather than from cracking open laid eggs. The two rare characteristics for reptiles, being warm-blooded and having water births, suggested to me an extremely special reptile, like Yao. Thus, Yao's offspring should be delivered by a water birth."

"I'm not sure I understand," asked Patti, "how you surmised that Yao was not born in present day versus about 200 million years ago."

"That is an excellent question," remarked Max. "When you were both gone from Yao's exhibit before it escaped, Tara asked to come over and do a scale biopsy. She had previously noted that several scales on its side had coalesced into one solid patch. I am now waiting for carbon-14 dating or another test to identify this reptile's actual age."

"Is it like counting a tree trunk's rings?" asked Blaze. He walked through the green door with anima mea on his right shoulder, Cali in his crossed arms. and Speedy flying above him.

Almost instantly, Yao rose out of the pool water. Speedy and anima mea flew over its head. Cali jumped out of Blaze's arms and scurried out of the pool room.

"Can I see the baby so far? Is it good?" Blaze asked.

Max looked to Patti. "Blaze, baby number one was not healthy and it passed away. Baby number two is doing well. Let's all look at what I call Mini Yao."

"Yeah, like the Mini Me in an Austin Powers movie," Blaze laughed.

"Right, everyone look to the ultrasound screen." Maxwell explained the fetus's features.

"Where are the extra holes or eyes?" Blaze asked.

"I reviewed amphibian, reptile and fish paleobiologist literature and the consensus is that this third eye is associated with the pineal gland and a photoreceptor organ still found in some lizards. In humans, the pineal gland is related to melatonin and our sleep cycle. The fourth eye, also found in frogs, is from the parapineal gland, which is an outgrowth of the pineal gland. It actually has a lens and retinal tissue found in a human eye and aids in the frog's circadian and seasonal rhythms."

"So where are they?" asked Blaze.

"They have regressed into the reptile's skull or are under its skin. Shall we discuss the time of the birthing process? A practical review," Max said and smiled. "The H-L machine remains out of the water. The domus vita remains slightly under the water's surface. I would like you ladies to be in the water with me, one on each side. I will stand right in front of the flap to open it and/or assist Mini Yao's birth or exit."

Yao stood a few feet behind the professor with both anima mea and Speedy on his head.

\*\*\*

**Two and a half weeks** passed. Mini Yao had grown at an even faster rate. Max was worried the domus would rupture before delivery time. The movement in Mini Yao's chamber caused surface concentric waves to be emitted from the domus, like when a pebble is thrown into a body of water. Even from poolside, one could see bubbling from the domus as proof of life. Each day Max moved the domus deeper to keep it submerged. He started thinking about how he would extend the tubing from the dry heart-lung machine to the wet domus vita. With every adjustment by Max, Yao watched.

Max had decided to send the nonviable fetal sac to an outside lab. The results came back with 52 XXYYY karyotype, having multiple abnormal and lethal chromosome trisomies or three chromosome groupings instead of only two. With this very poor result, Max had planned to perform two more ICSI procedures on number three and four donor eggs. Because this lost pregnancy was male, he chose Yao's female-carrying sperm for the two back up embryos.

Tara had given Professor Max a call with an update on Yao's dating process. "The initial carbon-14 dating reported Yao over seventy-thousand-years-old. So another two tests were used, which gave very contradictory results." Tara sounded apologetic. "I could meet you to uncover the more stimulating parts and together we could massage it until we both understood our results."

"I appreciate your willingness to spend your valuable time fingering through the rigid findings," answered the professor. "When you arrive, tell the front desk to show you to the second-floor conference room and call me."

Max closed up the lab facility when he received a call.

"Professor Maxwell, this is Jennifer at the front desk. I need to meet with you as soon as possible. I have some very important requests for you." Jennifer was then interrupted.

"Excuse me, Miss. I'm looking for Maxwell." Jennifer covered her phone and turned to Sheriff Gary.

Alisa came up behind the sheriff unnoticed. She then backed up and walked over to the MAAW research facility.

# Chapter 65

## *Orchestrating*

**Max went to the pool room** to see that the domus vita was still under water. The H-L machine gases, electrolytes, minerals and blood values were all in the normal range. Max turned to leave the pool room and saw Yao's green head emerge enough to have his glaring red eyes just above the water's surface. His last check before exiting the facility was that Speedy and anima mea were in their cages. Cali came to his feet and he picked her up for some brief cuddle time and then set her on the bench by her mama.

Crossing A1A, Max thought about his observation that Yao's head seemed less bumpy and its eyes were less red and more yellowish.

\*\*\*

**"I was hoping** for some private time with you, Max," said Alisa as she stroked his left arm. "Why don't you ever spend time in the condo you let me stay at?"

"How about I call you this afternoon and we will catch up?" suggested Max. "I have a few meetings to go to first."

After Max crossed back over A1A and entered the Marinescape parking lot, Sheriff Gary confronted him.

"Where is that evil creature of yours, Maxwell?"

"Good morning, Sheriff Gary and what creature is that you are speaking about? We have so many here at Marinescape, sir."

"Don't give me that worthless wordy backtalk. I know you're hiding that damn creature."

Max put his palms up. "I'm not resisting and I am answering your request."

"Don't put your hands on me." The sheriff pulled his rapid rotational baton from the back of his utility belt. With one swift motion, Sheriff Gary hit Max's back left thigh and Max collapsed to the ground. "You're forcing me to take you in," the sheriff said as he kicked Max's right shoulder and chest flat. "Show me your wrists." Gary pulled out his cuffs from his utility belt.

During the confrontation, Gary's peripheral vision caught Tara standing and watching from the Marinescape entrance steps. He stopped and stared at her. The sheriff put the cuffs and baton back on his belt.

"I'll let it go this time. Remember, no smart ass talk to me and no more physical threats on an officer." He walked back to his SUV and drove away.

Tara ran to Max's side and helped him up. "Are you O.K.? Can you get to the conference room?" Tara held up one of his arms as Max limped his way to the Marinescape entrance.

The two of them ended up in front of the conference room's open door. Tara pulled out a thin vanilla file labeled "Yao's dating."

Alisa entered the research facility calling Max's name. She saw Cali sitting on a padded bench. It gave Alisa a sideway glace as it rolled on its back, loudly purring.

"Cali, how are you today?" She gently stroked the feline's abdomen. Cali immediately curved up into a fur ball around Alisa's hand. "Oh Cali, your nails are sharp," said Alisa as she withdrew her hand with a few shallow scratches.

She wandered from room to room, ending at the pool room. "Well hello, Yao, I'm looking for the professor."

"Na, knee," Yao said in its improving English speech.

\*\*\*

**Max** stood in the hallway by the open conference door. From behind he felt touching.

"I'll be fine," he said as Tara ran her hand down his lower back and into his pants.

"Ah, my dear, I'll be back," he said as he slowly pulled her hand out. "Would you possibly wait for me inside this conference room, Tara?"

Shortly after, Max opened the door to his office and found Jennifer sitting behind his desk with her feet against it.

"Yes, young lady in the short skirt, how may I help you today?"

She spread-eagled her legs and stood up, approaching Max with her shirt raised. "I'm attending Keiser University, where the school's motto is 'Integritas, Veritas, Sapientia,' which means—"

"Purity, Truth, and Wisdom," said Max. "What's your future goal to be with this university?"

"That's what's cool. I'm working toward my baccalaureate, then master's and doctoral level degrees in resort, amusement and zoological park management. If you give me a recommendation and intern experience with you, I could be very grateful." She stroked his forearm.

"I like your snappy appearance with that navy blue and sky blue skirt and blouse. I know they are your school's colors."

Max grabbed the doorknob and started to exit his office. "I need to take care of a client. I'll be back in about a half an hour."

Back he went to the conference room and locked the door. Tara immediately kicked off her shoes, dropped her slacks and under apparel and sat with her legs up on an overstuffed chair.

Max responded appropriately. "So let's go into depth of what you are revealing to me." Max evidentially got the gist of the reptile's multiple dating results, but still no answer to the question of Yao's beginning. Max stared at Tara. "Is it a metamorphic result of eons of natural selection, environment exposures and survival adaptation of one and the same reptile now called Yao? Or is Yao just the newest generation result of many generations surviving environmental pressures? I appreciate you are driving here, Tara. I really appreciate this enjoyable and confusing presentation of your assets."

Tara ended up facing Max with her outstretched legs on top of his. "You didn't hear the latest news that Mr. Yuma Manta has used a poison that resulted in a lot of dead fish on the river, but no Yao. Also, Sheriff Gary believes the professional animal trackers HHMI-LPA hired are trying to anesthetize or poison Yao also and they don't really care if they capture Yao alive or retrieve its dead body. They also have killed a lot of fish.

Deputy Sheriff decided to ticket only Mr. Manta, less chance of legal repercussions."

Max just smiled as both of them slightly wiggled toward and away from each other.

"Why are you smiling? It feels so good … for … for … for meeeee!" reverberated Tara.

"We both feel good," said Max as he caught his breathe. "Fish are poikilotherms, or cold-blooded, as are amphibians and reptiles. Mammals are homeotherms or warm-blooded. Rotenone works on only on cold-blooded creatures. Aquacalm works on both cold and warm-blooded."

"Maybe Yao just drowned from the poisons and then sank to the river bottom and the current took it out to the ocean," Tara suggested as she tilted her body back and forth, holding Max's arms like she was rowing. After redressing and reviewing the dating processes of Yao, they parted.

Max returned to his office. The door was locked. He knocked and spoke. The door opened a crack. As he entered the office, the door quickly closed and locked behind him.

"Jennifer, I see your school colors are also evident in your see-through underwear as well." Max stood straight out and smiled.

"I wanted to pay it forward, to show I was serious," she said as she walked around toward him.

***

**When Max entered** the pool room, he reaffirmed Mini Yao was still stable. He rang Alisa.

As her phone rang, she walked into the pool room and sat on the vegetative wall's bench. "Fond memories, I believe, for both of us here," Max said as he followed her over.

"True, but can we move to another room?" asked Alisa. She looked poolside. "Does Yao's head seem less bumpy to you and its eyes less red? Anyway, I'm spooked by Yao's emerging head with no water disturbance around it. It's too eerie for me, if Yao watched us."

"Good point. I really don't know how much it would understand or if it would smell one of your pheromones, which could bring out its primal 'fight for your mating' territory and result in violent actions toward you and me."

They departed and locked the green door behind them.

Max did have a small research office in this facility. He opened the door, revealing piles of journals and other papers. They saw the one and only small table also covered with piles of papers.

"I don't think so," said Alisa and she pulled Max to the floor on top of her in front of the open door.

"Comfortable?" With his affirmative nod, Alisa wiggled to get herself situated on top of him. "I'm ready for my next rodeo ride. Giddy-up, ride-on!"

\*\*\*

**"Any chance** you have time to stop at our police station in Crescent Beach, Mr. Angel?" asked Sheriff Gary. The two met that afternoon. "My purpose for meeting is simple. I want to put pressure on Maxwell about how the reptile escaped and where is it now. He's always been close to the creature. I can't believe he doesn't know where it's hiding. Of course, I'll be ready to arrest them and press criminal charges again if I find them together. I might have to shoot, maybe kill them, if they resist."

"You mean the creature, right?"

"I will interview the professor about an update involving Yao. Remember, Howard Hughes Medical Institute-Live Prehistoric Animal has a vested interest in the professor. We're putting him at risk of them negating their earlier contract for his early jail release and sending him back to jail. He would lose his position at Marinescape," responded Mr. Angel.

"Good riddance. Humiliate him and publish some trash to spread around him like peanut butter," said the emotionally-charged sheriff.

"I wouldn't call what I publish at the *Palatka National & Local News* trash. I only report accurately and write about significant issues of the day, so our readers are the most informed." Mr. Angel reacted to what he considered a slam against his profession, his paper and his reputation.

"I apologize for my sharp, inaccurate and insensitive remarks. I always get hot when it involves that arrogant weasel. You do know about the water poisoning by two different sources?"

\*\*\*

"**Thank you** both for being here to assist in the birth of Mini Yao. Its intra-chamber movements have become quite violent. Because of this and its extremely rapid growth, I am ignoring the due date," spoke Max. "Today will be the day."

"We are ready!" Patti and Alisa held hands and bounced their clasped hands up and down one time.

The trio waded into the pool by the domus vita.

"Before we start, Professor, how did the water poisons not affect Yao?" asked Alisa.

"And why did the poisons not flow into the water coming into the pool via the connection with the Matanzas River?" added Patti.

"Excellent questions ladies. How lucky I have been, that the two of you joined this amazing scientific event." Max grasped each woman's open hand to form a circle. "This circle represents the trust and love among this trio. Manta's poison only works on cold-blooded or ectothermic, creatures. These organisms depend on its environment for heat. HHMI's hired trackers used poison that works on both cold and warm-blooded or endothermic animals. Yao is the latter. Do you feel a slight current on your legs? During the construction of the Marine Anima Aquatic World research facility, I anticipated that the Matanzas River might one day become polluted. As a safety precaution, I had an underground ocean pipeline constructed, which flows into the pool causing positive pressure flow. So the ocean water flows into the pool and out into the Matanzas River. So as long as the ocean is free of poisons, fresh, uncontaminated salt water is always available in the pool.

Patti and Alisa looked at each other and then at a grinning Max. The three changed their focus to the domus. Patti and Alisa each choose a side and Max stood at the domus chamber's number two's flap. Unnoticed behind them, Yao was just below the surface with its beady yellow-red-colored eyes.

"The green door is locked. Blaze knew we're busy in here."

The chamber's flap was barely below the water's surface.

"I really do know what to expect with this new creature, Mini Yao. It could go deep in the pool water, turn toward the pool's shoreline for land or swim out into the Matanzas River."

Max exhaled loudly. "May this be a landmark date in humanity's written history, a giant genetic leap for plant, animal, science and humans."

"A birthday for Mini Yao," excitedly added Alisa.

Professor Maxwell slowly opened the flap. Before it was completely open, a creature, soon to be called a monstrosity, leaped out and jumped on top of the domus. The three humans fell backward into the water.

"What is it?" Patti yelled out. "May the Lord help, forgive and protect us!"

\*\*\*

**As** Professor Maxwell would later describe: "A reptile with a somewhat flattened, shortened crocodile head from front to back, three red glazed eyes, one in the center of its head and one on each side of its head, above what appeared to be ears. If it had a human face, it would be expressing confusion. Four limbs, upper shorter than the lower. It had a waistline and bent over, like most reptiles and amphibians. Dark green skin with ridges, like scrunched up carpet or very thick wrinkles, running left to right on its body. It was hard to tell if it was related to scales. Finally, it had a short, thick, scaly tail that Mini Yao could lean back on like a kangaroo." The reptile Mini Yao opened its mouth, revealing three rows of teeth and actually spoke. "Ah ... hee ... oh ... ah," it roared continuously.

As Patti and Max fell back into the water, they moved backward doing the Australian crab walk toward the pool's shoreline as fast as they could while still watching Mini Yao. On the other hand, Alisa became frozen in her position next to the domus. Mini Yao looked to her and spoke with its vocal roar again. It started to lunge for her, with its open mouth snapping open and closed. Its front limbs extended claws a surge of water splashed toward them both. Mini Yao's head became severed from its neck entire body was pulled under water. The wavy pool water slowly became green and red, followed by smooth-like-glass pool water.

Max rushed to Alisa and swept her entirely wet body into his arms and walked to the pool's edge. He placed her on the ground next to a reclining Patti, who immediately hugged her and tried to comfort her by talking and rocking her back and forth. Max ran from another room, carrying a blanket to put over her shoulders. Alisa stared into space, seemingly in shock.

"You are safe now. You're all right now. You can relax, Alisa," Patti said as she continued to hug Alisa while stroking her hair.

"Ah, please, not me!" Alisa screamed several times, each time not as loud.

Professor Maxwell looked to the pool and saw a head pop up with its yellow-red eyes.

"Yao, thank you … for your rescue of us," Max called out.

Yao brought its arms out of the water and then its body to waist level.

"Aye kep all saf … kep Al … Lisa safe." Then Yao disappeared in the water.

"Help me, somebody," screamed Alisa. She cried until she realized she was safe and felt Patti's body heat and saw and felt Max massaging her right hand against his face.

The three left the pool room. Then they sat on the multi-ceiling room's bench.

Max rubbed his covered neck where he felt scaring of what once were childhood gill slits.

"Is your neck O.K., Professor?" Alisa's voice suggested she was mentally back.

He nodded. "All is copasetic for me. And you?"

There was the faint sound of weeping. They both turned to Patti, who had her head low and between her hands.

"Patti, Alisa, I am so sorry you had to be here, to witness this violent, monstrous event." Max put his arms around both their shoulders. They both hugged back. Patti still wept with a hidden face. Alisa moved around to hug Patti with Max.

"Patti, it's over, we're all safe," Alisa paraphrased Max.

"That's not the reason … for my grief. This pool experience has actually brought up some very bad memories," Patti mumbled through the hugging arms and her hands squeezing her face.

Max kissed the top of Patti's head and Alisa tried to bring Patti's face up.

"I've never told anyone before, not even the people at my workplace."

With Patti's upright, the three heads were up like a group of three peas in a tablespoon, peas touching close enough to be kissing.

"Once I was happily married or so I thought. My husband was the kind of guy who would easily make conversations with everyone. If it was a woman, he'd keep constant eye contact. I don't think he ever blinked. You'd think you were the only person in the room, in his world. When he shook your hand, his gentle grasp held on to you during the entire conversation, with an attention-getting squeeze revealing a reluctance to release." Patti wiped her eyes with her fingers.

"I'll go get some Kleenex," offered Max. Patti pulled him back, not letting him leave.

"I had a five-year-old, Joshua and another seven-month pregnancy coming along. I finally couldn't take it anymore. The three of us were in the back yard, by our inground pool.

Patti's tears started to leak out. "I exploded like Mt. Vesuvius and confronted him with the name of his latest whore he was fornicating with, screwed, and fucked. He pushed me back and I fell on the ground." Patti's eyes became a faucet.

"Joshua started to run toward me along the pool." as Patti tried to speak clearly through her rain cloud. "Joshua slipped and hit his head on the side of the concrete pool and fell in. He never came up. My husband jumped in to no avail. The pool slowly turned red as that disgusting man stood waist-deep, covered in red, holding my limp, innocent, dead child in his extended arms. In a flash, Joshua was taken from me. The paramedics and police came. After they took the lifeless body from the bastard, he got out of the pool, showered, dressed and jumped in his Dodge truck and drove away with the smell of burning rubber."

"He didn't say a word to you?" Alisa gasped.

Patti now collected herself emotionally and physically and shook her head in a vigorous no.

"Blaze was my child I was carrying that day. God blessed me with this healthy boy."

"Wouldn't God want you to forgive Dad and remember the good things about my older brother, who is resting in heaven?" Blaze asked as he hugged his mother.

"Oh Blaze, I never, ever wanted you to hear this," she said as she covered him with kisses.

"So this sight was frightening to you with terrible memories being brought back to the present," softly surmised Max. "I will document what I saw. The two of you may or may not want to document your experiences and read each other's. Reviewing what has happened, I wonder if I should just abandon my goal of reproducing Yao's future offspring," the professor pondered.

No response came from the two women who had also experienced the petrifying monstrosity.

"Since all is calm, I must now leave with Blaze. Is it O.K. if tomorrow I bring him to play with his three friends?"

"That is fine with me. I'm sure they will enjoy it."

Once Max and Alisa were alone, she snuggled up to absorb some of his serenity. She wondered how he was always so calm. "Max, I was so frightened. I'm so sorry I was worthless as your assistant under such stress."

Max wrapped his arms around her.

"Make me feel good, like you have before, to frolic in each other's loving land?"

# Chapter 66

## *Featureless*

**Max continued the next day** with a mindless frustration, circular thoughts and indecision. Patti found him in his cluttered office staring into a mountain of journals, thinking the journey through them was worthless. As always, Blaze could be heard giving commands to one of his three amigos.

"I can see you are still in a conundrum." Patti massaged his temples down to his neck and squeezed his shoulder muscle. "You need to clear your mind and relax. When you revisit the problem, your mind fog will be gone."

They both smiled. *"Joe Versus the Volcano*, how funny is that?" Max laughed.

Patti continued her massages to his muscular waistline, down to his thighs.

"I didn't know you were a skilled masseuse." Max's two hands embraced her head and brought her to his lips. "Shall we go to another room?"

"No, this place is quite cozy. I'll just situate myself on your lap." Their hands made the needed adjustments of their clothes for comfort and pleasure.

\*\*\*

**"It** is imperative that your net drags from the river bottom to the surface. Start where the water turned green and red in color," instructed Doctor Amy Adamoffski. "Also, collect the green water from several depths. This may contain clues as to what happened to the reptile Yao."

"Yes, Doctor, I understand that any evidence of this prehistoric animal is our goal," responded the spokesman of the hired animal trackers for the HHMI-LPA.

"Please make sure to drag the Matanzas River in the opposite direction of the river's current and for a quarter mile in both directions. The first thing is to put our nets at each end of the dragging area so as not to lose anything with the current," she added. "Also, you should get the X-ray plates and photograph every inch of the river's bottom."

"Doctor Amy, I see you are meticulous with your scientific searching," spoke Sheriff Gary, who stood next to her at the river's edge.

"Do I know you?" she asked.

"I'm the County of St. Johns Law Enforcement Agency, Sheriff Gary." They shook hands. "Our department has had an ongoing investigation into and search for the same reptile as you. I caught the creature once before—before this recent escape. This creature has committed multiple crimes against the local public citizenry, including at least three capital murders."

"I originally hoped to retrieve a live prehistoric reptile for an incredible opportunity to study it. We would have been seen as the cat's meow of the scientific world and by the general public if the marketing was done well," replied Doctor Amy.

"If you find definite evidence that Yao is dead, please send a memo to the sheriff's office so we can close its file," said the sheriff as he walked away.

"If we find only parts, we'll still have a landmark find. We may answer the question of whether Yao was a recently born reptile or truly a survivor over hundreds of millions of years."

The sheriff stopped walking with Doctor Amy.

"One of my staff, Tara, has carbon testing report that Yao is more than seventy-thousand-years-old. Other testing suggested it is several hundred million years old. She is waiting on still another test method for dating," Gary informed Doctor Amy.

"Thank you for that information. May I contact her directly?" The sheriff reciprocated with her phone number.

"With body parts, we will also run dating testing."

Doctor Amy and Tara met and exchanged information about Yao and many unrelated but interesting factoids.

"What you, the crime scene investigators and I, an evolutionary biologist, do is basically the same thing," revealed Amy. "We gather information and evidence and put them together to reveal the truth. For me, this job is my party down with many epiphanies."

"You're describing me," Tara said as they both laughed and gave each other a high five. "I love my job. There are times I'm lost with confusing evidence. I redirect to find supposed inconsequential and hidden evidence, which turns out to be the case breaker and then ... case solved."

"Tara, a call from Director Leon coming down to you," relayed Mary Jane.

"Tara, this is Leon. I just heard there is possible scrutinized evidence from the Matanzas River that confirms Yao's death. I want you to go down to the river and observe, review and make your own conclusions, with a written statement to me."

"There is a difference between our jobs," declared Tara. "I have a boss to answer to."

Doctor Amy and Tara discussed the similarities of their occupational testing of evidence.

"Now Tara, I know you have several techniques to discover and document fingerprints," stated Amy. "Most reptiles are diactyl, meaning each foot has five toes fused into a group of two and three toes, each with its own claws. It's a biped reptile, one that walks upright on two limbs, like humans. However, they usually walk on their toes, called digitgrads."

Tara listened and wondered why Doc Amy was giving her a reptile anatomy lesson. "I'm sorry, Doctor Amy. Yao is not your typical reptile. Yao had friction ridges on its five separated digits and palms. It has flat feet like an elephant, so one could also get footprints."

"Did you find any unexplained and unusual fingerprint patterns at you crime scenes?"

Tara immediately pulled up all her potential markings from the shoreline murder sites, Mr. Manta's scratches and blood impressions, pharmacy floor, glass enclosures impressions and the onboard yacht rape at Washington Oaks Gardens State Park boat basin. She included the deck surface, towel and clothing evidence.

"Not only reptiles, but also amphibians, marsupials and mammals have recognizable friction ridges classified as loops, arches, whorls and bizarre patterns," added Doctor Amy.

"I feel we're going to be great friends," said Amy as she gently placed a hand on Tara's hand.

Tara smiled. "I also feel that way."

"Since we agree, may I ask you about Professor Rory Maxwell? I've met him." Tara slowly withdrew her hand from physical bonding. "I was curious if the professor is always so friendly and sexually forward with all women?"

"I can only speak for myself. Professor Maxwell has always been friendly and professional with me in his actions," Tara said with a slight smile.

***

**With time**, many relationships seemed to become less important.

Reproductive Nurse Patti and her son stopped calling or spontaneously coming over to Marine Animal Aquatic World.

Alisa changed her contract to only work for Marinescape and Dolphin Adventure. Her boisterous personality and factoid-filled guided tours quickly made her the most requested person at Marinescape. A representative from Dolphin Alive Park on the Georgia Atlantic coast knew of her success with a subsequent pay raise. This allowed Alisa to purchase a Nissan Sentra and her own apartment. Max's condo became empty, with his car and condo keys on the kitchen counter.

Max got a text from Jennifer that she was changing her major to just Hotel and Resort Management and would like another letter of recommendation.

Tara sent a text to Professor Maxwell that she was still working on verifying Yao's age and wondering if Yao was dead.

Doctor Amy, being the official HHMI-LPA representative, emailed Professor Maxwell that she was waiting for laboratory verification of Yao's death by blood and body parts from the Matanzas River dredge. She stated she had collaborated with Tara.

Max rocked back and forth on an upholstered chair in the main Marinescape conference room. "What am I doing? Why am I here? Should I just publish my MAAW finding, creations, genetic engineering methods, yada, yada, yada? What some find as exciting science, I now find unfulfilling with no successful Yao offspring."

# Chapter 67

## *Offerings*

---

**Max's new work list** included four items.

First, the professor always thought that there was an application for humans with the green blood found in reptiles from bile and biliverdin. These came from red blood cell hemoglobin breakdown or metabolism in reptiles and humans. Then, in humans, the biliverdin was further metabolized to bilirubin, yellow in color.

The alarm indicated that someone had entered the research facility.

"Max, Max, you here?" a woman's voice rang out.

Cali jumped from her bench cushion and ran toward the sound's origin. Max followed the cat.

"Alisa, how nice to see you," Max greeted her. "I was wondering why you stayed away so long?" He tried to hug her. "Did I somehow offend you?"

"I've been busy and I didn't know if you needed me around anymore."

"I always need, want and love you. I'm so sorry you experienced the horrific Mini Yao tragedy. I was going over a list of possible new projects for me."

As Max went over his list and Alisa made remarks, in the pool room, the yellow-red eyes with a less bumpy head surfaced and listened to them talk.

"The green-yellow Jaundice, caused by elevated bilirubin, is a common problem in newborn babies. It is seen in 60 percent of full-term and 80 percent of premature babies. The reptile's green blood is also caused by bilirubin which I found the responsible gene for its blood traits. Medical treatment for baby jaundice might be genetically directed treatment. The liver makes green bile, green biliverdin and yellow bilirubin which increases in people with compromised liver function and failure might be genetically treated."

"Having green blood, as in a few amphibians and Yao must have some evolutionary advantage," proclaimed Alisa.

"And this is why I need you working with me. The advantage, as I see it, has to do with these animals having high blood biliverdin levels which help Yao red blood cells fight the continuous high concentrations of bacteria and a parasitic protozoa or plasmodium like malaria."

"Maybe patients with red sickle cell disease, which actually decreases the person's risk for some types of malaria?" smartly added Alisa. "Maybe your genetic work could help humans without sickle cell disease?"

"My second work is to write about the amazing Yao, its advanced mental capacity, development of speech and finally physical changes within the same animal by either natural selection and/or genetic adaptation. The proof is its ability to survive to an age of hundreds of millions of years."

"I'm excited to help and read your final conclusions," said Alisa. "It's a mind-blowing exercise that this single creature has metamorphosize itself in response to environmental stresses."

"I'll end the paper with thoughts on Yao's disappearance."

"I remember the motto in one of my university classes that the teacher had displayed in the front of the auditorium. It reminds me of your attitude," Alisa smiled.

Max looked to Alisa and waited. "Alisa, you are such a tease," he laughed.

"The motto was 'Intellectual curiosity is the most powerful energy in the world.' What is your next area of interest?"

"This idea is an extension of the previous one. Knowing the artificial genetic manipulation or engineering I did in my research lab, why not think about de-extinction?. That would be investigating the mammoth's hemoglobin that helped it survive such extreme temperatures and its" possible human applications. Why stop there? I can get an elephant's and the mammoth's suspected DNA sequencing and combine them for a more environmentally tolerant elephant-mammoth," enthusiastically stated Max.

"Yes, it would be an Elemoth or Mamephant or Mamelemothephant?" laughed Alisa.

"The Proboscidea Mammuthus Elephantidae," Max smiled. Then he frowned. "The elephant has fifty-six chromosomes; the mammoth has fifty-eight".

"Next idea, this is fun!" Alisa clapped to encourage Max to come up with another.

"I believe inflammation is one of the components of nearly every class of human disease, as found in genetic single and multiple chromosomal sites."

"So how does that work?" Alisa asked.

"Well, visualize this scenario. After an acute injury or illness, white blood cells will launch an attack on bacterial or viral invaders or irritating self-made proteins. This attack results in swelling, maybe a fever and local redness as other human-made cells come to the site. Inflammation decreases as a cut heals and the illness disappears. Consider the opposite, which is low grade chronic inflammation. This may occur with high synthetic sugar foods, high fat diets, diabetes, a female condition called endometriosis, arthritis and cancer. In fact, we need to look at each of our organ systems. They may operate normally or in an inflammatory mode, leading to chronic disease. Can we alter how the immune system responds? Genetically make it curative and less destructive?"

"That is such a wonderful goal."

"Great expectations, I feel so unfulfilled. I feel painfully lacking in skills in immunobiology, immune-engineering, molecular, cellular and developmental biology."

"But you're already so good," Alisa hugged Max, "so good at genetic engineering." She followed up with a few hand and face kisses.

"Think of high fat diets. Why not help people who love cream and chocolate filled donuts, potato chips, pies and cakes? In animals, there are gut receptors sending signals to the brain, which then assess the carbohydrate and fatty content. It knows when to stop eating."

Alisa looked to him with her index finger up. "You forget about dogs?" Alisa giggled.

"The brain signals to stop eating when the energy levels are met."

"Why don't humans have that?"

"They do, but the synthetic foods and pastries fool the brain to ignore the receptor signals. Food manufactures know three elements to include in food to make it addictive, they are?"

"I know: fat, carbohydrates and sugar, usually super sweet corn syrup."

"And the psychological response of some people is to eat, even if they are not hungry. Eating relieves stress, frustration, guilt and replaces love," Max sighed.

"I'm not into comfort food. I'm more into receiving comfort and giving comfort sex."

After a long pause, Max looked down. "Alisa, my one regret is that I never was able to create a being like Yao, a being that could change its genes in response to its environment, thus evolving and then physically change its appearance in its lifetime. This would—"

Alisa put her hand up to stop Max and took her shoes off.

"You know we're alone here in this research facility," she said as they started to undress each other while standing, followed up with a few waltz dance steps, which led them to the padded bench where they created multiple alphabet letter shapes with their bodies. They completed with echoing symphonic sound patterned after the familiar rhythmic *1812 Overture* finale. Alisa was sitting on Max in the inverted T position, lying back onto Max into the sideways Y, both facing up.

"Hey, want to go take a shower together?" cheerfully asked Max.

"Say what, a shower? All this time and you never said there was a shower here?"

As they both sat up, Max lifted her in his arms and carried her to an unlabelled door, which Alisa opened. He then opened the shower door.

"You Tarzan, me Jane," the warm water ran down their statuesque standing bodies. The bathroom was lit while the shower stall was not. Intriguing shadows danced between and on each other. Lathering the other's body intensified new feelings for intimacy. Soaping up and rubbing off enhanced the excitation of whatever was being touched. The artificial rainstorm continued until both were exhausted. They held on to each other not to fall down. Wrapped up in towels, Alisa and Max laid as two cocoons on the bathroom's throw rug and fell asleep, all spent.

When Max was conscious, he turned to be face to face with her. "I have something I need to tell someone. I'd love to stay, but I'm already late. I have a newbie at Marinescape I need to train. Remember when we first met?"

"Your glowing face of happiness, pent up excitement and energy, but you also looked to be anxious and somewhat fearful, I believe," Max grinned at her.

"I definitely was all that and afraid you were going to shut me down and send me back to Michigan like a scolded, unwanted feral cat." She started to get dressed. "Can't we talk later? I owe you some cream filled donuts," Alisa laughed.

Max nodded with a small regretful smile.

***

**Weeks passed** and Alisa never came back to the research facility or called Max. He kept busy, mostly writing. Again he seemed to isolate himself. Once he called over to the Marinescape front desk and Jennifer answered in her usual joyful voice.

"I was wondering if Alisa still works here at Marinescape."

"Oh yes, but it's hard to know what she's doing." She sounded indifferent and emotionally distant to him.

"Why are you so indifferent, Jennifer?"

"She and her intern, Garth, are always running around and hiding somewhere. I'm tired of calling her all the time."

Another week passed. Patti called, asking if she and her son could come over. They met at the front door of the research building.

"So nice to see you two guys." Max, Patti and Blaze immediately formed a hug bundle.

"Let us all come inside."

Max talked about his list of goals. Blaze talked about school and how he liked being in this lab. Patti reviewed how she had hired another nurse because the infertility center practice was getting busier.

"You know, happy pregnant patients make the best referral source." Patti listed the IVF pregnancy rates per age group.

"You know, Max, when Blaze isn't with you, he talks about you as if you were his father." Patti laid a hand on Max's knee.

"What happened to his father?"

"I tell Blaze his father died in a head-on auto accident with a drunk driver. In reality, his dad was a worthless heavy drinker and womanizer, as I told you and Alisa about my lost child and him just driving off." Patti glanced from Max to the floor and back. "He also had a gambling addiction. Somewhere, I fear, he became over-extended in debt at the local Atlantic casino cruises, or farther south at an Indian casino. Whatever, he left one day and hasn't returned in eleven years."

"Blaze is a wonderful and amazing child," reflected Max. "He is respectful of other people, thoughtful, inquisitive and thinking ahead about the consequencences of his actions, but most important, he has imagination with an attitude," said Max. "All is possible, I once said to Blaze. 'Without faith, all seems impossible … with faith, all is possible.'"

"Thank you for your kind and insightful remarks." Patti placed her hands on each side of his face and landed a long, hard, deep tongue-based kiss on him. This was followed with a few hand moves of intimacy. Patti called out, "Blaze, what things are you up to?" while looking at Max.

Max released Patti and turned to see a running Blaze, who had all three friends around.

"Blaze, I am glad you're here. With your mother's consent, would you like to take all three amigos home?"

Blaze looked to his mom. Patti appreciatively looked back to Max. The three looked back and forth at each other.

"Well, Mother Patti, what do you say?"

She finally smiled. "As long as you take complete care of them and all the responsibilities which goes along with them, Blaze."

"Remember your oath and agreement of privacy when you first entered the research facility?" Max asked, staring at his eyes.

"No one can ever know what has happened, has been done here, as long as I live and cross my heart." Blaze's right index finger pointed skyward to God.

"All right, who is or are the winners?" asked Max.

"After much deliberation—"

"Deliberation is such a wonderful choice of words," interrupted Professor Max.

"I'll take ... all of them, as you offered, and pledge my oath to Max and my mom." Blaze and his amigos left to play gleefully in another room their running leader, his two flying amigos and a Calico fur ball.

"Patti, before we talk further, I would like to confide in you something very private, something I never told anyone and I wish this information to not go beyond this building's walls." Patti's eyes flickered and went back and forth with a pensive facial expression. "I am sorry. I didn't want to put you under such obvious pressure. Forget that I—"

"No, no, I'm just taken aback that you would trust me so much to—"

"I do, I feel we are so very close." He embraced Patti again. "Let us go to my office." They closed and locked the door. "Do not worry, these walls are thin and we will be able to hear if Blaze calls out."

Max moved his rolling, reclining, leather chair next to Patti's straight back stationary chair. "Do you plan on reading all these journals and papers?" inquired Patti.

"I have read most of them already."

They sat quietly for several minutes.

"So ... congratulations on your highly successful career here in America," said Patti.

"I don't know who my father was ... or is."

"More kudos to you and your mother who raised you and that you believed in yourself."

"I am not sure who and if I have a mother."

"Of course you have a mother; everybody has a mother."

"I was raised by a Brazilian Roman Conception nun, Sister Joana Angelica Jesus, belonging to the Reformed Order of Our Lady of Conception." Max looked into Nurse Patti's eyes.

"I think you were blessed to have such a devoted woman raise you."

"She was born in Capitaincy of Bahia, Brazil ... in 1761."

Patti gasped and grabbed Max's right hand but said nothing.

"Sister Joana Angelica is a martyr of the Brazilian movement for Independence from Portugal. She died at the age of sixty from a bayonet stab on February 19, 1822. She became the first heroine of the Independence of Brazil. I believe the other Sisters actually raised me after her death.

Patti still remained speechless.

"I was told my birthday was on *Sete de Setembro*, September 7, Brazil's Declaration of Independence Day from the United Kingdom of Portugal, I just don't know what year."

"Did the nun birth you?" Patti mumbled.

"I don't know. I think one of them did; however, on a simple piece of paper was one cursive line that said, "Baby was born of water.""

"Let me get this straight." Patti held her head with both hands. "You are saying you're about two … hundred …years … old, plus or minus a few years?" Patti shook her head.

***

**"Hello**, Professor Maxwell, can you tell Alisa to mind her own business?" said an angry voice on the other end of the cell phone line.

"Excuse me, who is this?" Max asked as he still was eye to eye with Patti.

"This is Jennifer, your protégé, intern … you're my sponsor." Her voice became calmer.

"Yes, I am sorry for my lapse of recognition. What is it exactly that you want me to do?"

"Well, Garth and I were having some intimate conversation and that bitch Alisa found out. She pulled and pushed me from Garth, yelling at me. After Garth separated us, she started making demands of me and threatened to have me fired." as Jennifer was on the verge of crying.

"And Garth is who?"

"He's Alisa's new intern for Marinescape maintenance."

"First, you are not getting fired. Secondly, I will speak with Alisa, but I cannot promise anything about improving your relationship with her." Patti embraced Max with a kiss, sealing the end of his phone conversation.

"I don't believe your age thing; it doesn't matter to me. How many women do you know who've made love with a more than two century old man?"

Max slipped his hands under her summer dress. Her legs parted as she wiggled onto his lap's most comfortable spot.

407

# Chapter 68

## *Phoenix*

---

**Professor Rory Maxwell asked** Patti and Alisa to spend some time in the research facility in three days. They agreed. The time came and he found the two talking on a bench in the Marinescape lobby. Alisa got up as Jennifer approached her. Patti walked to Max.

"Patti, how are Cali and the flying duo doing with Blaze?"

"Oh, they're all inseparable. The flyers go in their cages at night. Cali sleeps on Blaze's bed. I was wondering … how long do cats live?"

"I believe the average life span in human years is twelve to fifteen," Max replied. "There is speculation that for cats and dogs there is some gene sites that turn off, others turn on, which lead to rapid aging and death between those ages."

"Why?" Patti and Max sat on a more secluded bench. "You're pulling my leg?"

"I thought I was somewhere between your legs, not pulling them," Max whispered.

"Right, smarty pants. I know you're not wearing underpants."

"Neither are you." They both giggled.

"You'll know when I'm pulling, stretching and squeezing your legs."

"Be serious now, Max."

"The aging control sites are mostly gene sites having to do with body function changes. This would include increased inflammation, oxidative stress, altered immunity, slower or absent DNA repair, decreased energy production getting to cells and less effective protein metabolism." Max hesitated.

"Isn't that what happens to us humans?" concluded Patti.

"One other factor is that I altered Cali's chromosome telomere deterioration with each DNA repair is set to zero, so that it should extend the cat's life maybe another thirty-five years."

The MAAW front door opened. Max got up from the bench to approach the expected visitor.

"Hi, Alisa," "everything resolved over at Marinescape with the personnel?"

"Good enough, at least for now." She saw Patti and did a low, short wave. "Let us go into the pool room."

On passing through the green door, they immediately saw the H-L attached to the repaired and submerged domus vita.

"I think you know why we are here." Patti followed Max and Alisa stopped at the green door.

"I have tried again with two new donor eggs and ICSI with Yao's frozen sperm, sperm favoring female offspring. Ultrasounds have been very good with no internal organ variation from humans, especially the heart, aorta and most importantly, facial structure."

Alisa slowly approached the poolside.

"Are we ready?" Max looked to the smiling Patti and frowning Alisa. "Where is Yao?" he asked, looking over the pool's surface. Max waded into the water and pulled the domus flaps above the water surface. He prepared to open the compartment number one.

**"Doctor** Adamoffski, several local newspapers and TV stations reported that an archeologist has found the skeletal remains of the Matanzas Reptile Monster Yao!" the HHMI receptionist relayed.

There it was, breaking news on Orland TV.

*"Behind me is amateur archeologist and fossil collector Charles Bartholomew Dawson, Jr. We'll listen to the official, worldwide historic presentation of Mr. Dawson."* The reporter turned toward the speaker.

*"You see before you, ladies and gentlemen, the oldest of cold cases. A thick portion of a reptile-ape-like-human skull, partial jawbone, cone-shaped canine teeth and fused reptile scales."* Mr. Dawson put his hands up. *"Please hold all questions to the end of my findings and conclusions. I do believe and verify that I have found the remains of the murderous monster, Yao and more importantly, a pre-hominid that lived before Homo heidelbergensis and before Homo erectus. These findings are actually from the first occurrences of the spilt of bipedal ape, bipedal reptile to the bipedal hominid. This is the elusive 'missing link.' I call him Yanthropus primis aurora dawnicus, or Dawson's first man of dawn. Questions?"*

Doctor Amy turned to her assistant, who was also watching the TV. "Call this Mr. Dawson and see if we can get some DNA samples from his specimens. We'll want to do spectroscopic, radiographic and genetic techniques for our own verification," grinned the doctor. "I'll contact CSI Assistant Tara for finger ridge impression and DNA verifications from her crime scene evidence of Yao. No answer on Professors Maxwell's phone or his assistant, Alisa's, phone." Amy shook her head. "I don't believe this Mr. Dawson. People want to believe him, but there have been many frauds presented before him."

"Doesn't Mr. Dawson have many scientific papers published?" the assistant asked.

"Yes, over fifty publications of questionable merit or just reiterating other people's work. He's also the one accused of finding, making and staining supposedly two-millennia-year-old 'scribed Roman bricks,' which were all found to be fake."

\*\*\*

**Max** brought out a squirming baby girl, which made one strong push against his hand and jumped or fell into the water. The baby started to swim along the pool's edges just visible below the water's surface.

The three witnesses applauded and gave verbal encouragement.

"Let us see if Mini Yao 2 will imprint and bond with me." Professor Max placed his hands palm upward, elbow deep, in the path of the swimming Mini Yao 2. All waited as it approached his hand ... and stopped belly down on the open hand.

"How wonderful is that?" the women paraphrased each other.

"O.K., who is next?"

Each signaled to the other to step forward.

"Both of you move to the domus chamber flap number two, please." They stood opposite each other and reluctantly held their hands, waiting for the other to swim out with the flap opening.

"One or both of you together open the chamber flap."

"No, I can't." Alisa waded out of the water and ran out of the pool room.

Patti and Max looked at each other. "I'm ready. I am ready and here we go." Patti opened the flap and saw an apparently normal girl, wide-eyed and looking up at her. It made no attempt to crawl, climb or jump out of the domus chamber.

"Reach in and bring her out and place her in the water." Patti reached in with her left hand and brought the newborn out and into the pool. The baby just lay in her open hand. All the time it stared at Patti's face without blinking.

"Max, why do you keep looking around?" asked Patti.

"I am looking for Yao. So far I do not see it here. Mini Yao 2 is still swimming around. Mini Yao 2 seems to love to swim. I briefly glanced at its neck and I think there are gills."

"I removed my hand to the side to let Mini Yao 3 swim freely. Instead, it barely swam and gently grasped one of my fingers and rolled over on its back," Patti observed. "It ended up with its yellowish-red eyes staring again up to my face. Mini Yao 3 just lay there, no maneuvers under water, just staring."

"Do you see gills on its neck?" asked Max.

"I'm not sure. There might be, but you know how water distorts your vision. Max, do they eat human or reptile food?"

"I cannot believe I didn't think about that. For now, let's see if they tolerate life on land."

The two newborns were placed on the dry poolside. First, Max had to catch Mini Yao 2.

"Patti, have you noticed anything happening?"

"Well, my Mini Yao 3 is still growing."

"I agree with you; both have noticeably gotten larger."

"Except maybe not the head of Mini 2," added Patti.

"When first born, Mini Yao 3 was barely the length from the tip of my middle finger to my wrist. Now it is an inch longer than my middle finger," noted Max.

Over the next few hours, Patti and Max watched the newborns go from rolling back and forth on their backs to crawling to becoming unsteady bipeds. Max went over and locked the green door.

"Where are we going to keep them?" asked a concerned Patti. "Oh, Mini Yao 2 fell down."

They watched.

"It's not getting up."

Max rush over, picked it up and placed it in the water. It showed minimal movement. Max ran out of the pool room.

"Where …what are you doing?" asked Patti.

Max came back in less than a minute, pulling a cart with vertical canisters, tubing, a frost covered probable cooling condenser and a noisy compression pump.

"When a human or animal has a cardiac arrest, two organs have a short survival clock ticking. The heart can tolerate up to twenty minutes without a beat. But cells are dying." Max plugged in the cart's main electric power line and flipped a switch from DC to AC power. "Once blood flow stops, the blood's oxygen supply is absorbed by the cells and depleted in a mere ten seconds and a patient loses consciousness. The brain is the second organ, even more fragile."

Max flipped Mini Yao 2 with its face up and inserted a narrow tube directed by a laryngoscope through its throat into its bronchus or airway, to the lungs and turned on the cart's AC pump. Max reviewed the checklist for the multiple devices on the cart while observing its effects.

"By five minutes, all oxygen and glucose, both needed by the brain, are depleted to zero, resulting in permanent total brain death."

Mini Yao 2 started to wiggle and tried to cough up the inserted tube. Max pulled the tube out and flipped the power off the cart. They waited as Max held the newborn under water.

"It is moving … swimming away." Max looked at Patti, who hurried over to the vegetative wall bench and reached under. Patti returned with the little Mini Yao 3, which held on to two of her fingers, waddling like a duck. "Max, I'd like to call her Leben, meaning 'life' in German. I'll nickname her Libby."

Max sat at poolside watching Mini Yao 2 swim around the pool again. Patti led Libby to the water's edge and it jumped in.

"What was all that rigmarole with that cart and stuff?"

"Back in the mid-1960s, researchers showed that a mouse could survive submerged in liquid perfluorocarbon, which carried oxygen. The mouse actually absorbed the oxygen. This liquid ventilation has been used for adults in respiratory failure and premature babies with immature lungs. Later it was found that creating mild hypothermia or lowering the body temperature by 7.2 degrees Fahrenheit, in dogs would increase the time of brain cells absorbing oxygen from five minutes to ten minutes before death." Max stared at Patti during the entire explanation.

"So I see the cooling unit, liquid unit, oxygen canister and mechanical pump to keep all elements flowing in Min Yao 2," smiled Patti. "I understand it all."

Mini Yao 2 took longer and longer to complete its circle of the pool.

"I'm going to give Mini Yao 2 another round of liquid oxygen ventilation."

Libby had come out of the water as Patti extended her hand to her.

"Where is Mini Yao 2, Max?"

They both searched the water.

"Look to the back edge by the inlet wall, the whirling water," Patti pointed.

Just under the water's surface, they both saw two yellow-red glowing lights ... eyes ... of Yao. Green-red color filled the far end of the pool. Is that Mini Yao 2's blood? The swirling pattern dissipated, the eyes were gone like a dream with the vanished Mini Yao 2.

\*\*\*

**Doctor Amy** from HHMI-LPA division, CSI Assistant Tara and Lab Assistant Rick reviewed all the evidence they had gather concerning Yao's age, location and suspected death. Seeing the three at a table, CSI Director Leon decided to join into their discussion.

"The Permian extinction wiped out 95 percent of all marine life and 70 percent of all species on earth. Very little literature is dedicated to this earth event 250 million years ago," stated Amy Adamoffski. "Most people are excited about the dinosaur world domination and demise, with extinction 66-65 million years ago. This mostly was brought on by a meteoric impact followed by earth solid particles becoming airborne and eventually circling the globe, blocking sunlight. The Yucatan Peninsula is the suspected location of this devastating event. The Permian extinction was probably from a comet or asteroid impact also."

"A comet is mostly ice, so its impact would have a much smaller world effect," butted in Rick.

"I agree," supported Amy. "An asteroid or meteor impact would launch clouds of debris and corrosive gas around the earth and block the sun for years. That caused a drastic drop in temperature, with resulting acid rain and snow. What's the difference between extinctions?"

"Are we in class here?" smiled Rick.

"The difference and why the Permian extinction was worse for all animal and plant species was…?" Amy hesitated.

"In the Permian Period, the earth's land mass was one … the Pangaea," added Leon.

They all looked at him in surprise. "Undergrad class in college," Leon said.

"In that world, hippo-sized amphibians and reptiles walked the earth with several story-high plants surrounding them. Eventually the splitting of Pangaea into the present day seven continents occurred. Now we come to Yao's story."

"Doctor Amy, should I start taking notes?" Rick pointed to Tara for a comic relief.

"Only a few species survived through these two massive, worldwide extinctions: starfish, clams, sea urchins and"—Doctor Amy looked around the table. "No takers? The family Crocodilia, made up of the crocodile and later alligator."

"So how could one of these crocodilia adapt through natural selection to be such an evolutionary miraculous creature of today called Yao?" asked Rick.

"The question that really needs to be answered is: Is Yao a product of hundreds, thousands or millions of generations or an animal that could change itself to adapt and progressively be closer to humanoid in one generation?" Tara posed this to the small group.

Sheriff Gary and Deputy Sheriff Keith entered the room. "I heard the last question presented to your group," Sheriff Gary said. "More importantly to the law enforcement agency is the issue of the general public safety and my personal oath to recapture or kill this monster reptile. Is that damn creature dead, as claimed by that Dawson guy?"

Deputy Sheriff Keith stood behind Gary and seemed more interested in Tara.

"Sheriff Gary, I believe we have met. I'm Doctor Amy Adamoffski with the Howard Hughes Medical Institute—Living Prehistoric Animals and the Smithsonian National Zoological Park, which has endorsed me. CSI Assistant Tara and I have shared information with each other concerning Yao, Mr. Dawson's evidence, which I had the opportunity to analyze and our own river collection evidence. We have made several conclusions."

"I'm sure we all are happy to hear those conclusions now or do we have to wait for it to be published by the media?" satirically responded Sheriff Gary.

Doctor Amy looked deeply into the sheriff's eyes for approximately ten seconds.

"First, from Tara's biopsy of melted together scales on Yao, multiple isotopic dating methods and blood-scale-human crime scene injury site's DNA analysis, we know Yao is approximately between 255 million to 230 million years old. Second, Tara, would you state your findings."

"Yao is a genetic chimera, which means its cells are instructed by more than one chromosomal source. This makes Yao even rarer, unbelievable in that it has four groups of different chromosomal instruction sources for its cells. This may have helped Yao heal and adapt so quickly. This would result in Yao being one of a kind adaptive creature in documented human history."

"I'm unclear on the chimera thing," interrupted Sheriff Gary.

"Pregnancy results from the fertilization of one egg and one sperm, each providing half the number of chromosomes. Now we have a zygote or an embryo grow to become one baby. This chimera called Yao has grown from the combination of four zygotes. This is four different chromosome groups, combining into one animal." She looked to the sheriff to see if that was a clear enough explanation. "It could also be that one egg was fertilized by four sperm," suggested Tara. "Or could the normal one sperm, one egg combining their chromosomes one time then divide again and recombine several times in the same embryo or zygote?"

"I get it but don't really understand why this creature happened to choose my county and why this monstrosity is still alive."

"I don't know," grimaced Tara.

"Third, what we do know is that Mr. Dawson's find is not Yao's remains," added Doctor Amy as Sheriff Gary slapped the table top and Deputy Sheriff Keith swore. "Mr. Dawson has a partial human skull, shark jaw, crocodile skin and scales, anteater's claws and the bone marrow of a humanoid Neanderthal." Amy didn't reveal that she was waiting for a return call from Professor Maxwell to ask if he believed Yao was dead or alive.

As the group broke up and Amy was outside, Rick jogged up next to her and they started walking together.

"Doctor Amy, where do you think the Permian extinction meteor or asteroid hit the earth?"

"The dinosaur extinction at 65 million years ago was caused by a meteor hit by the Yucatan Peninsula. It was a ninety-three miles wide, twenty miles deep crater and equal to one billion atomic bombs dropped on Hiroshima, Japan." Amy stopped at her black Porsche 911. "Do you have time to go get coffee or something?" Amy touched Rick's arm.

They both entered the car with tinted windows. She fired up the imaginary horses through a throaty and rumbling exhaust. The car went north on A1A.

"My educated guess would be the world's larger Vredefort impact crater in South Africa, which was 118 miles wide, started the Permian extinction. Crocodilians are the only still living member of the ruling reptile group that survived the Permian dinosaur and flying reptile extinctions. I believe Yao is of the crocodilia, a crocodile or alligator, survived and transformed." Amy moved her right hand up and down Rick's left thigh. He feverishly nodded. "Where are we going?"

"Ricky, you have the dowsing or divining rod. I'd like to experiment with overhand or underhand grips. Thus I would find out which of these grips will bring forth you're within spouting spring?" Amy turned her car off A1A and into the Frank B. Butler County Park, just north of the 206 SR Bridge. "I have a nice view from here ... of the Intracoastal-Matanzas Waterway and you." She seemed to act excited.

Doctor Amy's cell phone vibrated and rang with a North American mockingbird's series of different songs. "I'll have to call you back. My hands are on a mission." She turned off the cell and the car and they started to turn on each other with their arms extended to the other over the car's middle console. "Pretty quiet here," smiled Rick with his hands roaming about her assets.

Amy put up both windows and now focused on Ricky's progressive rigidity and growing situation. Amy felt confident she could handle whatever came. "We will bring some rock and roll to this place," she smiled, as all four hands strummed their selected instruments.

The setting sun across the waterway was a romantic end for lovers ... for intimate friends ... for?

"Ah, such a wonderful aura created here for having both our happy endings." The couple got out of the car to watch the glowing sunset. Amy and Rick slowly climbed on the Porsche's hood.

"Nice to see you again," They said as they turned toward each other to caress and kiss.

"What the hell was that?" They both heard vocal sounds and violent splashing of water in front of them. They scanned the river and sunset. The last vision they had was of a very tall, dark, human-like silhouette.

# Chapter 69

## *Finality*

**Patrolman John Brenner knelt** by the two victims' bodies. He heard two different sirens approaching.

"What do you have here, John?" called out the approaching paramedics.

"A semi-conscious Caucasian woman with multiple bleeding cuts, slashes and torn clothing." A dispirited John stared toward the water's edge. I believe this is Doctor Amy Adamoffski." He turned toward a severely disfigured male body. "Rick LaGrande is one of our own." John started to cry.

The paramedics examined both individuals. They prepared the women for immediate transport in their ambulance.

"I'll call for CSI and Doctor MacGrath," said John sadly.

The team pulled into the Butler County Park where John's patrol car's flashing red and blue lights reflected on the black Porches' scratched skin. The five vehicles unloaded where John knelt.

Tara stopped at seeing a crying John. CSI Director Leon started documenting possible evidence. Doc Ian MacGrath pronounced Rick dead at the scene. Leon and Detective Brett sadly continued surveying the crime scene. On the ground, they placed numbers, labels and photographed potential evidence. Brett documented the digital pictures.

The coroner's van left while Sheriff Gary and Deputy Keith continued searching the park and shoreline for evidence.

"Mary Jane, I need you to call the county police scuba team to search Butler Park shoreline and surrounding waters," ordered Sheriff Gary.

"Is everything—"

"I'll tell you when I return."

"You know what we have to do." He stared at Keith.

***

**Max** called Alisa and Patti to an emergency meeting in MAAW facility.

"I regret to tell you that Yao has committed another murder. CSI Laboratory Assistant Rick."

Patti and Alisa were aghast.

"Biology paleontologist Amy Alla Adamoffski from HHMI was severely injured. All this was told to me in confidence by CSI Assistant Tara.

"So what should we—"

"Patti, how are you doing with Leben?"

"Oh, she and Blaze have become best of friends. The three amigos love both of them."

"Leben?" asked Alisa.

"She's a successful offspring of Yao, thanks to Professor Max," smiled Patti. "I call her Libby for short." Patti touched Alisa's arm.

"The last thing Tara said to me in anger was that there would be retribution and rightfully so."

Maxwell had said nothing in response to Tara. "My plan is to save my work to be used as stepping-stones for future human medicinal and animal veterinarian advances. Alisa, I need you to photograph everything—equipment, cages, walls—in all the rooms and then close these rooms up."

They heard gunshots in the distance.

Alisa nodded. "It will be done."

"Alisa, I signed over my Jaguar to you for one dollar and my condo is signed off to you for one dollar. Both are paid off. You still have to pay the condo maintenance fee of $290 per month."

"No way, it's not—"

"No arguing, dear, it is already done." Max waved off her protests.

She became teary eyed and did her usual bear hug of gratitude.

"Patti, do you think Blaze would want and seriously keep and care for Speedy, Cali and anima mea?"

"I'm sure he would and will take on the responsibility." Patti too became teary eyed and hugged Max and Alisa.

"You know, many cultures consider cats of colors, like a calico, as good luck. Germans call them 'Glückekatze,' and in the US they are called 'money cats.' Japanese sailors have calicos on ships to prevent misfortune." Now Max showed some moist eyes to complete the weeping threesome. "I have already packed away the most important items, including the nitrogen frozen donor eggs, Yao's sperm specimens, Yao's skin, genetic materials and a sample of the pool room's wall of genetically engineered vegetation. Patti, I will let you take this small travel nitrogen canister because you can recharge it at your workplace." Patti agreed while still weeping. "To avoid confusion and inquisitive questions about the canister, I labeled it 'Lachlan's blood samples.'" The two women looked to Rory Fergus Hamish Lachlan Maxwell. The three grinned and chuckled while wiping their eyes.

"Finally, I bought a place for you, Patti, Alisa, Blaze, Leben, Cali and friends. A vacation cottage or later a home to live at if you choose. In this sealed envelope is a trust and will concerning the property and funds in both of your names if something should happen to me."

Alisa and Patti both began weeping as a thunderous rainstorm started outside.

"I am crying too." Max looked around "This place has ended its glory time. Patti, call this phone number should I be brought in for my end game."

***

**Sheriff** Gary called the entire law enforcement agency under his command. "Keep looking out for the murderous reptile. If and when the creature is visually identified, the perpetrator should be terminated with extreme prejudice.

"I have also again asked the Coast Guard to participate in the murderous creature hunt. Other local authorities have been notified, as has the media. Mr. Angel has agreed to run a full page warning to all residents to be on the lookout and immediately notify the police of its

420

location if the creature is seen. Citizens should *not* try to apprehend the reptile on their own."

***

**Maxwell** waited for Yao to appear in the pool room with no success. He then easily walked the Matanzas River banks, since the rain had stopped. The river bank was where Yao had appeared in the past, but this time with no success. Coast Guard, private helicopters and low flying planes filled the sky above Max. Police vehicles and yahoo bounty hunters drove up and down A1A into riverside parks and parking lots. HHMI-LPA placed a $100,000 bounty on the reptile, dead or alive or for significant portions of the creature's carcass.

Max returned to the outside of the MAAW facility. He saw the bench between the north side of the facility and the river. A light rain started.

As Maxwell sat looking at the slow flowing river, with rain on his face, he asked out loud, "Yao, why, oh why did you do this? Why Yao! Why... Yao?" Max closed his eyes and shook his head in grief.

"I bad, I not stop me ... I not wan ... to do, bad fee ... in me, forg ... e me?"

Max opened his eyes and found Yao standing before him. His head was more rounded, like a human's. Its hands had shorter claws, more like long fingernails. Its skin was less like scales and more like human ichthyosis. Its feet were smaller but still webbed between distinct toes with no claws. Yao's sad eyes were now dull green-crimson in color. Its overall body was not bright green, but a duller, olive green with patches of dark tan or earth tones.

Max stood up. "Oh Yao, you have been very bad. What you have done ... I cannot help you out of this." They stood looking at each other. Max moved closer as if to carefully touch or even hug the giant towering figure over him.

The rain became harder again.

"Professor Maxwell, move away from the creature Yao," two voices rang out.

Max looked around to see Detective Brett and Patrolman John Brenner pointing their firearms at the two of them. Yao started to move toward them and Max put his arms out and stepped in closer to Yao to stop its movement. The sound of multiple shots echoed off the research building's walls. Max fell to his knees and then to the ground, face-down with blood showing on his left leg, right shoulder and left lower side-chest. Yao's chest oozed green blood from several areas. Actual small patches of skin or scales fell off Yao to the ground. Yao grabbed Max's right arm as it stepped backward and fell into the Matanzas River.

"Where did they go?" called out Detective Brett as she saw red and green colors on the grass before them and in the water's surface where they'd fallen in. The colors disappeared as the river continued its flow as if nothing had been disturbed.

Brett took off her jacket and laid it on the grass of red and green before the rain washed the evidence away.

"I might have shot the professor," spoke Patrolman John as water dripped off his cap.

"We both did, but he was trying to help the reptile escape," yelled Brett as she spat water.

"Or to protect us from the approaching creature ... or to protect the creature," said John.

"We were told to use lethal force," explained the detective as they stood at the river's bank looking for the two wounded or dead individuals.

"I've never killed anyone before," said John as he pondered what had happened.

"John, your actions were in the line of duty. You had no choice," explained the detective. "We may receive some award for our actions."

*** 

"**Mary Jane**, tell the rest of the team to come now to the north side of the MAAW research building. We have shot the Yao creature," Detective Brett called in on her right shoulder microphone. Strapped also on her right shoulder was a digital recorder camera that captured the events that had just transpired." The detective checked that it had been on and still recorded in the rain.

"We had no choice but to fire our weapons," again explained Detective Brett.

The rest of the law enforcement and CSI teams arrived as the rain stopped. They went through their usual procedures, as they had done many times before concerning the reptile. All hoped for the last time.

After all investigative members had left the scene and driven northbound, a call came in.

"Sheriff Gary?" Mary Jane called on his cell phone. "The MAAW research building is on fire after an explosion, as heard and reported by several Marinescape personnel. I called the fire department, who called for assistance from two other local fire stations."

\*\*\*

**A week later,** Alisa put in her resignation at Marinescape and received her final paycheck. The management gave her a week to reconsider, with a pay raise and the title of Marinescape Aquatic Marine Biologist, as well as two interns and an option to redesign a new research facility for research if she desired.

She sat in Max's Jaguar at the Atlantic Ocean with the top down. She listened to the breaking waves and screeching seagulls flying above her. She placed a hand on her abdomen and slowly moved downward. As the morning sun rose, it beat down on her face, which was covered by Jackie Onassis style sunglasses. A dragonfly landed on the passenger seat's headrest, big eyes staring at Alisa.

She started to sing—

> Birds fly high,
> Sun in the sky,
> Fish in the sea,
> River runs free …
> Dragonfly, you stare at me.

"Should I drift on until I find my new direction? Or take on Marinescape's lucrative offer?" Alisa smiled and started to reminisce. "I had a few good times with that Max." She sat in her parked Jaguar and hugged herself and rocked back and forth. "Thank you, Rory Maxwell," she laughed. "You were the greatest mentor I could have ever imagined. I'm now professionally confident and very proficient in my field." She closed her eyes. "Wherever you are, here's my love!"

Alisa pulled out of the Marinescape parking lot to A1A. "I can go north … I can go south. North it is to the South Beach Grill for breakfast. Ha, going north for the South." Alisa grinned.

As usual, she parked in the restaurant's sandy parking lot facing the ocean. She noticed Sheriff Gary's SUV parked at the very south end of the parking lot.

"I'll take that table," she told the waitress, Gabe. "Good morning, Miss. Table for one?"

"Wait, I see friends." Alisa changed direction. "Hi, Tara, may I join the two of you?"

The man looked at Tara.

"Our pleasure," he said as he stood and pulled up a chair for her.

"Alisa, this is Mr. Yuma Manta, an acquaintance from work." Tara looked at Yuma. "Actually a casualty I met through work." He smiled and placed a right hand on her left.

***

"It's nice to have a day off, now that everything is quiet again." Yuma moved over to the woman and kissed her smiling face.

***

"Well, good morning to you, Gary. I have only one call for you. I feel you are up … to it." Mary Jane pulled him in tight. "And I accept your standing offer."

***

"Jennifer, you would be a great cover model for my *Successful College girls of Florida* publication," promoted Deputy Keith, "really?"
"I did do some acting in high school and posing for the yearbook," she responded with pride.

"Oh yeah, this magazine exposure could lead to a TV commercial or even more." Keith held both her hands while they laughed.

\*\*\*

**Director Leon** sat with his wife, Linda, at dinner.

"Anything worth telling me about your day, Leon?" she asked.

"Nothing to speak of. I believe our community has become quiet again, at least crime-wise," he responded with the sound of relief. "Great, we'll have dinner and dessert, dear, as always."

"For this night's entertainment, shall we listen to classical music, opera or take turns playing our practiced piano composers we've chosen for the month?" asked Linda.

"I'm all for Mozart or Chopin, my dear." Leon kissed her check.

\*\*\*

**Mary Jane** sat at her desk looking remorseful. Several people passed her with no remarks.

"Mary Jane, what's bringing you so down?" Tara stopped and pulled up a chair.

"I was reminiscing about the people who died as a result of the reptile Yao, about their grieving families and friends. Where's their justice?" Mary Jane angrily spoke. "Are they just collateral damage of progressing science?"

# Chapter 70

---

## *Epilogue One*

**"How does the story end?"** asked R.F. Angell. "Happy, sad or just several displaced people? Do the lovers find each other? Does the creature Yao disappear to reappear in another location, another century, return to the Amazon River or die? Is Professor Rory Maxwell found to be a great or evil scientist by society and history? Does the law enforcement team finally find justice for their persistent efforts and the community?"

***

**One year later ...**

"Blaze, Libby, come on in, it's getting dark," called out Patti.

A seemingly sleeping curled-up fur ball was actually watching the two from the shore under the shade of a Bismarkia nobilis palm tree.

Libby and Blaze jumped out of the moored boat to a dock. They ran up the dock toward the two-story building. Cali stood up and followed them into the weathered structure.

"No running on the dock! You both know better," again called out the familiar voice.

Libby was as tall as Blaze. Cali was now the size of a bobcat or lynx, the names referring to the same animal. The two flying friends of Blaze and now Libby had grown to the size of large black crows. "Come on, you guys," Libby said as she held the door open for the three following amigos. "Wash up and come to the dinner table," ordered Patti.

Cali pranced to its food bowl. Speedy and anima mea flew to their respective open cages with their appropriate food holders.

"Should we wait for—" asked Blaze.

"No, you know he's unpredictable when he's out there exploring or performing some experiment," smiled Patti. "Let's eat."

In the middle of their meal, they heard a knock on the front door.

"I'll get it," said Blaze and he left the table to answer it. The other two watched him, as did Cali, looking up from its bowl.

"Oh, I'm so happy to see you!" Blazed hugged her and wouldn't release her, just like a barnacle on a boat's hull.

"I don't believe it … you found us," Patti got up and also gave her a brief hug. "Come in, please come in." Patti looked out the front door in both directions as Alisa walked in. She saw Max's old Jaguar parked outside. "Alisa, what happened to your Nissan?"

"I sold it; I've become accustomed to the feel of the Jag and its memories."

"How did you find us?"

"I called your place of work. They said you retired. I then went and had Tara unofficially use the state-wide police data base and she found you here in Key Largo." Alisa smiled at the three. "And who is this young lady?"

"This is Leben. I call her Libby for short. She's a friend of the late Professor Maxwell."

Alisa walked over to her and gently took her right hand and stared into her multicolored light red, gray-green eyes. She grinned, hugged Alisa and continued the hug as she had seen Blaze had done.

"It's so nice to meet you, Libby. I think I was around at your birth?" Alisa looked at Patti, who winked with a following nod.

"We're having dinner. Why don't you join us? Did you drive straight from Marinescape?"

"Yeah, it was about seven hours from there to here. I have the digital photos of the research facility, also some of Max's records he asked me to save. I reviewed the over two hundred digital pictures. It brought back some wonderful memories." Alisa looked up at Patti.

"So are you still working at Marinescape?"

"You're looking at the Marinescape's Marine Biologist with interns!"

"That's Great news, Alisa," as Patti briefly smiled.

"Oh, that's marvelous!" Blaze again hugged Alisa with a deeply felt chest compression. Libby ran over and joined the hug.

"O.K., Blaze, that's enough." Alisa pushed Blaze to an arm's length. "And when did you start using the word marvelous?"

"That's Blaze's favorite word now," answered Patti.

"I really missed you and the fun we had together," chuckled Blaze.

Alisa put her arm around Blaze's should. He tried to re-hug her. "Ah, no you don't," she whispered to him. "Me too, that's why I tracked you guys down."

"Why didn't you just read Max's letter?"

"I wanted to make sure it was real; that's why I used Tara."

"What kind of records did you bring?" Patti inquired.

"A lot of genetic notations, hypotheses and conclusions Max wrote. I had to look up a lot of his words. I got the gist of most of Max's original goals and results." Alisa moved in close to Patti and whispered, "like creating genetically engineered insects, animal and Yao's offspring. Did you know the research building blew up and burned down with only the outside brick walls remaining?"

No immediate response.

"What has it been, about a year since Yao and Max got shot?" asked Alisa.

"It could be," answered Patti.

"This place has an interesting floor plan, like a hotel would have." Alisa walked around the great room, which could have been a lobby with second-floor room doors facing inward.

"It was from the 1930s and 1940s and named the Caribbean Clubhouse. I think it was a movie location or something," answered Patti. "Are you staying awhile?"

"I was hoping to. I sold Max's condo. I just resigned yesterday from Marinescape again. I have a month to get my position back. I can pay rent," informed Alisa. "I'd like to be here with you, Blaze and company. I really miss Max and if I stay with you guys, I'd feel closer to him."

"You don't have to pay rent; it's half yours. We'll get your bags and I'll show you your choice of rooms."

"What about the records and digital photos on the camera Max gave me? It shows the interior of his laboratories?"

"I'll take them and store the items in a room with other things of Max's ... in memory of him," hesitated Patti. "I was thinking of writing a Maxwell biography of his work, dreams and maybe his non-scientific life."

"That's a great idea. Maybe I could help, if you think it's the right time," smiled Alisa.

The next morning, Alisa awoke and looked out her second-story window to see the rising sun on the horizon. "What a beautiful day. Hey, look at that enormous boat," she said out loud. "I have to go down there and board her." After getting dressed, she hurried down and looked around for Patti. She was nowhere to be found. She saw the room where Patti had put Max's stuff. She quietly turned the doorknob, but it was locked.

Once outside, she saw Blaze and Libby playing on the dock. Patti was seated on the *Santana*. *What a great name*, Alisa thought as she went down the dock. She passed Blaze and Libby, who both shoulder hugged her, as controlled by Alisa. She stepped onto the boat's port side gangplank.

"Nice to see you awake and about," remarked Patti.

"Boy, just like the house, this boat is quite weathered."

"And seaworthy," finished up Patti. "The house and boat have survived several hurricanes. We got the boat with the sale of the property, as well as the house that Max got us. The previous owner claims this fifty-five-foot yacht belonged to some movie actor or writer."

"Was it the writer Ernest Hemmingway? He loved the Florida Keys."

Patti again didn't answer immediately. "No, I think it was a movie star from the 30s and 40s, Humpfrey Beauregard?"

"What a beautiful and relaxing location," commented Alisa as Patti moved to a starboard rotating chair to look southward.

Alisa sat on the port side chair and swiveled to look over the dock northward.

"Are these chairs for fishing?"

"Probably," replied Patti. "We've gone out to view the life on the ocean bottom and its scientifically interesting items," nodded Patti.

Alisa got up and looked over, "I can see the sandy bottom and some coral." Alisa turned around with her hands behind her on the boat's rail.

"You know, Patti, we both have a history with Max," she said, staring at her.

Patti just smiled.

"We both have — had a close friendship, relationship — an intimate history with him."

Patti's eyes looked down.

"At last … we can admit … We were meant for him. And he was meant for us," recited Alisa. "Nature fashioned him, and when she was done, he had all those good things rolled into one."

Patti got up and walked to the port gangplank. "The skies above were blue when I met him. I found a dream I could speak to." A teary-eyed Patti stopped and turned to see Alisa also weeping. "A thrill I've never known before — he just smiled and the spell was cast."

They approached each other, hugged and wept as one.

"You're right," said Patti. "I have missed you so much. Of course, Blaze even more, if possible. I admit we have always had so much in common." Patti continued their hug in wet joy.

"I can only hope Max," whispered Alisa. "I have prayed it to be possible." She wiped her eyes.

"Hey, everybody, look who's here?" called out Blaze.

The two women moved and stood at the port side rail of the boat to see Blaze waving. Max's head popped out of the water with Libby on his shoulders. Behind them appeared Yao, with an almost human looking head.

"I knew they were still alive!" Alisa started to weep again.

***

**It's hard to tell** if a human remotely triggered it or if the heating and cooling system's wiring just wore out and it spontaneously caused the fire, Sheriff Gary." The arson squad captain was reporting to the CSI team. "Unfortunately, this utility room was situated in the middle of the building, resulting in rapid and complete burnout, except for the brick walls."

"The recovered Doctor Amy Adamoffski and I were able to definitely verify that the remaining debris and blood came from the reptile Yao. This supports the creature's demise," concluded Tara. "Also, the evidence showed that Yao was the murderer of Rick LaGrande and the violent attack and attempted rape of Doctor Adamoffski." Tara looked around the team's faces.

"There were human blood cells mixed with Yao's materials. Unfortunately, the suspected blood specimens from Professor Maxwell for comparison didn't match his prior chimera blood history, so I couldn't conclusively match him to the blood at the scene. However, this blood does have HLA, human leukocyte antigens, which are cell surface proteins responsible for the human immune system response. Yao also has HLA cells, which do closely match the blood from a related human to Yao found at the river death scene!"

The members of the team remained quiet. From the back of the room spoke Detective Brett. "Are you saying that the—"

"So you can't tell us if that damn son of a bitch Maxwell is dead?" asked the angry Deputy Sheriff Keith.

"After all this testing, this is the best you can do?" ranted Sheriff Gary. "I can't believe with all the forensic science, your conclusion is 'probably.'"

"Thank you, Tara and the arson squad for your diligent investigating," interrupted Director Leon. "We will all forever mourn the death of one of our own, Assistant Laboratory Director Richard LaGrande. We all understand the stress and frustration you're feeling, Sheriff — that we are all feeling. We will do what we always do when confronted with insufficient answers." Leon pointed around the room.

"We are a team—let us continue to act like one."

***

**The happy group** of Patti, Alisa, Blaze, Libby and Max were having their nightly meeting to discuss the day's events at the dinner table. Each person relayed their adventures. Max expounded on some new idea and new experimental results in the now unlocked door to his recreated genetic manipulating laboratory.

"Alisa and I have a list of animals we want to read up on and then look for their habitats," excitedly stated Blaze.

"And what would those animals be?" asked Patti.

"Loggerhead turtles, starfish, sea urchins, sharks and crocodiles—"

431

"Of course, not all in one day," added Alisa.

"Pretty much the survivors of the Permian extinction?" stated Professor Max.

"I expect Alisa to keep Blaze and herself always safe," Patti said in a strict motherly voice.

"What?"

"Did you hear that knock at the front door?"

"I'm closest. I'll get it." Patti walked over and unlocked and opened the front door. "Ahh Tara. What are you doing here?" Patti turned and frowned at Alisa.

"Is the professor here? I have more information about Yao's age," Tara said as she scanned the room.

Patti spoke up again, "I thought—"

Tara opened the front door wider and stepped aside.

The room filled with flashing red and blue lights from several police cars. The house vibrated from the rotating helicopter blades. Bright lights illuminated the ocean-facing windows from two Coast Guard vessels on either side of the moored *Santana*. Shadows holding rifles stood on the residents' long dock.

Sheriff Gary T. Sellack stepped past Tara. Multiple officers stood behind him, including Brett and Brenner, who were now both detectives. "We're here to arrest the reptile calling itself Yao, his son and conspirator."

"Do you mean his daugh—" Patti started to say.

"Rory Fergus Hamish Lachlan Maxwell the IV, you are under arrest for illegal entry into the US, collusion, obstruction of justice and as the accomplice to a total of four capital crimes of murder, including Richard LaGrande. If you resist, we will use extreme prejudice to secure our position and your capture, dead or alive. There will be no escape."

All heard a helicopter above and two Coast Guard ships' sirens on the eastern Oceanside behind the Caribbean Clubhouse.

"We are going to recapture the monstrosity reptile Yao," continued Sheriff Gary, "for four capital murders, including Richard LaGrande, five assaults, including Professor Amy Alla Adamoffski, breaking and entering, vandalism and danger to the general public. If Yao resists, we will be forced to use extreme prejudice, terminating the reptile."

*Donec obvium iterum*, until we meet again…

Story written in honor of Ricou Browning…

Ricou's underwater swimming style won him the part of the underwater scenes of the lifelong loved *Gill-Man*. He captured the audience's interest in *Creature from the Black Lagoon* (1954). Browning co-invented the mobile underwater camera for filming the moving *Creature*. Prior to that, only fixed, standing and non-moving underwater cameras were used, requiring the "action" to swim by the camera. Everyone who saw the movie remembers Julie Adams swimming on the water's surface as the Gill-Man swam under her as the underwater camera moved along with them.

Ricou was born in Fort Pierce, Florida, the state where the underwater scenes for the *Creature* film and its two sequels, *Revenge of the Creature— Gill-Man* and *The Creature Walks among Us*, with Ricou playing the underwater scenes. Filming occurred at Wakulla Springs, Weeki Wachee Springs, Marineland and Hollywood. He also co-wrote the movie and TV series *Flipper*.

Browning also directed underwater scenes in *James Bond: Thunderball* (1966), *Caddyshack* (1980), *Never Say Never Again* (1983), *Police Academy 5: Assignment Miami Beach* (1988) and *Boardwalk Empire* (2010).

The world premiere of *Creature from the Black Lagoon* took place in Detroit, Michigan, on February 12, 1954. A boy named Alex never forgot the film and was later inspired to write this update of the Creature Existence.

***

### Footnotes

**Movies:** This book was inspired by the 1950s and 60s B movie storylines exploring new life forms created on or invading earth. Such examples are *The Blob, The Beast from 20,000 Fathoms, Godzilla, Creature from the Black Lagoon, The Deadly Mantis, Attack of the Giant Leeches, It Came from Beneath the Sea, Revenge of the Creature, The Creature Walks Among Us, The Woman Eater* (a tree in the Amazon jungle), *Them, It Conquered the World, The Giant Claw, Attack of the Crab Monsters, Frankenstein, Earth*

*Vs. the Spider, Cat Girl, The Wasp Woman, The Giant Gila, Monster from the Ocean Floor, The Alligator People, The Fly, Tarantula, The Mole People, The Killer Shrews, The Black Scorpion, The She-Creature, The Monster That Challenged the World,* and *The Indestructible Man.*

**Vespucci** navigated at least four voyages crossing the Atlantic Ocean. He discovered Venezuela, the entire eastern coast of South America, including Brazil and the mouth of the Amazon River.

**Rabbit's Foot** is considered lucky by the bearer of the preserved foot. Cultures around the world desire to possess this amulet. This includes people from Europe, China, Africa and the Western Hemisphere. In the legend, the rabbit and person sacrificing the animal must have certain attributes: the one sacrificing must be a cross-eyed man, it must be the rabbit's left hind leg and it must be sacrificed in a cemetery, under a new full moon, on a rainy Friday or on Friday the 13th. Today, however, such sacrifice is not performed, and a "lucky rabbit's foot" can be purchased in a store.

**Native History:** In the nineteenth, twentieth, and twenty-first centuries, controversy remained over what to call this group of native inhabitants. Europeans never considered what the natives wanted to be called. They were referred to by the continent they lived on (i.e., North American) or by their tribal names or the state they lived in (i.e., American Indians, Florida Indians). The Canadian government refers to these native inhabitants as First Nations People. Interestingly, the well-known Seminole Nation didn't seem to appear in Florida or have writings about them until the 1700s.

Originally, the Native population only had to survive and co-exist with nature and animals. Then new struggles arose when the aggressive Europeans arrived. The French, Spanish and English explorers and their settlers planned on using violence to displace and eliminate the Native way of life and beliefs in renewing the spirits of land and wildlife. The spread of "white man's" European diseases among the Natives was another lethal weapon.

The Matanzas (meaning "massacre" in Spanish) River is in northeastern Florida, which was originally occupied by the Timucua Native people.

Having children for many native Ameriicans was a joyous event, birthing either a boy or girl. What was important was that the child had all of their limbs and other parts. A good, vigorous breast-feeding was essential for strong body and spirit development. Water was important, from the safety of the mother's nurturing womb, with its still, warm waters, to the baby's introduction to Mother Earth's turbulent, cold and always changing river waters. The initial rinsing in water symbolized the new baby's ever changing spiritual life ahead. The heaven above brings forth rain to form trickling lines of water that become creeks. Multiple creeks will become babbling brooks. The babbling brooks will grow to serpentine streams. The streams join together to become strong and forceful rivers. Eventually, all spirits, good and bad, flow into the big waters with its waves and tides. Their spirits remain there until the Great Spirit has chosen the ones to rise into the clouds. There the human spirit waits with forest and animal spirits, some being game animals. All wait to return to Mother Earth. Some return gently in a bath of tears (rain); others, quickly and violently return in lightning, thunder and windblown rain and clouds. This is how all new life comes about as one Native legend explains.

**Homo Sapien:**

Homo sapiens (Latin for "wise man") have always been concerned only about themselves and then about other humans over nature. People in today's world live and work with the newest technologies and medical advances, which have resulted in life extension for many species, not just of humans. Each human generation believe they will have the best life experience. These lives are classified using their birth day.

| | |
|---|---|
| Baby Boomer Generation | 1946 to 1964 |
| Generation X, Baby Bust | 1965 t0 1979 |
| Generation Y, Millennial | 1980 to 1995 |
| Generation Z | 1996 to 2010 |
| Gen Alpha | 2010 to 2025 |

Each generation believes they enjoy even greater advancements in technology, newer and greater recreational opportunities, general health and lifespan compared to the prior generations. The Gen Alpha generation has been estimated to potentially live to an average age of 104. What about naturally selected evolving non-human life forms? Does past history matter? Do they care?

**Jaguar:** This car was originally made in Britain but is now owned by Tata Motors of India. Jaguar's creator, William Lyons, made this car to create a world-class sophisticated sports sedan. The car emblem is a pouncing Jaguar portraying "grace, space and speed."

**US Highway 1 (US 1):** Road designated as the highway along the Florida east coastline when the United States Numbered Highway System was established in 1926. US 1 run 545 miles from Key West, Florida to the St. Marys River, Georgia.

**Donor Egg:** Most women under thirty years of age may be egg donor candidates. Each woman is tested for sexually transmitted disease (STD) before being accepted to continue. They will take egg (follicle) stimulation, usually shots. The egg retrial will be just like an IVF cycle, except instead of a fertilized egg/ embryo transfer, the eggs will be frozen. The female donor will receive starting at $5,000 or more for six or more eggs retrieved.

**ICSI (Intra Cytoplasmic Sperm Injection):** This highly technical procedure is performed under an optical magnification of 200–400 x by a qualified embryologist. He or she has previously selected the best (washed, normal shaped, mobile) sperm and identified eggs at the egg retrieval. The sperm has three parts. The head contains the DNA, the mid-piece provides energy and the tail is for movement. The embryologist then takes the selected sperm and breaks the tail by using the pipette right at the mid-piece. Now the non-motile sperm is aspirated into the pipette, tail first. Finally, the pipette punctures the egg's outer membrane, called the zona pellucid, goes into the gel-like cytoplasm and deposits the sperm's DNA next to the egg's DNA.

### Animal and Plant Chromosome Numbers
Fruitfly—8
yellow fever mosquito—6

slime mold—12

Kangaroo, Koala—16

carrot, radish, cabbage—18

cannabis, maize, corn—20

Snail—24

Dragonfly, male—25 (XO), female—26 (XX)

Giraffe, Butterfly, pistachio—30

European Honeybee, Yeast— 32

Porcupine—34

Earthworm—36

Cat, domestic; Lion, Pig, Raccoon—38

Mouse, Ferret, peanut—40

Rhesus monkey, Wolverine, Rat, oats, wheat—42

Dolphin, Rabbit, Jellyfish, coffee—44

Homo sapiens, Neanderthal, Denisovan; Beaver, American—46
(other Huminidae and early great Apes—48, because the chromosome
number 2 is an end-to-end with another ancestral 2 chromosome 2),

European Beaver—48

Chimpanzees, Gorilla, Orangutan, tobacco, potato—48

cotton—52

Sheep—54

Elephant—56

Woolley Mammoth—58

American Bison, Cow, Yak—60

Donkey—62

Mule (sterile)—63

Guinea Pig—64

Hawk, Roadside, Elk, Red Deer—68

Deer, white tail—70

Dog, Dingo, gray Wolf, Chicken, Dove—78

Turkey, Pigeon—80

Great white shark—82

Carp—100

Rattlesnake—184

Red king crab—208

# Acknowledgements

I would like to thank several people for their contributions, help and guidance to making this book possible, including Nancy L. Kirk and Mary Jane Maximovich for their text readability suggestions, Embryologist Michael J. Kirk for his experience, continuously high IVF pregnancy rates and frontline techniques in Tennessee and Michigan. I personally worked with him for over ten years. I also thank another dear friend, Gary VanderMeulen, a retired Western Michigan Sheriff, Deputy Sheriff and Patrolman of twenty-three years. He helped police departments change from oil-based fingerprints to digital imprinting. I mention another close friend, Leon Pedell, M.D., who convinced me to change the direction of my book after reading the first draft. Finally, I want to thank Tellwell Publishing, Canada, and their personnel, especially Project Manager Gezel B Zozobrado, assistant Mary Apple Bertulfo and Kelly Wilson for story flow, grammatically correct text and my official editor with great directional comments and encouraging remarks. Finally, Cathi Wood for helping me navigates the Microsoft program to write this book.

# About the Author

Alexander Maximovich, M.D., (Dr. Max) recently retired from hospital and private practice. Early in his career, he spent a six-month externship with Chief Medical Examiner of Wayne County, Michigan (which includes Detroit) and Medical Examiner of Oakland County, Michigan, Dr. Olson. He assisted in up to twenty-one autopsies a day. Dr. Maximovich was present during detective/coroner discussions of forensic pathology. Later, he spent forty-four years specializing in obstetrics and gynecology, treating female issues through laparoscopic laser and robotic surgeries, treating infertility, endometriosis and performing in vitro fertilization. He taught hospital attending physicians, resident doctors and medical students from four medical schools in his field of expertise. He taught at hospitals and universities in several US states, four Canadian provinces, Europe and Australia. Dr. Max received several teaching awards from his peers, hospital doctors, students and nurses. He now lives off the I-75 corridor between Michigan, Tellico, Tennessee and Stuart, Florida.